"Whitley Strieber works magic . . . summoning forth ancient evil, bringing it into the world of today, and with the wizardry of his words, casting you under its spell. This book is exciting!"

—Robert Bloch, author of *Psycho*

"Perfect summer reading . . . [Strieber] aims to scare the reader half to death and he does it brilliantly."

—Cleveland *Plain Dealer*

"Strieber's updates and additions to Lovecraft's original ideas . . . provide ample suspense. Horror enthusiasts will find his central concept chilling."

—*Publishers Weekly*

"The action and danger in this novel are exciting . . . and the story works well as a Lovecraft-style tale brought into modern times."

—*Library Journal*

WHITLEY STRIEBER

THE FORBIDDEN ZONE

AN ONYX BOOK

ONYX
Published by the Penguin Group
Penguin Books USA Inc., 375 Hudson Street,
New York, New York 10014, U.S.A.
Penguin Books Ltd, 27 Wrights Lane,
London W8 5TZ, England
Penguin Books Australia Ltd, Ringwood,
Victoria, Australia
Penguin Books Canada Ltd, 10 Alcorn Avenue,
Toronto, Ontario, Canada M4V 3B2
Penguin Books (N.Z.) Ltd, 182-190 Wairau Road,
Auckland 10, New Zealand

Penguin Books Ltd, Registered Offices:
Harmondsworth, Middlesex, England

Published by Onyx, an imprint of Dutton Signet,
a division of Penguin Books USA Inc.
Previously appeared in a Dutton edition.

First Onyx Printing, May, 1994
10 9 8 7 6 5 4 3 2 1

PUBLISHER'S NOTE
This is a work of fiction. Names, characters, places, and incidents either are
the product of the author's imagination or are used fictitiously, and any resemblance to actual persons, living or dead, events, or locales is entirely coinciden-
tal.

*This book is dedicated
with heartfelt appreciation to
H. P. Lovecraft, the old one.*

ACKNOWLEDGMENTS

I would like to acknowledge the patient and determined help of my editor, Kevin Mulroy, the often surprising insights of Elaine Koster, publisher of Dutton Books, the careful attention of my friend and longtime reader Michael J. P. Smith, and most especially the inspiration and editorial skills of my wife, Anne Mattocks Strieber, who has struggled with me through twenty-three books.

The Forbidden Zone: An area around an extremely energetic object which normally cannot—and must not—be entered. But once it is entered, then time, movement, all events stop, everything changes. Within such a forbidden zone lies a state beyond mere destruction. It is a condition of chaos, absolute derangement.

—William N. Holmes, Ph.D.
"Large-Scale Transitions and
Quantum Derangements,"
The Journal of the Physical World

ONE

1.

To the middle of a perfect summer afternoon came a long, trembling scream. Because it was so faint, Brian Kelly feared at first that it was a memory. It could have been, certainly. His young and pregnant wife, who was lying in the grass beside him, didn't seem to hear it. He would have looked to his dog for reaction, but she was off on a wild chase after a rabbit.

The scream died away. He sat up and gazed out across the wide view. Perhaps he would see a column of smoke from a burning house, or a wrecked car on a roadside. But Oscola seemed quiet, and the southern range of the Adirondacks that rose beyond the town dreamed innocently in the blue haze of summer.

He could see past Judge terBroeck's house down Mound Road and on up Main into the center of town. In the other direction, he could follow Mound almost to its intersection with Route 303, which wound off toward Ludlum thirty miles distant.

In all of this expansive view, nothing was amiss. Maybe it had been an animal or a bird, or the wind.

The sun was warm, and he soon closed his eyes, letting the quiet of the hour transport him toward a nap. Time possessed him, that strange substance that had been the focus of his career and his life . . . time, his beloved mystery.

In the past he would come here with Mary. But she never cared for the mound. She was an indoor person, an intellectual—a genius, really, the best physicist he had ever known.

Her young death, with work and life unfinished, had left so many echoes.

He kept listening, worrying that he was going to start hearing her death screams yet again, and that they were indeed going to be like the scars on his chest, with him forever.

He reassured himself that this little mound was not a place for dangerous memories. People in Oscola had been coming here on summer afternoons for generations. Kids sledded here in the winter, always had. Judge terBroeck, who owned the place, didn't approve of casual trespass, but the town had long ago become indifferent to his many dislikes.

Ever since Mary and Kate had been killed, Brian had been hearing screams. His doctor had been the first one to speculate that he might hear them for the rest of his life. Initially, this link with his loved ones had seemed in a strange way reassuring. But once he found a new love, it had come to be an imprisonment. For his own sake and for Loi's—and for the sake of their baby—he had to let his dead family go.

Trying to escape, he found a state remembered from boyhood afternoons lying in this very spot. "I can almost feel the earth turning," he said. Loi answered with a contented murmur.

Every time she heard his voice, looked at him,

touched him or felt his passion, she reminded herself of her good fortune. For a woman whose life had been almost entirely unfortunate, finding him was a great piece of luck. He meant escape from the past, the dreadful memories of the Chu Chi tunnels, the soul-breaking anguish of the Blue Moon Bar in Bangkok. There was nothing in Vietnam, and very little in the rest of Asia, for a woman born of a G.I. father and a French-Vietnamese mother.

Before Brian, she had felt that a brutal life had robbed her of the ability to feel joy. But his gentle, persistent ways, his blazing, devoted love, had planted a new seed in the brown dust of her heart.

Brian would have thought nothing more of the scream if there hadn't been another—this one hard and loud and long. It was the kind that made you sick inside, a scream touched by death agony. But his wife still didn't stir. "Loi, did you hear that?"

She opened her eyes. "I was just dozing off."

He raised himself on one arm. "I'm definitely hearing screams again."

She turned to him, her stomach shifting heavily. Despite her grace of body, eight months of pregnancy had made her clumsy. "Oh, my poor Brian." She kissed him, hoping that the unfortunate ghosts of his Mary and Caitlin would finally go to their rest.

"I think they were real."

Dutifully, she listened. "There's nothing, Brian. You must try to forget the past."

"I am, Loi."

"Maybe I can help you." She shifted herself again, took him to her and embraced him. Very deliberately this time, she kissed him.

How she could kiss, he thought. She did it with a

combination of attention and sensuality that never failed to thrill him. Her kisses were so careful, yet so hungry. For a rumpled old physicist, and a damaged one, she was quite an extraordinary catch.

Mary, also, had been considered a catch. Poor Mary had burned alive.

Loi could tell by his stillness that his mind had retreated to the tragedy. She broke gently away. "You used to come here a lot?" If her predecessor had made love to him here, she must be very careful or her own efforts would only strengthen the power of the ghost.

"Not often enough. Mary wasn't an outdoor person."

She stretched luxuriously. "I love it so much outdoors."

He watched a smile envelop her face. As it did there emerged in her black eyes the trembling glance of a girl. Normally, her face—the neat, sad mouth, the hints of wrinkling under her eyes—communicated hurt. But these smiles when they came were miraculous.

He knew that she'd had a terrible life: her very refusal to say much about it revealed this. And yet, somehow, the tight little woman he'd met while she was waitressing at the Waywonda Inn had become this fabulous lover, tender and vulnerable and passionate.

There was a crash in the brittle summer brush, and Apple Sally came bounding up barking. "Hey, Sal." She sat on her haunches, whined. She was not happy, which was very strange. "Sal? C'mon, babe, take it easy." His tone quelled her nervousness, and she lay down with her big face between her paws.

There came another cry, one of total despair. It stopped abruptly, as if stifled.

Loi sat up. She'd heard that, all right. A look of agony came into her poor husband's eyes. As he dragged in a frightened breath, she took his hand. "These screams are real."

He felt a great familiar vise enclose his chest and begin to squeeze.

Mary shrieked, and then she turned and she was burning—

Another cry erupted, this one as clear and sharp as the crack of ice on a winter night. "We go for help, Brian!"

Apple Sally started digging, her claws ticking against stones, throwing back earth and bits of grass and flowers.

Brian leaped to his feet, stared down. "Jesus, they're coming from *inside* the mound!"

Loi could hear that it was true. There was certainly somebody in there. But who, and where? It was just an earthen mound, hardly even a hill. Could Mary be in there, she wondered, her ghost still suffering from the flames of her death?

Brian ran the twenty feet to the mound's bare summit. He peered around, pitifully trying to find some kind of an opening. His face was twisted, his eyes glistening.

"We have to get Bob," Loi called. His best friend was a state trooper. She started off down the hillside as fast as she could go.

When she saw Brian lean toward the ground, she returned. From below there came a long, echoing scream, lost in despair, indeed a cry from hell. "Brian, come." She tugged on his shoulder.

Sweat was pouring out of him. He was shaking like an old tree rattled by the monsoon. "Brian, we get help!"

The next scream spoke of absolute, almost inconceivable suffering.

"We've got to go!"

Beside him Apple Sally dug with the fury of the possessed. Maybe she could smell the poor woman, Brian thought, maybe she was actually close to the surface. Brian joined the dog, yanking up tufts of grass, trying to drag back the heavy, unyielding soil.

To Loi it appeared that he was going crazy. "That doesn't do any good! We need help!" She ran a little way, then saw that he was still ignoring her. She wanted to pull him away, but she dared not be so disrespectful.

He dug, he struggled, again there was a scream. He began to gasp, to grunt with the strain of his useless work.

She saw that he was entering a hypnosis familiar from her childhood. When soldiers did this, their officers slapped them back to their senses.

To treat an honored husband in such a manner was unthinkable. He was no common soldier—but he was digging like the animal beside him, grunting, panting, lost.

He felt something slam into the side of his head. Stars snapped behind his eyes and then he was on his back, his hands clawing air. Loi stood over him, all five feet of her, and she shouted in a trembling, unsure voice, "We have to get help at once!"

His cheek stung, his ear was ringing. He watched her shoulders hunch, saw her take her guilty right fist into her left, squeeze it until her hands shook. "I meant no disrespect," she whispered. "Please forgive me."

Chiefly, he was amazed at how strong she was. He sat up, realizing that he was being incredibly stupid, on some level reliving the moment he'd tried to dig through the wall of the burning kitchen where Mary and Kate had been trapped.

Another scream came and it was terrible to hear. "You come with me now, work the car phone!" Digital technology mystified and angered her. She took his hand, forced all the authority she could into her voice. "Come with me, Brian, if we are to help."

They went headlong down the mound, Loi rolling along with what Brian saw as all the grace of a small tank. He hurried behind her with his arms out, protective lest she take a fall. Apple Sally bounded through the grass beside them.

Loi ran because she had to run. Somebody was in agony, somebody was dying. Brian Ky Kelly bounced within her.

"Slow down, honey! Take care!"

As Brian hurried to keep up with her, his knowledge of local topography brought a frightful possibility to mind. He thought that a sinkhole might have opened up, maybe the ceiling dropped out of an old cave. Given that somebody was already inside, it was likely to be on the path. "Loi, stop!"

She ignored his cry.

"Loi!"

She shot off like a deer, racing wildly, heedless of her condition, unconscious of the danger. He dashed after her, past the clumps of daisies and dandelions, into the spreading view of Oscola, St. Paul's church spire and the town roofs awash in the green of summer trees.

He reached the base, looked desperately for her. "Loi?"

Silence.

No, please, not again. Not another wife killed, another baby. He ran madly toward his truck; he didn't see her in the cab. *"Loi!"*

Just then she sat up. She'd been bending over, pushing buttons on the phone. "It won't make the dial tone," she cried. He jumped in the cab, turned the phone on and punched in the number of the state police.

"Lieutenant West, please." Bob came on the line. "There's screaming coming out of the mound. You'd better get out here."

"Screaming, Brian? You're sure about this?" Bob knew all about Brian's problems.

Brian handed the phone to his wife. "Tell him."

"I hear it, too, Bob. And the dog, she is upset."

Bob said he'd be there in ten minutes, and Brian put down the phone.

Instantly, the thrall of summer reclaimed the moment. Bees were working through a soft white cloud of Queen Anne's lace in the field that led up to the judge's ruined pear orchard. A songbird warbled in a stand of hemlocks beside the road. Brian uttered a sort of whispered groan.

"Sometimes waiting is what we have, husband." She took his hands and began wiping them clean as best she could with some Kleenex. "Why did you do this crazy digging? Already your poor fingers are scarred."

"It was stupid."

She looked toward the mound. "I don't like it any-more."

"It's just a little hill. Some kind of—well, a small hill. A geologically trivial feature."

"Yes, my husband."

"There may be a sinkhole opened up around here. We've got to be careful."

"Yes." She noticed then that his temple was flaring red where she had hit him, and longed to touch it. But her shame was too great. Let it not become a bruise, let it fade.

Finally they heard a siren. The next moment a Chevy Blazer in state police colors swerved to a stop behind them. Bob climbed down out of the cab. He was in his usual shabby, unkempt uniform, and his wide, gentle face was grave.

He came toward their truck, running hard. Loi watched him through the rearview mirror. When she had been a child working for the Vietcong, he had been an American soldier. His unit had pumped liquid fire down the tunnels; her worst dreams were haunted by that same fire. When he had heard her side of the story he had shed silent, unacknowledged tears. Bob was the sort of tough-tender policeman who spent his off-duty hours coaching Little League and doing charity work. One of his secrets was that he corresponded with many of the men he'd put in jail. If they wanted, he'd be there for them when they came out.

2.

Apple Sally began to woof with excitement. She knew Bob, and her tail bounded against the bed of the truck.

" 'Lo, buddy," he said into the window. He barely glanced at Loi. They'd both left parts of their souls in Vietnam, and their relationship was complex. Sometimes when their eyes met, she would see something that frightened her a little. She could not tell if it was suspicion or anger or simply part of his pain. When they'd been getting to know one another, she had wondered if they could find forgiveness in their hearts, two soldiers who had lost dear friends to each other's armies.

"Show me where she is."

Loi would not be left behind; she also descended from the truck.

To Bob she looked ready to explode. He'd never seen anybody so pregnant. "You'd better stay here," he said. "Until we've got an idea what we're dealing with."

"Brian needs me," she said, afraid he would panic again if the person in the mound continued screaming.

"He's right, Loi. Somebody's already fallen in."

His tone told her that he wanted very badly for her to obey him. Normally, Brian did not insist. But when he did, she had to concede. Not to obey now would cause him loss of face. She bowed her head.

Bob was already running up the mound as she got back into the truck.

Brian put his hand on hers. "I'll be all right, Loi.

I swear." Then he started after Bob, checking the path ahead, looking for any sign of an opening. Sal ran beside him, her dewlaps flying. They weren't halfway up before she started baying.

"What on earth do you think you're doing?" came Judge terBroeck's voice from behind them. The old man must have been alerted by Bob's siren.

Brian was surprised to notice that the judge was changed, even from a few weeks ago. Where was his prissy, self-important way of walking, his easy arrogance? Now he dragged along, a wavering reed, his thin hair chalk white, his face all wrinkles and angles, his lips a bitter line.

As a matter of fact, he looked meaner than ever. A good deal meaner.

"There's somebody trapped in the mound," Brian shouted back at him.

"There's nowhere in there to *get* trapped."

"We know that, Judge! But she's there."

When the judge began to hurry, his spider legs pumped comically. The way he swayed reminded Brian of a great cornstalk blown by the wind. He arrived puffing hard. "My liability insurance covers me, thank God," he gasped. "I've never cared for people coming here! Why do they do it? They all know it's private."

"It's been part of this town forever."

"So has everybody else's backyard, Brian!"

With a terrific jerk Apple Sally abandoned all her years of training and ripped her leash out of Brian's hands. "Jesus," he cried.

Seconds later she reached the site of the original rescue attempt. She dug in a frenzy, her whole body pulsating with effort. Dirt and stones flew up around her.

As if the woman heard the sounds of renewed digging, she began to shriek again. "My God," Bob said, "she hears us!"

"That doesn't sound like screaming to me," the judge announced.

Sal's frenzy increased. She became a blur of flailing legs, her ears flapping like flags in a hurricane, her eyes bulging.

At first Brian was proud of her, but then he began to see red flecks on the stones she was throwing back. She was tearing her paws to ribbons. "C'mon, girl. C'mon, easy! Easy, Sally, back! *Back!*"

The wailing, pleading screams continued.

Something awful was happening to the dog. Spittle sprayed from her flapping dewlaps, and she made noises Brian had never heard her make before. "C'mon, Sal," he shouted, "back!" He grasped the dog around the midriff and started to tug. She turned, snarling and snapping. He released her. "Goddamnit!"

She used the moment of freedom to jump back into the hole she'd been making. The red flecks became gobs of bloody earth. The screaming rose. Then Sal's huffing growls changed to the desolate moans of a dying hound. Brian grabbed her tail and tugged. She skittered around, dug in with her feet, snarled and twisted.

Brian had hunted with dogs all his life, but he'd rarely seen a hound in a state like this. The whites of her eyes were showing, her teeth were bared, her muzzle sloppy with foam. Despite visibly torn paws she was still digging hard even as he dragged her back away from the rough pit.

Her whole body flopped and writhed, she twisted around, her jaws snapped, her bulging eyes gleamed. She began making undulant, humping movements, her skin quivering, her fine, clear voice gone to cracking, whispered barks.

As if responding to the sounds of the dog's effort, the screaming reached extreme frenzy.

"It isn't human screaming," the judge said. "It's some damn coon."

"It's gotta be checked out," Bob responded.

"You're a damn nut," the judge snapped at Brian. "All this over nothing!"

Abruptly, Sal collapsed, as if she'd been turned off with a switch. One moment she was in full cry, struggling to get back in her hole, the next she was a heap of floppy brown animal with froth pouring out of her slack mouth.

"My God," Brian said. He lifted her head, listened at her nose, looked into her eyes. "She's dead."

When the sound of Sal's digging had stopped, the woman in the mound had begun to sob. "We're coming," Bob shouted.

Silence.

"Just hang on, ma'am!" Bob's voice was shaking.

The response was terrible to hear, as if she had just made a new and hideous discovery, something awful beyond belief.

"Oh, Christ, get a backhoe, Bobby! Get a damn backhoe!"

"Don't you dare! You'll tear my property to pieces."

The screams dropped low, became gurgles, finally stopped.

"Listen," the judge said. "Nothing. So you don't need a backhoe. Not for a coon that just died."

As Bob ran down the mound, Brian gathered the dog into his arms.

"You let her overdo it," the judge said, "you let her run herself to death trying to dig out a coon."

"Hell, she wasn't trying to dig anything out, Judge. Don't you know a single damn thing about hounds?"

"Well, I—certainly!"

"Judge, there's something in there that Sal wanted to kill."

Both men looked down at the roughly ditched ground. Brian knew his dog. Sal had died of hate.

TWO

1.

When the phone rang Ellen Maas was—as usual—alone in the office. It was eight-fifteen on a Saturday night and this week's edition of the *Gazette* was supposed to be put to bed, but she was working desperately to expand the all-important local gossip column, the one with everybody's name in ALL CAPS. The more people she could fit in, the more papers she would sell.

She stared at the ringing phone. Surely it wouldn't be a bill collector, not on a Saturday night.

Between rings, she listened to the moths fluttering against the screens. There was a mutter of thunder; she blew sweat from her top lip.

"*Gazette.*"

"This is Harry terBroeck."

She sat up a little straighter. You wanted the extremely powerful, deeply respected, profoundly unpleasant Judge terBroeck on your side around these parts, you sure did—especially if you were the new owner of a broke newspaper. "Hello, Judge."

"I have a story. You know the way the paper used to run the local news on the front page? Well, this is that kind of thing. It's not going to be up there with a presidential visit to China, but it's interesting to us yokels."

The new girl in town had just been criticized. OK. She could handle that. "Great," she enthused, "I'm always looking for a big local story."

"Well, this is big, I mean, for us yahoos."

He waited for her protest that they weren't really yahoos, that they were terrific, that she just loved the town, gush, gush. The expected words got stuck in her throat like a backed-up corn fritter.

He went on. "The state police are out on my mound. You know the place?"

"Of course. What's the story?"

"They're tearing it all to hell. Making an awful mess of my private property without so much as a by-your-leave!"

Ellen tried not to sound impatient. "Right," she said, "shoot."

"Shoot?"

"Tell me the rest. Why are they there?"

"Well, I'd never let 'em do it, and if there's nobody in there I've got a fine cause of action against the state."

"Nobody in where?"

"The mound! *My* mound! They're tearing it apart to find a supposed woman. Been screaming."

"What woman would that be?"

"The one that's supposedly trapped in there. Nobody told you anything yet?"

"Why should they? This is just the newspaper."

He cleared his throat. For Judge terBroeck the paper was chiefly a forum where he could publish letters about the many liberal plots he detected in the affairs of the community. Evil forces on the town board trying to put in streetlights, hippies from downstate with their communistic recycling schemes, that sort of thing. "A dog—badly handled, poor damn thing—already died trying to reach her."

"You heard the screaming?"

"I heard sounds that I personally connect with a raccoon in distress. Brian Kelly said it was human screaming, of course—which he would, given that he's more than a little off balance on that particular subject, poor man. He was out there trespassing with that peculiar new wife of his when they first heard it."

"The woman in a cave or what?"

"They haven't found any woman! The story isn't the damn fool alleged woman, it's the invasion and destruction of my property, you stupid creature!"

She wanted to slam down the phone on him. She swallowed hard, then forced herself to thank the judge with dutiful and agonizing care. She hung up and went to the steel locker to get the ancient Speed Graphic that had been there when she bought the paper. It had been slated for immediate replacement, of course, considering that it was fifty years old, weighed twenty pounds and required old-fashioned glass plates that had to be special-ordered from Kodak.

"Immediate" had come to mean the end of her current five-year plan—if said plan could be realized somewhere this side of bankruptcy court.

Lugging the miserable hunk of photographic iron and an old Bloomie's bag full of plates, she went down the angular stairway onto the street. It was dead quiet, of course. Early on she'd discovered that Oscola nightlife ended when the Mills Cafe closed down at nine. She'd been a night rider in New York, as often as not starting with the theater or a concert and ending when they flushed out the after-hours clubs at dawn.

A Crown Victoria slid up Main Street, the frail driver sitting stiffly erect. The car moved like a hearse. Why? Small towns tend to be elderly, and old drivers can't see spit after dark. Plus, streetlighting was a liberal plot.

If she walked out in front of that Crown Vic, there wouldn't even be the flicker of a brakelight. Still traveling at a stately fifteen miles an hour, it would roll over her like a bump.

It being past eight on a Saturday night, Oscola was as dark as a cave, except for dim light coming from the Mills Cafe and Handy's Tobacco. The Rexall Drugstore was dark, as was Mode O'Day Fashions, which was like an antique clothing store where everything was still new. They had black patent leather belts and slack suits along with boxes of hair ribbons in the glass-topped counter and a rack of $2.98 harlequin reading glasses.

But Main Street was lined with big old oaks and maples, and down at the end where it became Mound Road there was one streetlight, a wonderful old iron creation meant to resemble a sapling, complete with iron leaves cradling the lamp.

The smell of pipe tobacco that floated out of Mr. Handy's open door was pleasant, and the faint clink of dishes coming from the Mills communicated the peace of the entirely ordinary.

Farther off something revved and died, probably some of the town's smattering of teenagers tuning a pickup out at Fisk's Garage. The "blown" pickup was Cuyamora County's ultimate muscle car. There were no Porsche Carerras here, no Acura NSX's. But then again, there were also no orthodontists in mirrored sunglasses to go with them, which was a plus. She'd had her fill of mirrored orthodontists, especially ones named Ira Bergman.

Still, something appealed about those breezy early-morning runs to East Hampton in Ira's Porsche with the wind in their hair. That was back when the relationship was still in the battlefield maneuvers stage, before the actual war had started.

Well, hell, what was love compared to owning a dying newspaper?

People around here hadn't stopped buying the *Gazette* because it was bad, but because she'd breezed into town and bought it and she was a city person and a fancy former *New York Times* reporter into the bargain.

She pulled her ancient gray Duster out of the parking space in front of ludicrously named Excelsior Tower. It was two stories tall, for God's sake. Then she drove the mile out to the mound, the Speed Graphic on the seat beside her.

As she turned into the long driveway beside the judge's house her ears drank the newsy snarl of heavy machinery out on the mound. A glance in the direction of the old terBroeck place told her that the judge was at home. She could see him in his kitchen, still on the phone.

Ahead she observed dancing red light bars, and up on the mound itself the glare of portable floodlights. She opened her door and jumped out, hefting the camera.

Passing the jumble of cars and trucks at the base of the mound, she noticed Brian Kelly's exotic wife asleep in the cab of their truck. The way the story went, he'd met her while she was waitressing at the Waywonda Inn in Ludlum. Discreetly turning tricks was more like it, Ellen thought. She was one of those desperate, unwanted souls coughed up by Southeast Asia, a Vietnamese all mixed up with French and American blood. As a child, she'd allegedly been used by the Vietcong as a tunnel rat. God only knew how she'd made her way to Oscola, New York. Ellen leaned into the cab. "Mrs. Kelly?"

Loi's eyes opened, but there was no sense of her being startled awake. Maybe the tunnel rat story was true. She certainly displayed the elaborately careful attitude of a person who's lived with danger.

"I'm Ellen Maas, Mrs. Kelly, with the *Gazette*."

Finally, Loi smiled. "I'm tired," she said apologetically. It wasn't surprising, considering the advanced state of her pregnancy.

"What do you know about the woman in the mound?"

"You must ask my husband." She made a movement so sudden that it shocked Ellen. The woman was as swift as a cat, but all she'd done was glance at her watch. Then she came down out of the truck and moved off up the path, her huge belly making her rock from side to side.

Ellen had the feeling that Loi Kelly was running away from her. So naturally she followed, stopping when Loi did among a group of men standing under the lights. They had a large chart open between them. She stared right back at the trooper eyes that were now regarding her.

Trooper Numero Uno was here, Lieutenant Robert West. His big, open face broke into a grin. She was not deceived: West was a sweet man, but he was no hick. And he was very careful about the press. She knew why: this particular Medal of Honor winner had gotten his award for doing some very hard things, very hard indeed. Very brave, also, but it was not West's nature to be proud of killing people with his bare hands.

She'd made the mistake of doing research into his medal. He'd begged her not to print the story. "Tell about my Little League work. Tell about my Great Books stuff. But leave the medal alone." She'd complied: her feature about him had quoted his thoughts about Aeschylus, but not Westmoreland.

She walked toward him, working on her mask. Don't smile like an idiot, just look very professional. Reticent though he was, the man remained a hero. How do you share a secret heroism?

Of the men with West, Ellen knew only Brian Kelly, now standing hand in hand with his wife. Her face had gone soft, the almond eyes melted with love, the full, heart-shaped lips revealing what Ellen thought was probably pride.

He'd lost his daughter and his first wife in a fire, and Ellen had looked that up in the newspaper's morgue, too. The fire had been attributed to a defective propane line under his ancestral home. He'd been burned half to death attempting to save them. He and Mary Kelly had been extremely close. She'd been one of his students, and after she got her doctorate they'd taught as a team.

The fire had crushed him. He'd walked away from his university job and become a hermit, gone on a two-year bender. Then he'd suddenly met Loi and astonished this half of the state by bringing her into his distinguished old Oscola family.

Ellen took a deep breath. West, with his obsessive concern for safety, was already asking one of the men to help Loi back down the mound. She'd be next, she knew, if she wasn't careful. "Any luck?" she asked in a voice that came out so husky it could have pulled a dogsled. Too many cigarettes.

Bob West glanced at her, then hid his face under the shadow of his hat.

"I'm sorry, but I've got to ask a few questions. Is she in a tomb?"

"More likely a cave," West responded. "And you'd best wait in your car until we've found the opening."

She rushed on. "Well, isn't it an old Indian mound? Maybe it's full of tombs."

"Now, ma'am, we've got a lot of heavy equipment working out here, and—"

"I'm press, Bob, you know that."

Instantly the head lowered, again the eyes disappeared. "I just worry that it isn't safe."

She sighed. "I have to stay. It's my job."

"You keep near us," Dr. Kelly finally said. "We don't want anybody else falling in holes."

"Thank you," Ellen responded.

"We think a sinkhole has opened up," Kelly explained. "Our theory is that she's fallen in and she's wandering in our hypothetical cave."

Fifty feet away the backhoe growled again. The machine rocked, its operator clamped his cigar in his jaws, a jet of exhaust fumes shot up past the lights. The hoe turned and the debris went pouring down into a pile near the base.

Ellen cranked up the Graphic and took a picture.

"Kill the backhoe," a man bawled from the dark summit of the mound. It ground, coughed, rumbled, finally went silent. All that was left was an occasional random crinkle from its hot exhaust manifold.

Ellen could just barely see the face of the man who had called out. It was visible in the faint green glow of some sort of electronic device. Smelling more story, she started up toward him.

"Quiet," the man yelled. "Hey, lady, *quiet!* Don't move, don't even breathe!"

Little pinging noises started above, continued for a few moments. Then the man stood up, removed his earphones, stepped out of the glow coming from his instrument's screen. He hurried down toward Bob West, who regarded him with eyes so full of pain that Ellen wanted to cuddle the poor man up in her arms.

"It's solid earth, in my opinion," the man said.

"You're sure?"

"There's nothing in there. It's exactly what it looks like, a small glacial tip without geologic significance. Certainly there are no caves."

"Then what did we hear, Danny?" Brian's voice was much too smooth.

Danny, who Ellen surmised was a state-owned geologist, rubbed his left hand against the stubble on his cheek. "I just don't know. Maybe it was a trick of the wind."

The Speed Graphic began to feel awfully heavy.

"There's somebody in there," Brian Kelly said. His voice had taken on the low, ominous note of a threatened man. "I can't buy your finding."

"Well, you have to," the geologist replied blithely. "It's reality."

Kelly tucked his chin into his chest. "She was in a hollow space. We could hear the echoes."

"Well, it wasn't in this mound! I'm telling you, there's nothing in it. Zero. Zip. *Natha.*"

"That's bullshit, Danny."

"Then dig the goddamn thing up yourself, Doctor! You've got a backhoe here, raze the damn thing."

Bob West spoke. "Let me ask you a question."

"One I can answer, certainly."

"Are you willing to say I should abandon this rescue, given that a woman—a human being just like you or me—could be in there dying in agony? You're that certain?"

"I can only tell you that my instruments do not support the notion that this mound is anything except what it appears, a pile of broken schist and stone."

"Come on, Danny," Kelly interjected, "you're dealing with a government surplus echo sounder that was designed for work in water. It's next to useless here. Even a dumb old physicist can tell you that. The resistivity of the soil isn't going to allow a meaningful reading."

"It's been recalibrated," the young man snarled. "Of course."

In the motionless air, the mutter of thunder became more defined. Off in the west the dark was thick.

"I've never liked this place much," the backhoe operator said. He'd been standing at the edge of the group. "Back last month the wife and me was up here and the whole thing sort of shook. It spooked us and we took off."

The geologist wiped his brow. "Admittedly there's evidence of some earth movement. The schist's probably loose. Changing temperature, degree of dampness—a lot of things can cause small-scale earth movement. Even the Towayda fault could be involved."

"The woman was screaming," Kelly repeated.

In support of her husband, Loi Kelly became fierce. "I heard her, too, Danny!"

Ellen made a mental note never to tangle with this woman.

"You might as well go ahead and move this equipment out," the young geologist said.

Brian Kelly roared. "No you won't! You sure as hell will not!"

Bob looked at him. "I can't get a budget for it if the expert says there's nobody in there."

"What expert? He was a failure when he was at Ludlum, and he's a failure now. That's why he works for the state!"

"How dare you!"

"Hey, Brian, come on. He's still my official expert. He's the guy I've gotta rely on."

Kelly went up to West, face-to-face. "Somebody's dying in there!"

"Brian, I don't have enough evidence. And what about the judge—he's already been after us to get out of here. I continue this dig without good cause, I've got a lawsuit on my hands."

"If there turns out to be a story here," Ellen said to West, "could you please give me a call?" She started off down the mound.

"Take care," Brian Kelly called after her.

She waved, and was soon negotiating the dark with the dubious old penlight she kept in the bottom of her purse.

She was past the halfway point when she felt a

sort of lurch. A distinct vibration began pulsing up from the ground. It stopped her dead. "Jesus," she heard herself say.

It hurt her bones in a way she'd never felt before, as if the marrow itself was vibrating. She imagined a crazed dentist boring into her jaw with a bone-burning drill. The vibration was accompanied by a metallic shrieking noise, like a very large buzz saw going berserk in the distance.

Lights flashed, the sound hummed off into the sky. She turned around to see the floodlights swinging on their poles. Shadows darted as men jumped to hold them steady.

She heard a new sound, painfully loud, like the squeal of a desperate child. Ellen turned toward the group she'd just left in time to see Loi Kelly stagger backward clutching her belly.

2.

The buzzing sensation was so intense that Brian slapped his hand to his jaw, instinctively going for the pain that was screeching through his head. But Loi's agonized shriek made him forget himself, gather her in his arms. "Baby," he said, "oh, baby!"

She felt the fire of a bayonet plunging into her womb, a thing she had seen done. She wanted to scream, but fought against it. Best to maintain a serene appearance.

Before anybody could react further there was a faint, tremendous clang, as if a door the size of a mountain had been slammed shut.

Bob threw himself down, listening. "Hey," he

shouted at the ground, "hey, lady!" Then he crouched. "Nothing."

Loi felt a tickle along her inner thigh. She turned away into the dark, bent over and reached her hand up under her loose outfit. Yes, the worst. She straightened abruptly.

"Loi?"

She hated to reveal weakness, but she had no choice. This was urgent. "Brian, there is no cause for alarm, but I would like to be taken to see the doctor now."

"Is the baby—"

"No, Brian, he is not coming. But we must go at once, please." Always in the back of her mind was the fear that Brian would reject her if she lost his son. Love was wonderful, but even American men surely had their practical considerations.

Brian fought down the churning acid in his own stomach. He must not let Loi see how frightened he was.

Ellen Maas reappeared in the swaying pool of light. He was startled by what it did to her face, making it appear alternately hard and soft. It struck him that she was an unusually beautiful woman.

"We go now," Loi said. Eight months was much too late for blood.

"I can take her," Ellen announced. She was fluttering her long hands at Loi, communicating concern. But Brian sensed something a little predatory in the gesture. A reporter always wanted something from you.

"I'll do it," he said.

His arm around Loi's shoulder, Brian guided her down the slope. He should have taken her back to the truck the minute she reappeared, not let her stay like this.

As they left, Brian heard the geologist telling Bob that the earth movement theory had just been confirmed.

Brian didn't believe it for a moment. But Danny wouldn't have been the first scientist who wanted to dismiss a mystery rather than explore it.

To both him and Loi it seemed a long, long time before the dark shape of the truck came into view. He helped her up, belted her in, then got in himself. He started the engine and began driving carefully toward the road, avoiding ruts and bumps as best he could. "Call Dr. Gidumal's office, hon, tell 'em we're on our way." He started the phone for her, trying to control his shaking hand.

When they finally reached the relative smoothness of Mound Road, he floored the accelerator and the truck jumped forward, tires squealing. They went racing through the dark and out onto Route 303, then down toward Ludlum and the hospital.

He shifted in his seat. She reached over, squeezed his hand. She was very scared, but she wanted him to be reassured, to think well of her. "I am a strong woman, I have a good womb." Was it true, after all the abortions, some of them done by casual midwives, others by well-intentioned friends? At the Blue Moon Bar they used to abort each other with a long instrument provided by the management. She had no idea of the condition of her womb.

He looked over at her. She was sitting with her head pressed far back into the seat, one hand on his. He reached the hand to his lips, kissed it. Her hand was as soft as a little bird. She seemed so brave and so vulnerable. He was terrified: he could smell his own sweat.

She finished the call to the hospital and put down the phone. "I am very healthy, Brian. I will give many sons!" She could feel the blood coming out steadily now. Baby Brian was jumping a little, as if he was beginning to become distressed. Sometimes she thought she could feel his beautiful young soul lying within her, like a golden shaft of light in her womb. He must not die, not now.

"We'll be there in twenty minutes, honey."

The ache was growing, becoming touched by what felt like heat down at the bottom of her belly. She forced back an urge to moan. The heat began to spread into her thighs, up her back. She sat as still as stone to stifle what she knew could quickly become agonized squirming. She turned to him and gave him a smile. "I am admiring your skillful driving. Please hurry."

That brittle, terrible smile told him that she was in agony. His own breath began coming hard and tight. It would have been easier for him, he thought, if she had not been so composed.

Her mind drifted on long waves of pain. The birds called softly in the garden of the Emperor of Jade Pagoda in Saigon, while little Qui Thanh Nguyen crouched in a secret place, a small girl in a white *bao dai*.

She'd changed her name to Loi because the white-eyes couldn't pronounce the "Q" sound correctly. She loved her white-eyes husband, though, no matter how he spoke.

The pain dug at her. Touching herself, she brought up blood on her fingertips. In the light of the dashboard they gleamed as if darkened by wet paint. She snatched the evidence out of sight, wiped it away under her blouse. The smile remained fixed on her face.

Although Brian knew every twist and turn, the trip seemed to last forever.

When they finally saw the lights of the hospital, the big red sign that said EMERGENCY, Loi was drifting into soft blackness. She came back, feeling the pain like a saw grinding between her legs.

Brian raced into the ambulance bay honking his horn.

Nurses came running out, followed by Dr. Gidumal.

"Help us," Brian said. "Please help us."

3.

A couple of minutes later she was in an examining room in stirrups, and Dr. Gidumal had a speculum poised as delicately as a wand in his gloved hand. The pain was now slamming up from her gut in great, red waves. She could no longer maintain even a fixed, rigid smile. But Dr. Gidumal was a stranger, and before a stranger one must be composed. She was breathing too hard. She tried to be more quiet.

"We went on a picnic," Brian said. "We heard someone screaming, called the state police. Loi is very gentle. She got upset."

The doctor stroked her forehead. "You experienced a sudden pain before you noticed the blood?"

She was silent. To speak of the pain would be to let it capture her. Now her womb felt like a great balloon filled with boiling blood, compressed, packed, being penetrated by white-hot needles.

"She is like the women of my country, she prefers not to reveal pain." The doctor looked at Brian. "You must tell me."

Brian looked into his wife's face, seeking an answer to the doctor's question. Her sweated skin gleamed in the hard fluorescent light. "I am going to have such a healthy boy," she said. "You will be very pleased with him!" Her voice was a harsh whisper. Her face was something carved.

An American woman would have been howling, Brian thought. He reached out his hand, and she pressed a clammy cheek into his big, rough palm. "She's suffering terribly," he told the doctor.

It was awful, like fire within! Brian Ky Kelly was jumping, also. She could feel his distress now! "A happy baby," she managed to whisper.

The doctor examined her. "There are no signs of labor. This baby is not going to be born today." He plunged his gloved hand into the bloody passage of life. It took only a moment. "As I thought, there is a tear," he said. "We may be able to repair it with fast work."

Barking orders to nurses, he went quickly away. Moments later Loi felt her stretcher begin to roll, saw the ceiling sweeping past. The suddenness of it all caused her composure to fail her. "Brian," she shrieked.

"I'm here, baby." He was trotting along beside the stretcher. They went up an elevator, then down another hall that ended in two huge and familiar double doors. The old, awful smells assailed him, the iron reek of iodine and the fuzzy aroma of alcohol.

He remembered the burnt-meat tang of his own skin on the morning they'd brought him in.

Another doctor hurried through the doors, leaving them swinging back in Brian's face. He peered into OR-2. She lay on her back draped in rough green sheets.

"Good luck, baby."

Loi's voice came back, thin and high, "All will be well!"

When they closed the inner doors he went to the waiting area, all bright colors and cheer, equipped with coffee machine, Coke machine and plenty of magazines. Four years ago his father had waited for him here, bearing the knowledge that Mary and Kate were gone. Yellow curtains or not, blue chairs or not, you could smell the fear in this place.

Brian waited, feeling like a dog left out in the rain. For a time he stared blindly at an old copy of *McCall's* magazine. He was counting the tiles on the floor when a shadow appeared. His heart jumped, but it wasn't the doctor. Instead, he found himself looking into the beautiful face of one of the very last people he would have chosen to see.

"Hello, Dr. Kelly."

"This isn't going in the paper."

"Shouldn't that be my decision?"

"I'd appreciate being left alone."

She pulled a chair up in front of him and plopped herself down. "What happened out there?"

"She was injured."

"Yeah, I noticed. But what did it? What was that noise, for God's sake? It went through me like a knife."

"Look," he said, "I don't want to be rude—"

"Then don't be."

"I want to be alone, Miss Maas."

"Ellen, if you prefer. It's just that I don't understand—"

He had no reserves of politeness left. "Leave me alone!"

"Do you know what the noise was?"

"My wife might be in there losing our baby and I want my privacy!"

"I'm sorry, Dr. Kelly, really I am."

He shook his head wearily. Then he walked to the window, stared into the black glass. Behind him, he could see the reflection of her arm reach out, hesitate, then drop.

She waited for a full minute. Finally her reflection turned away and went off down the hall. Her head was bowed and her shoulders were stooped, and he found himself feeling a little sorry for her.

But she was gone, and it was a relief.

Over two hours passed before the doors to OR-2 finally opened and Dr. Gidumal came out. Brian, who had been resting on three chairs pulled together, clambered noisily to his feet. Flecks of Loi's blood stained the doctor's green hospital gown, and for a moment Brian had a horrible thought.

"She's fine and so is your son," the doctor said in one quick breath. Brian sagged. Suddenly he felt absolutely exhausted. The doctor guided him to a chair. "But I want to know what happened to her, Brian. This is a violent injury. There ought to be a police report."

"She—I guess she got upset. All the excitement."

"No, this is wounding of the uterine wall. She has

lesions. We have repaired all we could, but this is caused by one thing—concussion. Hitting."

"That's impossible. She didn't fall, and she certainly wasn't hit."

The doctor nodded, his face screwed into a deep frown. "This injury is the result of a concussive force against the womb. An explosion, a blow. Nothing else could account for it."

"Nothing exploded," Brian said. He heard a high note in his own voice. "There was a little . . . tremble in the ground, I guess. But nothing exploded."

The doctor folded his arms. "That wouldn't do it. Was she—well, to be frank, Brian—was she beaten?"

Brian knew that his hair was wild, his face stubbled. He probably looked very much the part of someone who would strike his wife. "I'd never hurt her."

"Of course not. I meant if there had been an assault. A stranger, of course. It's just that I don't understand this injury. You say no explosion. You say no blow. So I say, something is funny here."

"Wait a minute, there was more than just a little tremble. It was a strong vibration coming up from the ground."

"There are houses down, trees uprooted? No, Brian, you would see this if she had been in a terrorist bombing, or gotten a kick in the belly."

Brian made an effort to keep his voice level. "Nothing like that happened," he said. "I want to see my wife."

"Yes of course. She will wake up soon, I expect."

Brian followed the doctor into the recovery room. And there she lay, a pitiful, delicate vision. "Loi," he said.

"Oh . . ."

Suddenly Dr. Gidumal pushed Brian aside, leaned into Loi's face. "Did anybody hit you, Loi?"

"No . . . it was the humming . . . the humming that hurt me . . ." She closed her eyes, suddenly asleep.

Dr. Gidumal straightened up. "Certainly this was not caused by any humming." As he had when he first saw her, he laid his hand on Loi's forehead. Brian saw the tenderness and understood at once. Both of them were far from home, both were Asian, both must have known the acute hurt generated by all the small, silent acts of prejudice in a self-involved little community like the Three Counties. Dr. Gidumal obviously felt protective toward his fellow emigrant, and worried that she was being abused. "She will doze for a little time more. When she awakens fully, you must be present. There must be no upsets to her. She is in a delicate state. There are many microlesions. Any one of them could open up, with the right sort of stimulus." Here he paused, gazed at her. When he looked up, it was with a frank plea in his eyes. "A delicate condition. We will keep her in hospital for two days' observation. Then she can go home. But you must be careful, careful, careful."

"Yes, Doctor."

Dr. Gidumal gave him another long look, then took his hand. "We will not fail," he said.

Brian wished that he hadn't said that, it sounded awfully ominous.

He stayed with Loi until eleven, when the nurses convinced him to go home and try to get some sleep.

That proved to be a great mistake.

THREE

1.

Ellen drove along Route 303, returning from the hospital in Ludlum to her little cabin in Oscola. The uneasy ratcheting of her Duster clattered in her ears. Getting stuck out here alone would mean a long, dark walk, and probably a wet one too: lightning was flickering against the horizon, thunder guttering off in the mountains.

Oscola was hidden deep in a wild country. The woods were not friendly. More than one small plane had crashed into these mountains and never been found. Every summer campers and hikers went out and never came back.

Much of the region—which fifty years ago had been a thriving community of foresters, apple farmers and dairymen—was now abandoned. Orchards so ancient that the trees appeared to be deformed clung to the few arable valleys. Abandoned houses, their windows covered with plywood, their interiors gutted, were all that remained of families who had made their livings here for ten generations.

It was a beautiful country, though, with sundappled valleys and laughing streams the locals called kills, using the old Dutch word. Its dangers were known—the isolation, the size of the forest, the tracklessness of the mountains. Getting hurt in the woods, getting lost—those were the things you worried about around here.

No matter what the state police had decided, she wasn't going to drop the matter of the woman in the mound. Even if it was as empty as their smarmy geologist claimed, there was still a story in that agonizing sound. Loi Kelly was lying in the hospital. Ellen could still feel an ache in her bones.

Now, what on earth had done that? Certainly not any of the equipment they'd had up there. It had come right up out of the ground.

There were brighter flashes of lightning. Thunder boomed back and forth, a deep and savage argument. She turned down Mound Road and passed the judge's place, a stone house with a gambrel roof and narrow second-story windows. The first floor was more graceful, as if the old Dutch patroons had attempted to recapture in a small way some of the elegance of the world they had left behind in Holland. But the effect of the tall windows and imposing front door was to make the house look crudely unbalanced. At this hour the place was dark and silent, the mound behind it a great, curving shadow, black against the tumbling clouds. A few moments later she was approaching her own place. From the road there was virtually no indication that her cabin even existed. Even the dirt track twisting off under the trees was hard to notice.

As usual it was shuttered in silence—the silence she hated. After the first six weeks, which had been grim indeed, she had decorated her three rooms with chintz curtains, rope rugs and Adirondack views from the Mountain Gallery in Ludlum. Even while she had been shopping the Sears catalog for curtain rods and cutesy cuptowels, she hadn't known exactly why she was dropping her sloppy old ways and doing the *hausfrau* two-step.

But she soon admitted the obvious: she was lonely as hell. Living the life of a backwoods hermit was an experience so oppressive that she had endeavored to disguise it by making her lair as warm, old-fashioned and cozy as she could. Maybe there was a little sympathetic magic in it. If she made a place that looked homey enough, perhaps a companion would show up at the breakfast table one morning.

A steady drip of water was the only thing breaking the present silence.

She looked at the phone. The only person she might conceivably call was Ira, and he didn't even have the same phone number anymore. For all she knew, he'd packed his collection of Ray-Bans and aimed the Porsche for Taos.

What would she tell her mythical phone companion—that she was lonely and in need, that she was past thirty and found her eyes caressing other people's kids, that she had foolishly bought a dying small-town newspaper and was tailspinning toward bankruptcy and spinsterhood?

She was headed for a white nylon dress and an order pad. The only real question about her future as a waitress was, did she have the feet for it?

A flash briefly lit up the front yard. She sighed, went into the kitchen, opened the pantry cabinet. Tang, Swiss Miss Cocoa, Café Français. She was turning into a rural frump with a junk-beverage habit. Vague, listless thunder underlined the thought. Somewhere out there the storm slipped through the night like a prowling cat.

As she was taking the cocoa out of the cabinet it crossed her mind that she could spend her sleepless night productively. She could work on the story.

The mound was out there, nobody would stop her, she could snoop to her heart's content.

Underground screams, a killer sound—there was a story all right.

Come morning, the judge would either be guarding his precious property line or the mound would be swarming with state cops again, in which case she'd have to negotiate both his tearing rage and their hostility.

She had a penlight. All she had to do was avoid the judge. How? Her car would shatter the tomb-like silence that shrouded Oscola at night.

She could walk. Along the road it would be a mile. But through the woods it was less than half that. It was rough, though, and full of animals. Black bears abounded. She'd seen them humping along like bridge trolls even during the day. They had strange, pointed faces, cruel, empty eyes.

Going out at this hour would be nerve-racking, no doubt about it. On the plus side, though, she couldn't get lost even if she walked. All she had to do was follow the path along Coxon Kill, the stream behind her house. After a quarter of a mile the forest opened into meadow. The mound would be directly ahead.

She stepped out onto her porch to assess the possibility of actually doing this insane thing. She tossed her hair, a gesture of defiance that had been with her since she was a child. She moved down to the loamy forest floor that formed her front yard. Another flash of lightning reminded her to count, one thousand, two thousand, three thousand . . . She reached eleven before she heard a faint patter of thunder. So the storm was probably not going to be a factor.

Shining her penlight ahead, she set off into the blackness of the forest. Soon she could hear the babble of Coxon Kill. Last winter it had frozen solid and its rapids had looked like quartz. She could touch them, run her hand along their wrinkles and curves. She'd fallen sort of in love with the kill then. A month ago she'd found a swimming hole about fifty feet long and eight feet deep, the water so clear you could count the trout ghosting along the bottom.

She could walk naked from her cabin and swim there, doing the breaststroke until the water turned her blue. She had adored the astonishing sensation of being naked in the woods, of feeling the cool forest air caress her breasts . . . God, she wished she had a man who was gentle, poetic and sexy. A nice man.

Her light flickered in a thicket of mountain laurel. Sharp stars of flowers shone pale. Far above, the enormous pines whispered on the slight wind. When the kill was so loud she was beginning to think she might stumble into it, she finally found the path.

Twenty minutes later the forest gave way to a wide field and the brook became sluggish, its banks muddy and indistinct. The mound stood before her, a low and unimposing shape blotting the horizon.

As she advanced, she saw light in a couple of the judge's downstairs windows. When she observed that it was flickering, she stopped. This light had an odd purple tinge, reminding her of the arc of a welder's torch.

Was he running a gas space heater? Surely not in this stifling weather. Maybe something was burning.

She went over to the house, moving swiftly through the ruined pear orchard with its twisted, twig-choked trees, and up the uneven brick walk that led across the garden to the kitchen door. This close, the house breathed out its own intimate smells, the odor of its cellar and the faint suggestion of the evening's meal that had been prepared in the kitchen, and another scent that was harder to define. Maybe there was a dead opossum in the crawl space.

Given that she was a tall woman, it was easy for her to look in the window. She discovered that the source of the flickering wasn't a fire, it was a huge television set.

The set was a room away, facing in her direction. Before it was a chair, and she could see the judge's head lolling to one side. Was he asleep? It looked like it.

The odd thing was the image on the screen. It was smoke—thick, roiling, purple smoke billowing end-lessly past. An after-the-bomb shot from a war movie might look like this, but such a shot would only last a second. This never ended.

What in the hell was it, she wondered, and why purple? Smoke was black. When stations went off the air, didn't they go to static? Who would leave an endless loop showing nothing but this?

Well, they had, and the judge had gone to sleep watching it. No doubt it was some regional station manager's concept of a cool idea, purple smoke in the night. Her experience with the world of small-town media was that it contained a high quotient of morons. Look at her, she'd given up a decent salary, a secure job, an orthodontist with a good car and the city she love-hated for this.

She was about to turn away when she saw the judge's long, thin hand come up to his face. The fingers spread, hesitated in the air, then fell against his cheek and slowly slid down out of sight.

She backed away from the window, repelled as much by the bizarre sensuality of the gesture as by the realization that he was awake. Now that she knew that he wasn't sleeping, it looked as if he was in some kind of weird state of tongue-lolling ecstasy.

What if he was an addict? Wouldn't *that* be a lovely story to print? She watched him. My, but it would be fun to beat up the old creep in the paper.

Now he was nodding up and down. She could see that his mouth was wide open. He was jerking. She realized that he must be masturbating.

Her impulse was to run, but she stopped herself for fear the sound would stir him. She'd interrupted a private moment, and her cheeks began to burn.

She crept off, feeling decidedly perverse.

2.

When she reached the summit of the mound her feet began to crunch in gravel. There'd never been any reason for her to come here before, and she'd always assumed that the summit would be like the rest of the mound, lushly overgrown with weeds.

It wasn't hard to find the place where Dr. Kelly and his Saigon Sally had heard the screams: that was where the backhoe had done its work. She went over to the black scar it had left. As she approached, she could smell the sick-sour odor of the raw soil. Once this would have surprised her, but she'd smelled enough cut dirt in this area to know that soil isn't necessarily sweet. A city dweller expects black, rich-smelling earth. But the reality is very different. Wild earth smells of death and decay, for it is a killing ground and the home of a carrion multitude.

She lingered at the edge of the ditch, not quite willing to commit herself to inspect that soil. She imagined black beetles, earthworms, grubs, moles, shrews, massive high-speed snakes. The ditch was an open wound bleeding confused little creatures who wanted so very badly to rush up her legs.

A reasonable compromise was to lie in the dandelion-choked grass that gave most of the mound its green surface. She pressed her ear against the ground, closed her eyes. After a few seconds she felt the most appalling sense of vulnerability.

She got to her feet. Looking around, she noticed a glow at the far end of Mound Road. A car. She turned off her penlight. Who would be coming down here at this hour? Then another glow appeared behind the first, and a third behind that.

A whole procession of cars was coming down Mound Road. She didn't like this at all. Maybe the judge had seen her, had called the sheriff's office or the state police.

But no, the first vehicle was an old pickup with a rattly bed. There was nothing official about these vehicles.

She crouched down, watching. A total of nine cars approached, parking along the sides of the road and in the clearing where it dead-ended at the judge's pear orchard. When they turned off their lights it was too dark to see, but she could hear the doors opening and closing as they got out.

She got ready to run. But then the front door of the house opened, pouring white-purple light out into the yard. The people filed into the judge's house, men, women, and children, all walking stiffly, as if they were—what? She didn't know what. They were just walking funny.

What the hell was this, a midnight meeting of some kind? Old communities are full of secrets. She ought to go back down there, try to find out what was happening.

Old communities also tend to be mean about keeping their secrets.

The judge had been flinging his fish. Was this some sort of wildly perverted backwoods sex club meeting going on here?

Then she heard low voices, saw lights going on throughout the house. Not exactly a secret meeting, after all. As the light got brighter, she could hear shouts.

The story was still out here. Again she stretched herself out, pressed her ear firmly to the ground and listened. The grass beneath her head crunched. There was nothing else . . . or . . . no.

Yes! A deep, deep sound. Underground stream, some kind of machine?

She raised her head, trying to tell if she'd been listening to the rush of her own blood. No, that deep, throbbing note had nothing to do with her.

It was a sound of engine power coming from a place where no engine should be. She took the cassette recorder out of her fanny pack and turned it on, pressed the mike into the soil.

But then it went still, almost as if—but no, that was impossible. But it did seem as if it had stopped *because* she'd been listening.

For a moment she wondered if she was going crazy. There weren't any machines down there.

Again she looked at the ditch. Would going down in a three-foot-deep cut really help her hear better? The mound was at least fifty feet high. On the other hand, what if the woman was in a tomb near the surface, too exhausted to scream? Maybe—if she'd heard anything—it had been the booming tremor of an exhausted voice.

She clambered down into the ditch. Did earwigs really run into your ears and start digging wildly toward the interior of the brain?

There was a bright flash of lightning and an immediate roll of thunder. That was all she needed—the storm had decided to come back. After the thunder subsided it grew very quiet. It was dark, too, like pitch, like ink, like the emptiness of profound sleep.

She leaned down, far down, and worked her ear into the muck. It was thick, giving stuff, but not nearly as gooey as she'd imagined. In fact it had a light, friable quality that was quite unexpected. The mud of the forest floor was as dense as wet concrete.

Suddenly she remembered a coke tailing she'd found behind an old silver smelter she'd once done a story about. This was what extreme temperature did to some types of stone.

She was rewarded with another noise, this one clear and close and quite ugly. It made even less sense than the deep rumbling, this rapid slithery noise. It was frantic, a lobster scrabbling in the pot, the whipping body of a snake whose head is being crushed under a boot.

She instantly leaped out of the ditch. Her impression was that the thing had been right under her.

There was no question about this sound: it had been big—very big. Not an eel in a pot, an anaconda in a caldron. Good God, what was *in* there?

It was time to get out of here.

She started down the mound—and was stopped at once by what she saw below. Cars now choked the dead end. There must be twenty of them. And there was activity in the house, a great deal of activity. Every curtain was drawn, but she could hear the hum of many more voices . . . and a sort of sizzling noise. There was also lots more purple-white light, strobing behind the curtains.

Risky or not, she knew she had to get a closer look. She moved quickly down the side of the mound—the path was well worn—using her penlight as little as possible.

The pear trees were gnarled and full of branches that seemed designed to stick her in the eye, but she found that they also afforded good cover. She could come within thirty feet of the house without showing herself.

This close, the purple light was really intense. It was odd, too, the way it made her feel kind of . . . trembly inside. Trembly and warm, a bit like sex.

Inside the house it must be intolerably bright. And the voices—it sure wasn't any fun party they were having in there. People were choking and bellowing, children were wailing, it was an altogether dreadful sound. People burning, people drowning, people being torn apart—these were the images that the screams brought to mind.

She moved out of the cover of the orchard, stepped quickly across the dry grass of the back lawn. She reached what was probably a dining room window, heading toward a bright chink of light that was leaking out from between a parting of the curtains.

Close up, the house was really rocking and the cries were ghastly—too hoarse, too loud, too . . . lost.

Her stomach twisted, she swallowed. She wanted to run, to get out of here, to go home and bury herself under the covers.

But there was a story here, very certainly.

Closer yet, the voices were even worse. They weren't simply sounds of agony. She recognized something she thought must be pleasure. It was a mixture of pleasure and torment. She pressed her face to the rusty screen and peered into the lit interior.

The light was so bright she was blinded. She had nothing more than an impression of movement—not even the sense of shape. People were leaping, jerking, flailing so fast that their bodies were blurs in the purple-white ocean. She felt a sensation leap through her eyes and right down to her groin, a sensation that ended in a tickling so intense that it caused an instant convulsion.

She screamed, she couldn't help it. Then she threw herself backward, sprawling in the grass. The pleasure was so great that she was momentarily helpless. However, she recovered herself and dashed off, running wildly away toward the orchard.

She crouched among the trees, breathless with fear. Nobody emerged from the house. She rubbed her left eye, which tingled furiously. What was going on in there? She'd been—it was like instant climax. More than climax. She sweated, her body tingling at the memory. Her eye was numb, though, and she wasn't sure she could see clearly.

The light had hurt her. Maybe it was a retinal burn. Perhaps she'd looked into a laser.

She began to back out of the orchard. When she was parallel to the end of the road, she decided to risk trotting across it and running among the cars. She didn't recognize many of the vehicles, which meant that they weren't Oscola folk but people from nearby towns. She knew most Oscola cars by sight.

Could it be a secret society—the Order of Purple Light Freaks or something—here to have an electronic orgy?

She had already crossed the road when she noticed that one of the cars was running. It was making a deep, throbbing sound, the growl of a monster engine.

Then she spotted it, parked facing outward with a clear run to Mound Road. It was a sports car, a convertible with the top down, low and mean, of a shape unfamiliar to her. It was a taut machine designed to dominate. Gas-guzzling sports cars left her cold . . . and thrilled her. She'd always been conflicted about Ira's Porsche. But this was no European jewel-box. This car had USA written all over it—the shape said tough and smart and powerful.

She moved closer, her eyes on the glowing instrument panel, which could be seen inside the open interior. The closer she got, the more obvious it became that this car was something very special. When she was just behind it, she could see the nameplate. It was a Dodge Viper. She was stunned: what was something like this doing in the Three Counties? This was the ultimate muscle car. The paper had gotten some press releases about it. A Viper was the kind of thing that belonged in Arnold Schwarzenegger's driveway, not Judge terBroeck's. She went around to the door. There were no handles, so she leaned over and peered at the odometer. Everything came up zero. According to its instruments, this car had never traveled a foot.

Was it stolen? What in hell was a stolen car doing here?

Then she heard another sound, one that made her stop dead. Somebody was breathing, slow, regular, deep. And it was coming from up under the dash, as if a dwarf was hiding himself by pressing into the car's cramped foot well. She started to shine her penlight, but then hesitated. The feeling of being watched was overwhelming—and absolutely terrifying. She backed away from the car. "I'm sorry," she said.

There was a grumbling sound from the dark—and what felt like a tangle of threads landed on her right hand, encircling it.

She leaped back, yanking her arm away. Had she gotten in a spider web?

It was then that she noticed the lightning bugs. They appeared suddenly, because otherwise she would have seen them before. As far as she was concerned, fireflies were one of the pleasures of country life.

But she wasn't interested in enjoying them now, even though they were drifting up from a hole behind the judge's pear trees in a graceful wave. They were coming in a tight group, gliding across the lawn.

If she didn't change course, they were going to collide with her.

The sky erupted with a lacework of lightning. It was rendered fuzzy by low, nasty clouds, but it was nevertheless an astonishing display, accompanied by guttering, persistent thunder.

In the silence that followed a breeze came up, at first welcome in the wet, sucking heat. But the breeze got harder, fast. Soon it was wind, cutting and mean. Huge drops of rain began to strike her.

Even though she was out of the pear orchard, the lightning bugs were still behind her. She wasn't being chased, of course, but it sure felt like it.

When a firefly landed on the back of her hand, she shook it off. Then she noticed one was in her hair. She reached up, brushed it away. Another came so close to her face that she could feel the breeze of its wings.

And she could smell it, a cutting mix of acid and dirty skin.

She ran like a madwoman.

3.

The weeds cut into her shins. On the uneven ground she stumbled, flailed, twisted.

But the moment she slowed down a firefly landed on her face near her left eye. Before she could brush it off another joined it. Simultaneously a third started scrabbling in her ear. She thrashed, and her right hand came away dripping crumbs of pink-purple phosphorescence.

Her flight became headlong, hell-bent, desperate. She had not felt like this since she was ten and running down the middle of Garr Street in Montnoy, New Jersey, running through the dark from Steffi's house to her own.

By the time she reached the meadow her breath was coming in ragged gasps. She was no jogger, and her run dropped to a lope. Immediately a firefly came tickling into the hair along the back of her neck. She yanked it out, threw the body away. What on earth was the matter with them?

Others appeared, cruising around her, their little lights blurred by rain. Up close she noticed legs lit by the glow of fat, segmented bellies, and between each segment was a more deeply colored glow, purple and angry, suggesting intense heat. But fireflies aren't hot.

More appeared and yet more, and she began to hear a deeper note in their buzzing. She also became aware that a long shadow strode before her.

A moment later she tripped and fell across a stump that had looked in the light like a clump of weeds. She landed hard, rolling to break her fall—and then she saw what was behind her.

They flowed and undulated along the ground like a single creature, a burning snake five hundred feet long. This living band twisted and turned through the meadow, glittered in among the trees of the ruined orchard, glowed across the judge's lawn. It was emerging from that hole back in there, which glowed with purple haze.

They were literally pouring out, swarming fifty feet into the air in a burning geyser.

She stared, for the moment too amazed to feel her fear. This is the state of frozen terror the snake seeks to induce.

The great mass darted at her with the speed of lightning. She felt a hot finger between her legs. Her belly shuddered with pleasure so deep and intense that it almost incapacitated her. A terrible sense of menace came with it, though, and she knew she had to run, must run, must get away.

They wanted to get her back, to take her down into their hole.

Then the Queen Anne's lace that choked the meadow was whipping her thighs, and she was racing with the wind in her ears and the rain jetting against her face, racing for the woods, and she felt—knew—that the race was against death. Her own shadow danced before her, darting and long and getting darker as the thing behind her grew, its light increasing. It became as bright as moonlight, then sickly day.

When she reached the woods she was once again enveloped in darkness, which caused her to founder helplessly until she turned on her penlight. Recovering herself, she dashed in among the tall pines. She couldn't find the path, not even the stream, so she just kept blundering ahead. She'd left lights on, and her hope was to see a glimmer among the tree trunks.

They came in buzzing and whirring, their abdomens so bright she could observe each fiery segment. In an instant she was surrounded by thousands and thousands of them, all scrabbling at her, getting in her hair, her ears, under her clothes. Where they remained on her skin there came a sharp sort of tickly pain—almost a pleasure.

It was loathsome.

They scrabbled up her legs, tickling and pushing until they were deep between her thighs. When they got in her they felt like a single thing, a thrusting, eager finger. It was a carefully intimate presence, probing, stroking, going in, up in, deep.

When she gasped ten or fifteen of them rushed into her mouth, and she found herself crunching into their bodies with her teeth. When she tried to spit them out more came in, plunging down her throat.

She fell back, too overcome by the thick masses of them that were filling her mouth and nose to utter the scream of abandoned pleasure that was making her heart leap up even as she choked.

There were so many she couldn't close her mouth, couldn't spit, couldn't swallow. She stuck her fingers into the writhing mass, into the crunching salty-sharp taste of them, and dug them out. They resisted, swarming down her throat, tickling horribly as they scrabbled along her esophagus. Then she lost complete control of herself, heaving great, rattling coughs, unable to breathe. Their sheer numbers stuffed her throat shut. She grew frantic for air. Even as waves of shimmering genital pleasure made her back arch, she began to suffocate.

She toppled over. A needle of fire cut into her face. For a moment she thought that they were setting her aflame, then she realized that it was water. Somewhere in the back of her mind a voice said, Coxon Kill, water, water will save you. She dragged herself forward, wriggling down into the stream like a grateful otter, sucking it in and spitting out jiggling masses of glowing material.

But the pleasure grabbed her and drew her back, made her ache for more. She struggled against the urge to throw herself onto the bank, to lie down and spread her legs to the undulating, buzzing creatures. The buzzing rose higher and the tickling came around her whole middle, began to infest her again, to break her with rapture. Again and again and again she came to climax, and each time the freezing water shocked her out of it. The fight continued between Ellen's will to live and the gruesome lure of death by pleasure.

As she struggled and writhed, she came closer and closer to the long, deep pool where in happier hours she had swum above the shadows of the trout.

She sank to the bottom of the pool. In an instant all the pleasure was gone and she was screaming, inhaling water and spitting out masses of bubbles thick with bug legs and broken cellophane wings.

By crawling along the bottom of the pool, coming up for gulps of air, she could more or less avoid the creatures. They impotently pummeled her back with their bodies. In this pure water she had no trouble seeing. The insects in their millions lit everything brighter than day.

Then it was dark.

Coughing, she sat up. Her mouth was still full of the jelly-like phosphorescence, and crisp bits that crunched when she worked her jaws.

Then she realized what they tasted like.

A wave of nausea hit her. She vomited a burning white stream of matter into the night. It arced over and fell with a hiss to the surface of the stream. She watched it float away on the quick current, its glow soon lost around a bend. Seeing the goop produced another attack of nausea, then another. She almost vomited her gullet inside out.

Slowly, the agony subsided. Grinding muscles went slack, helpless choking was replaced by long heaves of sweet air.

At last she stood and waded out of the pool.

It was then that she saw the tip of the swarm of insects. It was a glimmering strand in the reeds halfway down the length of the pool.

As she watched, it grew thinner and came closer, closer—then seemed to snap back against itself, exactly as if the millions of separate bodies were linked by unseen tendons.

Again it stretched toward her, the tip of it glowing fiercely as if with enormous effort. It *was* connected to itself, not a swarm but a single thing, and it had reached the limit of its range. It must be anchored down in that hole.

She fought to control the motion of her stomach but she couldn't do it, not with the taste, the memory of those awful things in her, the feeling that they were still crawling along her gullet—

Then she realized what they tasted like—blood and filthy, sweaty skin. If she'd licked somebody's naked feet, she'd have tasted the same complex mix of salt and dirt and stink.

Another spasm brought up more glowing debris. She went staggering off into the woods, thinking only of finding her cabin and getting this filthy, vile taste out of her mouth.

She left the thing behind her, questing and stretching against its limits. It had wanted to get her back. It had not wanted her to leave the judge's place.

Dear God in heaven, what was going on here?

After long minutes of blundering, she located the sparks of light that marked her cabin. The night deceived her, and what should have been a few moments' walk became a crashing battle with unseen ditches, rough tree trunks and deceptive paths.

At last she struggled onto her porch, weeping and crying out, and went into the house. Immediately she slammed the door, locked it. For a short time she leaned against it, crying like a baby. She shook her head, no, no, no, trying to eradicate the whole experience from memory, to somehow explain what had happened, to escape from this awful feeling of defilement, of having been literally packed with filth.

She crossed the living room, dropping clothes as she went. The taste in her mouth was sharp and strong, and she had an image of herself licking open sores.

In the bathroom she gargled with Listerine, pouring it down her throat, then spitting it into the toilet. Again and again she did this, until the bottle was empty. She smashed toothpaste into her hands and jammed her fingers in her mouth, working the paste down around her gums, in between her teeth, beneath her tongue. She brushed until her mouth was filled with foam, then washed it out.

Still the taste lingered, so she got some Palmolive dishwashing detergent from the kitchen and washed her mouth out with that, gagging from the bitterness of it, and she saw when she spit that there was a whole bug left. It was badly damaged, moving slightly. It looked like skin, like *skin*. Horrified, she managed to hold it just long enough to put it in a jelly jar, closing the metal top firmly and carefully.

Then she made a saltwater gargle, again she brushed, and finally felt a little cleaner. She took a long, hot shower. As she washed in billows of steam she heard thunder outside and moaned when the lights flickered. But she couldn't stop washing. She used Jergens soap and Ivory soap and Lava soap and would have used lye soap if she'd had any.

At last, lying on the floor of the shower, her skin aglow from the soap and the hot water, she began to feel a little better.

There was a terrific crack of thunder and the lights went out. A moment later the shower stopped. Of course—her well had an electric pump.

In the silence, she listened to the quick gurgle of water going down the drain. This was replaced by another sound—a peculiar sizzling like bacon frying. She got up, listening, struggling to find something to grasp—a corner of the shower, the wall. She was so scared and exhausted that it was almost impossible to control her movements.

That sound—she'd heard it before, coming from inside the judge's house. She found her way to the bathroom window, raised the edge of the blind.

Off in the woods she saw light—more than one light, as a matter of fact. But it wasn't fireflies, it was a group of bright winks of light like purple jewels. They were advancing slowly toward the house, and the sizzling noise was coming from them.

It was the most menacing thing she'd ever seen. Had she locked every door, every window? What about the crawl space, were the vents closed or open? And the flue—had she closed the flue in May after she'd made her last fire?

She began to cry, her throat tight with the frustration and the fear. This was worse than the worst nightmare, and it just would not stop.

Then the shower came to life with a roar. Startled, she uttered a scream. But the lights also came back on and that calmed her down a little. At least she could do something more than cower.

Her nakedness was making her feel horribly vulnerable. She grabbed a towel and dried herself, then rushed through the house checking window locks and closing curtains.

She could no longer tell if she was awake or asleep, in nightmare or reality. Naked, cold, damp, shaking and still deeply nauseated, she prowled her three small rooms, her eyes flitting from door to window, her mind alive to every creak and sigh.

A gust of wind made her run to the kitchen, grab her two biggest knives. She advanced through the house, her teeth bared, growling softly. At some point she'd put on her white terry-cloth robe, and it hung loose about her as she patrolled.

Finally she sat on a rigid dining chair, putting her knives on the table before her. There was an occasional dribble of rain, but no more lightning, no thunder. Then she realized that she could see the dim trunk of a tree beyond the picture window.

The night was over, the nightmare past. She thought she'd like some coffee.

She was putting the coffee in the percolator when

the true impact of what had happened slammed her as hard as a physical blow. She leaned far down over the kitchen counter, her eyes shut tight.

It had all been impossible.

Groaning, she held her belly as if her guts were spilling out.

A crackle from the woods made her snap to attention. Instantly, the knives were in her hands. She rushed to the window. All was still. But she knew the sound of a footfall in the pine needles that covered the forest floor.

She stepped away from the window, and then—following another thought—rushed through the house dousing lights. For a long time, she simply watched. Slowly, dawn began to define first the outline of the window, then the trunks of trees outside. Finally the first birds began their tentative peeping.

Full daylight came then, shimmering with dew. Today was Sunday. She had been planning to drive down to Ludlum, get an Albany *Times-Union,* and sit on the terrace of the Waywonda Inn and eat croissants and drink coffee.

But she would never reach the Waywonda Inn, would never read today's paper. Dawn or no dawn, Ellen Maas stood at the edge of a great darkness.

FOUR

1.

Night was the worst time for Brian. He'd wake up smelling smoke, hearing Caitlin's first, sharp shriek, hearing Mary's surprised shout turn to an inarticulate bellow of agony.

He sweated out the nights.

Before the fire his habit when under pressure was to retreat into the intricacies of mathematics. He would play with equations, carrying them to their angelic and logical ends.

No more.

When he'd first been released from the hospital, he had gone to the Ludlum campus, expecting to begin the return to his old life. But he'd seen Mary everywhere, heard her singing across the reaches of memory.

Memory frightened him, because his equations told him that every moment was happening forever.

They told him that Mary and Kate were dying forever.

He hadn't even entered the physics building.

After that experience, he'd begun to spend more and more time on his land. He'd fallen in love, a little, with the farm.

But he could not bring himself to repair the

house, not even when he'd brought Loi home as his wife. To provide her shelter, he'd bought a bigger trailer. It was dinky, in his opinion, but she'd been awed by it. She'd managed to decorate it pretty nicely, if you liked the pictures in *Trailer Home Designs.*

"Loi," he said to the empty, dark room. A glance at his watch told him that it was past two.

He looked around at her things, her furniture, her pictures, her beloved Laughing Buddha. It was plastic, it was chipped and scratched, but she loved it. He picked it up, wished on it that she would be well. Too bad it hadn't helped her today.

He sighed, wondering if he would ever get to sleep.

What in God's name had happened to her? No wonder Doc Gidumal was suspicious, he had every reason to be.

Apple Sally—she'd been attacking something. What? Could there have been one of those little black bears down in there? Sal hated bears.

There was her dish, still half full of Kal-Kan. She'd been a good friend, that busted-up old hound. He took a long breath, then tossed the dish in the trash.

No bear had made the noise that hurt Loi.

What would be the properties of a sound that could cause such an injury? Great intensity, enough oscillation to actually set cells in motion, enough power to burst them. It'd take an awful lot of energy to produce such a sound.

First somebody is screaming like a banshee, then you get something like that.

He went to the refrigerator, got a bottle of Bud

and returned to the living room. He sat in his easy chair, balancing the beer on its wide arm.

The nature of the sound continued to bother him. It had been a sort of undulant hum, a warbling acoustic discharge. The oscillation would have been what caused the damage; it would have set up the kind of motion that could burst cell walls.

Afterward, he'd had muscle aches and a fairly severe headache—far less damage than Loi, but he was a lot less fragile than a woman at the end of her third trimester.

Outside there was a series of brilliant flashes. The storm that had threatened earlier was hanging on the higher elevations, lurking back in the Jumper Mountains above the little town of Towayda. Right now it could go either way, stomping off into New Hampshire or coming back here to give Oscola a predawn pounding.

He swilled the last of the beer, tossed the bottle toward the trash can. It hit the floor with a sullen clunk. So much for any nascent Scottie Pippen fantasies. The living room clock bonged three times. He sat staring, wishing he had a fire to watch.

It was long after the crickets had stopped and the bats had gone to bed that his eyes shut for a final time, and a tired, uneasy man slept.

2.

It only lasted a moment. When he woke up he found himself sitting in a very different sort of a seat. There was a sensation of electricity going through his body.

Then he realized that he couldn't open his eyes. He heard familiar rattling. Sounded like he was in his truck. And why couldn't he move? Muscle spasm? Stroke?

He realized that he wasn't in bed at all. He was in a seat, his hands were on a steering wheel.

He *was* in his truck!

No, this couldn't be. How could he be driving his truck with his eyes closed?

This was crazy. No matter how it felt, how real it seemed, he had to be dreaming. He wasn't in his truck at all, he was still sitting in the easy chair in the living room.

There was a bump, followed by the rattle of the passenger door that had been bothering him for weeks.

Light flashed on the other side of his closed lids. Thunder rumbled.

He tried to open his eyes, tried again, raising his eyebrows until his forehead was deep with furrows.

Suddenly they popped open—and he was dead stunned by what he saw.

He was in the truck all right. His hands were on the wheel, his foot on the gas, he was driving down Kelly Farm Road in the direction of Mound. "What the hell?" The dashboard clock said it was five-fifteen.

He was going . . . was it to Ludlum, back to the campus, back to the facility?

He had a vivid memory of his old facility with its walls covered by the blue PVC pipe that contained the vacuum-sealed cables.

He was out of control. He was heading down

Kelly Farm Road toward Mound and he couldn't stop himself.

He fought. He willed his hands to move off the wheel, willed it until he groaned with the effort. His hands shook, his neck throbbed, he grimaced with effort—and suddenly his right hand did as it was being ordered. Struggling mightily, he managed to get the shaking, quivering fingers around the key, to turn it.

The truck stopped. For a moment he slumped over the wheel.

Then a tickle started down between his legs. For a moment he thought a rat was on him. Before he could even panic, though, the sensation blossomed into one of electrifying pleasure. It was a needle, hot, vibrant, incredible, stabbing deep into his solar plexus. He hadn't felt such a sensation in years, not since he was first touched there by a girl. He still remembered that pleasure, how it had stripped him of his will. Now it drew him out of the truck, into the woods.

Like magic he was walking somewhere, being drawn, being pulled. On some level the pleasure made him sick, made his heart weep. He wasn't going to the campus, not back to the facility, not at all. He was going somewhere else, to a house, a familiar house . . .

He thought he could feel something wrapped around him, threads that he couldn't see, hair-thin but wildly active, tickling as they raced about under his clothes.

He grimaced, shut his eyes—and the pleasure disappeared. He became aware that there had been purple light, deep almost to black, shining in his eyes.

When he opened them again, the purple light came back. He moved like a robot, or a puppet controlled by strings that gave him pleasure down to the depths of his soul.

Then he burst into the meadow beside the mound, and before him was an extraordinary scene: a burning woman with her arms over her head, followed by a long, swinging stream of white fire. It was something from another version of the world.

The vision of the burning woman was so bright that it left red ghosts in his eyes after he turned away from it. He saw Mary burning again, Mary in a flower of popping, blurry flames, moving fast, her hair a spreading blossom of fire.

He was close to her, only a few feet away, and he saw that the supposedly heavenly glow was actually coming from thousands of busy winged worms.

Her face was pale fire, her hair flying sparks. Behind her was the dark shape of the mound. He could also see the judge's house—which was bizarrely transformed. Its windows were pouring electric purple light so bright that silhouettes were visible behind the closed curtains, gyrating as if some sort of maniacal dance was taking place inside. But it wasn't a fun dance, he could see that.

Cars jammed the driveway, spilled over into the front yard.

He was being drawn here.

And he was in a fight for his life. He'd fought like this before in the burn wards at Ludlum Community and Midstate Catholic in Albany.

The pleasure drew him, dragged him, made his

hands shake as he tried to untangle the threads, weakened his arms when he sought to tear them away. Still, he lurched forward.

Desperate now, he concentrated all that was left of his willpower. Ahead of him the front door began to open, letting out a shaft of pure purple light. A silhouette stumbled past, horribly contorted. Long legs and arms as thin as sticks swam in the light. Inside, screaming mixed with caws and whoops and the continuous sizzling of a gigantic skillet.

It felt so good that he wept. He was aware that he was marching across the yard like a mechanical toy. The threads were all around him now, enclosing him like a deadly web.

His will was a single dot of white light in the center of his being, and that dot wanted to live, to be free. It wanted to live so badly that it began to grow, to get brighter.

Higher the pleasure rose, higher and higher, to greater and greater intensity. He groaned, he yelled, his skin quivered with it.

But it was death, he knew that, he could taste it, feel it in the coldness of their touch.

His mind fixed on Loi and the baby. On his son. He would never get to see his son.

No!

He was being dragged now, toward the open door, toward the angry purple flashes and the capering, twisted figures inside.

He tensed his muscles, stiffened his legs until his heels were digging into the ground, and he pushed. He fought, tearing at the threads, he flailed and yanked and ripped, he threw himself back against their strength.

A tall, angular shadow came onto the judge's porch. He could not see the face, but he felt watched, carefully watched.

Spittle flew from his mouth as he twisted and shook, his muscles strained to their limits as he fought the threads. All the while the purple light pulsed into him, causing his deepest soul to cry out in the agony of the pleasure.

The grave figure on the judge's porch gracefully tossed what looked like a thick cable in his direction. It fell before him with a dense thud and began scrabbling at the earth, trying to get closer. But it was stretched to its limit.

The tickling threads disappeared, the purple light went out, the figure withdrew from the porch.

He ran away like a frightened child. He kept running until he reached the woods at the far end of the meadow that surrounded the mound. Then he stumbled into Coxon Kill, lurched through it and collapsed on the opposite bank.

He felt as if every aching muscle had been pulled awry. He was soaked and cold and miserable.

A crow raised its voice in raucous anger. He could taste the sourness of its inhuman rage. He whirled around, looking for it. The tall, strange figure from the porch had followed him. It extended a long, thin arm toward him.

Absolute panic. A man running. Leaves whipping past. Little sounds, half-made screams. A man running, running and the blaze of dawn striping the horizon with perfect colors: long gold lines of cloud tinged with the black of the departing storm, the sky going from green to soft pure blue. Beneath this grandeur, a man running.

A brace of pheasant rose before him, their wings shining. When he first noticed the glow in among the trees he stopped, shrinking back like a terrified deer. But then he saw that it was a cabin with lit windows and smoke coming out its chimney. The logs were dark and old, the lights in the windows were dim.

It looked like something from a sinister fairy tale.

3.

A miserable Ellen Maas was waiting for the percolator to stop coughing when she again heard footsteps.

Nobody ought to be around here at this hour.

She grabbed the biggest knife.

"Who's there?" she asked. It came out as a thin, ineffectual whine.

A man's face appeared in the living room window.

It was waxy green, the eyes staring, the mouth slack. The eyes went to the knife she was brandishing, then the face reared back into the dark.

She threw down the knife, reeled away from the window. She was biting her knuckle to keep from screaming. It was Dr. Kelly out there and he looked as if he'd been in a wreck or worse. She dashed out into the living-dining room and threw open the front door.

"Dr. Kelly . . ." Her voice died away. The expression on his face was unlike anything she'd ever seen before. His eyes were wide, his lips open, his skin wet with sweat. He shuffled toward her. Instinct made her step back. All sorts of unspoken dreads began to rise.

Then he stopped, buried his face in his hands, trying to wipe away a thickness of sweat and grime. His hair was full of pine needles, his T-shirt was ripped almost to shreds, he was wet. "I'm sorry. I've had— had—" The hollow eyes met hers. They pleaded.

"Dr. Kelly?"

"Help me." As if the two small words had drained the last of his strength, he slumped forward. Big though he was, she had to catch him or he was going to fall. She reached out, was staggered by his full weight.

She was just strong enough to get him in the door, to aim him at the couch. He toppled down, hitting its old springs with a squealing crash. She didn't want that door left open; she slammed and locked it. What had happened to her was bad enough, and now look at this poor man.

Then she saw him fully in the light. His scars were clearly visible and she was surprised at how extensive they were. His chest looked . . . molten. She'd never seen such deep burns.

Her old percolator went from coughing to wheezing, indicating that the coffee was finally brewed. Looking back at him, she moved quickly across to the kitchen. The man had to be helped, but the damn thing would explode if it wasn't turned off. That taken care of, she rushed into the bathroom.

What should she get? What did she have? Alcohol and cotton balls, a tube of Mycitracin, some Kaopectate, lots of Mylanta. Obviously, her first-aid capabilities were a disaster.

"May I have some of that coffee?" he asked in a

beaten voice. At the hospital he'd been cruel to her. Now his eyes were anguished.

Brian couldn't get over how good the brew smelled, so rich and strong and familiar. Dimly, he remembered struggling through the woods, seeing the gingerbready little cabin, coming up to the door . . .

There'd been a beautiful woman in the doorway, wearing a fluffy white robe. Now she had a percolator in her hand and was filling a big mug.

In amazement he reached out, touched the terry cloth of the robe. He no longer felt able to verify reality merely by looking.

The green eyes blinked, regarded him. "Are you hurt?"

Her voice was as pure and refreshing as the water of Coxon Kill.

"Hey, listen up, Dr. Kelly! Are—you—hurt?"

He didn't know how to explain his pain, what to say that would identify the cause of his wounds.

"Please tell me!"

"I—I don't know . . ." He tried to remember what he'd just been through, but it all seemed so impossible, it was just a crazy jumble. He was exhausted, but he didn't think he was actually hurt. "I'm fine," he said. He realized that the woman was Ellen Maas. He'd come all the way to her cabin.

He didn't understand at all.

"You don't look fine." She thrust the mug of coffee into his hands. Beneath her tone of concern was a much sharper note. She was afraid of him, he decided. That wasn't too surprising.

He took the coffee, drank gratefully, deeply. "I'm sorry, I know it's early."

He got only a guarded shift of the eyes from her. She definitely wasn't happy to have him here, and he couldn't blame her. "Dr. Kelly, what the hell is going on around here?"

"I don't know!"

She watched him with increasing wariness. He appeared mad. But after what had happened to her out there, she was willing to give him a little latitude. But only a little. "Why are you here?"

He tried to explain himself. "I've had—an experience. Something happened to me that I can't explain."

He was surprised to see that this made her less uneasy. "I had a bad night, too."

They regarded each other.

"I'm sorry I burst in on you." He noticed for the first time that his scars were visible. Ashamed, he covered his chest with his arms.

"You don't need to do that."

"I'm sorry."

"You got them trying to save your family."

She went into the kitchen and began preparing her breakfast.

He followed her. "Will you give me something to eat, Miss Maas?"

"If you like."

The smell of coffee and bacon, the sound of butter being spread on toast, the clink of spoon against cup—these familiar things allowed him to do what he so desperately wanted to do, and that was imagine that life would return to normal. For her part, the familiar rhythms of cooking the meal and setting the table were what enabled her to return to the ordinary.

The terrors of the night sifted into memory.

Brian and Ellen were like deer who have glimpsed the hunter and run, and think themselves safe, and pause to crop the stems of autumn.

FIVE

1.

He ate mechanically, his eyes on his food. She hadn't wanted anything after all; she wasn't sure how long it would be before she cared to eat again. Instead she sat and smoked and watched him. He had the rangy build of a hardwork farmer, but his eyes betrayed the complexity of his intelligence.

"I think I'm feeling separation anxiety," he said.

"From your wife?"

"In the sense that I want to stay here. I want to hide."

A silence fell. She wanted to talk about what had happened to her, but she didn't know how to do that. There was no simple way to explain something so weird, not without sounding deranged.

Unless the same thing had happened to him. To find out, she would try an indirect approach. "What are those insects that come out at night—the glowing ones?"

"Lightning bugs."

"I mean that attack you. Like wasps."

He looked up from his food. His eyes now held a question. "None."

"Not anywhere? Not back in the mountains?"

"No."

She smoked, watching him carefully. So that wasn't what had happened to him.

So what had? Why had he come staggering out of the woods at six a.m.?

He wondered what she'd been driving at with her questions. Had something happened to her, also? No, he'd had a nightmare of some sort. "I'm sorry to disturb you."

"Do you know any entomologists at Ludlum?"

"Bug boys? Nah. I'm a physicist. Worked on esoteric particles."

"Star wars?"

"We were going to harness a new sort of particle. If we could find it."

"I want to talk to an entomologist."

"But not to a particle man." He cut across the second of his two eggs, dipped some toast into the yolk. "Thanks for this. I needed it."

She smiled a little. "My breakfast usually consists of cereal and a half grapefruit. I didn't even know I had those eggs. What kind of particle were you studying?"

"Generating. I was trying to generate it. A particle that would have moved backward in time. It sounds esoteric, but it would have been a very powerful particle. Capable of great things."

She went to the window and looked out a long time. He watched the shoulders of the shabby terry-cloth robe. Perhaps he should leave. Probably should. But he found himself pouring another cup of coffee.

"What happened to it?" she asked suddenly.

"It?"

"Your project."

He shook his head.

She came back to the dining table and sat down across from him. "So, have you figured out why you came walking out of my woods at six in the morning?"

He watched her movements, hasty, nervous. She was very tired, still wary of him. Still angry, he suspected. "Please don't put it in the paper."

"No, I won't hurt you. It's not my style." She smiled then, and it was quite wonderful to see, a sudden, fierce brightening of her tense features. But the smile disappeared abruptly. "You didn't answer my question, Doctor."

He had to explain more fully, he saw that. "I had a waking dream," he said carefully. "It's called hypnogogia. A commonplace of psychology. Apparently I walked in my sleep."

She nodded. "Go on."

"Well, that's the explanation."

She laughed in his face, but the laughter was gentle, it wasn't mean. In simple, straightforward language, she told him the craziest story he had ever heard, about killer insects that glowed.

"I can understand your interest in entomology," was the best response he could think of. It was a most curious story, though. "But you're talking about a nightmare, not a real experience."

She went into her kitchen, came back with a pickling jar, held it out to him.

"What?"

"On the bottom. Look."

The jar was empty, with a hole in the tin lid. Silently, he gave it back to her.

She unscrewed the lid, examined it. "Damn."

"A lightning bug that can bust through a tin jar lid. Not possible."

"You do have your pompous side, Doctor."

"I know my science! And I know that this hole was not, repeat *not*, made by any insect known to man."

"I know what I saw. I can't explain it but it wasn't any hallucination. Hell, look at Loi. Your wife's lying in a hospital bed because of this—"

"You're assuming that a strange sound and . . . lightning bugs . . . are related? That's more than a supposition, that's a leap of faith."

"Everything strange that happened out there in the last twenty-four hours is related!"

"What makes you say that?"

"The screaming in the mound, the injury to your wife, my experience, your experience—they've all happened within a few hours, and inside the same square-mile area. Of course they're related."

He felt sweat gathering under his arms. Acid twisted his stomach.

"You look sick, Doctor."

"Call me Brian. I'm just—"

"You're scared. Like me."

"I'm scared."

"It's time to tell me all about it."

He recounted his whole story.

"I saw those damn cars, too! I even touched one!"

"If this was real—" He fell silent. He had just realized something appalling. "Dear God."

"What?"

"You say you ran through the field behind the judge's place, and you were covered with them?"

"Totally. They were even in my mouth."

It was incredible. That image—that dream

image—must be real. "I saw you. I thought you were part of my nightmare—a burning woman. I often dream about people burning."

A prickling sensation told her that goose bumps were rising on her arms.

He was hunched, staring at his food. "You're trembling," she said. She held out her hand.

Silently, he nodded.

When he didn't take the offered hand, she withdrew it. She had only wanted to comfort him. "I think maybe that creepy judge is breeding some kind of tropical insect," she said at last. "They came out of a hole in his yard. Probably wants to drive people off his land."

"What about your theory that it's all related? How does Loi's injury fit in? And what about me?"

"Well, I'm a reporter. I'll do a little research. A lot of research. But you're a scientist. What's your considered opinion?"

"I can't even begin to formulate one. Except that I have a sense it's all very dangerous."

"That I know."

2.

Brian went out and located his truck, then drove home and fell into a deep, empty sleep. He awoke at noon and rushed off to the hospital, angry with himself that he hadn't been there the moment visiting hours began.

On the way down to Ludlum he pushed the truck through seventy. When he saw the low, white buildings of the hospital complex, he felt the muscles of his neck stiffen, felt his breath tighten in his chest. He was a man capable of intense passion, he'd always known that. But Loi's combination of beauty, vulnerability and determination had moved him very deeply. He had loved Mary and he always would, but this was deep, too, this was valid, too. Loi deserved every bit of love and loyalty he could offer.

He drove up to the big parking lot, got out and hurried through the heat waves rising from the tarmac. Grasshoppers ratcheted in the wide lawns that surrounded the buildings, and a gopher moved stealthily toward a shrub.

Brian went through the revolving doors, listened to his own shoes rattling on the linoleum floor of the lobby.

Loi was on the second floor, housed in a private room because of the need for absolute rest. When he appeared, a smile danced into her face. "You are late coming."

"I overslept."

"You look tired."

"Nightmares."

She reached out, drew him close, kissed him. "I am feeling much better. When the doctor saw me, he was pleased."

"I'm glad."

"What were your nightmares? Do you want to tell?"

He didn't want to worry her. "Just the usual," he said. "Screaming."

She nodded. "You need me home."

"Yeah."

There was at this moment an opportunity to say something about Ellen. "I sleepwalked."

"Oh. That is demons, make us do that."

"There's also a scientific explanation. Sleepwalking's well understood. It's a stress reaction."

"I gave you this stress, husband. I cannot apologize enough."

"An accident did it, Loi, not you. If anyone's to blame, it's me. I never should have let you get back out of the truck. I should have taken you straight home at the first sign of danger."

"What happened to me, Brian?"

"My best guess is that rocks grinding together created some sort of electrostatic field that set up the vibrations."

"I heard screaming also, Brian. I heard that poor woman!"

He took her hands, kissed them. She was so precious, so sensitive. "It could be that the geologist was right. Some sort of earth movement created the screaming sounds, too."

"But you don't believe it?"

He shook his head. He didn't know what to believe.

"You know, you and I have a real problem. Because I want to know what happened to me, and I don't. Dr. Gidumal says I must have been hit. But it didn't happen."

Now was perhaps the time to bring up a rather delicate subject. "Did you fall, perhaps?"

She looked at him steadily. "I did not."

"Loi, if you did, I won't be angry. I'm not like the people from your country, I don't treasure the child more than the mother. I treasure you both." He moved closer to her, drinking her in, smelling the soft fragrance of her hair. He embraced her.

"Brian, I didn't fall. I—maybe all the running. But that noise, Brian, it hurt! It hurt right in the middle of my womb!"

He remembered exactly how it had felt. "It hurt me, too, honey. And I have to admit to you, I don't know what it was all about."

Normally he told Loi everything. Normally he shared every detail of his life. But he did not share the terrible story Ellen Maas had told, and most certainly didn't tell Loi about his own bizarre experience. Those stories would scare her—they'd scare anybody—and he wasn't about to take that risk.

"I wish we were home in bed together," she whispered.

"Me too, Loi." He closed his eyes and felt her softness beneath his hands, and dreamed.

But visiting hours ended, and he had finally to go.

After he left her and got in his truck, he made a turn that he'd never expected to make again. He drove over to the campus, into the heart of his past.

Ludlum University was lavishly kept, rich with a hundred years of endowments and, more recently, a substantial amount of Defense Department funding. It wasn't large. Like Rockefeller University in Manhattan, it was highly regarded for its science programs. People came to Ludlum for physics and math.

It consisted of a cluster of red brick Victorian buildings, with a smattering of more modern structures on the outskirts of the campus.

He told himself that he'd come here for the peaceful drive, for the shade and the quiet.

And he knew that wasn't true. He'd come here because he was a worried, confused and very frightened man, and this was where he'd done his best mental work and solved his most challenging problems.

None of them had been as thorny as this one, though. None of them had even approached it.

For some time he drove along the quiet streets. There were few students about this time of year, giving the place an air of abandonment. The ancient oaks and maples spread their shade on the lawns and over the roads, and beds of flowers bobbed in the warm summer breeze.

He did not intend to drive past the physics building, where his lab and research facility had been. There was a very good reason for his reluctance, one that went beyond grief.

He was a man touched deeply by the mystery of time. His equations told him that the past was still there, frozen in memory, awaiting only the magic touch of physics to be restored to a sort of flickering life.

Perhaps the deepest reason that he had been unable to continue without Mary was that he thought—knew—that their time together still existed somewhere, a bud that was closed forever, and yet in some way alive. Just the right particle, aimed in just the right direction, might light it briefly in the magic space of the mind, making her laugh again, lift her eyes to him again.

With the equipment they had been building, it might have been possible to shine a light into the past. Remotely possible. Not to go back—that could never happen. But to look back, yes.

With twenty or so years of effort, he could perhaps have created such a light.

So he'd quit.

And maybe for that reason it would still be too painful to return to the building itself, to face the old places, the echoes. But he knew that he had to return to science, in order to solve the mystery that had ensnared him.

Which discipline, though? Geology, to explain the earth sounds that hurt Loi? Entomology, to identify Ellen's insects? Psychology, to heal his own mind?

Or was this a problem of physics? His mind was too well disciplined to allow speculation based on insufficient data, but it was also true that the manipulation of time could theoretically lead to some very strange derangements of reality.

His own equations had, in fact, suggested dangers—some of them profoundly serious.

What if there were parallel worlds, living by other laws, harsher worlds, perhaps . . . and what if somebody made a light and shone it pastward . . . but aimed it wrong and tore the fabric of present reality instead?

His work had been classified, his work had been dangerous, his work had been full of unknowns.

It had also ended—hadn't it?

He didn't intend to go in, but he decided to at least pass the old building . . . and—when he saw it—to stop in front.

The Physics Department was housed in a great Gothic pile with the crenellated roofline of a castle. Its tall, peaked windows seemed to glower down at Brian as he parked the truck.

For fifteen minutes he sat and watched. A couple

of grad students strolled up the walk and went in the big double doors.

After a time he saw a figure at one of the downstairs windows, looking out at him. It was a man wearing glasses. Maybe it was the chief of security, Bill Merriman. He'd have cause to be concerned about a strange truck stopped in front of a building where classified work was being done.

The last thing he wanted right now was an encounter with an old friend like Bill. Brian started his truck and drove home.

After he'd parked the truck he went into the trailer, made himself a ham sandwich, then spent the afternoon treating some of his older trees for borers.

When night came, he thought to call Loi, but he was afraid that he'd wake her up. No matter how optimistic she'd been, he knew that she needed lots of rest.

For dinner he threw some Lean Cuisine into the microwave, and ate it with a Coke. No more beer.

All afternoon, he'd been hoping that some good ideas would slip into his mind. In the old days he'd hiked the Jumpers to get ideas. Anything diverting helped, even a shower.

Tarring borer holes hadn't helped. Sitting here eating his grim little supper certainly wouldn't.

He needed somebody to talk to, somebody intelligent, who could at least pretend to follow his discourse.

Ellen Maas.

He didn't actually know Ellen's number, of course, but the phone book was only fourteen pages long. "Maas, Ellen, Bx 358, Oscola," and a number.

Just as he was about to dial, it rang. He snatched it up. "Hello?"

"Are you eating dinner?"

A thrill of happiness went through him. "Loi, hi."

"I want to know what you're eating. I'm concerned about you."

"I had Lean Cuisine. How about you?"

"Corn on the cob, roast pork. I ate gratefully."

"In other words, it was lousy."

"Not entirely perfect."

"Inedible."

"Yeah, but I got it down. I am having strong lonely feelings now, Brian."

"I miss you, too. I was just thinking about calling you."

"I am worried that you need me."

"I need you. But not sick. I need you well."

This brought a silence. Again he was bothered that he hadn't told her what had happened. It was eerie to conceal something of such importance from her, and distanced him from her in a way he didn't like at all.

"I am feeling very much love now, Brian."

"Me too. But I also want you to sleep. I don't want you to worry. I'm perfectly fine."

"Brian, I called three times this afternoon and you weren't there."

"Oh, Loi, I was out doing those old trees. You remember, the borers?"

"Oh, yeah, of course. I'm glad that you keep busy."

"I'm fine and I love you and I want you to go to sleep right now."

"OK, husband."

She hung up. He looked at the phone in his hand.

Dare he call Ellen and discuss temporal refraction and the instability of the reality constant? Poor woman, he didn't want to torment her like that.

Maybe it would be best to leave Ellen out of it. He could go over to the hospital in the morning and talk to Loi instead. She'd listen eagerly, even if she didn't understand.

But he didn't need a sounding board, he needed a foil. Ellen was a bright, sophisticated and—above all—reasonably well-educated person.

More importantly, she was involved in the secret.

He called her—and got her answering machine. He left a brief message, hoped it wasn't too terse. He wasn't an answering machine person.

He went out onto the small porch that overlooked the driveway and the barnyard.

The whippoorwills were thick tonight, their voices echoing in the woods. He'd always found their call the most beautiful next to that of the loon, and he stood for a time listening.

The moon rose in silence, and the evening star followed the sun westward.

Until deep night, he was fine.

Then he began to pace the trailer's few small rooms. He turned on all the lights and locked the door. He would have turned on the air-conditioning, but something made him prefer to hear the night. Katydids argued, the whippoorwills continued their gentle talk, and the night wind hissed in the pines.

He found himself listening. But for what?

Maybe Ellen was out doing research.

Would she be fool enough to return at night to the scene of her experience? No, surely not.

He watched the news at eleven, then went to bed.

That night he had more dreams, terrible dreams. In them he was being dragged toward the judge's house, toward the open door, and there were huge shapes inside that radiated malevolence like a foul purple gas.

3.

Ellen began work at once. Unlike Brian, she was not hampered by excessive respect for something as cumbersome as the scientific method.

She proceeded efficiently. On the *Times* she'd learned effective investigative techniques. The first thing she'd learned was that clams stay open until they perceive a threat. So she didn't question anybody directly. She resisted the temptation to pressure the old judge.

She spent most of a day just nosing around Oscola—and finding it a good deal more interesting than she'd thought. Towns reflect the deep nature of their people, especially old ones where certain small, critical things have become important. A wonderful old neon sign is not changed simply because the shop joins a chain. The tobacconist keeps stocking Borkum Riff even when he has few customers left for it, because of the atmosphere its familiar aroma gives his store. The druggist reupholsters the stools at his soda fountain in red marbleized vinyl because they've been like that for sixty years.

A town full of people with such sensibilities becomes in time fertile ground for an astute investigator, revealing things about itself at every turn.

At their worst the people of Oscola were narrow

and prejudiced. They suffered most of the weaknesses of the self-involved. But they also had good in them. They worked and did not steal. Generally, they were not violent. They knew beauty when they saw it, and that was reflected in the appearance of their town.

Essential to Oscola's beauty was the fact that it was so taken for granted by the townsfolk. It wasn't a model town, it wasn't a toy. It was just itself, and she found that she liked that about it.

Walking slowly down Main Street, passing Fisk's Garage with its splashy new collection of all-terrain vehicles and Mode O'Day with the latest tangerine pants suit in the window, she noticed a sense of emptiness even greater than usual.

At one o'clock the Mills Cafe had six customers. Usually, Betty Mills had easily twenty people in for hamburgers and fried chicken, and her mouth-watering meatloaf from yesteryear.

Maybe Ellen wasn't the only one who'd encountered the damned bugs.

The one person who knew what was happening behind the scenes in Oscola was Mr. Handy, who'd been the tobacconist for nearly forty years. When she'd first gone in the place she'd been tempted to buy cigars, but Mr. Handy was too nice to tease, and it would have shocked him deeply.

As she entered the store he pulled down her usual carton of Salems.

"Mr. Handy, what're those meetings at the judge's place? The ones that happen late at night?"

"I wouldn't know."

Oh, but he would. Mr. Handy was no liar. She could tell by the look that came into his face. "Come on, I'm curious. Maybe there's something in it for me."

"Don't put anything about that in the paper!"

"So you do know."

"Look, Miss Maas, it's private stuff. The people who go there are from downstate."

"You make it sound very mysterious."

He nodded, ringing up the Salems.

"But if the people are from downstate, then why do they all have local license plates?"

Color spread up his neck. He coughed. "Masons," he said. "That's what I think."

"But you're not certain."

He shook his head. "They wouldn't let me in, you know. All my life I've been here, and not really a part of Oscola. Forty years in the town, and they don't trust me even yet. You want to know why?"

"Weren't born here?"

Again he nodded. "In my opinion, it's the Masons. He's the grand master here, you know."

"They always meet late at night?"

"There's no way to know what they do. It's a secret society."

"Except that everybody belongs except you. Does Brian Kelly belong?"

"Not him. He's a Catholic. The Church won't allow it, and Father Palmer's really stuck on the subject."

She watched him nervously rubbing a finger along the top of his glass counter.

"Goodbye, Mr. Handy." He handed her the accursed cigarettes. Maybe this was her last carton, ha ha.

She looked up and down the street. Now the silence had a different tone. Cults, secret societies, the mean, autocratic old judge . . . and the insects.

They had been so vile, so aggressive. They'd wanted to eat her, drag her away—she couldn't imagine what they'd wanted to do.

She ought to go after that miserable old judge with a gun. But that would be a mistake, given that a gun wasn't her weapon of choice. Instead, she returned to her office and looked him up in the tiny morgue. There wasn't much, not from files that only went back five years. Prior to that, the morgue consisted of scrapbooks. They weren't much help, although she did find out that he'd been born, educated locally, then graduated Columbia Law back in the forties. Missed World War II by a hair.

In a controversial 1956 trial he'd sent a local man to the electric chair.

He wasn't a mobster, a sexual pervert or a violent man. In fact, he was a pretty good judge, if a bit conservative for her taste.

He was a nasty little man; arrogant and cold as stone.

It was time to confront him. The hell with this pussyfooting around town. This bunch of clams had been closed up tight even before she started. They were always closed.

She got in her car and drove down Main to the intersection where it became Mound. When she crossed it, she was in the judge's territory.

He answered his door after the third ring. Up close, it was obvious that he was very old.

"Judge terBroeck, can you tell me what goes on out here at night?"

He just stared at her.

"The cars. Dozens of 'em. I've seen them. What's it all about?"

"Get out."

"Goddamn you." Oops, that was a mistake.

His eyes widened. "I'll thank you to keep a civil tongue in your head."

"What about the bugs that live in your backyard?"

For a moment, his face was totally without expression. Then he blinked. "Ah."

"Come on, you know what I'm talking about. The ones that come out at night. Glow in the dark."

"Lightning bugs?" His voice was small. He'd backed a good distance into the foyer.

She advanced on him. She wasn't going to let him pretend he thought her crazy. "Don't give me any crap, Judge. I know they're there because they tried to kill me. And you know they're there too. You're a poor liar, Judge."

"I have no idea—"

"You sure as hell do have an idea. What are they, Judge? Something you imported from Brazil or somewhere to scare people off your property? Well, they're pretty scary, all right." She took another step toward him. "Let me tell you something. If I find one of those things—and I will find one, sooner or later—I'm going to take it to a lawyer. Not a bug collector, but a lawyer. And I am going to get him to sue you until you're left on a street corner with a cup of pencils, and they're my damn pencils!"

"They have nothing to do with me!"

"You're a liar!" Her heart was pounding, she could feel the blood rushing to her cheeks. All her pent-up fear and rage surfaced. She wanted to bash his face in, the arrogant old bastard.

"Listen—please—don't come around here at night. Don't do it!"

"Why the hell not—have you got Satan and his demons after you or what?"

His face had gone as gray as death. His hands shook, making a dry paper sound against his old suit pants. "It's worse, my dear. Worse than that." He raised his old claws, seemed to be seeking some sort of comfort. "Keep to your house at night. Do it for your own sake."

"What about all the cars? Other people come here at night."

He nodded. "Stay away, if you value your life."

"Melodrama won't scare me off either."

"Then you're a fool!" Now it was his turn to advance on her. "This is my property. Get off my property!"

She didn't want to stay. There were other ways to skin this particular cat, better, quieter ways. "OK, I'm going. But I want you to know that I'm a real curious person. And I'm gonna find out everything."

"Yes," he said, "you do that. You find out everything. And see where it gets you, young woman." His eyes were sunken, his lips were trembling. "See where it gets you."

He shut his door.

4.

Two days after her admission, Loi returned home.

The doctor had warned her to be extremely careful, and she became a fragile, gliding shadow of herself. She had been told to think of her womb as made of glass, and so got Brian to put pillows on all the hard chairs and generally arrange things in the trailer to minimize her chances of taking a stumble. She wanted to be wrapped in blankets, to be cherished. Above all, she wanted to be held close and often.

Sadly, they couldn't make love. Obviously it was a danger, especially with him being so big and heavy and getting so excited.

He consoled himself that this was safest. She was high fruit now, untouchable by a groundling like him.

Loi had been home a day when Ellen called. "It's the *Gazette*," Loi said, handing him the phone.

"I figured you'd be in for lunch." Her voice was taut.

"Yes."

"Look, I want to come talk to you about Judge terBroeck. I've interviewed him and it was strange."

"I'm not surprised." He glanced at Loi. She must not hear this. "I'll come to you."

"Fine. I'm at the office."

He hung up. Loi gave him a questioning look. "She's still investigating what happened on the mound. She wants to ask me a few questions."

"Oh, Brian, I want to forget it."

"I told her I'd meet her at her office. That way you won't have to be involved."

Loi smiled slightly. "This afternoon I am reading *The Winter's Tale*. We will discuss it tonight?"

"Sure. Gladly."

He went across the driveway and got into the truck. Even running the air conditioner full blast didn't cool it off before he turned onto Main Street, parked in front of the Excelsior Tower, and gratefully got out.

He'd never been in the offices of the *Gazette* before, at least not since he could remember. She was sitting at a steel desk like the kind of thing one might encounter in a welfare office. There were hard fluorescent lights burning overhead, and an ancient window unit ineffectually circulating the smoke-hazed air. Papers were strewn over every available surface. There were five or six insect books opened on tables and chairs, dozens of pictures of the judge and of his estate, some old, others obviously taken in the past couple of days.

He was shocked by these. She'd obviously been spying on the town's leading citizen.

She thrust a photograph into his hand. He found himself staring at tire tracks. "Taken this morning in the judge's front yard," she said. She gave him another picture. There were many fewer of the tracks. "Yesterday morning, same spot."

"Isn't Bob going out there to work on the mound?"

"The judge put a stop to it. No more equipment on his property without a court order. But I've been on his property."

"Obviously."

The whole office was devoted to his property, right down to a house plan that must have been obtained from county records.

"He's scared, Brian. I hated him until I realized that. The man is terrified."

"Have you got any more information?" He gestured toward the insect books.

"I went down to your old alma mater and described the things to a Dr. Soames."

Brian nodded. Soames was a biologist. "I wasn't aware that he has an interest in insects."

"Well, he seemed to know what he was talking about. But as far as my bugs are concerned, he drew a blank."

"We've got to get more information of some kind."

She took a long drag on her cigarette. "I've been working on that." She held up some sheets of paper. "Your friend Lieutenant West gave me these. The cops use them to identify what kind of tires make a given mark." She picked up one of the pictures. "Like this one. It's from a Michelin of the type they use on the Volvo 240. And this, a Goodyear Aquatred—an aftermarket tire. The size suggests something large, a Crown Vic or maybe a big Olds or Buick."

"Typical local cars, except for the Volvo."

"I've found out that there are seventeen Volvo 240s registered in Ludlum County."

"That many, in Ford and Chevy country like this?"

"Sixteen of them are Ludlum cars. Popular with your fellow professors. But one of them lives up in Towayda. And you know what? They're not at home. As of yesterday, they've been gone. Just packed up and left night before last. People are real curious. Evans is their name."

"Sure. Ritchie and Charlene. I know them a little. Charlene was on the debate team with me in high school."

"They went over to the judge's night before last. They haven't been seen since."

"And the judge says—"

She shook her head. "If I want to talk to him

again, I'm gonna have to take a gun. He won't open his door to me, he won't stay on the phone."

"Scottish Rite's a big deal around here. Maybe you've stumbled onto some sort of Masonic group."

"I know all about that."

"If the Rite's involved, everybody would be very secretive, especially with an outsider."

"You're not an outsider, so you ask him for me."

"I'm Catholic. Catholics don't join the Rite, at least not in the Three Counties."

"I found the hole where the bugs come out. The judge calls it a root cellar, but he's lying. It's deep, Brian."

Maybe a sinkhole had indeed opened up. It would be like the judge to conceal such a thing, for fear that the county would make him pay to have it filled in.

He dropped into a chair across from Ellen. "This work is brilliant. Why you're not still on the *Times* I can't imagine."

"Too many soft news assignments. I wanted the hard stuff."

"I think you got handed a little, I have to tell you."

"Unless I'm connecting dots that shouldn't be connected."

"Physical evidence of the bugs—that's what we need."

"So let's get a net and go back to the judge's."

"A strong net, given what happened to your jar lid."

"Do you believe me?"

He nodded. "Let's say that I've accepted your story because I respect you. You're not a nut and you're not a liar. But as a scientist, I sure would like to see that evidence."

She sighed. "I was hoping we'd make some progress bouncing ideas around."

He rubbed his face. "Jesus. I've thought and thought about it. My problem is, the connection issue. I drove past my old lab yesterday morning. Just sat there thinking about it." He watched her light another cigarette.

"I still don't really know what you did at Ludlum. Not the details."

"The details are classified. Let's just say it was a way of connecting with the past, using a stream of particles."

"So it's unrelated."

"Well, probably. But these particles—if they exist—would break all the laws of continuity. The math says that they might *also* break holes, in a manner of speaking, between parallel universes. That's a fairly silly way of saying that they would cause profound chaos."

"Goddamnit, Brian, I want to know what happened to me."

"So do I."

"It eats at you. Jesus!"

"Just don't be foolish."

"In what way?"

"By going to the judge's at night."

"It's the only alternative."

"We have to be methodical and careful. Given time, we'll make some headway. Scientific investigation always works like that."

"I'm a reporter!"

"Do it my way. We'll get better results." The clock

on the wall behind her head told him that twenty minutes had passed. "I have to get back to Loi."

"I'm sorry I bothered you."

"No, it was no bother, believe me. And who knows, we might be about to solve the secret of the ages."

"Is that what this is?"

"I think it could be." There was silence between them. Then he got up.

Ellen followed him to the door. "How is she?"

"Improving, the doctor says."

He was aware of Ellen's hand coming into his as they paused at the door. "You take care, Brian. Me personally, I bought a shotgun which I have no idea how to use. I keep all my lights on at night and my windows closed."

He drove home slowly, considering what their most logical next step would be. It seemed clear that insect bodies were needed. And they should follow up with the Evanses, be certain that they came back.

She was going to go charging off to the judge's, he knew it, and put herself in great jeopardy. Care was needed. To convince the outside world that this was really happening, an array of carefully gathered evidence had to be presented.

When he got home he folded Loi in his arms and kissed her deep and long.

She took him to their bed. In the way of some familiar married couples, they undressed without speaking. He lay with her, listening to the baby, kissing her breasts, her belly, tasting the sweetness of her skin. Very gently, she caressed his penis, and kissed him there in her modest way. She kept on until he rose to his full passion. Familiar waves of pleasure enveloped him, and he watched in amazement as the author of his pleasure moved her head in the gentle, rising rhythm that led to only one thing.

After he spent himself, she stroked his hair and gazed into his eyes. To his own intense annoyance, he found himself thinking about the problem.

"You frown."

"No, I'm happy. Loi, I'm so happy." He embraced her and kissed her long, tasting a hint of himself in her mouth, and loving her the more for her willingness. "Thank you," he whispered after the kiss.

They made a chicken stir-fry for supper. He chopped and she cooked. They had it with tart lemonade.

Afterward he sat in his chair reading the latest *Astronomy*. But he couldn't concentrate. He stared off into space, ruminating. He thought of the tire tracks, the missing people . . . and of fighting the steering wheel in that truck. If Ellen went anywhere near that house after dark, she was in danger.

Half an hour passed. An hour. He got up and phoned her. There was no answer.

"Honey, I'm gonna ride into town. Get a magazine."

"You were just in town."

"I'm restless. I'll just go down to Handy's and be right back."

He drove out into a dark, starry night. At the intersection where Mound became Main, he turned down toward the judge's house.

Mound Road was empty of cars—almost. Parked well off the road about thirty yards from the house, Brian was not very surprised to see a familiar Plymouth Duster, dark and empty.

He got out of his truck. The night was silent, very dark before moonrise.

Five minutes passed, then ten, then twenty.

He got back in and called Loi. He said that he had a flat. She sounded a little strange, but said she was fine.

He'd been there forty-five minutes when he saw the glimmer of a flashlight coming up the road. Relief poured through him as she came up to the truck. "You've been spying on him."

"Yeah."

"And?"

"I expected lots of cars. But I think I have to come back later."

At all costs, he had to deflect her from that course of action. "We should try to catch one of the insects."

"I think it's more practical to take pictures of the cars, get license numbers."

He took her hand, then almost as quickly released it. "Go home, Ellen."

"Let's compromise. You come with me tonight. If we fail, then we'll do it your way. We could meet at your place at about two. Go back through the woods, see what we can find."

This was a bad mistake, he knew it. But he couldn't let her do it alone. "We'll need a container."

"I have some jars with glass lids."

They parted then. He followed the Duster until she turned into her driveway, then accelerated toward Kelly Farm. Five minutes later he was home and wishing very much that he could explain things to Loi.

"You got the tire fixed OK?"

For a moment, he drew a blank. "Oh! Yeah, fine."
He glanced at his watch. "Look, it's pushing ten-
thirty. What say we turn in?" He wanted to get some
rest before it was time to go out. Above all, he
wanted to make certain that Loi was deeply asleep
when Ellen came.

"Sure, Brian."

He threw on the boxer shorts he used as pajamas
in the summer and got into bed. Loi soon followed.
They lay together, she reading a dictionary, he an old
Newsweek he'd grabbed. "I thought you went for a
new magazine."

"Handy's was closed."

Page by slow page, she perused the dictionary, re-
ferring frequently to a look-up list from *The Winter's
Tale*. Every so often, she would whisper a pronunci-
ation to herself.

An hour became another hour, midnight approached. He dozed, only to wake and find her still
studying.

"You really need your sleep," he said at last. But it
was nearly one before she turned off her light.

He lay awake, waiting.

When there came a light tapping on the front
door, he almost jumped out of his skin.

She'd done it.

He said nothing, only sat up in the madly creaking
bed, put his feet on the floor and went shuffling into
the kitchen. He even went so far as to get himself a
glass of water, on the off chance that Loi might be
vaguely aware of his movements.

Ellen appeared at the kitchen window. "I'm
scared, Brian." Her whisper was little more than
breath itself.

He pulled on a pair of jeans over the shorts, and threw a T-shirt across his shoulders. Then he slipped into his ancient sneakers. He went to the door, opened it a crack, hesitated. The hinges seemed to creak even more loudly than the bed. Well, no matter, he had to risk it.

They walked toward the woods. "We can go along that path by the kill," she said. "We'll be at his house in a few minutes."

"I know."

"Did you tell Loi?"

He didn't answer, and she didn't repeat the question. As they passed the ruins of his old house, he began to feel the cold. He put on the T-shirt.

Ellen's arm moved around his waist. "I'm afraid," she said. "I'm scared all the time."

"We'll get one of your bugs. Then science will react."

They were well beyond the ruins of Kelly Farm now. Here the woods were deeper, darker. The breeze sighed in the trees.

"You know, Brian, even being out here with you, I'm still real afraid. Are you as scared as I am?"

"For a couple of minutes I was totally helpless, moving toward the judge's house against my will. You're damn right I'm scared."

"I keep remembering the way they smelled." She shuddered.

"You have a sensitive nose."

"They stink like sweaty old men."

They began to hear Coxon Kill up ahead.

"This is where I got away from them—by diving into the water right there!" She pointed, then glanced back the way they had come. "I hadn't realized your place was so close to mine."

"Our old roads wind around a lot. The whole area's deceptive that way."

At that moment there appeared a glimmer among the trees.

A shock like a slap went through him when he realized that it was a long stream of light, like a glowing snake. It shimmered and undulated among the trees, the tip of it gliding about, seeking. Ellen's hand gripped his arm. "They're here."

She opened her purse, pulled out a Ball jar.

He was watching the thing, deeply fascinated. Was he actually seeing something from another reality, another world? "It's as cohesive as a single creature."

"We've got to go closer. You'll see it's actually a swarm."

She fumbled the jar open. They stepped forward. They were hand in hand, like two children.

The moment they moved, the swarm shot at them like a bolt of lightning. It stopped short fifty feet away. Brian could hear the sigh of many wings. It seemed to strain toward him. "I think it has a limit to its range."

"Yeah."

"Give me the jar."

She put it in his hand. Her heard her sob.

"Stay back, Ellen."

"Hell no."

Together, they moved into the pale light of the swarm.

Without warning he was covered with them. He screamed like a shot deer, grabbed at the legs scrabbling against his face—felt himself pulled hard from behind.

He fell back against her. There was a tinkle of glass. The jar had broken against the ground. "Run." Her voice was choked.

In moments they were in one of Brian's orchards. The trailer was visible in the distance, a black shadow. The swarm had extended itself again, and was now a hundred feet beyond where it had originally stopped. It was also a good deal thinner, like a long, glowing cable.

She was sobbing openly now, her shoulders shaking, her hands tearing her hair. "We're OK," he said, "we're OK."

She clutched him.

The glowing cable was undulating, and getting shorter and thicker. "Look at it, Ellen. It's pulling itself back."

He held her to him, comforting her.

Another voice spoke: "Brian?" Loi came out of the shadows, moving softly and carefully—but fast. She was very fast.

"Loi!" He pushed Ellen away. His heart started thundering.

Ellen said the worst possible thing. "I'm sorry, Loi!" She could not have appeared more guilty.

"Brian, please come with me now."

"He was helping me in an investigation," Ellen said.

"Ah. You are exploring sex?"

"I—he—Loi, there's something you should know."

"I guess so."

"It's not what it seems. He's helping me investigate the judge."

Loi looked toward the forest. "The judge is in the woods, then?"

Brian went to her. "Loi, it's not what it seems."

"Don't you dare tell me what it is or isn't. You think I'm stupid?"

"There really is an investigation—"

"And as for you, Miss Fancy Reporter, you get off my land right now. And stay away from my husband, or I'm gonna come after you the way we do at home!" Her voice crackled with authority. This was a very new side of his wife.

Ellen gasped, stepped back. Brian was so shocked he couldn't make a sound. Loi's tone had sliced through the air. She'd meant those words, they were no idle threat.

It felt to Brian as if the whole world was falling in on him. He loved this woman with all his heart and soul. "You mustn't think—"

"Come, husband. We go." With that she turned and began moving back toward the house. She walked fast, slipping through the night with the grace of a trained infiltrator. "Come," she called.

He hurried after her.

SIX

1.

For Loi the awful details of her discovery were the hardest part to bear. Brian's hurrying along home with her like some silly geisha; the way Miss Maas had nervously drummed her fingers along her jaw—these were the things that cut through the lies that they spoke.

A part of her sought blame and wanted to apologize. Another part wanted to do something to him with a knife. She had been a worthy wife, and wasn't she carrying his son?

She had seen all—and not two hours ago he had been making love with her. Was he never tired, never satisfied? Why were men slaves to their sticks?

She took him back to their trailer in silence, listening hardly at all to his protests. "Loi, I did not—" "Loi, it wasn't what—" At home a man discovered like this would not have further humiliated himself with such babble.

At home, indeed. What was she thinking? She was without a home. This trailer, this man and her big belly—these were her home. Without the man she might fall back into destitution. She would fall back. She knew well what awaited a little boy in the back streets of Bangkok. Was it also the same in the slums of New York?

The thought tightened her throat, made her stomp with rage as they passed through the brushy field that had once been Mary Kelly's vegetable garden. Her own far better garden was nearby, sited farther down the slope for correct drainage.

When they got back to the trailer, he spoke again: "Loi, please, I beg you, listen to me."

"Why you put me in a trailer? Why not rebuild the house, you've got the money, you old skinflint."

"I—Mary—"

She put her hands to her ears, she didn't want to hear that name, not now. "All of these women," she shouted. He grabbed at her but she pushed him away, turned from him. She did not even want to look upon the face of Dr. Brian Kelly.

"Loi, please. I can't bear this."

She went to bed. When he heard the springs creak, he came into the room, but she delivered a look that drove him out.

Let him go. Let all the white-eyes go. They were no better than the devils who had made her a soldier at the age of eight. The devils would never have put a pureblood child in those tunnels. Only a nigger girl, the child of a round-eyed colonialist whore and a dirty American, an ugly little embarrassment.

Loi lay imagining that she was a statue, as still and cool as the Emperor of Jade Buddha in his shady pagoda.

Within her she felt Brian Ky Kelly begin to move. She smelled the aroma of the cigarette Brian was smoking in the living room, and her soul reached into her womb and twined tendrils of it about her baby, imagining that the sweet threads of family still bound them all together.

She didn't want this new weight in her heart. But she was a proud and good woman, she did not deserve to be treated in this disrespectful and humiliating manner.

Her anger was so great that she couldn't sleep; she got up and went to the front door. Maybe the quiet of the night would calm her spirit.

"Loi?"

She thought she wouldn't answer him now. She stepped onto the tiny porch, surveyed the still, silent yard. The driveway was a pale shadow, beyond it the dark bulk of the barn. If she walked to the far end of the trailer, she would be able to see the ruins of Kelly Farm, where he had left his past life . . . his real life.

She was only his whore, not his wife.

The driveway was lit briefly by a lightning bug. It was a lovely, large one, like the ones that floated through the jungle at home.

She went along the path that surrounded the trailer, stopping when she could see the remains of the farmhouse. There were lightning bugs gleaming among the ruins, lending them a ghostly significance, as if spirits of the dead still lingered there. She went closer. One of the bugs came up and hovered before her. It acted as if it wanted to land on her belly. Idly, she slapped it away. The thing was big and fast, and it buzzed angrily and came straight back, bouncing against her stomach as if it wanted to burrow its way inside. Again, she brushed it away.

In each beat of her heart she felt her love for Brian. She wanted to turn it off, but she could not.

She looked back at the trailer. If he was really suffering as much as he pretended, then there was still hope. He would have to apologize, of course. He would have to do many things.

Two of the lightning bugs were hovering around her belly. They landed, she brushed them off.

Maybe he'd been seduced. That woman certainly had the capacity to do it. The need, too. She was alone in a small town. The only available men were either too young, too old, too mean or too drunk.

Annoyed, she pulled another of the pesky bugs off her stomach. It buzzed angrily, and two more came racing toward her. Then she noticed that a great swarm of them was coming up the field behind the ruins of the farmhouse, pouring out of the woods like a river of moonlight.

For a moment she watched this phenomenon. Its beauty distressed her, though, because she could not enjoy it, not through her new sorrow.

Five or six of the bugs began pummeling against her stomach like moths crazed by a light bulb. Waving them away, she began to think that it wasn't so pleasant to be outside now.

More angry at him than ever, she returned to the trailer.

From the dark of the living room, she heard a sound like a dove sighing.

Behind her lightning bugs began hitting the screen door. They were peculiar and unpleasant, not a kind she'd seen before. She shut the wooden inner door to make sure they wouldn't get through.

"What was that?" he called from the dark.

"Nothing." She went into the bedroom and lay down. Her body sank into the mattress.

Maybe she had wronged Brian, somehow hurt him. Perhaps the slap—had that driven him away from her? But no, he'd never even mentioned it.

The truth was that men were weak, feckless creatures, led by the stick, as the old grandmothers used to say at home.

Brian belonged to her, and she would not let his stick lead him away.

She was so much smaller than the American woman, so much darker. That was her real trouble. Ellen was as pale as a lotus flower, as tall as a goddess. Her eyes were beautifully round. Despite all her white blood, Loi's were more slanted than her own mother's. Slanted eyes were such a misfortune.

The dove sound came again, and this time she sat right up in the bed because she could hear that it was definitely coming from Brian. Was that the sound of his weeping?

She rose, went softly into the living room. "Are you all right?"

He looked up at her, his eyes hollow, his face gleaming with sweat. His reply was mumbled.

"Brian, I can't hear you."

When his words came again, they were like the rumbling memory of a storm, slurred echoes of speech. "I'm sorry. I was terribly insensitive."

She bent to him, took his face in her hands.

"Godawful things are happening," he said. *"Godawful!"*

"I know," she said.

"No, Loi, you don't know. You don't know anything!"

"I know all."

He pushed against her chest, so that she had to

rise to her feet, step away from him. "What do you know?"

"Her beauty is very great."

He closed his eyes, a look of pain.

"Are you going to go with her?"

He came up from the chair. "You're the best thing that ever happened to me!" His bulky body pressed against hers and he held her, trembling like a guilty boy.

He looked down at those rich, dark eyes, and was shaken, amazed by how much he loved her.

Somewhat roughly, she broke away.

"You have a right to your anger. But I still want to ask you to understand."

She looked down at the floor. He reached for her hand, but she drew away.

"I lose my face. All face." Her voice shuddered with emotion. For her, there could be no catastrophe worse than loss of face in her marriage. "I saw you embracing her. It hurt me so much!"

"Oh, my poor baby! I beg you, forgive me, some-how find it in your heart."

"Brian, I am wishing to but I don't think it's gonna be!"

He no longer had the option of telling her about the insects. How could he ask her to believe such a crazy story—it would sound like an absurdly clumsy attempt to conceal an affair. "Loi, this is a horrible misunderstanding."

"Nothing is misunderstood."

"No. She isn't my lover."

"What is she then, a concubine?"

He didn't answer. There was no way to answer.

She did not want to fight with him. This would

accomplish nothing. If he still loved her, she would find out soon enough—but only if she was careful. She gave him a smile. "It's a hot night, Brian. You're sweaty. If you'd like some lemonade, it's still in the fridge."

They went into the predawn kitchen together and she gave him a glass of the lemonade, watched him drink. "I am a good woman for you. Better than her!"

He could see what had enabled this woman to drag herself up from the bottom. Sometimes great human beings are born into very small lives. In the scheme of things, Loi's escape from her past was a small thing. But it had required the same kind of human greatness that enables big people to change history. He raised his glass to her. "Thank you, Loi."

"My lemonade is good, isn't it?"

2.

She watched him drink, his eyes pleading. For forgiveness? For rescue? What terrible thing troubled him, so big it was even more important than his infidelity? Better always to speak of big things in the morning when the blood was strong. "You're exhausted," she said.

"I can't possibly sleep."

He needed help, she could not deny that . . . nor that she had the desire to give it to him. Even so, she drew him to the couch, got him to lie with his head in her lap. "Ellen Maas does not even know you. She couldn't help you now."

He closed his eyes, let the whirl of explanations

fall silent. He dared not ask her if this small intimacy meant that he was being forgiven. Somehow he had to prove to her that he wasn't being unfaithful with Ellen. Maybe Ellen herself could do it. Together, the two of them could explain all that had happened. It would seem more plausible then. Yes, that was what had to be done.

In the meantime, it was so good here, with his cheek pressed against her stomach, his son communicating faint movements from inside. He closed his eyes. "Loi," he whispered, "I love you."

She did not reply.

He had not been asleep two minutes before he became troubled by a nightmare of a tall, black insect standing before him in the darkness, cloaked like a monk. There was a loud cawing noise, the sound of an enraged crow.

Her cool voice awakened him from the dream, then her soft caressing hands lulled him. "Nobody could do this for me, my love, nobody but you."

He sank away into deeper sleep.

When he woke up she was in the kitchen preparing breakfast. He sat up from the couch, saw her standing at the sink, sunlight pouring over her from the window.

He'd had more bad dreams, of being trapped down in his old facility, of seeing the charge in the waveguide rising and rising, going beyond redline, of the blue pipe shuddering and smoking and glowing orange, turning into a glowing swarm and rising into the control room—

But nothing like that had ever happened. It was just a nightmare. It symbolized his life going out of control, his brain humming on overdrive, everything flying apart.

Regret cut his heart. Between the two of them everything had changed. Her posture—shoulders stiff, head down—told him that the incident had penetrated the depths of their relationship.

He got up and went into the bathroom. He shaved, mechanically preparing for the day. Her peculiar and delightful Vietnamese singing did not fill the house on this morning.

When he kissed her on the back of the head she neither responded nor resisted.

There was a nice breakfast laid out: grapefruit, pineapple juice, yogurt filled with strawberries. A tiny incident, however, confirmed that nothing was forgiven. Usually, he took his coffee cut with milk, and he preferred American roast. She liked it as dark as she could get it, French style.

On this morning all the coffee was her way.

He drank it without complaint. He wanted to talk to her, but her silence was a wall. Maybe if he tried again, if he just plunged in. He took a swallow of coffee, looked up at her. "Loi, I want to be forgiven. I want it to be like it was."

"You should think of that first." Her eyes went to the window. "A truck." She looked out, cupping her hands around her temples to cut reflections.

He heard a rising roar, then the slam of a door.

Suddenly Bob West was coming in. Brian was glad, his appearance would transform this crushing atmosphere.

"We've got trouble up in Towayda," Bob said without preamble. "Another screamer. Down in the Traps, other side of Jumper Ridge."

"That's nasty country back in there. Not like the mound."

"Brian, I'd like you to come with me as a scientist. Tell me it's not the damn wind so I can order a proper search."

All of a sudden Brian wasn't glad anymore. This was the last thing he wanted.

Loi stopped what she was doing, looked hard at him.

"I'm a physicist," he said. "Not a geologist."

"You'll be the only scientist there."

"Brian." Her fingers touched his.

"I'm hoping this is nothing," Bob added, glancing at her nervously. "But I want you along, Brian."

"How will a physicist help you?" Loi asked.

"You don't want him to go?"

"I'm worried, is all." She glanced down at her stomach.

"Course you are, Loi. The last thing I'd want is to take him away when he's needed. But this isn't a fishing trip." He regarded Brian. "I would've leveled the mound if it hadn't been for that fool Danny. This time I want to go in with more than just a backhoe. I need your credentials."

A request like that from an old friend couldn't be denied. "I'm gonna have to go, Loi."

At first she said nothing. When she spoke, her voice was like velvet. "You will leave me." Her tone was low and sad.

"You make it sound like forever, Loi!" Bob said. He gave her a playful peck on the back of the head.

"Call me from the road," she told Brian.

"I will, honey."

"You go." She smiled wide, projecting an impression of happiness that she most certainly did not feel. "It's OK, really."

He left the small figure of his wife in the doorway, got in Bob's trooper-marked Blazer. As they rolled out toward the road, he looked back for a goodbye. Almost formally, Loi raised her hand, a gesture that suggested long farewells.

They drove down to Ludlum and got on the Northway.

"She seemed upset," Bob commented as they rolled out the driveway and turned onto Kelly Farm Road.

"She's worried about the baby."

"Can't blame her. What's Sam Gidumal say?"

"He's optimistic."

"She looks like she's gonna pop."

"That she does." He thought to himself: you've made your bed, Brian Kelly, now sleep in it.

Although it was only fifty miles to Towayda by the old road, the new highway with its smooth curves and moderate grades was faster. The site was sixty miles up the Northway, then ten more through Towayda, deep into the Jumpers.

For a time, they drove in silence. Brian's mind remained fixed on Loi. "Did she seem just normally upset, or real upset?"

"You've had a fight?"

"No. But she's been moody."

"It's the pregnancy. Nancy gets on a roller coaster at the beginning of the third trimester. And that's without the worry of complications."

He shared a lot with Bob, but he didn't see how he could share this, not any of it. "I hope that's all it is."

"You married a very special woman. You know how I feel about her."

"Yeah. A beautiful woman with all kinds of incredible assets."

"Would you look at that," Bob said, snapping Brian's train of thought. He was peering into the rearview mirror.

"Oh, beautiful," Brian replied dutifully. A brand new Dodge Viper was closing from behind. It was bright red, being driven by a cross between Nick Nolte and Cary Grant. Beside him sat the goddess Venus. Cars normally bored Brian, but this one was remarkable.

"Is that a vision or is that a vision," Bob said. He loved fine cars. He had an Austin-Healey he'd been rebuilding for years, but it was nothing like this. Chrysler's new competitor to the Corvette was the hottest car to come out of Detroit in thirty years.

"How fast are they going?"

Bob sped up so they wouldn't pass, paced them ahead. "Seventy-one. Nope, now they're slowing down. They've noticed the livery."

As the Viper dropped back, Bob slowed even more. Soon they were alongside. The car was all mean angles and seductive curves. To him its engine sounded like fabulous sex.

He peered down into the leather interior, looking directly at the perfect lap of the woman. "Oh, man, short-shorts." As he watched, the girl turned her young face and smiled at him. Then she made motions. She wanted him to roll down his window. He complied. She yelled, but he couldn't hear her over the throbbing engine.

"Say again," he shouted down at her.

". . . setups . . ." was all he got. But it was enough. He knew what they wanted.

Brian looked over at him. He'd heard, too. "You gonna tell her?" If Bob found out the location of the radar units ahead on the highway and told the Viper, he and Brian were going to get a chance to see what it could do.

"What the hell, let's find out." He went to the radio. Dispatch gave him the location of the next radar trap, a single unit at the one-six-zero mile marker.

They were still running parallel to the Viper. "They're at the one six zero!"

The driver saluted. He had thirty-one miles of clear road. "This is gonna be fun," Bob said.

"Is it legal?"

Bob laughed. "Course not." At that instant he noticed the driver's arms. They were jointless like snakes, and long, monstrously so, curving around the cockpit, looping down into the foot well. And the hands—long, muscular fingers that ended in black claws. "Goddamn! Can you see the guy?"

"Yeah."

"Look at his arms!"

Brian strained, but he couldn't see that far into the vehicle. Bob swung the Blazer toward the center of the lane but the Viper accelerated. As it did he caught a last glimpse of the girl. Now the pretty face seemed entirely changed. It was nothing but cheap plastic, something you buy in a dime store. It was cheap, painted plastic, and behind the dark eyes there were things glittering and rushing, as if the mask concealed a seething mass of bugs.

"Oh, fuck, Brian, look at that!"

Even though it had started at nearly seventy miles an hour the Viper was pulling swiftly away.

"It's a beautiful thing to see, Bob."

Bob hardly heard the words. His blood was rushing in his temples, his heart was rattling in his chest. That man had the arms of a—a—he didn't know what. And the girl—he'd wanted her, tasted her in his mind.

His stomach heaved; he only had seconds before it went on him. Swerving across the lanes, he caused a Lexus jammed with elderly ladies in designer hair to bleat its angry horn.

"Jesus Christ, Bob!"

He couldn't talk, all he could do was pull onto the shoulder. With little more than a glance back at the onrushing traffic, he stumbled out of the vehicle. Before he could get off the highway, his stomach turned inside out. A second later a UPS thirty-six-wheeler came blasting past, its airhorns blaring. Bob grabbed the door of the Blazer, choking as he swayed in the rig's slipstream.

Then he was out of control again, his whole insides seeming to twist against themselves, as if a fist was opening and closing in his guts.

Brian piled out and then he was holding him, lifting him from his helpless crouch. "What's the problem, buddy?"

Bob peered down the road. The Viper was half a mile away and going like the wind. "Did you see?"

"What?"

"They were—" But what could he say? He couldn't tell anybody what he'd seen, not even Brian. If one word of it got back to the Department, he'd be put on psychiatric report. He steadied himself against the hood of the truck. He was a state police officer in uniform, he could not reveal weakness like this in view of the public. People would assume he'd been drinking.

Another car passed, its horn blaring. He hopped back into the cab. "Too much cheap breakfast," he said as Brian joined him on the other side.

"You have eggs sunny side up?"

"Always. Good for the heart."

"Maybe it was salmonella. You can get that from soft-cooked eggs nowadays."

Off in the distance Bob could just make out the Viper, a dot on the horizon. Then it was gone. He had recovered himself enough to want to find out what the hell was going on in that car. He picked up the mike, thumbed it live. "This is unit two-two-eight on a detail passing marker one niner zero. We just had a red Dodge Viper through here at about warp speed. He's moving north, and moving is the word."

There was a click, some static. "We hear you and we appreciate," came an unfamiliar voice. The way troopers were shifted around these days, Bob wasn't surprised that he didn't know the voice from the radar car.

"You shouldn't rat on the guy." Brian remained completely unaware of what Bob had seen.

"Come off it. He's doin' a buck fifty at least. That qualifies as abusing the privilege."

Brian laughed. "You guys are all the same. Traitors to the core."

As he drove, Bob's stomach slowly settled. He began to think about maybe a cup of tea to complete the process.

"You sure you're OK, buddy?" Brian asked.

"You ever do lucy?"

"A couple of times. I saw Puff the Magic Dragon in a phone booth, as I recall."

"Ever flash back?"

"Nope."

"Well, I think maybe I just did. In that Viper— hell, I thought I saw—" He managed to chuckle a little. "The damn chicken!"

"What chicken?"

"The one that laid the egg that made me sick!" They both laughed. "Lookin' for a Dunkin' Donuts," Bob added.

"I don't believe it, you just don't quit."

"A cruller and a cup of tea'd set me up just right."

In Vietnam he'd dropped acid until it was coming out of his pores. He'd had to, he had a death job as commanding officer of a Long Range Infiltration and Intelligence unit. He'd take his squad of specially trained men deep into the jungle for patrols lasting a week, two weeks, three. Charlie hid rice in holes, but he and his men had no holes. Charlie had underground field hospitals, like the kind of place where poor Loi had worked. They even had field kitchens down there. Bob had stayed alive by eating water rats and sucking pond scum.

The funny thing was, acid had never tripped him out back then. His stress level had been so great that it had worked as a kind of tranquilizer. It made colors prettier, it smoothed over the cellulite on the thighs of Saigon whores. When the sun hit his face when he was on acid, he felt the subtle and deeply comforting presence of some greater force, some deity.

Maybe it was Brian's mere presence that had set off the flashback. His best friend getting a VC wife—could you beat that? She'd worked in the Chu Chi tunnels. After his stint in intelligence, he'd spent four months tunnel-busting, which meant blowing them closed and then pumping them full of napalm. To drown out the horrible sounds from below, they'd screamed their throats raw.

At first he'd thought he would hate Loi, then that he would be unable to face her.

Part of him was still at war, would always be at war. But then the two couples would sit down to a bridge game, and his heart would touch deep feelings of respect and friendship for Loi. Because it had given him these feelings, the war had come to seem in a curious way blessed.

He searched the horizon for the familiar Dunkin' Donuts sign. Tea and a cruller were his original comfort foods.

There was nothing at the next exit, meaning that he had to put down another eleven miles before relief.

They drove those miles without saying so much as a word. Brian never pushed anyone to talk, it wasn't his style, hadn't been since Mary died. Before that, he'd jabber physics until your ears dropped off. The friendship had sort of knocked along in those days. Brian had gone through the war on a student deferment, and Bob really resented that. Then he'd resented all the fancy professors hanging out at Kelly Farm, and been rankled along with the rest of Oscola by the way Brian let those fine Kelly orchards go.

But he'd come back to them, hadn't he, in the end?

The minutes crept past. Would the radar unit stop the Viper? Sure they would, even if they didn't get it on the gun. Just to remind the guy that this wasn't the friggin' Sahara around here.

Finally the exit showed up, and it had everything—a Roy Rogers, a McDonald's and a local place called the Franklin Inn and—praise the Lord—a Dunkin' Donuts. Bob went for tea with milk and two crullers, what the hell, he'd work it off later. Brian got the coffee with milk that he always drank.

Just past mile marker one-six-zero they spotted the radar unit. "Nicely hidden," Brian commented. "Cunning bastards."

Bob slowed down. "The better to get your ass with, civilian scum."

"That's how you guys feel, I know it."

The crullers were hitting Bob's stomach like a load of bowling balls. Maybe this was a combo flashback and stomach flu situation. Be just his luck.

Twenty yards down from the radar unit, Bob pulled over. They got out and walked up to the car. "You get that Viper?" Bob asked.

The station man looked up at him. "Never came through."

"Never came through at all?"

"Nah. Musta taken the Corey Lake exit."

Bob concealed the rush of emotion that this caused. He'd wanted to hear that the people in the car were wearing masks or something. That would put the whole thing to bed. But now he was just going to have to suffer.

They drove on. From time to time he glanced over at Brian, then stuck his nose down into his tea. No way could he afford to go crazy, he had kids at home.

He was glad when they reached Towayda and he could get his mind off LSD and weirdness, even if it was only to think about whether or not a horrible crime had been done here.

They drove down Towayda's main street. "Quiet this morning," Brian commented.

"Damn quiet." There wasn't even a car in front of the grocery store. "There isn't a soul."

"Well, you're a cop. What gives?"

"Fishing? Hunting? A mass migration to Atlantic City? I have no idea."

They passed through the town and headed toward the frowning Mount Jumper ridges. Bob had never much liked Mount Jumper itself, it was too rough and raw. People fell off, got themselves busted all to hell. The name had been conferred when an entire tribe of Algonquin Indians had thrown themselves to their deaths rather than accept captivity.

As the Blazer moved along, the ridges were arrayed north to south like a wall. The somber green of the pine forest opened every few miles to a rock face.

As they reached the summit of the Jumpers the views appearing below could not have been prettier: green fields, long stretches of forest, undulating hills. But just beside the road there was a brutal cliff. Dangling from it like a pretty spider was a girl in bright red shorts. For a long moment they both gazed at this apparition. She was hanging in her climbing gear eating a sandwich.

Brian noticed that Bob had gotten dead quiet. As

they ascended into the Jumpers, the road narrowed and became pitted with potholes. Finally the pavement gave out and Bob stopped briefly to shift the truck into four-wheel drive.

The road was now just a track enclosed by dark pines. And up ahead, through those pines, they could see the winking red of light bars.

SEVEN

1.

Bob hit his own light bar and accelerated.

Three minutes later they pulled into the tiny parking area near the Traps. Two trooper cars were standing parked with their doors still open. Beside them was an ambulance marked TOWAYDA RESCUE. But for the clicking of light bars, the silence was total.

They went off along the path to the Traps, moving as quickly as they could on the steep path. Around them the woods lived according to their own slow meaning. They were dark, black and silent. A man who grew up with the woods might enjoy what they could give him, but sentiment was for city people.

The path wound down, deeper and deeper into a rocky, forest-choked crevasse. It was in this sort of place that the desperate Algonquins had hidden, and eventually met their deaths.

The thick trees gave way to huge rocks jutting up on either side of the path, giving the sense that they had entered some vast, half-finished temple. But it wasn't beautiful: the sharp, jutting edges, the hard angles, the gray stone, made it a cruel place.

Then the crevasse widened, and suddenly what had been simply big became awesome. Enormous boulders, like prehistoric monoliths, stood every thirty or forty feet. And it became clear why the place was called the Traps: it was possible to get lost in the labyrinth, maybe for a long time . . . and if you wandered off a bluff, then it would be forever.

They moved carefully among the columns of stone. Only dim light penetrated, and the odor of mildew was strong. There was also another odor and Bob knew instantly what it was: human blood, lots of it. He had smelled it in Vietnam. He smelled it at the sites of bad accidents.

"Hello," Bob called. Now that they were among the stones, it was impossible to tell which way to go. The ground was softened by a layer of decaying pine bristles which muffled sounds and sprang back into footprints, meaning that any path would disappear in minutes.

A trooper burst around one of the huge stones. There was blood on his hands, his shirt was sticking to his body, his face running with sweat. "We got her half out," he gasped. Brian and Bob traded looks. The fact that somebody had been found here meant, also, that somebody had been in the mound.

Deeper and deeper, they followed the trooper in among the columns of stone. Now the silence was absolute. Not even wind penetrated this place.

Then they saw her. Brian made a low, trembly noise. Bob simply sucked in breath.

Brian had never seen anybody so wounded. She was covered from head to torso with bruises, cuts and scrapes. She looked worse than the raw, dripping ninety percenters on the burn ward. She was still half-buried in the earth.

"What happened to her arms?" Bob asked. They

were dark blue and narrow, the skin tight. They looked rubbery and jointless, as if the bones had turned to pulp. He was reminded of the arms of the man in the Viper.

But no, that was impossible, he told himself. What he'd observed in the Viper was a flashback, pure and simple.

Then he saw her eyes. His hand came up to his chin, he sucked breath. But he did not cry out, he fought it back just in time.

Those eyes were vividly aware, darting from face to face. The irises were invisible, the pupils huge and black. The whites were ash gray. Her eyes *almost* didn't look like . . . eyes. Not normal eyes.

"Can you hear me?" Bob asked.

"She won't respond," one of the troopers said.

"What's wrong with her?" Brian wanted to cradle her, to somehow make it better.

"It's some kind of compression injury," one of the rescue squad men replied. "We need to know more."

Her lips moved and she made a small internal racket. Her voice sounded like somebody was burning leaves in her guts. She looked to Brian as if she had to be dead, and yet she was not only alive, she was still conscious.

Bob, who was now the senior officer present, went down on one knee. "Ma'am?"

There was a sort of response, a crackle.

"What happened to you, ma'am?"

Silence.

"Ma'am, try to tell me."

The torso writhed, the face softened, the eyelids flickered, the teeth appeared behind half-parted lips. Her expression was unmistakable. Inexplicably and

horribly, whatever she was remembering was bringing her great pleasure.

"We want to help you, ma'am," Bob repeated.
"What did this to you?"

"Purple . . ."

"Yes? Purple what?"

The lips quivered, the eyes rolled. "Ma'am?" There
was no further response. "Where was she, in a
cave?"

"She's stuck in the fuckin' dirt like a grubworm!"

The eyes were moving again. Now the chief medic
tried to get through. "Lady, can you hear me?" The
eyes didn't slow down, the voice didn't even crackle.
"She's out to lunch," he said. He looked around.
"We gotta get her out."

They withdrew her from the earth with a sighing
pop, as if she'd been a giant cork, tightly jammed. A
congealing gel of blood coated the hole.

She began spitting and gyrating when the medics
tried to put her on their portable stretcher. It was a
hideous thing to see, like watching a corpse move.
The skin was so dead, and giving off a rotted meat
smell, that Bob found it almost impossible to believe
that they were seeing life here. But the damn eyes
were still going, moving like crazy, and the spray of
her spit was colored rose by blood.

The medics finally got her onto their stretcher,
strapped her down and covered her. They lifted her
and moved off, with the troopers giving assist.

Flushed and sweating, the chief medic hung back.
"What do I tell them in ER? How did the injuries to
her limbs come about?"

He was ignored by the flustered young troopers.
But he had a job to do, so Bob swung into action.

He reached out, grabbed one of them on the shoulder. "Answer the question."

The kid turned on him, his face gone white with fury. "We don't fucking know! She was screaming like hell and we dug toward the screams. Then we see hair, we get her face free, two hours later we got what you see. Until ten minutes ago, she was totally unconscious. For the first hour, we thought she was in a coma."

The medic's face tightened. He wanted to help her, too, but he couldn't do his best unless he knew more. "Her legs and arms—it's not a familiar pattern of trauma."

The trooper glared into his swimming eyes. "She's been in the fucking ground, packed as tight as a goddamn rock! Look, I don't know what the hell this is. You said it yourself—compression injury. Put that down on your damn form!"

The medic glanced toward the path, realizing that his patient had been carried far ahead of him. He set off at a fast trot.

Bob and Brian also ran, soon catching up with the others. "Y'know, it just never ends, these days," Bob said. "Any goddamn bizarre thing can happen."

The run up the steep path was exhausting. "Too much bridge," Bob said, "not enough medicine ball."

Brian was too winded to reply.

The tumble of rocks ahead was so tall that it seemed as if they must have gone all the way down the mountain to get to the Traps. But it was only a hundred feet or so.

Finally the path smoothed out and the woods dropped away. They had returned to the parking area.

Theirs was the only vehicle left.

The last echoes of the rescue truck and the troopers' sirens could be heard dwindling toward Towayda. They would be taking the victim to the hospital up in Saranac.

"Let's follow 'em," Bob said.

They were both grateful to get back in the truck. For a moment, Bob hesitated. He waited for his heart to slow down.

They went through Towayda and back out onto the Northway. Saranac was forty miles farther north, farther from Oscola. Brian wished that there had been time to call Loi, but that was obviously out of the question. "I'd about convinced myself that Danny was right," he said.

"God knows how it must've felt to that poor woman in there, when she heard us quit."

It was too hideous for Brian to comprehend, and he did not reply. His mind turned to Loi, and he wished yet again that there was some way to contact her. There was nothing to explain, there were no more apologies to make. It was just that he suspected that her pride might make her pack her bags and leave. That he could not bear.

The forty miles passed quickly, though. Bob was using his siren, driving fast. Once he cursed when the electrical system faltered and the siren cut out, but it began working again and he became silent.

Soon they were passing through the outskirts of Saranac. The hospital was close to the center of town. The parking lot was full, and Brian could see the rescue vehicle still parked in the emergency bay.

It turned out that the woman, now classified as a

Jane Doe, had been brought in DOA. "May I speak to the attending?" Bob asked the duty nurse.

"She died of massive internal injuries," the young doctor said as he came from behind a privacy curtain drawn around a bed. "Practically every bone in her body was broken. She was a victim of torture."

"I'd say so! She was buried alive."

"That was only part of it. Her arms and legs had been literally pulverized. The bones were liquefied. Frankly, we've never seen anything like it. Not remotely like it. They're gonna take her down to New York City for the autopsy. They've got pathologists down there who've seen everything."

"This'll be news even to them," Bob said.

Brian was relieved when he turned to leave, heading toward the glass doors that led from Emergency Receiving into the parking lot.

"Hey, Officer."

Bob stopped. "Yes?"

"You want to see her?" The doctor's face was grave.

Brian didn't want to. "We've already done that," he said. "We were on the rescue."

But Bob turned around.

"Because she's definitely dead. The brain's reading goose eggs right across the chart. But the left eye is still moving."

They went. She'd been taken to the hospital's small morgue, which contained three aluminum tables and four refrigerators. She was the only cadaver, and she lay on the central table. Except for a green square of cloth covering her face, she was naked. Her arms were at her sides. Like her legs they were black and unnaturally thin. Her belly seemed enormous.

The pathologist, who had been making notes on a clipboard, looked up as they came in. She was a woman in her twenties, and Brian was surprised that he knew her. She'd been in Physics III as a premed student. An efficient scholar, as he recalled.

"Oh my goodness, where in the world did you come from, Dr. Kelly?"

He fought for her name, but it didn't come. He smiled weakly. "I'm with him." He nodded toward Bob. "We have an interest in the case."

She wasted no time on pleasantries, given the situation. "She's an unidentified white female, approximately thirty-three years of age. Death due to traumatic injuries and shock. There are a number of strange factors. First, the condition of the arms." She lifted one of the loose, black appendages. It looped through her hand like a hose. "This is due to liquefaction of the bones. It's as if they were actually taken out and ground into a slurry of marrow and blood and bone, then poured back in. Obviously, that's not what happened because there are no corresponding wounds. We don't have any idea what happened to these bones."

"Why are her arms so black?"

"That might be a combination of bruising and cyanosis. Frankly, we're not sure about that either. It's one of the reasons she's on her way to Bellevue Hospital down in New York. Another is this eye." With that she removed the cloth covering the face.

In death, the woman's face had attained a hideous stillness. Hideous, because the expression was one of extreme pleasure, lascivious and wanton.

Brian must have groaned, because Bob dropped his hand onto his shoulder.

Silently, the pathologist lifted the lid of the left eye. The effect was startlingly lifelike. The eye moved, it seemed to rest on objects, people. You could almost feel curiosity—strange, malevolent.

"Cover it," Bob said quickly.

The pathologist dropped the cloth back onto the face.

"How can this be happening?" Brian asked.

"Obviously the muscles are receiving electrical stimulation. We've tested the voltages, they're low normal. But where's the energy coming from? It's a mystery."

"I gather that you never see this."

"Oh, absolutely not. None of it. Not the condition of the bones, not the eye. This is definitely the strangest cadaver I've ever seen or heard of."

It took an hour to drive back to Towayda, and on the way they followed the squawks back and forth as the state police brought heavy equipment up to the Traps and started digging for the answer to where the woman had come from.

For a long time nothing was heard from the dig. It was pushing five when Bob finally broke into traffic and communicated with the barracks in Saranac. "This is Lieutenant West. Could I hear a progress on that dig, go ahead."

"All the soil that was around her has been saved."

"What'd they find?"

"Nothing. Just the dirt."

Bob flipped the switch. "If that don't beat all!" He glanced over at Brian. "We've got a decision point here, buddy," Bob said. "Either we stop at Wally's for a burger or drive straight to Oscola. Choose your poison."

"I'd like to get to a phone when it's convenient."

That decided Bob on Wally's. He got off the Northway and went down into Towayda. "What's buggin' you, Brian?"

"What's bugging me? You must have nerves of steel! We've just seen an incredibly brutal murder and you're stopping for a burger."

"We have to eat."

"We let that poor woman in the mound die!"

"Now look here, Brian, it's time to settle down. She was probably in worse shape than this one, the way she sounded."

Bob pulled the truck into Wally's parking lot. It was a famous local place and the main reason to come to Towayda. The burgers were always perfect and the fried chicken basket could make a grown man cry on a night when Wally was doing the frying.

Brian called Loi from the phone in the foyer, but she didn't answer. "She must be at the grocery store," he said. He forced back the worry.

Wally's was a comfortable diner, open all the time, and often crowded at hours like three and four a.m. with hunters or fishermen. It was the real thing, too, made out of a couple of old railroad cars. There were pictures of the Republican presidents of the twentieth century on the walls above the window and a MARINE AND PROUD OF IT sign behind the counter. Wally was Mr. American Legion of Towayda township. The fact that Bob was not only a trooper but also a vet and a Medal of Honor winner made him always welcome. Money was not discussed, and if there were no tables, Wally would kick some city people out to clear one.

In the event, the place was a graveyard. Usually at the dinner hour in the summer, Wally's was hopping. On this night there were exactly two other customers, a man and a woman sitting together in a booth.

Bob looked around. "This is getting mysterious. I mean, there just plain ain't nobody in Towayda."

"They're lucky," Brian said. "Considering." He wondered about the Evanses.

"Yeah, that's for sure."

Amy, who had been waitressing here since the days of the ponytail, got their orders. It took Wally all of five minutes to roll out of the back with the two burger baskets.

He was a big, tough guy, but he had the disposition of an Irish setter. "You goin' out of business, buddy?" Bob asked him.

"If I don't get a few people in here soon, I am. Been like this for a week."

Bob told him what had happened, and he was just as saddened and disgusted as Brian. "Tell you one thing, Robert. You catch the creep, you give him to me. Just remember to pass on the chili for a while. Let the city boys eat it."

After their meal Brian called Loi again. The phone rang once, twice, rang again. He let it ring five times, then seven, then ten. Finally he hung up. "She should've answered."

It was after seven when they pulled out onto the Northway. *"Tempus fugit,"* Bob said.

"It's hard to believe it's been all day."

"Fear compresses time. You notice it if you do enough accidents."

"Are you afraid?"

"Yep." Bob watched an eighteen-wheeler with only one headlight pass in the oncoming traffic. Bastard. Who knew what else was in violation on that rig?

The Blazer moved steadily south, the western horizon slowly went from gold to orange to red, and finally to deep purple. The evening star hung in the perfect sky.

South of Corey Lake the road emptied and narrowed, and the evening was broken only by an occasional passage of lights. A deep tiredness began to filter through Bob's body. The radio drifted in and out of static.

It was pushing ten when the Cuyamora County sign passed on the right. The night around them was clear, and stars hung in multitudes above the pines that crowded the road.

Feeling the Blazer shudder slightly, Bob blinked, put both hands on the wheel. He swept the gauges. The alternator needle was oscillating a little, the way it had earlier. The vehicle wasn't being properly maintained. Budget cuts, no doubt.

Then the headlights started flickering along with the oscillations of the needle. The engine was obviously having trouble. Bob began to think about radioing for help.

When the faint hiss coming from the speakers died, he toggled the switch. Too late. "Goddamnit," he said.

That brought Brian back from wherever he'd been. "What?"

"We got a problem. Bad alternator. It's taken the radio down."

The engine coughed and died, and Bob began wrestling with the now-heavy steering, guiding the vehicle to the shoulder. As he did so the electrics failed completely. He watched the gauges and lights die. By the time the Blazer was stopped, it was also stone dead and dark.

"We'd better start walking," Brian said.

"A state trooper never walks. We'll put out flares and wait for the divisional car."

Brian didn't want to be away from Loi for another second. Why hadn't she answered the phone? She'd known perfectly well who'd be calling. "When'll it come through?"

"Well, before the midnight shift change, anyway."

Three hours to wait. "Jesus, I don't need this."

Bob turned the key. There wasn't even a relay click. "Gone."

"Bob?"

"Yessir?" When he turned, he could see that Brian was staring fixedly out the windshield. The shadows transformed his profile into a mass of black ditches and tight lines.

When he followed Brian's gaze, Bob was shocked. He couldn't grasp what he was seeing. It seemed as if an enormous black curtain had dropped onto the highway about a hundred feet in front of them. "What the hell is it?"

"I have no idea."

Bob saw that the blackness had depth as well as form, like a kind of opening. A suggestion of movement made him strain to see more clearly. "There's something there!"

"I know it!"

It was the same kind of awful rushing Bob had

seen behind the mask of whatever had been riding in that Viper. But this time it was huge, swirling around down inside the hole. He glanced over at Brian. It was incredible, but he was definitely seeing this, too. "Lock your door, Brian. Roll up the windows."

The rushing became a flickering, and suddenly a mass of glowing bright dots appeared in the darkness. For a moment they swirled as if in some kind of a vortex. They were so bright that they lit the walls of the opening, which gleamed as if it was wet. It was extraordinarily wrinkled, and the material was undulating rhythmically.

Then the glowing dots of lights resolved themselves into a tight ball, so bright that it was hard to observe directly.

Like a bolt of lightning they shot at the car. Bob was so surprised that he cried out. Brian was silent.

They came around the side windows, slid like a thick liquid down the rear window. In moments they had blotted out everything, and the interior of the Blazer was filled with their light.

Brian could even hear them scrabbling against the glass. His mouth was dry, his hands were trembling, but the scientist in him was observing. They were definitely insects of some kind, with six orange-red legs and fat, segmented abdomens. "We've got to get a specimen." He started to crack the window.

An iron-hard hand grabbed his wrist. "Are you crazy?"

Then the light went out. All of a sudden the vile, bright little things were gone—and both men were night-blind. Bob couldn't see the dashboard a foot from his eyes. Sweat was pouring down his face, tickling his underarms.

Brian saw an opportunity that must not be missed. He fought for control of his shaking hands, forced himself to open his door.

"Are you nuts, man?"

Brian's heart was leaping in his chest, his throat was so dry he could barely talk. "We need to gather a specimen," he managed to say.

"We don't need to gather anything, we need to pray!"

"Look, I'm scared, too, but I'm gonna go out there and do what I can, because this is important. It's so important, you have no idea."

Because he knew his fear would stop him if he didn't act at once, he stepped quickly into the dark.

Bob had never been so scared that he couldn't move, and he wasn't quite that scared now, but he was closer than Brian. He cracked his window. "Don't do it, Brian."

"We need that specimen."

"We need to stay alive."

"These things—they attacked Ellen Maas a couple of nights ago. We've gotta find out more. Without a specimen, we're nowhere."

Bob put his hand on the door handle, felt it, hesitated. God, he didn't want to go out there. But he couldn't let Brian down. He pulled the handle, opening the door into the cool night air. "What's that smell?"

"I don't know."

To Bob it smelled like an overcrowded drunk tank on a hot night.

Side by side, the two men approached the dark area. "Brian, what the hell is going on?"

"It's a nest. Or maybe some sort of a trap."

"Keep well back, man."

In its depths there was a faint purple glow. There was also a deep, persistent sound, impossible to identify. It was a mixture of buzzing and sighing, punctuated by the crackles of static electricity.

"Sounds like bacon frying," Bob said.

The purple light grew, and Brian backed away. He wanted no part of that, ever again.

Without the slightest warning a stream of insects burst forth. In an instant they were scrambling over Bob. He didn't even have a chance to scream. Then he couldn't because if he opened his mouth they were going to get in.

"Get one," Brian shouted, "get one and kill it!"

They clogged Bob's nose, stinking like sweaty farmworkers. He danced, a gilded man, plucking at them, trying to get them off him. Their legs were like wire, pulling at his eyelids, his lips. He struggled, but they were strong and they would not stop. They pried his lips open, poured down his throat, cutting off his screams. Then they came swarming up his pants legs and invaded his privates, pushed into his anus. The horror of it froze him.

Then he felt his feet leave the ground. He knew he was moving, and fast. It was so surprising and bizarre that his emotions turned off. He was watching a movie, Bob West being carried down a hole, Bob West going deeper and deeper and deeper and all of a sudden they were gone, all the light was gone.

He was in a damp, warm room. The floor was thick, like sponge. Great, rhythmic pulsations heaved all around him, and the walls got closer, pushing against him. He shrank away but the oozing, gulping motion became stronger, closer, until finally he was completely surrounded by a mass of what had to be wet, muscular living tissue.

There was a wet crackle and the flesh pressing against him flickered with purple light. He could see veins and some distant structure like bones far away in the seething, gelatinous mass. The flicker came again and he was for a moment knocked senseless by a burst of sheer, total pleasure. The sensation was beyond anything he had ever known. It made the best possible moment of bellowing, gasping sexual release seem empty.

It came again and again, and in the back of his mind a voice said: it's a weapon.

But the voice was drowned out, and he was overwhelmed by wave after wave after wave of shivering, glorious, soul-bursting ecstasy.

2.

Brian battled his way through the mass of creatures, grabbing for them. Their bodies were as pliant as rubber and their legs were springy and strong. Even so, he might have crushed one if they hadn't been so fast. If he got one in his fist it wriggled out between his fingers before he had a chance to bear down. Their curved pincers seemed almost artificial, so carefully burnished and sharpened were the edges.

Brian was awash in them, smelling their sweaty-skin stench, feeling them crawl over him. He fought to keep his reason. "Use your gun, Bob! Fire the

damn thing! Maybe we can get some fragments."
They were lifting him, they were actually picking up
a human being! "Bob, they've got me!" He struggled
wildly. "Bob, where are you? I can't see you!"

For an instant he glimpsed the side of the Blazer.
Then it was gone, a blur behind him. He pulled
them off in fistfuls, dragged them out of his throat.

He realized that he was being moved toward the
hole. Because he was neither confused nor surprised
by their appearance, his response was very different
from Bob's.

Instead of freezing as Bob had, he went wild.
Lunging, plunging, battling with animal fury, he
ripped them away from his face, took in deep
breaths of fresh air. He was thrashing, leaping—half
here and half back in the fire, fighting for his family,
for Loi, for his baby.

He felt something hard in his grip—the door post.
He pulled it, dragged himself ever closer. Then he
was inside the vehicle. Yanking the door closed, he
trapped at least a hundred of the insects inside with
him.

They changed instantly. Instead of remaining aggressive, they lined up with military precision
against the top edges of the window frames. They
were all turned toward him, their red eyes glaring. It
was like being face-to-face with the biggest,
meanest-looking hornets in the world.

Evidence, certainly. But too much of it. They were
revving their wings. They were going to attack. He
cracked his window, hoping a few would escape and
he could contend with the others.

With blinding efficiency and speed they flowed
out, every last one of them. "No! Oh, shit!"

An instant later it was night again. Brian waited, his breath catching in his throat. "Bob," he whispered.

There was no answer.

He managed to say it a little louder. Still nothing.

He realized that he could see the road stretching ahead, looking perfectly normal. No hole, not a trace. "Bob, I think we're OK." Then there came a truer sign, the chirping of a cricket.

Soon he heard the whine of an approaching car. He peered ahead. Headlights glared, then he glimpsed the slick red curves of a Dodge Viper.

In the headlights he thought he saw Bob running. The car shot past, its engine howling. He had only a glimpse of the occupants, who were sitting as stiff as dolls.

The bastards had come back! They'd been ticketed and they'd come back for revenge!

He jumped out of the Blazer, dashed off into the woods in the direction Bob had gone, calling him at the top of his voice.

Silence answered. Darkness enclosed him.

Around him the woods rustled and sighed. The memory of those red insect eyes still bored into him, the huge, wet opening gaped in memory.

He went back to the truck, stationed himself beside it with the door opened, and from there he called Bob again and again, his voice echoing flatly. He called until he was so hoarse he couldn't do it anymore.

All remained silent.

Brian threw open the Blazer's rear deck, got out Bob's large flashlight. "Where the hell are you?" he rasped.

The wind sighed as Brian walked around the vehicle. There were no footprints in the soft shoulder, not a single indication that anybody had ever been here but him. Also, the road was devoid of markings, despite the fact that a large opening had been there just a few minutes before.

He actually found himself hoping that Bob had been hit by the Viper. It was better than the other thing, the impossible thing. "Bob!" He played the light along the shoulder, back into the grass, trotted across the highway and searched the other side. "Bob!"

Alone with the night, Brian slumped against the truck. He considered—stay here or start walking?

No question: stay here with the windows closed and the doors locked.

Down in the valley he saw headlights. When the oncoming car was perhaps a thousand feet away, he went out into the road and started waving his arms. The car, an aging Buick, stopped. "Yes, Officer?" Because of the livery on the truck, the driver was assuming that Brian was a trooper.

He didn't bother to correct him. "This truck's broken down. Could you stop in Ludlum and call the state police barracks for me?"

"Well, I'd be pleased to do that."

"Get them out here right away. Tell them it's Lieutenant West's vehicle, and he's down."

"Down?" The man looked around.

"I think he's been hit by a car. I can't find him."

"Jesus, I'll do my best!" The driver accelerated away.

When the sound of his engine died, Brian was sure he heard the Viper again, now off in the dark somewhere, idling. He got in the Blazer and locked it up.

Ten minutes passed. Fifteen. What the hell was he going to tell them? Had he really seen Bob running in the lights of the Viper, or . . . how did he even talk about the other thing? They'd think that Brian Kelly had gone completely around the bend this time.

Quite suddenly the Blazer was awash in flickering light. A patrol car was coming up fast from behind. Finally!

As Brian got out, he found that a dark vehicle had somehow overtaken the patrol car. The Viper roared past three inches from his body, a red needle blurred by extreme speed. Brian was thrown against the door. Hot wind washed over him as the car disappeared into the dark.

The report of an officer down meant that the trooper car stopped instead of giving chase. "Jesus Christ," one of the officers said as he trotted up, "that guy's doin' more'n a C."

Brian swallowed, forced his throat to construct the words. "It's a sports car, a Dodge Viper. It's been after us because Bob turned it in to a radar unit this morning. I think it might've hit him. I can't find him!"

"Where'd you last see him?" one of the troopers asked. Brian noticed that both of them had their guns drawn.

"Over there," Brian replied, pointing weakly toward the shoulder.

They shone their lights around. "Why'd you stop?"

"Electrical problem."

"So he got out? What then?"

He could not lie. He did not know how to tell the truth. "Well, we saw some lights."

"Car lights?"

"I'm not real certain what we saw. We were observing what I think is a new species of insect."

"Insect? You stopped to look at a bug?"

"A lot of them. Very unusual. We got out of the truck, and then it all happened very quickly."

The theory became that Bob had been grazed by the fast-moving car, had become disoriented and wandered away. The troopers made a search, but could not find a sign of him. A helicopter was called in and it spent half an hour shining its searchlight from above, also with no result.

After another hour a mystified group of rescuers gave up, planning to continue at first light.

Bob's commanding officer drove off to perform the miserable task of informing Bob's wife and two boys that he was missing. Brian would have gone, but how did he explain things to Nancy? Her husband had disappeared. He couldn't show up with a story as crazy as the one he wanted to tell.

He wanted to compare notes with Ellen, but he didn't dare go near her. Instead he asked the troopers to take him home. He rode in silence, sitting in the cage of one of the patrol units. As the dark forest passed outside his window, his mind turned the day's events over and over again.

He felt the same disorientation that would have followed if he'd sighted a flying saucer or seen the Loch Ness Monster.

A new species of insect? Hell, it was a new genus, a new type of life altogether. He was very much afraid that it was a man-eater, too. But not Bob. Please, not him.

No, he'd seen him in the lights of the Viper, surely he had. The poor guy was probably unconscious, that's why he hadn't answered.

He had to think this through carefully, theorize and try to understand.

Women hidden underground like grubs—actually, that fit. It was very insectoid to encase caches of prey for further use. Typical behavior of colony-living insects.

Oh, Bob, where are you, my friend? When he'd been in the hospital, unable even to mumble, Bob had come every evening and sat there holding his hand and talking baseball.

He needed lots of help if he was going to save his friend. He needed entomology, but also biology, physics—maybe even the damned Air Force.

He felt a moment of relief when they pulled onto Kelly Farm Road. But then he worried. What would he do if the trailer was dark, the truck gone?

He saw a glimmer in the woods, then another. The trailer—it was lit, she was still with him.

But she didn't come out onto the porch when the car pulled up. The troopers said their grim farewells and drove off into the night.

When their car was gone the night enclosed the little place, the mobile home with its few dim lights, the ruins beyond. The yellow bug light over the kitchen door was surrounded by a cloud of moths, and at the edge of its glow bats squeaked and darted. A great white barn owl flew through the edge of the light, a pale shadow. A moment later it muttered softly off in the dark.

Normally, he would have felt a sense of peace, hearing the bats and the owl, and smelling the rich scent of apple blossom and corn tassel. But not now.

He went inside.

At first he had the horrible thought that she'd gone and left the lights on; he actually looked for a note.

But she was in the bedroom, apparently asleep.

As quietly as he could, he undressed and got ready for bed. She might or might not actually be awake. In any case, she did not stir.

Normally a big dinner would have been waiting, beside it a cold Bud or a glass of wine.

He slipped into bed beside her.

Her breathing was regular, even. "You asleep?"

No reply.

Outside, the owl muttered and coughed. The past hours were like a nightmare, a sort of tumor in the middle of memory. When he closed his eyes, he saw the insects, heard the sound of the destroyed woman being drawn out of the ground.

Vaguely he recalled that there were known species of insect that encapsulated their prey in the ground, injecting them with a drug that paralyzed but did not kill, so that they would be fresh when the larvae hatched.

The woman in the Traps had been like that, helpless but still retaining enough consciousness to suffer and to scream.

Was that happening to Bob right now? Was he three feet underground somewhere out in the woods, screaming bloody murder?

His hand slipped beneath the sheets, sought Loi's.

She let him hold it, but there was no response whatsoever.

They were man-eaters, these insects. He had to get a specimen, that was now absolutely essential.

He slept, and in his sleep saw red eyes, and heard Bob crying out again and again, from the depths of the earth.

He dreamed they were all together in a tiny, stifling cave, him and Bob and Ellen and dear Loi and all the rest, the people of Oscola and Towayda and Ludlum and all the land around, and there was an earthquake and the way to the surface was blocked. They were trapped here forever and something was coming, coming up from the depths, coming fast.

And he was right.

EIGHT

1.

Loi was awakened by the thuttering of a helicopter, a sound that always brought her instantly to full consciousness. Once she would have cried out, fearing the lazy track of tracer, the hiss of a phosphorus bullet burning out somebody's stomach. But since she had been with Brian, she had stopped allowing herself the luxury of nightmares. His were enough for them both. "Brian," she asked carefully, "did you call a duster?"

"No way, not this time of year." The sound had awakened him also, brought him suddenly to sickening recollection of all that was happening.

There was just enough thin light for the air search to start again.

It was time to tell Loi everything and damn the consequences. He didn't know how, but he would have to try. "Bob's truck broke down and there was some kind of bizarre accident. He disappeared."

"What is this?"

"We were outside the truck investigating an unusual incident. A car came past very fast. The next thing I knew, he was gone. They haven't found him yet." He gestured toward the window. "That's what the choppers are about."

"He was hit?"

"I couldn't find him, Loi! I called him and called him but he didn't answer!"

Her eyes widened, her hands went up to her cheeks in an oddly antique gesture of horror. "Nancy and the kids!"

"The troopers are taking care of them."

"They need their friends! You have left them all night without friends!" She went to the phone, dialed the Wests.

The line was busy. She dialed again, then slammed down the phone. "We go." They dressed fast. She wouldn't even let him shave. While he was still combing his hair, she marched out to the truck.

Brian didn't even consider the idea of arguing. She was right anyway. They should have been with Nancy and the boys from the beginning, that was obvious. The shock of what had happened had numbed him, shut down his mind.

Well, he had better get it powered up again. People needed him.

They went down Kelly Farm Road and turned onto Mound. It took ten minutes to get to Queen's Road and the little four-house development where the Wests lived. In that time he had decided that he was going to have to attempt to explain the insects to her.

"Loi, there's more." Out of the corner of his eye, he could see her nodding. He continued. "There have been a series of what I would characterize as unusual and dangerous incidents involving a number of people. I think they're related, but I don't know how."

"Brian, what is this you are trying to say?"

"There are apparent insects. I don't know how to say this. Something that comes out of the ground, that glows like a mass of coals—"

"You saw a demon."

If he didn't say exactly the right thing, this conversation was going to go off the deep end in about three seconds. He really didn't think that Southeast Asian animism had any part to play in it. "This is about something else. It all started with the screaming in the mound. On that night, Ellen Maas also had a very strange experience."

"What is her part?"

"She went out on the mound and saw a thing there. It defies description, really. A spectacular apparition, like a burning snake made of vicious insects."

"So that's it, a demon brought you together. I should have known! We must put a stop to this at once."

"Whatever. The thing is, Bob and I confronted something similar in the road. Strikingly similar. The same sort of glowing things menaced us. It could have been that they—well, that something dreadful has happened."

She sighed. "If demons took him he is gone, finished. There is no help for him. Now there is something more urgent than waiting with Nancy. She will have her grief a long time."

"Loi, this is all very unknown. Very confusing."

"They confuse you so you will not fight so much. But they will come back." She touched the edge of an eye. "Why Bob? Ellen has sinned, she tried to steal somebody's husband. You're OK, you've confessed and faced your wrongdoing. But Bob . . . it's very strange. Maybe they made a mistake. Maybe they'll return him to us after all."

She's lost in her demons, Brian thought miserably. "This is a physical phenomenon."

"We must try to save her, Brian. She is hateful, but nobody deserves such a fate. We go first to Ellen Maas."

Brian was so stunned that he almost killed the engine. "Loi, why?"

"To warn her! She must get out of Oscola at once. She must admit her sin and cleanse her soul. Otherwise—" She made a chopping motion.

So that was it. She was going to try to scare Ellen away with tales of demons, thus neatly removing the threat of her imagined rival. He did not want to pity his wife, but it was a pitiful stratagem. "There are no demons, there's only nature."

"Demons are part of nature. Turn around, please."

There was that sound in her voice again, that new determination. He obeyed her.

Ellen's cabin was back in the woods a few hundred yards behind them. Despite the hour, he found that it was blazing with light. He wasn't surprised.

Ellen pulled the door open before they got there; obviously she'd been watching since the moment the truck arrived.

"I'm sorry," Brian said.

She laughed, a brittle trill. "How about some Café Français? I've just been making some." She could not conceal the shock in her voice.

"We need nothing, thank you." Loi moved into the small cabin, looked around. "This is nice."

"Thank you," Ellen said. Her voice was wary.

Brian met the confusion in Ellen's eyes.

"Bob West disappeared," he said.

Ellen looked up at him, blinking.

"A demon has come. It has come and it is collecting souls. You must leave, Ellen. Your soul is in danger."

"Excuse me?"

"If you don't pack your bags and leave, it'll carry you off to hell while you're still alive. This is a very unfortunate fate, Ellen. It is reserved only for the worst of sinners. Such as women who have seduced the husbands of others."

"I didn't do anything of the sort! Your husband was helping me investigate the very things that have apparently caused this tragedy."

"We went up to Towayda yesterday, Ellen. There was a woman encapsulated in the ground. It was horrible."

"Oh, Jesus. So there was somebody in the mound, too."

"I'm afraid there was."

"If there is no sin, then why has the demon come?"

"There is no demon," Brian said patiently. "The only thing wrong here is that something horrible's happened to Bob."

"We don't talk about what happened to him. Bad luck." Then she went to the window, looked out into the brightening morning. "There is much sin here. Secret sin. Demons can smell it from a long way off." Her hands were on the two sides of her belly, protecting her pregnancy. Another helicopter came drumming along, its sound growing to a roar, then slowly diminishing.

When the helicopter was gone, Brian spoke

again—very carefully. "They're looking for him, Loi. If anybody believed he'd been taken to hell, they certainly wouldn't be doing that."

Ellen wasn't interested in Loi's demons, either. "What happened out there, Brian?"

He told her the story. By the time he was done, they were beginning to hear sirens. They rose in the distance, fell, rose again, became rapidly louder.

"Going toward the judge's," Ellen said.

More helicopters thundered overhead, started circling.

"Bob's been killed," Brian said. "They've found him in the mound and he's dead."

"I'm going," Ellen announced. "Instantly." She pulled her hiking boots on, got her heavy old camera out of a box at the foot of her bed, then headed for the door.

"We go, too," Loi announced.

2.

They followed Ellen's car. Loi sat with her chin in her hands. "She is very beautiful, Brian."

"Not as beautiful as you."

"So you say."

A state police car, its light bar blazing, stormed up from behind and darted away down the wrong side of the road. Brian increased his speed.

The judge's yard was swarming with people, state troopers, sheriff's deputies, the men from the Oscola rescue unit.

The dismal yard with its abandoned orchard and its weedy lawn was now an accident site. A rolling stretcher stood on the front walk, its white sheets gleaming in the bright morning sunlight. The judge hovered about in black trousers and a dirty dress shirt. He'd looked bad when they'd met on the mound. But seeing him now, Brian thought in terms of death.

Then he noticed the tire tracks everywhere, all over the grass, in every bit of naked soil. He glanced around, trying to determine if the police had done it. There was no way to be sure.

"Judge terBroeck," Ellen asked, "what's happening here?"

The judge stared toward the bottom of his yard, in the direction of the mound. Brian followed his gaze.

"That's where they came from, Loi," Ellen said. "They came out of that hole."

Bob, his hat missing, his uniform tunic ripped to pieces, was being pulled out of the old root cellar by a group of troopers and emergency workers.

The next moment Brian was running. "Bob," he shouted.

There was a shriek of tires in the driveway and another car stopped. Nancy West got out and started running also. "Bobby," she cried in a hoarse voice, "Bobby!"

As they pulled him up out of the ruined cellar he regarded his wife with vacant eyes.

It seemed for a moment as if he was going to respond to her, but then his eyes rolled back in his head and he slumped into the arms of the medics. Somebody brought the stretcher and they put him on it. Nancy came down to him, threw her arms around him.

She made not a sound, a silence that was as heartrending as it was impressive.

They took him away, Nancy moving along beside the stretcher, her eyes streaming. Loi went to her. "We are with you," she said.

Nancy hugged her. "The boys are at home. Take care of them, Loi."

"They'll be well with us."

The parade left, marching to the ugly chatter of Ellen's camera clicking and grinding as she shot and reloaded and shot again. She was not one of those people who are graceful in their work. There was something awkward about her, almost brutal, as she slung her bulky camera around.

Loi missed none of this. "Look at her, Brian, how greedy she is. It is greed that allowed the demon into her heart."

"There is no demon!"

"I am not wrong. They send him back because he is a good man."

Brian looked at his wife, at her hollow eyes. "Why would they take a good man in the first place?"

"This will emerge," she replied.

Ellen's Duster rattled off at the rear of the crowd of departing vehicles.

"Let's look in the root cellar," Loi said. She tugged at Brian's hand. "I will prove there are demons, show you their marks."

"I don't think so."

"Come." Loi marched across the yard.

"Loi, get away from there!" His shout made her turn toward him. As she did so her weight unbalanced her and she toppled backward, stumbled, then slipped down into the weedy, bramble-choked hole before he could reach her.

"Brian!" Her arms came up, barely reaching above the edge.

Brian dove after her, crashing down through the choke of roots that held her.

He landed hard, rolled. The first thing he saw was her legs dangling in the dimness above him. "I've got you, baby!" He reached up, took her ankles and pushed her. Despite her unaccustomed bulk, she scrambled up into the light.

"Brian, come on!"

"I'm right behind you, I'm coming."

He grabbed the roots, hauled himself up, kicking and scrabbling against the moldering bricks in front of him.

There was a grating sound, deep and close, and all at once the whole wall started crumbling. Musty air came out. Brian flailed, pushed himself back, struggled to get away.

He grabbed the weak, giving roots immediately above him. Soil poured down into his face. With a huge, howling cry he pulled himself up—and went crashing back down amid a mass of roots and vines and a great deal of dirt.

Above him there was a terrible, piercing cry. He could see Loi's face framed against the morning sky. "Brian," she shrieked.

"I'm OK!"

Then she turned to one side. "Get a rope," she shouted.

The judge's voice replied, apparently some sort of refusal. Probably he didn't have a rope.

"You find one!" There was a sharpness there that

Brian had never heard before. She leaned down into the root cellar. "He will find a rope," she said. "Are you sure you're not hurt?"

"I'm sure." He was looking into the blackness that had been opened up by the crumbling wall, trying to penetrate its inky gloom. This was more than just a root cellar, this was some sort of abandoned mine shaft or something.

People had once mined this area for iron, but that was over two hundred years ago.

From deep in the dark, Brian heard a sort of sighing . . . like the sound of many small wings.

Maybe the old mine had another opening, and it was the wind. But he didn't think so. "Where's that rope, Loi?"

"Coming. Remain calm."

There was an almost military sense of command in that tone. But Brian was not reassured. He was beginning to notice air moving out of the hole, and the air stank. It stank of sweat and skin, urine and feces, the smell of a concentration-camp dormitory, a man-jammed boxcar. "Hurry, baby."

Was that a glow down in there? And another sound, a low sort of popping noise?

He jumped toward the roots, missed them entirely, ran back the five available steps and tried again, straining with all his might. The fingers of his right hand closed around a thick vine. He dangled, bringing up his left hand, wishing he was in better shape.

He hung with both hands, his legs windmilling. From far below there came a flicker of light.

He pulled himself up, trying to somehow get his feet over the vine. As he struggled, he felt it give.

When he put even a little weight on it, the thing trembled.

He went crashing back to the floor of the pit.

The smell from below was strong now; the wind was blowing steadily. He could hear many sounds: buzzing, sizzling, a grating snick, like the snap of great scissors. The air was suffused with a purple glow.

He threw himself against the back wall, tried to somehow claw his way up the crumbly bricks. But they gave way like dry clay, collapsing even more.

Brian kicked, he tried to make chinks for his feet. "The rope, Loi!"

Finally it came dropping down. But it was too thin, it was nothing but a clothesline. "I can't climb this!"

"Listen to me carefully, husband. Tie it around your waist, bring it around the front of your right arm, take it across your back and under your left shoulder. Do you understand?"

He fumbled with the rope. "I'm not sure."

"You do it, and do it right. Now I get the truck."

There was plenty of slack to tie it securely. He just hoped he'd done it right.

A single glowing object, looking like a lantern, rose lazily from the depths, hung for a moment on the air, then winked out. Instantly, Brian felt something in his hair, something moving. He screamed, tore at it, grabbed it—and was suddenly swept straight up and out onto the grass.

He landed with a bone-jarring thud, was dragged a few feet before Loi could stop the truck. Then she was running back to him. "Brian, Brian!"

She came down to him. "Careful," he said, hold-

ing out his closed hand. "I've got one of the insects."
He opened it—and there lay the crushed remains of
a large but entirely commonplace wolf spider, a
harmless creature.

"That's an insect from hell?"

He threw it down without comment.

She rushed into his arms. "I was so scared for
you!"

The judge, his face pinched, peered at them from
his kitchen porch. He looked for all the world like a
vulture on a stump.

"Were they there?" Loi whispered.

Brian formed his words carefully, forcing the answer past a bone-dry throat, through cracked lips.
"They were there."

She went to the hole, looked down inside.

"Stay away from it," Brian said.

She stepped back, regarding him gravely. "We
have a great battle on our hands, Brian. A very great
battle indeed."

His first impulse was to get into the truck and
take her a thousand miles from here, and never turn
back.

And that, perhaps, is exactly what he should have
done.

NINE

1.

Brian and Bob and Nancy were like most Oscola folk, they went back to childhood together. In a small community, the people are woven of one another, they are not single and alone and isolated. This was happening to his best friends, to people he could not remember being without.

How had he ever left Nancy alone all night to worry by herself? How had he done that? He couldn't imagine, he was shocked at himself.

Brian and Loi reached the hospital a few minutes behind Ellen.

They drove up into the emergency room parking lot, got out and went inside through the swinging glass door that led to the emergency receiving area. The nurse in the check-in booth looked up expectantly.

"Bob West," Loi said.

"He's upstairs in the Brain/Mind Suite. Let me call them and see if he can have visitors."

That was the local euphemism for the psychiatric ward. Brian had the horrible feeling that Bob had talked about the wrong thing.

Ellen was already in the waiting room. "He's physically OK. But they've got him in the psycho unit." Her voice was flat.

"You'll put this in the paper?" Loi asked.

"No."

When the nurse finally called them, Brian found himself going down a familiar corridor. It had been on his route when he'd been struggling along with his IV tree six months after the fire.

Bob was in one of those rooms that had always been closed. When the door opened, Nancy looked up, and Brian was deeply touched by the way her eyes tugged at him. "What happened, Brian?"

"I don't know."

Bob spoke. "Blue pipe," he said faintly. "E. G. and G."

Those few words changed Brian's life, his view of himself, his understanding of the world. The room rocked, the ceiling whirled. He grabbed the door frame and hung on, looking in astonished horror at the man on the bed.

Bob stared at the ceiling.

"What blue pipe, honey?" Nancy asked.

The conduit that housed the miles and miles of wire involved in Brian's facility were made of light blue PVC pipe. "Where did you see it, Bob?"

There came out of him a howl as high and wild as any from the deepest woods. The power of it made Brian stumble away from him. Nancy covered her ears with her fists. The doctor reached toward Bob, tentative, his face grave. He muttered something about the Valium drip. "It's LSD," Nancy said miserably. "He did a hell of a lot of it during the war! He's having hallucinations all over again."

"That was a long time ago," Brian said.

"An LSD flashback," the doctor interjected, "can happen at any time. This isn't uncommon."

Again Bob howled. The sound rocked them with its deafening power.

Brian had not been aware that a human being could make a noise like that. When it finally stopped, Nancy turned on him, shrieking. "What happened out there, Brian? You tell me!"

What could he say? "I don't—"

"Tell me!" She was face-to-face with him, her eyes swimming, sweat pouring down her face, her top lip quivering. Never in all the years he'd known her had he seen Nancy in a state like this.

"I observed some insects. Wasps. Maybe something from the tropics, I don't know."

"What sort of insects?" the doctor asked.

Brian shook his head.

"Could he have been stung? I'm thinking in terms of a bizarre venom reaction."

"It's possible. They were all over him at one point." Brian did not expand on Bob's mention of blue pipe, but it had sickened him inside. That was the project, it had to be. They'd gotten that pipe specially manufactured. It wasn't anywhere except in the facility.

The room seemed very small, the hospital stink made Brian feel as if his throat was going to close. An awful coldness began creeping through his body.

He saw the dead eye of the woman from the Traps, that staring, dead eye, moving, moving, looking into him and through him, carrying with it a message from another world—and from his own past.

He felt his skin growing clammy, crawling beneath his clothing, smelled the oily sour stink of fear.

Nancy spoke again. "Brian, you're holding back."

"I don't—"

"Brian, *please!*"

He put his arms around her. Something about the way she leaned against him recalled a long time ago, before either of them were married, when they'd had a couple of very intense weeks together.

"My project involved the use of lots of blue PVC, and it was stamped with the logo of a defense contractor, E. G. and G. Bob must have somehow seen some of this pipe."

"Last night?"

"I don't know when else."

Ellen came into the room. "Where was he, Brian, was he in some lab? Did somebody use him as a lab animal because he used to be a soldier?"

"It was almost certainly a combination of the LSD and these . . . apparent insects," the doctor said, with more than a trace of self-importance.

Bob groaned.

Everybody stopped talking.

He growled.

The doctor raised his eyebrows.

With a hollow cry Bob leaped on Brian. They went down hard amid screams and toppling equipment. Brian saw his friend's face distorted beyond belief, hideous, the lips quivering, the eyes darting like—like—

The woman in the Traps. Her eyes had darted like that when she was alive, and after her death, the one eye had kept on.

Then Bob was being dragged away, he was being restrained, and Loi and Ellen were helping Brian up, he was brushing himself off, watching as orderlies piled on his friend, covering him with heaving bodies, until only his head was visible, jerking like the head of a trussed bird, his cries rending the air.

2.

Four hours later the howls were still echoing in Brian's mind, tearing into his heart.

They'd left because there was nothing else to do, gone like three wooden people out into the innocent morning. Brian and Loi had picked up the Wests' two scared boys, eleven-year-old Chris and his eight-year-old brother, Joey.

Now the boys sat in front of the TV, quietly watching through tear-drowned eyes.

Brian was pacing like a trapped animal, physics flying through his mind. How could Bob have been in his old facility? He had paranoid visions of some vast underground complex, growing like a cancer out of his own abandoned work while he spent his time tending his damned apples.

What on earth did gross anomalies like mutated insects have to do with his *work*?

Nothing made sense. He paced back and forth in the little trailer, trying to put together a functional scenario. But abstruse experiments in subatomic physics simply did not lead to . . . this.

If they had taken Bob underground, how had he managed to return? Why hadn't he ended up buried?

He imagined insects burrowing beneath the whole region, from Ludlum to Towayda, a distance of over sixty miles. They must be using caves, old mines, tunnels of their own, burrowing like ants or termites.

He had to make some kind of a case with Nate Harris, Bob's commanding officer. It shouldn't be hard to talk him into investigating the damned hole behind the judge's house. Maybe he could even get him to send a detective to one of the judge's little parties. "Look," he said to Loi, "I'm gonna go down to the state police barracks in Ludlum."

"I'm going, too."

He could see her filing a complaint about demons. "You stay here." He started to leave.

"No." She snapped her purse shut and slung it over her shoulder. "Boys, we'll be back in two hours. You aren't to leave the house. Is that understood, Chris?"

"Yes, Aunt Loi."

They rode together in silence. As was her habit, she fiddled with the radio, trying to tune in WAMC, the public radio station out of Albany. She was a voracious consumer of news.

"Listen, Loi, don't say anything to him about demons."

"Brian, I'm not stupid. But we should pack up everything we own and leave."

"Is that what happened in Vietnam, when the demons came?"

"Those demons wore uniforms," she said, "and burned our houses with cigarette lighters. But when they died, they had the faces of scared kids far from home."

She hadn't spoken so many words to him in quite a while. "I love you," he said.

She nodded solemnly.

The barracks was a brand-new prefabricated

building on the Northway about a mile north of the Ludlum exit.

As they pulled into the parking lot, Loi opened her purse and examined her makeup.

The sight of Bob's Blazer sitting alone and abandoned with an impound sticker on the windshield made him feel physically ill.

"Hey, Brian," Nate said as soon as they entered his small office. "Figured you'd be along."

"He's bad."

"I know it. He's gonna be on psychiatric leave for a while. Won't get paid, I'm afraid."

"It happened in the line of duty."

"The pencil pushers have this phrase, 'preexisting condition.' Send quite a few guys to the poorhouse with it." He crossed his legs, leaned back in his chair. "You got some more information for us?"

"Nate, I want you to investigate that root cellar over on the terBroeck place."

"Where we found Bob? I took a look around there. It's nothing much. An old root cellar built over an even older mine shaft."

"How did he come out of it? Where did he come from?"

"Look, I'm gonna tell you the same thing I told that *Gazette* lady—"

"Ellen Maas?" Loi asked.

"Her. He didn't come out of the thing, he was going in."

"You know that?" Brian asked.

"Well, it's obvious. Where would he be coming from, a mine that's been abandoned for two hundred years or more? I don't think so."

"The presence of that mine could explain the

screaming on the mound. That's reason enough to investigate right there. Maybe somebody got themselves trapped in there."

Nate sighed. "We did that two days ago. You know what we found in that mine? A shoe. A button shoe, in fact, with a big cut right down its side. Damn thing was probably a hundred years old."

"You might have a dead body back in there somewhere."

Nate's eyes narrowed. "Yeah, Brian, maybe we were just too damn dumb to find it."

"I didn't mean it that way, Nate. I only meant that a mine like that's a honeycomb."

"Well, we searched every inch. I guess your bugs ate your dead body."

Brian opened his mouth, closed it without speaking.

Nate went on. "The *Gazette* lady told me all about them. How they got in her—between her legs—excuse me, Loi. For God's sake, Brian, I think you'd better forget about these bugs. The wasps are heavy whenever we have a humid summer."

"Ellen Maas is a smart woman," Loi said. "She didn't lie to you."

Brian glanced at her. His wife was softening to Ellen.

"I wasn't implying that," Nate said. "But from what I hear around town, the *Gazette*'s on pretty shaky ground. If this was a really sensational story, she could sell it to other papers, bring in some dough."

"That isn't her style," Brian said. "She's very straightforward."

Loi gave him a sharp look, then slipped her hand into his.

"Look, I don't begrudge her the story. But she's gone a little bananas about it. At least, that's my impression. I don't know if you're friendly, or what."

"She's a levelheaded woman," Loi replied, much to Brian's surprise. "If she tells you something, you've got to think it's true."

"You'd have to show us some evidence."

Brian broke the silence that followed. "There's something out there, Nate. No doubt it's entirely explainable. But whatever it is, one person was roughed up by these things and another one's been hurt pretty bad. Others may have been killed."

"Again, I have to see something. I mean, the mound area is clean. That hole the things supposedly came out of—clean. So what do you want me to do, send up smoke signals? Rattle beads?"

Nate's hands were tied, and there was no use arguing. Brian got up to leave.

Back in the truck, he made a decision. He had to face his old life, at least enough to return to the physics building and see what in the world was being done in his facility.

"You are feeling OK with this?" Loi asked as they reached Ludlum University's tree-shaded gate.

"Not really. But it has to be done."

He guided the truck through the gate and up the winding street that led around the main building and curved past the physics building behind it.

The old Gothic castle was as forbidding as ever.

Loi said nothing as they went toward the building, but her eyes were big, taking in everything.

"Lovely, isn't it?"

"It's so big."

"Not actually. We needed more space three years ago. It must be bursting at the seams by now."

He took her up the herringbone-patterned brick walk, between the familiar rows of flowers.

Bill Merriman was at the proctor's desk in the central hall. He looked up in surprise as Brian came forward, then his face erupted in a smile. He got to his feet, his big glasses glistening in the sunlight that was streaming in the door.

"I don't believe it, Dr. Kelly!" Merriman's voice thundered like a foghorn.

"Hi, Bill. Bill, I'd like you to meet Mrs. Kelly."

There was just the slightest hesitation, as Bill quietly acknowledged the passing of a beloved friend. Then the smile resurfaced. "I'm so pleased to meet you, Mrs. Kelly. I just can't tell you how pleased I am." He pumped Loi's hand until she began to vibrate. Then he stopped, gave Brian a sly, twinkling look. "Am I the last to know?"

"What?"

"Are you coming back with us, Doctor?"

"Bill, I'd just like to take a walk through, have a look at my old facility."

"Well, I suppose you can do that. It's off clearance, so I don't have to follow you around with a gun." He chuckled. "There's no classified work being done here now, not since you left."

"None?"

He shook his head.

"You're sure it's OK for me to go in?"

"Oh, absolutely. That'd be Dr. Robinson's lab now."

"Active?"

"Under construction until the fall term begins. But there's not much of your stuff left. You know, when the funding went—"

"I know, my immortality went with it."

Bill laughed. "I wouldn't say that, Doctor."

Loi looked like a small child, peering up at the foyer's faded grandeur. Before them a wide staircase soared up to a wall of stained-glass windows depicting the achievements of practical physics circa 1897, the year the building was completed. A blast furnace belched fire, electric lighting dotted a cityscape, a locomotive came roaring out of a tunnel.

"I'm afraid we descend into the stygian depths," Brian said as he led her around the staircase to the rickety iron steps that led to the basement labs. "In the old days there was nobody in the basement but us trolls."

He had been trying to push the memories of Mary aside, but the smell coming up from the basement brought them flooding in. That familiar odor of slightly damp concrete—he hadn't recalled that until just this moment. He'd smelled it a thousand times through their life together, working down here.

Behind him Loi negotiated the steps with exaggerated care. As best he could, he helped her down the thirty feet. The basement was deep, its ceilings high. Originally, it had been a dormitory of some sort. It must have been a depressing place to live.

Brian's big steel door now had ROBINSON stenciled on it in black, but it was still possible to see where the KELLY & KELLY plate had been—brass, bought at the Door Store in Albany.

Brian opened the door, reached in and turned on the lights. As they always had, they glared down out of cheerless metal gratings. Brian looked up, and when he did his blood almost stopped in his body: the red tinsel they'd hung as a joke during the 1987 departmental Christmas party was still there.

"All right," he said, looking around the room, "let's see what's going on in here."

"This was your lab?"

"This was our lab." He pointed to a wall now covered by shelving. "Our control console was over there." The steel hatch in the floor near it looked much the same. "The waveguide was underneath."

"What is that?"

"An esoteric particle generator—or rather, detector. Although detection and generation would have arguably been the same event, in this case."

"I don't understand that."

"It was my main piece of equipment. The barrel of my rifle."

"The barrel isn't the most important part of a rifle. That's the firing chamber."

"Oh, OK. Then it was my firing chamber."

The work being done in here now clearly had nothing to do with particle physics. When he opened the hatch, he was going to find a ruined waveguide, blue pipe and all. "The service facility is just under the floor, and the device itself eighty feet farther down."

He went over to the hatch, which was partially occupied by the leg of a chair. "We used to call this place the forbidden zone."

"Because it was secret?"

"Because a forbidden zone is an area near a very powerful object that you can never escape, once you enter it. In a forbidden zone the laws of physics become deranged, everything changes, the world is turned inside out. You reach a point where time runs backward and you end up forever remembering that you've been destroyed, but never actually dying. That's the paradox of a forbidden zone."

Loi had twined her arm in his. "Step back," he said, "I'm gonna open the hatch."

"Is there danger?"

"It's just a ruin, it seems."

He lifted the ring, pulled. The hatch was sheet steel, but not particularly heavy. Disuse made it creak, but it came up easily. An odor rose, of mildew and dust tinged with sewage.

The service facility was pitch-dark. All he could see were the first two rungs of the ladder that led ten feet to its floor. It was here that he and Mary had gone to adjust the polarity of the waveguide, or aim it. The guide had to be absolutely straight or there would be dropoff when it was activated.

"Be careful, Brian!"

"It's OK, I know the terrain like the back of my hand." He descended the ladder and reached for the light switch. He flipped it, and the fluorescents flickered on. Two of them did, anyway. In the old days, they'd been able to flood the place until it was as bright as the surface of Death Valley on a sunny day. A good bit of their work involved extremely fine wires, which were always getting lost. They manipulated these wires with tiny padded tweezers called picks.

He had not expected the place to have been stripped to the bare walls. Every single piece of equipment had been removed, even the conduit that had housed the cables leading to the waveguide.

Most extraordinary, the foot of the guide was gone. In its place was nothing but the original well, now empty of the blue tubing that had housed the guide and its supporting cables.

Brian looked into the well. About ten feet down he saw concrete, and embedded in that concrete, the heads of ten massive bolts. "It's been sealed!"

"Brian, are you OK?"

He backed out of the hole. "I'm OK, I'm fine. But the guide—everything's been ripped out. And it's been sealed." He returned to the ladder, climbed up, closed the hatch. "Sealed like an atomic containment."

Her hands drifted to her belly. "There's radiation?"

"No, no. Our work didn't involve radiation. High-energy plasmas were used in the waveguide, but there was no radioactivity."

Brian stared at the closed hatch, confused—and for a moment, horrified—by a glow emanating from around its edges.

Again he opened it—and went back down to turn out the lights.

"You won't stay down there?"

"No." He climbed out.

She wrinkled her nose. "That place stinks, Brian."

"There must be some sort of mildew in the walls. Maybe down in the well."

"It stinks of the demon."

3.

He went upstairs. "Bill, where's my waveguide?"

"They took it out about a year ago."

"Who took it?"

Bill only shook his head.

"Don't tell me it's still classified."

Bill's face was reddening; it was obvious that he knew more than he could say, and he was extremely uncomfortable with this. When his beeper went off, he lunged with relief for the phone. "Excuse me," he said, dialing. He spoke earnestly into the phone. "This is Bill Merriman of the Physics Department. May I help you?"

Brian did not want to embarrass him further, and he knew there was no point in pressing the man. Merriman would never divulge a secret. "Thanks for all your help, Bill."

Bill cupped his hand over the receiver. "I wish I could do more, Doctor. It's not a day passes that somebody doesn't mention you—" He did not finish the sentence.

"You mean my work is still discussed?"

Bill shook his head, went back to his call. Brian could see that he wasn't going to get anything more.

When she was finally sitting in the truck again, Loi sighed with relief. "I am tired of carrying you," she said to her stomach. "You must come soon, my baby Brian Kelly."

Brian drove almost blindly. His facility hadn't been abandoned, it had been taken. And those bolts— dear heaven, what did they mean? Why would they see the empty well as so dangerous that they had to sink a million-dollar containment vessel to seal it off?

"We are not going home," Loi said as they passed the Northway exit to Route 303.

"Not just yet."

"Brian, I must go to the bathroom."

Brian felt urgently compelled to go back to the spot where Bob had disappeared. The state police had searched it thoroughly, but not for things like insect legs and bits of broken wing, things that would prove something to a scientist.

It wasn't hard to find the spot. Locally, it was a famous place, where the highway came down off the high ridge of the Jumpers into the Cuyamora valley. From where Bob's truck had stopped you could see twenty miles and more on a clear day.

He pulled over onto the shoulder. "This is where it happened," he said.

"I don't want to be here." Her voice was tight and high.

"I just need to take a look around."

She folded her arms. "Please hurry, then. This is a place of misfortune. Not a good place to bring an unborn child."

He'd never encountered anybody before for whom superstition was fact, and had no real idea of how to deal with his wife.

He got out of the truck.

Flooded with summer sun, this certainly seemed an ordinary enough place.

"Brian, I must pee now."

"You can go over there." He pointed to a clump of bushes.

She glared at him. Angry but helpless, she moved

off into the brush that bordered the shoulder. In a moment the forest had swallowed her.

He walked up and down, looking for some critical fragment. He and Bob had fought the insects fiercely. They must have broken a few of them, there must be some remains.

Soon he came to the place where they'd seen the hole, and noticed that the gravel here had a light, friable quality. It looked stony, but would crumble between your fingers. Clay, really, that was all it was. Nothing unusual about that, though. He couldn't bring the authorities out here and show them a little clay in a road shoulder otherwise composed of gravel.

The sun bore down on his neck, white clouds drifted lazily in the late-morning sky. From far off came a deep mutter—thunder back in the mountains. Day after still, quiet day the storms had been building back in there, and at night they marched forth like a discontented army.

He could see the thunderheads already bulging upward toward the stratosphere, a wall of mysterious caves and ranges.

Then he turned his attention to the ground.

On his hands and knees, he crawled slowly along, examining every detail. Bits of tar, stones and clay presented themselves, along with dandelions, teasel and other weedy plants, but nothing that seemed in the least unusual.

He extended his search back away from the gravel, into the cut part of the shoulder. There were slow grasshoppers grinding in the thick air, and quaking aspen rattling at the edge of the woods.

Another, softer sound penetrated Brian's consciousness only slowly. Without quite realizing why, he paused in his work. He found himself watching the aspens. Behind them was a thick stand of scrubby white pine, then the taller forest.

He began to listen, gradually becoming aware that he was hearing somebody breathing.

"Loi?"

No answer.

He peered into the forest, but could see only leaves and close-ranked pines. "Loi?"

Far off, a car was droning closer, its engine straining.

He went toward the woods. How long had she been in there, how far back had she gone? "Loi!"

The car screamed past so fast Brian couldn't tell the make.

In the silence that followed, the breathing became more distinct, and Brian realized that it wasn't Loi, couldn't be. This sounded like some kind of machine.

He heard a rattling sound, almost a sizzle, as if an electrical circuit was sparking.

Without wasting another moment, he went tearing into the woods, calling her at the top of his lungs. His voice shattered against the dim forest silence. His own crashing blotted out any other sound. *"Loi, Loi!"*

"Brian, yes!" She came rushing out from behind a tree, still pulling on her floppy maternity pants.

He grabbed her, threw his arms around her, kissed her hard. "Oh, God, I thought—" He stopped, fought for control. "I don't know what I thought."

"You scared me yelling like that."

"You were gone for so long. And I heard—sh!"

It was still there, only faster. And louder—it was getting louder. The rhythmic breathing was big, the crackling was sharp and steady.

They ran, both of them, ran headlong and jumped in the truck. Frantically they rolled up the windows and locked them. Then he started the engine and hit the gas, turning around in a flurry of dust and gravel.

When he looked back, he thought he saw what might have been a thick, black cable emerging from the grass onto the gravel shoulder. But he couldn't be certain, and he didn't linger.

"What do you think it was, Brian?"

He shook his head.

"It was horrible!"

He was beginning to feel the awful desperation of a child whose innocent play has unaccountably set the house afire.

The material world was very different from its appearance, very much less stable, he thought.

—There are an infinite number of possible universes. Reality appears as it does because of the way we look at it.

—Communication with past and future is happening all the time, and we know it. But we can't talk about it because we don't have the right verb tenses.

—The river of time runs between banks of chaos.

What hath God wrought? Or you, Brian Kelly?

"What have I done?"

"You?"

"I think maybe so."

The sound of his own words reverberated in the jittering cab.

"I don't understand you."

There are messages everywhere, messages from other worlds. That breathing—one, two, one, two—perfectly timed. The insects lined up along the window, as if they *knew in advance* that he would open it.

The brain is a quantum machine, filtering reality out of chaos. Rockets screaming in the sky, bombs sailing, children playing, cats screaming in the night—

Oscola passing the windows, a doll's town, the gingerbread trim on the porches, the arched windows of the Excelsior Tower, the flowers in the town common: a doll's town, full of secrets, dolls concealing secrets in their glassy blue eyes.

He saw where Bob had gone, down the hole of madness. He could go there, too, go and set up shop, build himself a little cottage of chocolate cement and candy.

He could attract the children of the world to his oven and bake them into obscure and terrible forms.

"I want to get home," Loi said.

He realized that he'd been driving up and down the streets of Oscola. He turned down Main, past the town square with its bandstand and its monument to Oscola's dead from four wars. "I was thinking," he said. "Trying to understand."

She made a small sound. Was it derision, or just impatience?

They drove out Kelly Farm Road, turned into the driveway. "When will you rebuild our house?" she asked.

He felt anger flare in him, then felt it transform itself, become something else. "Soon, Loi. As soon as I can."

4.

They got to the trailer, went inside. The boys were asleep in the tiny second bedroom that would one day soon belong to Brian Ky Kelly.

When she was comfortable again Loi made coffee and gave him some. He noted that it had milk in it. She sat across the kitchen table from him, drinking her own. "My name is not Loi Ky," she said suddenly.

He was astonished.

"That's my whore's name."

"Your whore's name?"

"Easy for the white-eyes to say."

"What's your real name?"

She regarded him. "I'm used to Loi Ky by now."

"Please tell me."

She smiled in a secret, inner way. "Someday I will. When all is well again." She kissed his forehead.

He spent the afternoon sitting on the front porch trying to come up with some useful ideas. He had a yellow pad, and he tried to do some equations, but he couldn't make anything work. The jump from his original work to the present mess was just too great.

The shadows lengthened, and he found that he was not looking forward to the night.

When the sun was turning gold and the voices of the larks were echoing in the sky, he put his work down. This wasn't about his theories. It was about something so far beyond his theories that he simply couldn't see it.

Evening brought sheet lightning, and wind heaved through the old trees around his ruined house. But the storm did not break. He wondered if there even was a storm out in the mountains, in the conventional sense. Maybe the lightning represented another sort of cataclysm altogether, too big to simply break of an evening and slip away by dawn.

Bob's boys were playing in the gloaming, their voices shrill in the shadows.

The TV went on, and Brian heard the familiar music that announced the Yankees' pregame show. The boys heard it, too, and went racing inside to watch.

The wind began flowing down from the mountains. It swept across the back fifty with its tall stands of white pine, whispering in the needles. When it reached the barn it moaned in its eaves, then splashed up against the trailer and Brian on the porch, and made him follow the boys into the bright living room.

Loi was reading, her eyes tight with concentration. She looked up at him. "Brian, listen." She read: "Why do you tremble at my doorway? A man of many hearts does not need me."

"What's that from?" He tried not to sound wary.

She held up the book. "Anne Sexton." She laughed a little.

"This man needs you."

She smiled, but he knew that she was still struggling to heal the pain that he had inflicted on her with his carelessness.

Silently, she handed him the book. The poem she'd been reading was called "The Interrogation of the Man of Many Hearts." In his wife's eyes he saw something entirely new.

"You shudder, Brian."

A roar came from the TV. "Line drive right into the glove of Mattingly," the announcer yelled.

Brian went down onto the couch. Chris leaned against his shoulder. He drew Chris closer, and tried to get caught up in the baseball game.

Soon, though, he sank into a black study, staring at the television and returning to the flow of theory that might have led him astray.

He thought that he must have inadvertently discovered a great poison, the most terrible of all poisons. He still didn't fully understand. But whoever had removed his equipment, then sealed his facility with steel-reinforced concrete understood.

He was deep in thought when Loi got up and went to the door. He hadn't heard the tap that had announced the visitor. "Your friend is here," Loi said, stepping aside as Ellen's striding entrance brought him to his feet.

She came straight into the room, and she came straight to the point, too. "I'm at a dead end," she said. "I've played out every lead. The judge has ordered me off his property at the point of a gun." She locked eyes with Brian. "Midnight. His root cellar. Breaking and entering."

She stood there in the light, her flawless skin glowing, her soft round eyes sharpened by determination, her lips a rigid line.

Loi's eyes widened. "We have been in this man's house as guests. We won't go as thieves."

Ellen knew that she had to be very careful here.

She sat down in the big easy chair, crossed her legs and took out a cigarette. "May I?" Loi went into the kitchen, returned with an ashtray. "Look, Loi, I know that you don't want him to do this. I don't

blame you. I don't want either one of us to do it! But
it's my obligation to discover the truth of what's happening here and tell the public. Brian has an obligation, too, because he's a scientist."

"Didn't Nate Harris tell you that he'd gone
through that place? You don't need Brian to help you
do something the police have already done."

"The insects come out of the same hole Nate said
was clean. Therefore it is not clean."

Concerned lest the boys overhear upsetting talk,
Loi sent them off to their room. She pulled their
door closed. "I know something's crazy," she said
quietly. "But I don't see where my husband has to
get in the middle of it. Skulking around playing rob-
ber! What use is it, Brian? What will you accomplish? Let me tell you, the more you place yourself
in their way, the more you tempt them. Eventually,
they will strike again."

"Just for a second open your mind to the idea that
this isn't demons," Ellen said. "Consider the idea
that it's something so completely different that we
can hardly even begin to understand it. Something
totally new."

"I know about demons from a long time."

On the television, the crowd roared. First base-
man Don Mattingly had just hit a stand-up triple.
Chris peeked out of the bedroom. "Can we come
back out, Auntie Loi?"

"Yeah, boys," she said. "We're finished with the
private stuff." She gave Ellen a guarded look. "We
keep it *Reader's Digest* from now on, OK?"

"Brian, we can get our evidence, I know we can!
It's down in that root cellar, I'm sure of it. That's the
lair."

Loi put her arms around Brian.

Ellen wanted to yell at her, but there was nothing to say, nothing she *could* say. Finally she let out a long exhalation of smoke, slumped. "Brian—"

"I know what it is! And I'm not going back in there."

"You went in?"

"Fell."

"And—"

"I'm not going back. I can't."

"You're a funny kind of a coward."

"We need more information. The direct approach is too much of a risk."

"It's all we have!"

"People are getting killed!"

Little Joey began to cry. "Stop this," Loi said. "Both of you, shut up!"

Ellen got up and left without another word.

"She's a damned fool," Brian said into the sudden quiet.

Their eyes met. They had both felt the faint, deep vibration that could have been a big truck out on the road, or maybe the engine of Ellen's old car starting roughly. And they both knew that it could have been something else.

Ellen lingered a moment on their porch, furious at them and at herself. Here the vibration was too small to be noticed. She peered out into the night, which was rushing with wet wind and not a bit pleasant. She'd come to hate the hours between dusk and dawn.

She'd searched the woods looking for strange nests. She'd even searched her house trying to find where the thing she'd put in the jar had gotten out.

Eventually she'd located a neatly burned hole in the top of the bathroom screen, and she'd patched it with a square of duct tape.

She walked down the stone path into the sleepy argument of katydids and the deep rhythm of frogs. Her car was a shabby ghost in the driveway. She turned around, and the light flowing from the windows of the trailer seemed to her to possess a special gold.

Down in the woods she could see lightning bugs. She tensed, watched.

They were ordinary.

She resumed the walk to her car. What she was about to do was insane. She ought to go home and lock her door and windows and pray. Her habit now was to sleep from five a.m. until ten, never in the deep night. To keep going she floated in coffee, which made her irritable. She was smoking like hell, too, like she had when she was first starting out in the newspaper business and she thought it made her look more reporterly.

She reached her car and got in. The Speed Graphic was on the seat, beside it the large flashlight she'd gotten from Ritter's Hardware this afternoon.

She caressed the cold steel box of the camera, then picked up the flashlight and turned it on and off, testing it.

Do it, woman. She had her principles, and one of them was to get to the bottom of a story.

Quite near the car a lightning bug shone and faded. She rolled up the window with fumbling hands.

The question was, how scared could a person be?

Was fear like cold, with a final, ultimate extreme, or was it like heat, that would just keep rising forever?

The mound, the root cellar . . .

Don't think, do.

She turned on the car, pulled out into Kelly Farm Road. Once an opossum's eyes flared like angry little torches, another time some deer were briefly caught in her headlights, but the drive to the terBroeck estate was otherwise without event.

She drove as far down Mound Road as she dared, then cut the lights and pulled off, letting the car roll into the woods, hoping the tires wouldn't sink. She cracked her window, inhaled the fresh night air. Ahead of her stood the judge's house, as dark and quiet as a tomb. At least there were no cars here tonight, and no dance behind the curtains to the purple light from hell.

Far off a powerful engine guttered, began to whine, then settled into a steady rumble. It echoed in the darkness, mingling with the mutter of thunder.

There were answers out here somewhere, she could almost smell them. She clutched the steering wheel.

TEN

1.

For a long time she sat without moving. Every so often a lightning bug would glow nearby. She held the flashlight, flipping it on, flipping it off, trying to gain courage. These were only ordinary lightning bugs, after all, slow, beautiful, a little mysterious.

She watched moon shadows dance along the ground. The moon was only half full, but it shed plenty of light when it emerged from behind the rolling clouds. She fingered the door handle. This was a little like diving into a cold swimming pool. The point was to start.

No. It would be insane to take one step out of this car. She sat, her hand on the door handle, wondering if a thirty-year-old could have a heart attack, just from fear.

She wanted a cigarette, she wanted water, she wanted a gun. Most of all, she wanted somebody to help her.

She took a deep breath, let it out slowly, reflecting that the Ellen Maas of even a week ago would never have come out here like this. This was somebody else, a secret Ellen Maas that she hardly even knew, a strong, determined woman who was capable of pulling this door handle like this, and shifting in the seat, and putting her feet on the ground like this, and standing up.

She took two wide steps into the middle of Mound Road. In three minutes she could be in the judge's yard. Thirty seconds later she'd be at the root cellar.

She stood dead still. Using her flashlight, keeping it pointed low, she tried to get a look into the woods. It wasn't hard to picture the insects waiting back in there with their little lights turned off. Could they fly without their lights, were they doing that now? Or were they coming along tunnels, ready to burst up out of the ground wherever it suited them?

It was difficult to tell through her boots, but she had the impression that some sort of vibration was rising from below. She bent down, pressed against the road with her outspread palm. Nothing.

When she stood up, though, a gust of breeze brought a distinct sound: somewhere in the dark, a powerful vehicle was in motion.

More carefully, she moved forward, going down the side of the road, keeping to the shadows. Was that a crackle in the woods? Yes. Probably an animal.

The memory of that first night she'd seen the glowing insects remained vivid. People had been dying in the judge's house, she was sure of it. She reached the edge of the property. The house was dark and quiet.

Carloads of people had been here that night. Their cries came back to her, full of dreadful ecstasy.

The judge had not been forthcoming, he'd ordered her off his property, he'd threatened.

She proceeded past the house, forcing authority

she did not feel into her stride. Even this close to the house, the windows were absolutely dark. Was he in there? The old Cadillac was in the garage.

As she came closer to the house the forest gave way to a wide lawn. The wind snatched at her hair, seeped down her collar. She increased her speed. The small hairs on the back of her neck tickled. Glancing behind her, she almost stumbled over the stones that lined the judge's driveway.

The silence was not the silence of sleep, but of watching.

Jagged clouds raced across the sky, pouring down from the north, and suddenly she saw coming toward her, across the hills and forest tops, a great wave of silver light. Then she was in a flood of moonlight so bright she could see the bobbing heads of dandelions in her path.

Hurrying now, almost running, she crossed the shaggy lawn to the root cellar. Quickly she squatted, thrusting the flashlight down into the tangle of undergrowth, then turning it on. She could see an open area below, and in it long black coils.

They were entirely motionless. Could they be roots?

She pressed down into the undergrowth, wishing she had a stronger light.

Then she thought that they must be a garden hose, old and tangled, long since discarded. Beyond them she could see a collapsed brick wall, and considerable evidence of work—footprints, scrape marks, bricks organized into piles.

Ironically, the police investigation might well have destroyed vital evidence.

She shifted, dangled her legs into the opening.

The air was cool around her exposed ankles. For a long moment she hesitated. She fought to prevent her thoughts from forming into definite shape.

But that was a battle she couldn't win. The only thing to do was drop down, and at once.

She hit the floor of the little chamber with a jaw-snapping thud. Her light got away from her, the beam casting wildly among the roots and brush. She ran to it, grabbed it, shone it in the direction of the strange tangle she had seen from above.

There was nothing there.

She went to the spot where the hose had been, but there weren't even any marks in the earth. Then again, the ground was packed hard.

Her light revealed an opening behind the collapsed wall of bricks. This must be the entrance to the iron mine that Nate Harris had talked about. She moved through the burst wall, careful to avoid dislodging any of the loose bricks still hanging overhead. If they all caved in at once, they could trap her.

The iron mine was little more than a hole leading downward at a steep angle. There were no supporting beams, no steps, no little miner's railroad. This was an old, old mine of the kind that had been run by slave labor back during the Colonial era, before slavery had been outlawed in the northern states. Her flashlight revealed the scars of chisels and hand drills. The granite had been penetrated with muscle and blood.

As she moved deeper, she cast her beam first at the floor, then at the walls, then the ceiling, continually seeking the bit of wing, the dried carcass, that would prove their case.

Within minutes she had to bow her head, then to crouch. Here the footprints of the state troopers ended. She went on, noticing that the floor of the mine had become curiously springy and soft. She reached down and felt a smooth, giving surface, cool and a little damp. It felt as if it was made of the flesh of mushrooms. But when she tried to tear some off, she found that it was extremely tough, like leather. There was an odor, too, that first tickled the back of the throat, then burned. She sneezed, recovered herself—and realized that the tangle of coils she had seen from above was now two feet in front of her.

She backed away, suddenly very aware that she was deep underground in the middle of the night in a terrible place, and she didn't have the faintest idea what that thing was.

It was completely inert, but from this close very obviously not a garden hose. It seemed to be the source of the acrid odor. Carefully, she peered at the tightly knotted coils. Was there a faint pattern in the surface? She couldn't be sure.

This was something alive, and not a normal something. It was unlike anything she had ever seen or heard of, not a snake, certainly not a worm.

She coughed, and the sound went echoing off down the mine like a shot.

Shaking now, feeling the sweat trickling down her face, fighting not to choke on the odor, she forced herself to go closer to the thing. The whole knotted mass of it was about two feet across, a foot high. Conceivably she could pick it up, probably even push it out through the growth above to the surface. Gingerly, she touched it with the edge of the flashlight. Then she prodded it harder. Totally inert. She pushed it with her toe. It had heft—maybe it weighed as much as ten pounds.

Pushing harder, she shoved it onto its side. Shining her light, she could see considerably more structure underneath. Eight of the thick, snake-like appendages came out of a center that had the tightly wrinkled appearance of an anus.

This thing was in no way normal. It wasn't even something you'd find in the tropical rain forest, not as far as she knew, and she felt sure she'd know about anything this odd. They'd have them in zoos, or stuffed in museums.

To get the thing out, she was going to have to pick it up in her bare hands. She was going to have to touch it, and she didn't know if that was possible. Again, she shoved it with her foot. It was upside down now, still totally motionless.

But it had come in here. So it could move if it wanted to. It wasn't dead, and she must not allow herself to forget that. On the one hand, she had to be careful. On the other, if it slipped away down the mine, then what was probably the story of a lifetime would have slipped through her fingers. Not to mention the danger, and there was no doubt in her mind that this thing represented danger.

She reached down, grabbed the two most prominent coils like handles and lifted the thing. There was a lot of weight, more than ten pounds. But this was gold, proof absolute, the most valuable scientific specimen in the world, the biggest story.

Staggering, she carried the thing up out of the

mine, lurched through the hole in the brick wall, and dropped it onto the floor of the root cellar itself.

Catching her breath, she shone her light upward. Soon she found the place where she'd come down. She would have to shove the thing up, then grab roots and haul herself hand over hand to the surface. Too bad she hadn't kept up her aerobics. She was going to need every bit of strength she possessed.

But when she picked the thing up and held it overhead, she realized that she was going to need more than strength. She had miscalculated the depth of the root cellar.

When she saw that she was trapped, she cried out, a brief shout, stifled almost at once.

Frantic, she cast her light around, looking for a hanging root, maybe a ladder.

The piles of bricks—she could build up a platform.

It took time, and she discovered that the bricks were soft, old and of poor quality.

As she worked, she watched the coiled creature, which never once moved, never an inch.

In fifteen minutes she had a platform three feet high. When she stood on it, her head was pressed up into the tangle of brush and roots above.

She picked up the coiled creature and put it onto the flat surface. It landed with a wet sound, and seemed to quiver a bit. Getting up onto the platform, she heaved the thing upward, gripping its slick, cool coils in her dusty hands.

The roots and briars overhead seemed almost to come alive, fighting its passage to the surface. She struggled, found that she couldn't get it quite to the edge of the hole. She had to wedge it in among the roots, then climb up herself.

As she climbed, it slipped, falling toward her, and she caught it against her chest. She pulled up with her arms, struggling desperately now, her feet seeking purchase, not finding it. The thing was knobby and knotted, as hard within as wood, but the surface was taut and felt as if there was a muscular fascia immediately beneath the skin. It was slippery and, she realized, also beginning to flex. She kicked, slipped back, kicked again.

The smell that had hurt her throat was strong now, and easily identifiable: the thing was sweating urine, and she was being soaked in it. The wetter it got, the more slippery the skin became.

She could feel the wetness soaking through her blouse, running along her midriff, tickling down her belly and inner thighs. A wave of nausea rocked her, making her gobble back her own gorge. Then she slipped, felt the thing collapse down on her shoulders, felt the urine running down her face and neck.

She grappled for purchase, slipped, slipped more— then found a long loop of root. As she straightened her leg she burst to the surface. The bundle in her arms fell to the ground and she sprawled out beside it.

She sat up. She had the damn thing. Immediately she gathered it into her arms, embracing it to prevent its slipping back into the hole. The surface of the thing was now covered with a sort of mucus, as slippery as boiled okra.

Moonlight flooded down, glimmering on the ooze that covered her hands. She raised her head, trying to escape the stink.

She went off toward her car, charging fast. She got it into the front seat, pushed it down onto the floor under the dash.

The next and urgent step was to get herself cleaned off. Coxon Kill wasn't far from here, running clean and fresh. The urine was so acidic that her skin was beginning to sting.

Using her flashlight, she crossed the road and dashed into the woods, went at an angle to the mound, toward the place where the kill turned and crossed the meadow where she'd originally been chased. Soon she heard the burbling of the stream. She threw off her wet shirt and sat down beside it, splashing herself with water. She splashed furiously, rubbed, then soaked her shirt. She rubbed it along the bottom stones, squeezed it, then drew it soaking out of the black water and sluiced herself, her face, her chest, her abdomen. As the freezing cold water poured down her, the stinging diminished. This was the second time that water had delivered her. She decided that she loved Coxon Kill.

Cold as it was, she got her shirt back on. Now she had to do one more thing, and that was to get Brian and get this thing to the authorities. He'd know scientists who would do the right thing with it. She wasn't ready to turn it over to the state police, not without knowing how they would approach the investigation.

She reached the edge of the woods and stepped into the road. Darkness, silence. She began to walk, her heart slowing, her breath coming more easily. Her car was fifty feet away, and she started feeling in her pocket for her keys.

The Viper, when it came, came like fury, its engine

pulverizing the silence. She leaped back, falling into a clump of weeds, feeling briars dig into her back.

At once there was a screech of brakes, the sound of tires wailing in protest, a red shadow turning in the dark, then the cruel, rising snarl of the engine.

She was still rolling but she wasn't going to be fast enough; the car was going to kill her. As she rolled, her flashlight flew to pieces around her.

As the moon went behind clouds the car shrieked past not three inches from her twisting body. She was jerked hard by its slipstream, it had come that close. Then she was in the woods, a big pine with sticky resin on its trunk shielding her.

Clawing at the tree to steady herself, she fought back the panic. The engine guttered, began idling.

Terrified now, she peered around the trunk. It was pitch-black, almost impossible to see. A wave of fear and frustration brought hot tears to her eyes. The Viper was right beside her Duster.

But it looked empty. She could see no movement. But she had a distinct impression—a taste, really—of *somebody*. It was easy to think that she was being watched by baleful, cunning eyes.

Evil. Horribly so. She was stunned at the power of it, and at the sense of there being an actual personality behind it, as if the whole array of terrors was being orchestrated by a single individual.

She could smell him, taste his foulness.

Another sound came, a sharp curl of breeze . . . or a whisper. She listened. There it was again—a definite whisper in the woods behind her. She couldn't make out the words. She cupped her hands behind her ears, faced the sound.

Another whisper. My God, it was coming right

down on her. It seemed to know exactly where she was standing.

And it wasn't alone: there was now a chorus of quiet whispers.

When the moon came out again, it cast mottled gray shadows on the forest floor. But it also made it possible to see, at least a little.

She tried to remember how the roads went. She had to cross Mound and try to sneak out through the woods to Queen's Road, then double back to her place.

She heard another sound, intimate, growing. Slithery. Something huge was slithering toward her through the leaves.

The moonlight disappeared, but even so she ran. Almost instantly she careened off a tree trunk, tumbled cursing into the dead leaves of the forest floor. It hurt, but also brought her to her senses. She wasn't going to get away by running, not in a forest this dark. Why wouldn't the moon stay out, just for ten minutes?

Two careful steps later she fell again, tripped by a low branch. There was a flash in her head, a pain, the momentary sense that the ground was on top of her.

The slithering came again, something brushed against her thigh. That did it: she scrambled to her feet and slogged off, all sense of direction gone, blundering and crashing aimlessly.

She hit the road so suddenly that she almost fell flat. She stopped, peered up and down the strip of tarmac. Mound? Main? She trotted along, her side flaring with a stitch, her breath coming in hot gasps.

At last the moon returned, sailing majestically

from behind an angry tumble of cloud. She was horrified to see a dark, familiar shape on the immediate horizon—the mound. And off to the right, the judge's place.

This was Mound Road and she'd gone in a circle.

She crossed it, began to double back. But then light flickered in her eye, followed by a shudder of pleasure that made her heart jump. Just across the road were a dozen dots of purple light, a hissing like a gasoline lantern.

To keep back the scream she jammed her fist in her mouth. She forced herself to retreat . . . back toward the woods where she'd heard the slithering.

She took a step, then another. Behind her she was aware of more flashes.

Where the light touched exposed skin—the back of her neck, her arms—it left a rich, seductive tingle, like the slowly drawn finger of a gentle and subtle man.

She plunged off into the woods, crying out when she was slapped by limbs, smashed into tree trunks.

Ahead was a gleam.

"Dear God—"

But it wasn't purple, it looked like the moon on a metal surface. She crouched, moved forward as slowly as she dared. Everything she did made noise—her feet crackled leaves, her breath rattled, she bumped loudly into trunks.

It was a car in the woods. She became cautious, barely moving. It must be the Viper.

She was fifteen feet away when she recognized her own car. She was thunderstruck. This was worse than being in a funhouse. You just did not get anywhere, not one damn *inch!*

It was right there where she'd left it, seemingly unmolested, seemingly empty. The Viper was nowhere to be seen.

Had she escaped, or was this a trap? Was the car really in the same place? She moved toward it. The keys—she got them out of her pocket. She reached the door. Feeling blindly, she found the lock.

At that moment the moonlight again disappeared. But it was no matter—the interior light would come on when she opened the door. She got the key in the lock, turned it, heard a click, pulled at the door.

No interior light.

There was a stink in the car so horrible that it knocked her head back, made her gag. It was like pressing your face into the underarm of a corpse. She looked down into the dark beneath the glove compartment. There was a thickness there, very still. Maybe the thing had died.

Holding her breath, she moved toward the open door. She rolled down the driver's window, then reached inside and lowered the one behind it.

She got into the driver's seat, reached over and opened the window opposite. Fresh air came in. This was better, she was going to be able to handle it. She put the key in the ignition, stretched her foot out to the gas pedal.

A black arm snaked up the dash. At the end of it she thought she could see a narrow hand.

Then the moonlight returned and she saw that the hand was to all appearances human. Before she could so much as cry out in amazement the fingers spread and the black, claw-like nails dug into the thick plastic dashboard, cutting it as if it was modeling clay.

Another hand came creeping up her inner thigh. It was cool and damp, its palm as soft as deerskin. Razor nails tickled her flesh.

She kicked, momentarily popping her right leg loose. The response was a flash of purple light, a spangle of pleasure.

Her skin crawled, she was almost drowned in a wave of the warmest, sweetest, most delicious sensations, wonderful little tickling penetrations that went deeper in her than she'd thought delight could reach.

The hands got their grip on the dash, the arms rippled with muscular contractions. Under her feet there commenced a flopping and heaving so great that the car began to shake.

The moonlight disappeared.

With all her might she smashed her foot down into the muscular, writhing mass. Again she kicked, again and again.

A third hand shot out, barely visible in the gloom. She heard its claws sink into the back of the front seat with a popping rip of leatherette.

She wanted to close her thighs, but the claw tips pressed into the tender inner flesh.

Some deep instinct she knew nothing about sent a rush of white-hot adrenaline into her blood. Her muscles turned to steel, she reared back on the seat. The three hands all detached themselves from their various moorings and came clawing toward her at once.

With a great boneless flopping and writhing, two of the hands grasped for purchase, one clawing the ceiling and ripping it down, the other popping holes right through the metal door.

She was so stunned by the violence, by the bizarre ugliness of what she was witnessing, that she lost consciousness in the middle of lunging back away from the thing between her legs. This caused her to fall limp, and the sweeping, grasping hands clutched air barely an inch from her neck.

The impact of falling against the ground brought her back to consciousness just as a fleshy coil poured out the door. She pushed away from the car, leaped up and started running blind, her arms wind-milling before her.

She blundered into brush, into trees, arms flailing. As she skittered away, pushing herself with her heels, her whole being contracted into a dot of savage terror. Ellen Maas wasn't there anymore, she had been torn from her moorings. An animal was all that remained, a terrified animal.

2.

Into her view there came the vague image of two rough old boots, two jeans-clad legs.

"Ellen! Hey, Ellen!" Brian jumped away from her panicked flailing. "Hey, it's me!"

His truck was idling at the roadside, the door open, the lighted cab glowing. She was beyond the reach of words. She choked and gagged and clawed the air. He tried to stop her, but she yanked away from him.

She could see nothing, but the slithering sounds in the woods behind her held a terrible meaning. Close beside Brian she could discern movement.

Her impulse was to jerk away, but when she did he tried to hold her more tightly. "Take it easy," he said.

Then the moon came out.

Two hands were quivering, fully extended, not a foot from Brian's head.

She swallowed, gasped.

"Ellen, it's gonna be OK."

The arms undulated, stretching. The hands came closer.

"Brian!"

The claws extended. To get away she threw herself backward—but he grabbed her, clutched her to him. The claws now vibrated an inch from his head. "Take it easy," he repeated, his voice shaking. She could see that the flesh of the arms was pulsating, getting thinner and longer, the fingers wriggling, now questing, now a mere breath away.

In another instant they would tear his head from his body.

She pummeled his leathery chest and bellowed, desperate at her own incoherence.

His response was to press her against him harder. "It's all right, baby, you're fine now, you're fine."

The pulsation of the arms was getting faster. They were getting thinner and thinner, jerking spasmodically. He reached back, absently brushed his head as if he thought a bug had landed there. But his strong left arm held her tight.

Other parts of the thing were swarming out the windows of the car.

No matter how hard she tried, she remained unable to control her own screaming. All she could think of was being touched again by those fingers.

Brian had come out here largely to stop her from

getting hurt or getting in trouble. Now she was having a breakdown right in his arms. He thought she was going to shatter his eardrums.

All of a sudden she gave him a vicious knee to the groin. He jackknifed, gurgling with agony as she wrenched herself free of him. Digging with her heels, sliding down the path on her back, she dragged herself toward the road.

Fortunately, she hadn't incapacitated him, and he was able to rise almost at once. As he did so something slapped the side of his head. It hit him hard enough to jar his vision. He turned toward it.

The four strangest, most lethal claws he'd ever seen were spread out in front of his face, trembling in the moonlight.

For a long second his mind was totally blank. Then he saw details: an ordinary palm. The claws had been carefully sharpened. He could see the serrations left by the fingernail file. This terrible hand was manicured.

On the finger pads were prints; the hand was so close that he could see even this tiny detail.

Another joined it. As he pulled back, the two of them closed just in front of his face with a sound like springing rat traps. Then he saw what looked like stiff cables in the moonlight, leading back from the hands all the way to Ellen's car. More writhing arms were pouring from every window.

A slight movement in the brush drew his attention to the fact that another of the appendages was slinking along the ground off to his right. Then he saw a fourth, this one looking like a black fire hose reaching into the trees above the car.

A deep, visceral shock went through his body.

He thought: my shotgun, my shotgun is in my truck.

He ran so fast he caught up with Ellen, who was just clambering into the cab. He could see the barrel of the shotgun, blue in the dim light. Throwing himself past her, he dove in, grabbed the weapon.

With one hand he pushed her down. "I'm gonna shoot!" She cringed as he braced the gun against the steering wheel and pulled the trigger. The gun spat blue fire. Ellen screamed. Again he fired, and again, the thunderous reports blasting away her cries.

Then there was silence.

With a thud one of the hands dropped onto the hood. The diameter of the arm was now no thicker than that of a rope, and it seemed almost devoid of strength, able only to flop weakly forward. But then it contracted, and the claw-like nails slid right through the steel hood. Instantly the arm went tight and the truck lurched. It began to be dragged toward the deep woods, like a fish on the hook.

Then the moonlight went yet again, and they could see nothing outside but dead, inky blackness.

The truck lurched and shook, being dragged farther into the woods.

He turned the key, listened to the engine cough, cough again, die. Again he turned the key. The truck jerked forward, stopped. Again and again he tried the key.

Finally the engine struggled to life.

He threw the transmission into reverse, started to let out the clutch. The engine roared, the truck pitched, the tires whined in the damp, loose soil. A stink of hot tires filled the cab. Oil pressure and water temperature began to rise toward the red lines.

When another of the hands flopped against her window, Ellen practically leaped into his lap. The claws tapped furiously against the glass.

The truck engine was powerful, but the gauges were climbing steadily and it was only a matter of time before a gasket or a tire blew.

Mound Road was just a short distance behind them.

Something shook the truck as if it was a toy. Brian jammed on the gas and the engine's whine rose to a shriek, the tires wailed.

Despite all this effort the truck lurched forward, moving deeper yet into the woods.

The hand must still be embedded like a hook in the hood, reeling the truck in. Brian threw the gearbox into first and smashed the accelerator to the floor. The truck shot forward much faster than the hand had been dragging it. In the glow of the headlights Brian could see the arm, which had been wiretight, flopping in helpless tangles across the hood.

He threw the door open, leaped into the tangle and grabbed for the hand. The extreme stretch of the arm had caused it to lose its strength. Under him, however, the coils pulsated and wriggled. They were warm, getting hot, getting rapidly thicker. Faster they pulsed, faster and faster.

By the time he had grabbed the hand at its wrist, it could resist. As he tugged it toward the windshield, away from the hole it had made, the muscles pulsed. The arm was now the thickness of a bicycle tire. Under his fingers the flesh of the thing bubbled like a thick, hot liquid.

From the woods came a flicker of purple light. He

was surprised to feel deep, warm stirrings come up from the depths of him.

While he paused, confused by this unexpected sensation, the coils surged faster, getting thicker and thicker.

Then Ellen appeared, also yanking the hand. It came out of the hood with a clanging screech, the claws doubling up on themselves so fast they made a sound like the crack of a whip.

"Drive," she bellowed, "for the love of God, *drive!*"

He threw himself back into the cab, ground the gears, backed out onto Mound Road.

They were free. "Thank God," Ellen whispered. "Oh, thank God."

He went bolt upright, he couldn't believe what he was seeing.

"Jesus," Ellen said.

Stretching off into the distance was a line of cars, all heading toward the judge's house. Against the sharp spikes of the pines that blocked the view of the house from here could be seen a constant flashing of purple light.

Every car was filled with people—men, women, children. Worse, he knew them, they were familiar faces. "It's Will Torrance—hey, Will!"

"Don't stop, Brian!"

Brian hardly heard her. He put on the brake, staring in amazement at his fellow townspeople. "Look, there's Mike Mills, Betty's boy, and his wife's with him! And the Robertsons and old Mr. Hanford—"

"Brian, get us out of here!"

With a hissing sound, a great shape slid out of the nearby woods, flowing toward them like a massive snake. Before he could react, pale purple light flashed right in his face. Reflected in the rearview mirror, it emanated from the headlights of a car behind him. He recognized this vehicle, low, mean, red. A terrific wave of pleasure hit him. He felt himself spring erect, found his eyes glaring hungrily into the reflection.

It was all he could do to shove the mirror out of adjustment. That broke the spell.

He returned to his senses. "Ellen, open the glove compartment, get out the shells. Can you handle a shotgun?"

"Not yet."

"Then be real careful, please. Put a couple of shells into the breech, lean out the window and fire. But don't look into that friggin' light!"

"I know about the light."

She was clumsy with the shells, she dropped two or three of them, but finally got some loaded. The Viper was right on their tail. A floodlight was filling the cab with purple iridescence.

It was the light of heaven. He began to go weak. The truck's speed dropped as he unconsciously lifted his foot.

A roar followed and the cab went dark. Ellen screamed, threw herself back from the window, tossed the smoking shotgun to the floor.

Instantly the pleasure ceased, and Brian felt a brief, black sense of loss. Ellen pitched back against the seat.

"Ellen?"

She did not answer.

3.

He turned onto Kelly Farm Road, drove hard for five minutes. He had only one thought: the worst thing in the world was somewhere in these woods, and Loi was alone.

When Loi saw the way the truck was racing up the drive she came onto the porch, then hurried toward the driveway. He jammed on the brakes. "We gotta get inside," he yelled.

Loi reacted instantly, pulling Ellen's door open. "Oh, Brian, look at her legs!"

"Get her into the light!"

They took her onto the porch. Loi pulled away torn cloth. The lower part of Ellen's pants legs were shredded. For a moment Brian thought he'd accidentally shot her. Then he saw the pattern of the injuries—dozens of puckered, red dots, each leaking blood and pus.

"What is this, Brian?"

As best he could, he swallowed his terror. He peered out into the dark.

"Pour water on her head," young Chris yelled, seeing that they were supporting her and assuming that she'd fainted.

"Get inside at once," Loi told the child, "at once!"

Astonished at sweet Aunt Loi's change of voice, the boy retreated.

With Loi's help Brian walked Ellen into the living room. He shut and locked the front door. "Loi, the windows."

"What?"

"Lock them!"

His tone of voice caused an automatic response: she raced through the trailer doing as he asked. Then she returned to the room. "Tell me the problem."

"Something's out there," Ellen breathed. "Something—"

"It's beyond belief," Brian said.

"What is?"

"You don't want to know," Ellen said.

Brian remembered those hands, the pared nails.

"Well, we have to see to you," Loi told Ellen. "That's the first thing." She went into the bathroom and returned with alcohol and cotton pads. "Boys," she said, "go in your room." She looked at Ellen. "You will suffer, I'm sorry."

She poured alcohol over a pad and began methodically washing the injuries. To Ellen it felt as if her skin was being rubbed with a hot iron. To prevent a scream she bit her lip.

Brian was looking out the living room window, his hands cupped around his eyes. He was watching for any kind of unusual movement. The driveway seemed empty, but he didn't believe it, not for a moment.

"Brian," Loi said. "Call the state police."

He obeyed instantly, realizing that he should have done it before, even from the truck. He dialed, listened to the familiar clicks—and got nothing.

Again he dialed, hoping that he'd done something wrong.

The phone was stone dead. He held the receiver out, stared at it.

There was a plan at work, a strategy. Whatever

was out there, it could not only act, it could think ahead, it could be cunning.

He had to get the shotgun out of the truck. And now he also had to use the cellular phone to call for help. With a quick, nervous motion he stepped onto the porch.

There wasn't a sound, not a cricket, not a grasshopper or a frog. It was like being in a cave lit by the moon.

The ten feet to the truck seemed a very long way. From the darkness around the side of the trailer he heard a distinct whisper, almost a word, but not one he could understand. For a moment more he listened. Nothing. It could have been a raccoon snorting at him, but he didn't think so. He moved closer to the truck.

When the whisper came again he whirled. There was something out by the ruins of the old house.

He went quickly to the truck, got in, opened the glove compartment and dug out the box of shells, loaded it with the five that were left.

When he turned around he was horrified to see Loi coming across the driveway. "Go back in!"

"No."

"Go back in the house, run!"

She came up to the truck. "Give me the shotgun." She held out her hands. He gave her the gun and she took a position in the middle of the drive, porting the gun across her chest. "Now make your call." Her voice was trembling.

Brian turned on the ignition and started the phone. He waited, but no dial tone came. Finally he turned off the truck.

"It didn't work either?"

"No."

She was staring out into the dark. He followed her eyes and was appalled to see a thick, black hose of a thing lying across the drive thirty feet behind the truck.

"It is like a snake," she said, "it hides in its stillness."

He ran into the trailer. Loi came rolling after him across the driveway, wielding the shotgun.

"It's unwise to run from a snake, husband." She leaned the gun against the wall near the door and pulled up a dining chair, seating herself across from Ellen, who was nursing her legs, tears of pain in her eyes.

"We've got to get out of here," Ellen said. Her voice was a moan.

"Ellen, it's in the driveway." Brian touched her cheek, full of compassion for her.

Loi folded her arms. "Brian Kelly, you will tell me all that has happened since you left."

"All right! I'll be very specific, but I warn you, Loi, this ain't gonna help your sleep!" He described what he had seen.

She nodded, taking it calmly. "The demons."

"We're dealing with anomalous taxonomy. But it's entirely physical, believe me."

Ellen lit a cigarette. Silently, Loi reached over and took another from her pack. She didn't like smoking much, but she was too worried. She didn't mention the sensations that were radiating up from her uterus, the dull, long pains.

"It'd help if there was a name," Ellen said. "I wish I knew the name."

"There is no Bureau of Monster Nomenclature," Brian commented.

A long, sighing scrape crossed the roof. "That's the sycamore blowing."

"No, Brian." Loi took off the shotgun's safety.

A moment later a mournful howl rose, then died away into the night. The three of them huddled together.

"That could be one of the Flournoys' cows," Brian said. "If she's lost her calf."

Silently, Loi pointed to the trailer's low ceiling. All three of them knew that the sounds had both come from directly overhead, and that the Flournoys' dairy herd was at least a mile away on the other side of dense forest.

To Brian the howl had seemed much more human than animal. It had been a conscious sound, full of the deepest woe, as lonely and sad as any he had ever heard.

Then there was another noise, this one from the driveway. It was distinct, something scraping through the gravel. Loi positioned herself before the door. To a stranger her face would have appeared to be without expression. But Brian knew different. She was expertly concealing her fear; she'd looked like this during the hemorrhage. "Watch at the windows," she said softly.

He went to the living room window, parted the drapes. For a moment he didn't understand what he was seeing. Thick black cables surrounded his truck, thrusting up out of the ground. "Give me the flashlight," he said, trying to discern some detail.

Ellen thrust the light into his hands. He turned it on, pressed it against the glass to reduce reflection.

Each cable led to a hand, and every claw was buried in the body of the vehicle.

The cables went taut, the truck shuddered, the ground beneath it began to seethe. Dust clouds rose and the truck went down. When it was half underground there was a pause. Then the hands shook, the vehicle shuddered, more dust rose.

"My God!"

Loi abandoned her post, joined him at the window.

The truck sank slowly into the driveway. As it disappeared the gravel surged like disturbed water.

Moments later, all was still.

The lights went out. Ellen screamed, Brian cried out, lurched back into the room. Both boys rushed out of their bedroom, crying and fumbling among the confused shadows being cast by the flashlight in Brian's hand.

"Get into the middle of the room," Loi said. "Brian, push the couch against the door."

"What's wrong, Uncle Brian?" young Chris cried.

He started to speak, but the words died in his throat. He couldn't tell the truth to an eleven-year-old, he didn't know how. "There's a—we think it's a bear. There's a bear outside."

"Oh, those little blacks ain't any bother." Chris started strolling toward the door. Brian froze as the boy put his hand on the knob. "You just shoo 'em off."

Loi got to him, drew him back into the room. "Not that kind of bear," she said.

Joey started to cry. Loi got the boys away from the windows, then went once more for the phone. Silently, she shook her head.

"The floor's hot," Chris announced.

Brian bent down, felt with wide sweeps of his hands. Hot, so hot in places that it stung. *Mary is burning, Kate is burning.*

What strange meaning was ghosting about behind the facts? He felt the floor again. A lot hotter.

The first fire—Mary and Caitlin's fire—had started exactly the same way, under the floor. "We've got to get out of here!"

"Brian, we can't!" Ellen's voice had a desperate edge.

A line of dancing orange flames appeared along the wall behind the television. Loi lunged for her precious Laughing Buddha. Before she could get it, Brian grabbed her, lifted her into his arms. "Not her," he shouted, "not her!" A sheet of fire rushed up the wall. Ellen and both boys shrieked. The flames boiled dark red and orange across the ceiling.

Mary and Katie were howling, dancing in a curtain of fire.

It would be fast, he knew that, almost instantaneous. He threw the door open, pushed Loi out, grabbed the nearest bit of shirt and pulled. Joey. "Ellen, Chris, come on!"

Ellen was pressed against the kitchen closet, the narrow little pantry that never offered enough space, her face as expressionless as a statue. Frozen by fear.

Brian went for her, knocked her to the floor just as the fire tumbled from the ceiling. The linoleum began curling like bacon. He knotted her shirt in his fist and tugged. Help came in the form of Chris, who half dragged, half pushed her.

Then they were on the porch, and a hungry maw of flame was all that remained of the doorway. Brian pitched away from the slicing heat, Ellen flopped and flailed, regaining her balance. Chris shrieked as fire danced on his back. Loi leaped on him, rolled him in the gravel.

When the flames were extinguished she cradled him. Sobbing, his brother crying with him, he buried his face in her bosom.

"We're gonna get you to the hospital, son," Brian said. He couldn't imagine how.

An owl's muttering made him look up, and he saw in the fire-bright trees a white barn owl, its baleful eyes staring.

With a sighing roar the trailer exploded. Brian shepherded them toward the barn. "We'll get the tractor," he cried over the rush of the flames.

"It only goes ten miles an hour, Brian," Loi said.

"Well, it's what we've got!" Maybe they could use it to go cross-country to Route 303. "Form a chain, everybody holds a hand." Thus linked, they began the journey across the driveway and down through the weed-infested barnyard.

"Look for things like cables on the ground," Loi said.

"And if you see any purple light anywhere—turn away," Ellen added. "No matter how it makes you feel."

The boys, who had been silent with shock, began to whimper. "My back hurts," Chris said.

"Be brave, guys," Loi told them. She was between them, holding their hands firmly. "Be as brave as the bravest man in the world."

Behind them the fire flickered and hissed. Brian couldn't stand to look back. His wife simply walked along, her head down, putting one foot in front of the other. This was like a natural catastrophe, a storm, an earthquake, or it was like a war. She'd probably walked a hundred miles just like this, a refugee.

There was a low, vibrating sound in the air around them. Fifty feet ahead of them dust was rising from the roof of the barn, glowing in the moonlight like smoke. Brian remembered that sound and grabbed his wife, trying desperately to shield her with his body.

It came again, like an immense groan from deep in the earth. His teeth vibrated, the boys howled, Ellen clapped her hands to her ears. The barn shuddered, seemed almost to be going out of focus. The whole front wall loomed over, and Brian saw that it was collapsing. "Run!"

It hit the ground with a huge thud and a cloud of dust, and in the dust the rest of it came to pieces, beams crashing down, walls, finally the roof itself tumbling into the destroyed heap.

Brian didn't even stop to look for the tractor. "We've gotta try to walk out," he said. But in his heart he asked a question: why don't you just kill us? Why torture us like this? He knew the answer, it was no mystery. People were not being killed, they were being *summoned*.

Well, not everybody was willing to go, Brian thought angrily.

They came straggling along behind him, still clinging hand to hand, and started out the long, dark driveway.

From the grass on both sides he heard steady rustling. He just kept going, not even hoping anymore.

His understanding of the world had been gutted. There was nothing left to do but struggle blindly on.

Loi drew the boys closer to her, her eyes searching the shadows.

"You can hear it," Brian said. "That slither."

Ellen hesitated, then took a jerky step back.

"Take it easy, Ellen," Brian said. But then he saw where she was looking. There was movement in the brush, coming toward them.

Then he heard a siren, thin but unmistakable. He let a moment pass, another. They all listened, nobody making a sound. The boys knew how to count the changes in tone as the vehicle maneuvered through the town. "It's turned onto Main," Chris said.

"It's the fire truck," his brother announced. A policeman's kids could tell just by the note which service was involved.

Brian saw what looked like a long, thin tree limb appear above the line of the weeds.

The hand spread, the claw-filed nails arcing to hooks. Then a second one appeared, gliding above the moonlit grass. Behind them another shadow slipped across the driveway.

He heard more slithering, this time very close.

A long wire rose over them, looking for all the world like a gigantic lobster's feeler. It danced in the air, swept down, touched Chris's shoulder. He skittered away, slapping at himself.

"Only a moth, Chris!"

"OK, Uncle Brian." But he continued to clutch the place on his shoulder where he'd been touched.

The timbre of the siren changed. "It's turned," Joey announced as the sound faded.

A coldness clutched Brian's heart, the dark seemed about to suffocate him. He ran a few steps down the driveway. "It's going down Queen's, it's leaving!" The raw bellow of his own voice shocked him.

Loi slipped a hand into his, squeezed firmly. "It is on its way up Kelly Farm Road, husband."

He looked down at the gleams of moonlight on her black hair.

Then the volunteer fire brigade arrived, their truck lurching into the driveway. Air brakes hissed as the big old truck rocked to a stop. It was a mess, pumps dripping, hoses looped crazily in the back. The men looked exhausted, their slickers smeared with ashes and dirt. "Everybody outa there, Brian?" the driver asked. It was grizzly old Mort Cleber.

"Everybody's out."

The truck snarled, dug in, moved slowly toward the flaring ruins of the trailer.

Loi spoke quietly to her husband. "Brian, I am bleeding again. Just a little." She leaned her head against his chest.

Tommy Victor had followed the truck in his pickup. He stopped and leaned out. "Anybody hurt?"

"I am," Chris said. His voice was choked, but he was being brave. "I got burned."

"My wife needs a doctor, too."

"My legs are hurt."

"But nobody's dead?"

"We're all accounted for," Brian said.

"You're lucky. The Jaegers were killed about an hour ago. Whole family."

"What's happening, Tommy?"

"Cold snap in the summer, you always get the

fires. Better get in, we wanta get you people to the docs."

Brian was so stunned he was left speechless. They didn't know, not a thing! He looked at Ellen and Loi. Their expressions confirmed his helplessness. There was no way to tell the story.

They rode out, Loi and the boys inside the cab, Ellen and Brian in the hay-dusted bay.

To shelter from the night wind, the two of them sat silently together with their backs against the cab. Brian watched the ruins of the trailer recede into the night. "Thank God she's still alive," he said.

"She's still a soldier," Ellen commented, "every inch of her."

Brian considered the idea. Little Loi, with her constantly lowered eyes, her scuttling feet, her quick kitchen hands . . . a soldier. "A refugee," he said. "It must be killing her. That trailer was the best thing she ever owned."

"I'm sorry." The wind whipped Ellen's hair into Brian's face.

He brushed it away. "What for?"

She was silent. They were both watching car lights behind them, glowing, then going dark as they were lost in a curve of the road. The thick forest flashed past on both sides.

When the lights disappeared and stayed gone, Ellen spoke again. "I went down in the root cellar. Back in the mine. I got something—a creature—I put it in my car. The next thing all hell broke loose."

"It came after you."

"And kept after me. All the way to your place."

"Did you find it in the mine?"

"Yeah. It was like a—well, a big, curled-up spider. But ten pounds at least. It wet on me."

"Wet?"

"Urine-type wet. It was so vile!"

The car lights reappeared, this time much brighter, much closer. Ellen's hand gripped his.

Even over the roar of the slipstream and the rattling of the old truck, they began to hear the deep thrumming of a powerful engine. "Oh, God, Brian!"

The purple light—it would be fired directly into their faces. They'd go mad. "We have to get in the cab!"

The car came closer yet, pounding around the curves, its lights slashing the darkness.

Brian rose up, went to the side of the truck, leaned his head into the surging air, until his face was beside the driver's door. "We're gonna come in," he yelled.

The truck started to slow down.

"Don't stop! And don't look in the rearview mirror."

Tommy was peering at Brian out of the corner of his eye, obviously aware of his reputation for being a little crazy.

The car came closer, closer yet. The engine was drumming, thundering, howling. Ellen covered her face with her hands. Brian went around to the passenger side. "Loi, roll down the window!"

It came down.

Ellen was behind him, clawing at him. He put a leg over the side of the truck bed, pulled his way forward. The truck swerved onto the shoulder. "Don't slow down, Tommy!"

"Brian, you're going to be killed!"

"Tell him to keep driving!"

The car's lights were flaring now. Ellen's face was white in their glare.

And then, very suddenly, the car passed them.

It wasn't a Dodge Viper, it wasn't even a sports car, and it wasn't red. It moved off, heading innocently south.

Brian returned to the truck bed, slumped down beside Ellen. He looked out at the blackness of the night. Being here, now—this was *alone*. And he didn't just mean himself and Ellen and Loi and the other people in the truck.

He had a feeling that every living soul was about to find out what a few people had already discovered: this little world of ours, lost out here in the dark, is very much alone.

ELEVEN

1.

Shock numbs, but unfortunately not for long.

At first they all welcomed the lights of Ludlum, the familiar cluster of fast-food places out at the Northway interchange, their signs challenging the dark.

The tall Rodeway Inn sign invited Ellen. "I'll never, ever go back there again," she told Brian. "At dawn I'm outa here."

Brian hardly heard her. Again and again his mind went over the events of the night. The fire had come up through the floor, just like the first time. The first one had been attributed to a defective propane line, but was that really true?

He shivered, clutched himself. It was nearly two in the morning. He looked up at the sky, the moon red against the horizon, the stars like eyes, diamond-hard, cold as ice.

He wanted to hold Loi, to enclose her precious body in a protective embrace.

He couldn't protect anybody.

"Two hours ago I was thinking in terms of moral obligations and major stories," Ellen said carefully. "Now I'm thinking in terms of saving ass. We've got to get out."

And where did she think she would go?

Then the truck was turning, and the buildings of Ludlum Community Hospital appeared ahead.

When he got down off the truck, Brian embraced his wife. "How's it going?" he asked.

"The bleeding stopped, Brian."

He closed his eyes, felt relief wash through him.

Young Chris was hunched over. Brian picked him up. "It's gonna be OK, guy," he said.

"It's hurting real bad, Uncle Brian."

"I know that, Chris. I know all about burns."

As they entered the emergency room, Joey said, "Our house burned up." Nurses came, there was a brief admission ritual, Loi was put in stirrups and Chris was laid on his stomach for an examination. Brian could tell at a glance that the boy's burns weren't serious, but those red welts must hurt like the very devil.

Loi and Chris were in cubicles side by side. Brian stood between them. Chris cried when the ER doctor began dressing his burns. "You're lucky this wasn't worse," the young doctor said.

"There was a bear out there," Joey announced. "It had long arms like a snake."

The ER doctor didn't even look up. "We got a lotta bears coming down this summer," he said. "They like the landfills. I went to see the ones up in Long Lake. You ever see those, Chris?"

"No, sir."

Dr. Gidumal arrived for Loi. Brian slipped into the front end of her cubicle and kissed her cheek.

She smiled at him, then closed her eyes as the doctor examined her.

"This is doing well," he said. "You have a little bleeding, maybe, but this is doing well."

Brian kissed her again, whispering in her shell-like ear, "Thank God for you, thank God for you." With a quick motion of her head, she gave him a peck.

The doctor put his hand on Brian's shoulder. "How are you feeling, Brian?"

"I'm good."

He took Brian by the shoulders, looked into his face. "No, I beg to differ. You are not good. You are in shock."

"I feel fine. I'm—yeah, I guess you'd say that."

"You have lost your home, you are in a terrible time. You are not good."

"Doctor—"

"Do you two have a place you can go? Relatives, perhaps?"

Brian did not want to go to any relatives. He wanted to do three things. The first was to get Ellen and Chris and Loi in a condition to travel. The second was to find Bob and Nancy and get them out of here. The third was to run.

Ellen's leg was examined by a bored intern who announced that she'd brushed against nettles and experienced an unusually strong allergic response. She reflected on the futility of telling him what had actually happened. She'd already had Nate Harris laugh in her face, and Bob was on the psycho ward for blurting out his story.

The doctor gave her antihistamine cream. "This'll keep the itching down. If you're not better by tomorrow afternoon, come back and we'll take another look at it. But I'm sure this is a very minor problem. You must have gotten in the nettles running away from the fire. Lucky that was all that happened. You're all very lucky."

"You're sure it couldn't be anything else?"

Smiling, he shook his curly young head. She read the easy condescension in his face.

She wanted to yell a warning from the rooftops, but what could she say? Hey, my name is Ellen Maas and I think that Oscola's full of creepy crawlies. Please strap me to a bed beside Bob West.

It sickened her to realize the truth: the enemy had been breathtakingly efficient. There were no hordes of refugees claiming to have witnessed the impossible. Only four people who knew what was happening had gotten away—Loi and Brian and Bob and a very frightened outsider called Ellen Maas. Not even Bob's children understood the truth.

When she left the treatment area, she found the rest of the emergency facility quiet. Brian and Loi and the boys were gone. Looking around at the sudden emptiness, she felt hurt.

The quiet, the soft voices of the intern and the resident talking together on the nurses' station, the distant whirr of the air-conditioning system, even the familiar hospital smell, combined to enforce upon her a sense of deep isolation.

She would never return to Oscola, not even to get her belongings, not for any reason whatsoever.

She paid her bill with a MasterCard. There wasn't any insurance, so the $270 would just eat a little further into her credit limit. It was possible to see a welfare office in the future, if she couldn't find work somewhere.

"Did the Kellys say where they were going?" she asked the desk clerk.

"No, ma'am. But I don't think they left the hospital."

"Was Mrs. Kelly admitted?"

"None of 'em were. But that guy with the truck, he told 'em goodbye. So I figure they're still here."

Of course they were, and it was perfectly obvious where they had gone.

She went through the long, echoing corridors to the so-called "Brain/Mind Suite."

"I'm here to see Lieutenant West," she told the nurse at the station.

The nurse peered along the hall. "They're all down there. Two-forty-three. Are you a relative?"

Ellen walked into the open room, confronting a tableau of complex human emotions. Loi and Nancy were standing side by side, Brian was leaning over his friend. The two boys were in a corner, their eyes open wide.

Their father was under restraint, his body wrapped in long, soft hospital-green clothing of a type she'd never seen before. There were lots of belts and straps. It froze her insides to see a human being treated like this. She'd never dreamed that this sort of thing was still done. Shades of Bedlam, with the mad chained to the walls.

"Miss Maas," Nancy said. "Please—"

"She is with us," Loi interrupted. "She has great courage. And you need to listen to her." Their eyes met.

"Thank you," Ellen said. She turned to the bed, where Bob was straining against his straps, his face gleaming with sweat. The poor man was struggling to get up. Ellen looked to Brian.

"He's absorbing it. Aren't you, buddy?"

His voice when it came was a deep, throaty rumble, vastly weaker than Ellen remembered it. "It's . . . all of it . . ." Then he looked to Ellen, a fierce question appearing in his eyes.

"It's true, Bob. I've seen them. You're not hallucinating."

"You're not psychotic, Bobby," Nancy said. "The things you're remembering—the things with the arms and all—"

Slowly, it sank in. Deeper and deeper it went. They could see the wonder come into his face, followed by a flicker of relief, a sudden turning of the head, a sigh as if a weight had lifted, then a widening of the eyes—wider, wider—and a great, long, rolling groan mixed of relief and triumph and abject terror.

Followed by sudden silence.

Then his eyes seemed to look into some far distance. "Get me out."

Ellen began working the straps, then the others joined her, and they all untied him together. When he sat up in bed he wobbled a little, but then he was on his feet, swaying in his hospital gown, going down on one knee as two very excited boys flew into his arms. "You're gonna be OK, Dad," Chris said. Joey snuggled against him, burying his face in his father's chest, drinking his returned power.

"I'm fine, boys, but I don't think the Yanks are."

"Yes they are," Joey said, suddenly coming to life. "They just won six games in a row is all."

While Loi and Brian and Ellen waited in the hallway, Bob dressed. "I really think we ought to all go to a motel," Ellen said.

Loi looked at her. "We certainly can't stay in Oscola."

"I thought I had some kind of an obligation, but this is beyond that."

"Yes," Loi agreed, "our obligation is to survive." She put her hand on her belly. The pains had faded, but she did not feel strong.

During the fire Loi had seen that Ellen was a very strong, mature woman. Somebody who was cool in the face of the unexpected, who was efficient at times of high danger, was not also an emotional baby. That woman would never try to seduce a married man.

She hadn't lost Brian, she could see the love in his eyes. But she had certainly lost all her curtains and dishes, her marvelous dresses she'd bought at the Mode O'Day, her pretty furniture.

She'd also lost her collection of books, the mathematics and physics texts she was studying, her poetry, her *Great Novels in Outline*. She had lost the papers that identified her as a new American and the wife of an important man: her citizenship certificate and her marriage license.

She had lost her beloved Laughing Buddha, that was her luck. She was just a barefoot on the road again.

She had stopped crying years ago. Weakness must never be revealed.

"We gonna go home," Joey piped as the Wests came out of the room.

Bob hushed his son.

Quietly, the whole group of them went to the far end of the hall and down the back stairs. It wasn't difficult to leave undetected; the hospital wasn't guarded.

Now that the moon had set, the sky was filled with stars. Ellen did not like going out into the parking lot where there were only a few cars, did not like being in the dark, under the sky. "What if they're here?"

"It's possible," Brian replied, "but I don't think so."

"Well, why not? I mean—"

"They're apt to be confined to the area of Oscola and Towayda, at least for a while. We've seen that they have limits, a sort of range."

"But they'll spread?" Bob asked.

They had reached the Wests' Taurus. "Oh, yes," Brian replied.

"The bears?" Chris asked.

"It's not bears," his mother replied.

"Something else," Loi added. "We do not know for certain what it is."

"Look," Brian said, "there's almost no chance that we can fight this on our own. And I doubt very much that we can get the evidence we need."

Ellen looked at him. "Do you realize what you're saying?"

Brian glanced down at the boys, nodded. Ellen thought she had never seen such sadness in a human face.

"We go to the Ludlum Inn," Loi said. "Wait until dawn." She was holding her own shoulders. "I don't want to stay outside any longer."

They got into the car, all except Ellen. There wasn't room for her. She leaned into the driver's window.

"I'll catch up with you," she said. "Take a cab."

The car pulled away, leaving Ellen to face the dark and silence alone.

2.

She hurried back to the hospital lobby. The car had obviously been jammed, but something about being left behind still hurt.

The corridors were so quiet that she could hear the humming of the fluorescent light fixtures on the ceilings.

So, where was she going to go? Following the others to the Ludlum Inn was one alternative. But she could also rent a car and just start driving.

"Excuse me, ma'am." The maintenance man stood before her in his blue uniform, his keys in his hand.

"Yes?"

"You can't stay here at this hour."

She used the phone in the entryway. When you need something after midnight in a small city like Ludlum you call the cab company. Sure enough, the Tru-Serve dispatcher knew of an all-night car rental. Allomar Texaco was also an Avis station. She took a cab there and soon had wheels again, a green Escort with a complicated stain on the front seat.

She drove out to the Northway, intending to crash at the first motel she found. There was no point in trying the Ludlum Inn. Only well-known locals could get a room there without a reservation. Unlike the higher Adirondacks, the Three Counties were not much of a tourist area, so there was a possibility of getting a room on short notice in the summer season.

Even so, the Suisse Chalet was full, the Rodeway Inn likewise. She finally found a room at the Days Inn. On the way in she bought a Hershey Bar and a 7-Up from vending machines. She didn't even like the walk down to the room from the lobby. It was all she could do not to run.

She called the Ludlum Inn, but they hadn't arrived.

Sitting in the middle of the bed in her ripped jeans and dirty sweatshirt, she ate candy and flipped from channel to channel on the TV, trying to blank her mind. The memories of the past eight hours were not to be touched, not if she wanted to stay sane.

McLaughlin was bellowing on CNBC, tonight's "Larry King Live" repeating on CNN. "The Brady Bunch" flashed past, followed by a chunk of *Fort Apache*, followed by a story about a school prayer scandal on *Headline News*.

It should have been reassuring, but instead it was eerie, like peering into a dead man's eyes.

Without realizing it, she fell asleep. A soft sound . . . a tickle along her right arm—and she leaped back against the headboard screaming bloody murder.

She clapped her hands over her mouth, horrified that she'd get thrown out of the motel. There was nothing on her arm, nothing unusual anywhere in the room.

She sighed, drank down the dregs of her 7-Up. It was warm, which surprised her. Then she noticed that she could see the swimming pool.

Incredibly, it was seven-fifteen. She'd slept for three hours. The last thing she remembered, she'd been sitting in the middle of the bed.

She grabbed the phone and called the Ludlum Inn again. This time, they were already gone.

Next she called the Wests' house. Would the phones in Oscola be working?

Nancy answered.

"This is Ellen."

"What happened to you?" She spoke off line. "It's her."

"I'm sorry, I accidentally fell asleep."

Brian came on. "We were worried sick."

"Brian, what in the world are you doing back there? Are you people insane?"

There was a pause. "Look, Ellen, we can't just turn our backs on this."

"We have to!"

"I'm gonna try one last time. I didn't come back for somebody else's shirts and underwear."

"Brian, you took those children, your pregnant wife?"

"It's broad daylight. So far, everything that's happened has taken place at night."

"So far."

"What I'm going to do is look for fragments over near your car, where I did that shooting. And the Wests are packing a few things."

She should put down the phone right now. She should not say what she was about to say. "I'll come help you."

"Ellen—"

"I'll come," she repeated as she hung up. She sat on the bed, fumbling in her purse for a cigarette.

Lighting it, taking the first drag, she relaxed a little. Then she daubed her tongue on the shoulder of her shirt. Smoking was a nasty habit. It made her taste bad and smell worse. It made her look weak or stupid or both. But she sure as hell was stuck with it, especially now. She took another drag, a long one.

This problem would not blow away with the smoke.

After washing her face she went to check out, stopping in the hall to buy a cup of vending-machine coffee.

Coffee in hand and cigarette in mouth, she passed the restaurant. There were a couple of people in booths, a couple more at the counter. The morning papers stood near the door in stacks, still tied. Outside, crows perched on the motel's sign, calling to one another. The leaves of an aster quaked in the morning breeze.

Nothing was wrong, nothing at all.

She signed her credit card receipt and went out to the Escort.

Driving back, she watched the road narrow, the woods close in, watched the rolling mountains behind Oscola, thought about what lurked in the shadows, in the depths of the ground, thought of the quietly growing number of empty houses.

She approached Belton Road, the last turnoff before Route 303's unbroken run to Oscola. This was the point of no return. "What are you?" she asked the humming silence as her car passed through the intersection.

Her foot touched the brake, hesitated, wavered, then pressed harder. Just beyond the intersection, she rolled to a stop. She raised the windows and locked the doors.

She drove fast, alert for the least sign of movement back in the woods. But 303 seemed abandoned. Nobody passed her, she overtook no other cars. She reached River Road, then crossed the bridge onto Mound, then turned onto Queen's Road at the intersection.

At the Wests' house, she turned off the engine, got out and went up to the front door. From inside came the familiar smell of cooking bacon.

This was one of those small moments that is really huge, and for once she knew it. She was making a commitment here, a big one.

She knocked.

There had been soft voices inside, which now stopped. "It's me," she said through the closed door. She stepped back, suddenly certain that this was a mistake. The door opened a little.

Bob West dragged her inside.

Behind the closed curtains the lights were on. She found herself in a cozy living room. A big photograph of an Adirondack stream hung on the wall above the entertainment system. The room was filled with solid Early American furniture. Some of the pieces were obviously very old. She had seen family antiques like these in everyday use in many Oscola homes.

"Ellen," Loi said from her place lying on the couch, "welcome." The smile seemed warm, but Loi's personality had so many subtle twists and turns, it was impossible to be certain.

"How are you doing, Loi?"

She touched her stomach, smiled. "We are well."

Ellen looked around for the boys. "Chris?"

"He's going to be fine," Nancy said. "There's still a good bit of pain, though."

"Burns hurt," Brian added. He gazed at her. "I've got a theory in place."

She raised her eyebrows, questioning.

"Some of my equations suggested that we could crack a hole in space-time. Somebody must have done it. Built a device and done it."

"They took my husband's work, twisted it."

Bob walked over. His wide, kind face reminded Ellen of her own father. "I remember being in a room full of blue pipes and broken equipment. I was swallowed, for God's sake. Like Jonah in the whale." He paused. "Somebody talked to me, tried to get me to see it his way."

"Who was he?" Ellen asked.

"I remember a tall shape. Blacker than black. A sense of great dignity and . . . what I would call evil. Essence of evil."

Loi sat up. "The demon."

"Satan," Nancy added.

Loi gave Bob an appraising look. "Did you feel like you wanted to help him?"

"I don't know what I felt. If it was Satan—"

"This isn't about the devil," Brian snapped. "I'm talking about a derangement of reality on the deepest and most subtle level."

"I remember him as being . . . insectoid. When he moved, it was slow and stealthy until right at the end. Then—wham—he was at your throat."

Nancy went closer to him.

Ellen was fascinated by the idea of just sitting across a table from somebody from another reality, if that was the right way to describe it. "You said he was evil. How could you tell?"

"It radiated from him like a stench. Total contempt, total hate. Like nothing you can imagine."

Loi, who had gone to the kitchen, put a plate of bacon and eggs on the table with a bang. "We've got to eat," she said.

Brian took some eggs. "Then I'm going out to make the last try at evidence."

Again, there was that terrible sadness. Poor Brian. Ellen could see how responsible he felt.

Nancy called her boys and they were soon loading plates with food.

Brian stared into his own plate. "We're pawns. I'm my own pawn. Or the pawn of my own inaction. Ironic." His voice went low. "My grief over the loss of my first family has placed my second in mortal jeopardy."

Ellen's heart went out to him, but it was Loi who tended his sorrow, putting her arms awkwardly around his big shoulders.

A moment later he looked up from his food, stood, and without a word strode out the door.

"Gotta go, baby," Bob said to Nancy. They kissed and he hurried off behind Brian.

Ellen watched them go in Bob's sedan, watched it kick up dust at the end of the driveway, then disappear around the corner of the house.

Soon Loi and Nancy began to pack, with Loi cooing over Nancy's humdrum wardrobe as if it belonged to a princess royal. The boys turned on the television. Ellen went over to the picture window and opened the curtains. She stared as far as she could see down Queen's Road.

"You don't wait well," Loi said, coming up behind her and putting her arms around her waist. "Best to work." She grasped her shoulders and turned her around. "Put the fancy monogrammed linens in the cardboard box in the hall."

Ellen worked, but her mind was turning over and over, she couldn't stop it. She was worried about Brian and Bob, and that was a fact. She possessed none of Loi's fatalism.

The two men had been gone thirty minutes by the time the women were finished with the packing. "Loi, we've got to go out and look for them."

"Ellen, I am *waiting*. I will wait a certain time that is in my heart. Then I will go."

"Do you—I mean—I know nothing about Eastern religions. Do you pray for him? What are you?"

"I am somewhat a Buddhist. As much as Brian is a Catholic. Also, my people have their beliefs. Their understanding." Suddenly she went to the front door, threw it open.

"What?"

"Be still."

The sedan appeared.

The three women streamed out into the driveway, followed by the boys. Brian leaned out of the passenger's window. "Your car's gone, Ellen. Not a sign. Just treadmarks."

"Any—"

He shook his head. "The site was as clean as a whistle."

"So we're leaving, then?" Nancy's voice had an edge in it.

"Let's go, Dad," Chris said.

His younger brother added his voice. "Dad, I don't like it around here at night. There's *bears!*"

They divided into two groups: Ellen and Brian and Loi rode together in Ellen's rental, and the Wests went in their own car. The plan was to continue on to Albany, and meet up again later.

They went in procession down Queen's Road to the four-way intersection where Main became Mound. From here they could see up into the heart of Oscola. "It looks as empty as Towayda did," Brian said. The fact that the roads weren't yet full of refugees seemed a bad sign. He felt sure that each empty house represented a dreadful tragedy. "Turn on the radio."

The Oscola fires were the big story. "Prominent local farmer and professor Brian Kelly" was mentioned as having survived one of the two fires that had struck the Oscola community the previous night.

All the land seemed to be smiling, so beautiful, so completely benign, so harmless.

They were about halfway to Ludlum when they came upon the first sign.

"What's that?" Loi asked.

"I don't know."

Ellen peered beyond the windshield. A cloth object, torn, lay on the roadside. "It's a shirt. Was."

"Look at the red on it." Loi's voice was small.

Then they rounded a curve and found a car lying on its side amid a great tumble of possessions. There were shirts and sheets and toys, furniture that had been tied to the top, a lawn mower, an exploded television, all manner of smaller debris.

Brian hit his brakes, and so did Bob behind him.

An instant later Bob ran past. Everybody else crowded out of the cars. "It's the Michaelsons," Bob shouted. He clambered up onto the wreck.

"Boys, stay back," Nancy said. She and Loi took their hands. Ellen went forward with Brian.

Bob looked around. "Not a sign of 'em." He dropped back down to the road. The group came together.

"Should I know the Michaelsons?" Ellen asked.

"They're new people over from Rochester," Brian explained. "I don't think the family's been around here more than thirty years or so."

"They must've walked away from it." Bob peered into the woods. His words sounded hollow in the roadside silence.

"How many kids do they have?" Ellen asked.

"Three," Bob said.

"I think I see someone." Loi was looking toward the tree line.

"Where?" Brian asked. His voice had become soft. He could smell the death, too. They all could.

"Get the kids in the car, Nance." Bob's hand went to his hip. There was, of course, no pistol there. He ran a few feet toward the trees. "Hey there, you OK?"

The figure did not move. But its outlines were clear. There was no question but that a man was standing in the woods about two hundred feet away.

"Hey!"

"Could be in shock," Ellen suggested.

"Maybe." Bob went forward. Both of his sons grabbed him. "Daddy, no," the smaller boy said.

"Get in the car! Nancy, take care of 'em!"

"Stay here, Bobby."

"I'll do it." Brian took a step toward the woods.

"No!" Loi threw her arms around his waist.

Silence fell. Nobody moved. Obviously, the fathers and mothers could not take the risk.

3.

Ellen began to walk toward the forest. Nobody stopped her and that was all right. "Are you hurt?" she called into the silence.

The figure didn't move or speak.

"Everything OK?" Brian called.

"So far." As she walked forward Ellen recognized a new set of reactions—lack of muscle control, extreme tightness of throat, whistling breath. This was a state of fear she had never entered before. Then her vision blurred. She shook away a great flood of tears. Her heart was humming, her face was hot, every cell in her body screaming at her to turn and run.

Brian stayed back, unwilling to leave Loi's side, yet also unwilling to completely abandon Ellen.

She took a jerky step forward, then another. This was ridiculous, she was barely in control of her own body. Instincts she didn't even know she possessed were being engaged. If she'd had a pistol she might have done something outrageous, like empty it right into that shadow.

The drone of flies was loud. She could see the definite shape of a man, even that he was wearing a blue denim shirt. "Hello? Can you hear me?"

No reply. She took three quick steps closer.

"Be careful, Ellie!"

She sucked in a breath, let her hands go to fists, and forced herself to step into the forest, pushing aside the leaves of some maple saplings.

Her first clear impression was of a glaring eye. Then teeth, a tight smile. She did not exactly scream, but rather made the kind of gasp of surprised agony that comes from stepping on a scorpion or having a centipede bury its red legs in your thigh.

She twisted against herself, her fists coming up to her throat. There remained a tiny spark of self-control. But when she saw the horrific distortion of the man's neck, she shrank back in panicky confusion. It was a ropy stalk an impossible three feet long. It was the color and consistency of dried beef jerky.

Then she saw the left arm.

She shrieked, a terrible, inarticulate wail that brought them all running down from the road, even the boys.

Brian was the first into the woods beside her. "Ellie!"

"God help us all!" She threw herself away from it, as if the mere sight of it was a slamming, crushing blow across the face.

Brian gagged, bent double, stumbled back.

Under its ripped, bulging clothes, the body was a great mound of tight, twisted flesh jutting with bones. Knots of muscle and fat distorted stomach and thighs.

The right arm was a bloated dirigible of black, wet skin, covered almost completely with flies. It was as if all the man's fluids had been pushed into that one arm.

The face above the hideously stretched neck was

grinning, the teeth visible all the way back to the molars. Unlike the right arm, the head had been sucked of every molecule of blood. It was the face of a mummy, the eyes pulled wide, the cheeks sunken against the bones. Flies raced between the teeth, and the tongue within was the shape and color of a rotted fig.

The neck was as tight as wire, and with every stirring of the air the head bobbed on its spring-like neck.

But they weren't looking at the head, not at the swollen right arm, not at the bulging humps.

They were watching in horrified fascination as the left arm grew and grew and grew. It seethed, its fingers turning to claws, its muscles bunching and popping, an awful, crunching creak coming from the torsioned bones.

This was the fate of the people who went to the judge's house: before their eyes was unfolding the future not only of their little community, but of all mankind.

A smell filled the air, of hot electric wiring, as if a machine somewhere nearby was working at extreme speed.

"We've got to go," Loi rasped.

Suddenly Bob grunted, plunged off into the wall of leaves. He charged forward rapidly, thrashing through the dense foliage. Then he was coming back, and the others saw the dangling arms and legs of a child.

Bob emerged carrying the poor little burden, a dead naked girl. Her hair was blond and long, still done up with a pink plastic barrette. There was no visible damage. Even her skin still seemed to glow with life.

As they got closer, though, Ellen saw that this was very far from the case. In some infinitely delicate and inhuman operation, the outer layer of the girl's skin had been eaten from her body.

And the glow came not from life—it came from something *inside* the child, something packed in tight under the remaining skin.

Ellen had seen them before.

"Drop her! Oh my dear God, *run!"*

Then young Chris cried out, "It's Lizzie!" His voice was high and clear, and stopped the grasshoppers that were singing in the meadow. Chris sat down on the ground. His mother hid her other son's eyes. With a child's insatiable curiosity, he fought her. "I want to see, Mommy!"

"Jesus," Brian cried.

Lizzie's body surged in Bob's arms. "What the hell?"

Grabbing her by the hair, Ellen yanked the child clear of him and hurled the wet, breaking mass of her as far away as she could. The force broke the carcass open and they came pouring out, swarming, their wings buzzing, their red legs scrabbling.

Bob lurched back, astonished, then horrified. He gagged, frantically brushing his chest.

"Evidence," Brian cried, "it's evidence!" He plunged toward the mass of insects. But the father's long left arm whipped around, and suddenly Brian was confronting one of those clawed hands in the light of day.

All of them ran out of the woods and across the bordering meadow, and dove into their cars. "It's evidence," Brian moaned, but he started the engine as the hand swarmed out of the woods and the insects followed in a mass as cohesive as a jelly, dashing toward them like a shark in air. They took off at full speed toward Ludlum and safety.

"They were trying to get away," Loi said. She looked down the road. "They also knew."

"Don't anybody panic!" Ellen's own voice told her that she was about to do just that. Loi heard it, too, and touched her shoulder, a gesture Ellen found curiously reassuring.

She cried a little bit as the car moved down the road. In the front seat Loi sat stiffly erect, staring out the windshield. They climbed a hill, and the tires complained around a sharp curve. The forest was thicker here, drawn close to the road on both sides. They drove in its dense shade.

Without warning Ellen was thrown forward, her head hitting the back of Loi's seat. "Brace yourselves," Brian yelled, but too late. The car pitched, there was a terrific jolt, followed by an explosion of white dust.

Silence. Both airbags hung out of their housings, deflated. "Are you OK?" Brian asked. With shaking hands he reached toward his wife.

Loi was clutching her abdomen. "I think so," she responded in a careful voice.

Ellen was completely confused. "The airbags went off?"

No reply. Then, from Loi: "Why did you stop?"

"I didn't. Jesus!"

An enormous coil rose in front of the car, higher and higher, unwinding itself in the light. It was dead black, filled with rushing musculature.

Loi shrieked in short, sharp bursts. Brian leaned back, staring, his teeth bared.

Ellen jumped out onto the road. The thing was coming up from the ground, clumps of flowers and chunks of pavement ripping away as it surged out.

Hundreds of gray threads surrounded the car like a web of fungus.

Ellen tore at them, yanked Loi's door open. She and Brian scrambled out. Ellen struggled, ripping at the curtain of threads. Where they touched her, they made her skin itch fiercely.

There came a piercing sound. Brian shouted, Ellen shrieked, Loi went stumbling back toward the Wests' car. The heavy coils were dropping down on the rental, crushing and pulverizing it.

From the woods came a snapping, sizzling sound. They began to see purple light winking among the leaves.

Then Bob was beside them. "Let's *move*," he cried. The whole group of them forced themselves into his car, crowding in, falling all over each other.

They turned around, going in the only direction they could—right back into Oscola—the trap.

TWELVE

1.

The car hurtled down the curving road, pushing through fifty, sixty, seventy. Brian drove hard, the images of what he had seen in the woods burning in his mind. Surely those masses of sweat-stinking insects couldn't think, couldn't remember what they'd been. But the other things—those long, long arms, those hands . . .

The filed nails he'd observed on the hand last night took on a whole new meaning. That had once been a person's hand, those nails had probably been filed in a local home before the horrible transformation took place. Maybe he'd been face-to-face with an old friend.

"It's all because of me," he said.

"Shut up," Ellen snapped. "Quit apologizing."

"You are not responsible, husband."

"Brian, it's an awfully long jump for me from some esoteric physics experiment to—what we're up against." Bob spoke for them all, Brian felt sure.

"Jump or not, it's real. Otherwise you'd never have been in my facility."

"I saw blue pipe. I can't remember much else. That E. G. and G. logo. It could have been a lot of different places."

"No. That pipe was made especially for us, using an experimental fabrication process. It's unique."

As they passed the Michaelsons' wreck, Brian noticed that Loi closed her eyes. Ellen made a raw, empty sound that could have been a sob. Nancy held her boys' heads down.

The sentinel trees whipped past.

"There," Loi said.

"What?"

"Just where the road curves. Something is moving there."

He floored the gas and they raced past the spot at ninety. Purple light flickered in the corner of his eye. In the seat behind him, Nancy sighed and squirmed. Her younger boy's head popped up. For a moment he drank in the light. "I like that," he cried. "Stop. Stop, Uncle Brian!"

Brian pressed the gas pedal to the fire wall and the car leaped ahead.

Purple light, sizzling sounds . . . and pleasure—howling, insane pleasure: it didn't hurt to be transformed bone and brain and gristle into one of those vile nightmares, it *felt good*.

"If it looks like they're going to get us, I think we should consider suicide," Bob said.

At that Chris burst into tears. His brother, now sucking his thumb, made no sound. "Bob," Nancy said with soft reproach.

"I don't want the boys to end up like—God help us!"

Ellen barely moved her lips as she spoke. "I want to win this."

"I agree. We must win." Loi slipped her hand into

Ellen's, and Ellen laid her head against Loi's shoulder.

They all fell silent, all hearing the same thing—a drumming sound was coming up the road, moving fast.

"The Viper," Brian whispered.

"Let's get the hell out of here!"

And go where? There was only one road between Oscola and the outside world, and this was it. The alternative was to go up to Towayda.

"It's not the Viper," Loi said. "Listen carefully!"

When it appeared, the vehicle proved to be an ordinary pickup, blue and tired-looking. It was piled high with household goods.

Brian got out and walked into the middle of the road waving his arms. He knew the family, of course. It was Jimmy Rysdale and his wife and kids. The Rysdales were really Ruisdaels, one of the original settler families. They had come with the Dutch landowner, the patroon, who had settled the area in the eighteenth century.

When they stopped Bob gave them the story of the Michaelsons, speaking quickly, his voice so low that he sounded as if he was sharing a pornographic secret. He omitted the terrifying details of what had happened next, saying only that something very, very dangerous was guarding the way out of Oscola.

"But you can't cut off a whole town," Jimmy said. "What about people tryin' to come out here? FedEx and stuff, and the grocery truck and the beer wagon? And calls. What about phone calls?"

"Our phone is dead," Loi said. "Was before we were burned out."

"Yeah, well, ours has been dead since last night. That's what decided us."

"Some phones are working," Ellen said. "I got through to the Wests from Ludlum, remember."

Brian thought: you were probably meant to get through. He thought also that the enemy was a careful planner, that he had a remarkable head for details and a highly developed sense of theater. But he was careful. He did not want them to lose what little hope they had, for he did not want death or suicide. He was herding them into his lair.

Jimmy Rysdale was on the near side of fifty, balding and a little dumpy, but a good farmer and a smart businessman. He owned a piece of a specialty lumbering operation that made out pretty well. He and Brian had hunted grouse and deer together, and Annie made about the best venison sausage in the Three Counties. Their youngest, known as Annie Junior because she looked so uncannily like her mother, was ten, solemn, and said to be a math whiz. Their boy, Willie Rysdale, was a starting pitcher for the first time this year on the Oscola Patroons, and a pretty good one from what Brian had seen.

"Let's go, Jimmy," his wife called from the truck. She had red O'Shaughnessy hair, and the flashing green eyes of that clan. "Jimmy, start the truck. We're getting out of here!"

"I don't think that'd be such a good idea," Brian said. "Our enemy must know he can't keep a town isolated for long."

Jimmy stared off down the road. "Which might also mean this is the last chance."

"It's past that, Jimmy."

Rysdale did not respond directly. "We're gonna spend a couple of weeks with my sister in Saratoga, make a few visits to the track." The races would be in full swing down there at this time of year.

He got back into the truck.

"Mr. Rysdale, don't do it," Ellen said. "Think about your kids!"

Jimmy looked at her in amazement. "What the hell do you know, Miss New York hotshot newspaper lady?"

"Too much," she said.

Jimmy lowered his head, closed his eyes a moment. "Them things that've come," he said in a mean voice, "we hear 'em tunneling under the house."

"They want us," Annie said, "they're gonna get the kids!"

"Shut up, Annie! The less we talk about it, the better."

"We can tell these people, Jimmy! They're like us, they won't go to the judge's. So them things, they were coming up under the house. And the closer they got, the more you could hear . . . voices."

"It was people screaming, Mom!"

"If we could get word to the military," Jimmy said, "they could come in here and fix this. That's why we have to leave, it's not just to get away. We aren't quitters. It's for patriotic reasons."

Brian shrugged his shoulders. "What're you gonna do? Who're you gonna tell?"

"You tell people the truth, you're gonna end up in a padded cell like I did," Bob said.

"We've been trying and trying to get physical evidence," Brian added. "Now that we're trapped here, it's there for the taking. We're up against something very smart, very careful, very determined. And why not? He's fighting for his life, just like us."

"With every blow, a demon grows stronger. To fight back we must be cunning also." Loi's eyes were steady. She believed in her demons as much as she did in her own breath.

Brian recalled the sound of little Lizzie Michaelson's body falling open, the soft, tearing whisper of the skin parting, and then that hideously energetic buzzing as her contents spewed into the air. In the thoroughness of its evil, the attack was indeed profoundly demonic.

But there was another side to that, wasn't there? The old Greek word for demon, *daimon*, also means soul, or source of knowledge. To look into the eyes of the demon was to see the truth.

There was movement in the pickup and Willie emerged. He was still his handsome, athletic self, but he looked as if he'd been crying. "Let's get going, Dad." His voice was sullen.

"The Michaelsons," his father said, gesturing ahead. "We don't want that."

"So we don't pull over or slow down or do whatever they did. Come on, Dad!" The boy hefted a shotgun, pumped a shell into the firing chamber with an efficient snap.

Now the daughter came down off the truck. "I don't want to die." She tugged her father's sleeve. "I'm staying here, Daddy!"

"Shut up, sis!"

Jim Rysdale looked down the road. Brian followed his eyes. "You could go examine the Michaelson wreck, buddy. Convince yourself."

Willie climbed up into the truck bed, stood behind the cab and ported his gun. "Let's move out, Dad."

Just then something shifted behind the roadside screen of trees. All eyes turned.

Loi saw it first, a slick black worm a foot in diameter uncoiling in the grass. Locusts leaped away from its gliding progress, as it exuded itself from the ground, its tip probing ahead.

How quick you are to make your point, Brian thought.

Bob was the next to see it. He cried out, an inarticulate bellow. Willie fired his gun, which discharged with a bone-jarring boom. The pellets tore through forest leaves with an angry clatter.

Pouring blood, the worm slid back into the ground. "See, Dad? Now, let's go."

A hand shot out of the woods on a long black arm and dug into Annie Junior's hair. It started dragging her toward the woods. She was too stunned to cry out, but her eyes widened, her hands went up and fluttered uselessly against the thing.

Her mother's fists went to her temples, her whole body lurched as if she'd been gut shot and she shrieked, a raw, resounding cry of astonishment and anguish. *"My baby!"*

Willie aimed his gun. Now Annie Junior shrieked, kicked, tore at the claws.

"You'll kill her, Willie!"

"I can get it, Mom!"

Loi started after Annie Junior. Brian didn't even have time to call her before she had her arms around the girl's waist. Then she was ripping at the shrieking child's hair, trying to extract it from the monstrous fingers before the long arm retracted into the woods.

Brian could see more coils gliding up among the leaves, their hands flexing, claws spreading.

Loi and the child were moving fast now, their bodies making a rasping sound as they were dragged across the summer-dry grass. Loi's stomach ground against the earth.

Brian ran after her. Stretching out his arms, he hurled himself at their feet and grabbed his wife around the legs.

The poor child's hair was torn right out of her head, and she screamed in agony.

The hand shot into the air on its long, curving arm, its fist full of bloody blond tufts.

"Baby, baby," Annie cried, dashing to her little girl.

There was a thunderous boom and the shotgun spat white smoke. The shot slapped the wall of leaves and the gray shapes within undulated.

Then Annie Rysdale had her daughter in her arms. The child was bawling, gripping her temples with fists like gnarled white nutmeats.

A moment later the two vehicles were speeding off in the direction of the town. To relieve the congestion in the Wests' car, Brian and Loi rode with the Rysdales. Annie Junior was on blankets in the truck bed, cradled by her mother. Willie was with them, clutching the shotgun to his chest.

Brian put his hand on his old friend's shoulder. "Jimmy buddy," he said.

"They are from the world underground," Loi said. "They've broken loose. We must get them to return to their world."

"That may not be possible."

"That was a very brave thing you did, Loi. I don't know what to say—you saved our baby."

"You would have saved mine."

2.

All the way to the Wests' house they saw broken telephone and power poles, lines down everywhere. Just in the past half hour, great destruction had been done. Worse, they observed half a dozen more wrecks along Route 303, and a tall column of smoke rising from the direction of the Jackson place out on the Towayda Road. This time there were no sirens raised in response.

When they arrived back at the Wests', Pat and Jenny Huygens were waiting in their car with the windows locked. They opened them as the little caravan drove up. "Bob," Pat said, "you gotta get the state police—"

"I'm gonna try to use my radios."

Everybody went into the house. They made sure all doors and windows were closed, and most of the windows curtained. Nobody wanted to risk so much as a glimpse of the purple light, day or night.

During the next hour more people came, drawn to the authority represented by Lieutenant West, and because they saw the other cars there.

The growing carnage along Route 303 had been what turned them all back.

In addition to the Rysdales and the Huygenses, old Mary Yates, Brian's cousin Dick and his wife Linda, and Father Palmer from St. Paul's church came. He was followed by the Reverend Simon Oont, the Dutch Reformed pastor.

Dick and Linda brought a bucket of fresh eggs, which made more sense than the family heirlooms and favorite clothes that tended to clog the trunks of the other cars.

"We're the accidents," Brian said, "the ones who've been missed."

The seventeen people present cramped Nancy West's living room. "We oughta go on a rampage, kill 'em all," Dick announced.

"That'd be smart," Bob responded. He'd been trying his handheld radio. It appeared to be working, but he couldn't break in on any of the calls. "Funny, the division's still patrolling the Northway as usual. No emergency's in effect or anything."

"Don't they ever come back in here?" Jenny Huygens asked.

"Not normally. Just the sheriff."

Mary Yates barked out a laugh. "So *that's* why we're being eaten by devils from hell."

"Let's inventory our weapons," Bob said. "We have to know where we stand."

There were five shotguns, seven deer rifles, a couple of .22s and five pistols.

"We need a plan," Mary Yates said. "We need to sit down and work it out right now."

"The things are getting bigger and stronger," Jim Rysdale responded. "How do you plan against that?"

Brian wished he had more information. But he could scarcely imagine the bizarre permutations of his elegant theories that had led to this disaster. A theoretical particle traveling back through time doesn't lead to . . . monsters. "I suspect it's going to go very quickly now. I doubt we'll be left alone for long." He looked around him. "My thought is, every single survivor from Cuyamora County is right here in this room. Look at it this way: we've been very efficiently rounded up. Now for the *coup de grâce*."

"I think you're right about that," Father Palmer said.

"I have an idea," Dick Kelly announced. "I say we work out a fuel line from Fisk's to the judge's root cellar and pump as much gas as we can down there. Then just strike a goddamn match." Dick had black hair cropped close at the back and around the sides. The curls left on top looked curiously artificial, but Brian knew that they weren't, having yanked at them many times when they were boys.

"A two-mile fuel line—that's a technical problem and a half," Pat Huygens said. He'd been a civil engineer. He was retired now. "What're you gonna do, get every garden hose in town?"

"Well, maybe something like that."

"Those old pumps over at Fisk's aren't going to move a volume of gas like that. Even if you got the line charged somehow or other, the gas'd be too heavy for 'em. You wouldn't even get a dribble out the other end."

"We could use a tanker truck. Could we get one?" Dick looked from face to face.

Everybody knew the answer, so nobody replied. The closest gas tanker would be at the Texaco distributor in Glens Falls.

A sound outside set everyone to frantic activity. In moments every window in the house bristled with gun barrels.

A blue Acura Legend came down the driveway and parked.

"It's Dr. Gidumal," Loi cried. She went out onto the porch as the Gidumals got out of their car.

Nobody went down the steps, though. Sam and Milly came in quickly. Their real names were Sanghvi and Maya, but the town had changed them to something easier to remember.

There were brief greetings, people automatically observing amenities that were now meaningless. Then Dr. Gidumal was taken to Annie Junior, who was lying on the Wests' bed with a blood-splotched turban of towels around her head.

Dr. Gidumal, it developed, had tried to call the hospital this morning. An investigation had revealed all the phone lines down. Then the power had failed. They'd been picking their way out toward 303 when they'd seen the cars here. They knew nothing of what had happened, and had difficulty believing what they were told.

As Loi watched and listened, she grew increasingly impatient. They were letting time pass, maybe too much time.

"To fight something this powerful," Milly Gidumal said at last, "it would seem important to know exactly where it is weak."

Brian shook his head. "I probably ought to know, but I don't. I mean, I was working on a project in theoretical physics."

"They are demons," Loi said. "We cannot fight them directly." There was acid in her voice.

Ellen disagreed. "This all has a scientific explanation. It seems like something supernatural only because we don't understand it."

"What does *she* know," Mrs. Yates commented *sotto voce*.

Ellen heard, and turned to her. "If hell's opening up, we obviously aren't going to get away. That's the trouble with that kind of thinking."

"Father," Pat Huygens asked, "could a door to hell actually open?"

"Well, now, we're not sure about that. But I suppose it might."

"I concur," Oont announced solemnly.

"We're ignorant, helpless and we don't have much time." Brian looked from face to face. "That's the truth of it."

"What about the judge? Maybe we ought to go over in a body and interrogate the judge." On the surface Pat Huygens' suggestion was reasonable.

"An awful lot of people have gone there and not come back," Ellen said.

"We stay away from the judge, folks." Brian put all the authority he could into his voice.

Willie Rysdale flared at him. "I say we take every gun we got and go over there and shoot everything that moves, then torch the place!"

People glanced nervously at each other.

"I'm capable of facing who I have to face," Loi said. "But I don't think we should attack frontally." She regarded the Rysdale boy with cool eyes. "Only fools do that." Her words caused a silence. She was not used to being the center of attention, and she felt sweat tickling her temples. But she continued. "I was born to war, raised in battle. This is war, I am a soldier. And you, Bob, you also."

"You won our war, don't forget," Bob said.

"The Americans were brave."

Bob nodded slowly, regarding her. The feelings now passing between these two former enemies were very deep.

"What about your baby?" Ellen asked. "You're not exactly strong."

Loi tossed her hair out of her eyes. "If I fight, my baby has a chance. If I don't fight, he dies."

"I say we form a box and go out armed to the teeth. We fire at anything that moves."

"That might work!" Willie's father was enthusiastic, but nobody else supported them. People were trying to imagine themselves winning a pitched battle, and having a hard time doing it.

"Maybe we should wait to be rescued," Bob said.

Brian thought that was at least as dangerous as the banzai charge idea. "Bob, that's a gamble. I mean, I'm looking at this as a minute-to-minute thing."

"Let's go!" Willie hefted his shotgun.

"We've got to have a more practical plan," Loi said.

Father Palmer, who had been in the kitchen with Nancy trying to put together food for the group, now returned to the living room. He was carrying a tray with boxes of Wheaties and Quix cereals on it, a couple of dozen boiled eggs from the bucket Dick had brought, a bowl of pickles and some salami. "Let's all try to eat," he said. "We need food."

"What's your take on this, Padre?" Pat Huygens asked. "The door to hell gonna close, or do we all gotta burn?"

Brian respected Father Palmer, but a theological explanation wasn't going to work. "I think we'd better forget fighting and concentrate on survival."

"My husband is right," Loi said. "It's getting toward noon already, and the last thing we want is to be caught in Oscola after the sun goes down."

"God save us," Reverend Oont said.

"Somebody sure as hell better," Mrs. Yates responded.

That stopped conversation. Husbands and wives moved closer together, gathered in their children.

Morning was gone, and the shadows of afternoon were emerging. The day was no longer young.

THIRTEEN

Loi was watching the street. "There are clouds forming up again off toward the Jumpers." She looked back at Brian. She feared that her husband felt helpless, that he was freezing like an untried soldier.

She listened to the murmur of voices. So many people were here, most of them not well known to her. Except for Bob and Nancy, she had made few friends in Oscola.

Even so, she wanted them to live, all of them. If they would not find a way out for themselves, she would do it. Her hands went to her belly, to the baby within. No demon could attack a baby, young innocence was too powerful, it drove them back.

But she could lose her baby.

Mary Yates, the owner of Mode O'Day Fashions, where Loi often shopped, suddenly rose from the couch. "OK, folks, this is official. I've panicked. So what I'm gonna do before the shadows get another inch longer is, I'm just gonna drive right on up the Towayda Road, turn out when I get to Corey Lake and go down that old logging track up there. I can slip right across to the Northway. I'm asking for volunteers."

Jim Rysdale narrowed his eyes. "You gonna do it in your Oldsmobile, Mary? That logging road's probably washed out up beyond the first ridge line. God knows, nobody even hunts back in there anymore."

"It may be hazardous, Mary," Sam Gidumal said. "If you were to get stuck, you'd be helpless."

"I've got front-wheel drive." Again she glanced out the window. "Better than being shut up in here waiting to die."

"Mary, *please!*" Nancy held her boys close to her.

"Daddy says we gonna commit suicide," little Joey said. His voice was hushed, exactly as it would have been at a wedding or a funeral. His brother shushed him, then glanced over to their mother for approval.

"Look," Mary said, "I don't want to commit suicide or die or end up God knows what way, like the folks that got caught out on 303. Which is why I'm going to take my rifle and my pistol and I'm just gonna go." She smiled, but her fingers were twisted together like a tangle of worms. "Jimmy's right about one thing, though. My trip's gonna be dangerous. I need another car at least, in case we have to help each other through."

Loi pulled back the curtain. "The clouds are getting dark. That logging track won't be passable in another hour."

"All the more reason to get our tails in gear."

"I'll go," the Reverend Oont announced. "I have my four-by-four Cherokee. We can leave the Olds here."

Mary went to him and threw her arms around him. Others milled. Nobody seemed ready to follow them. Father Palmer wished them luck.

Brian watched Loi as she went to the table and

carefully ate a hard-boiled egg. Rather than cracking it against the edge of the plate, she cut the shell with a fingernail, and removed neatly cut squares of shell.

There were hugs all around, and more than one pair of eyes went wet as the two prepared for their departure. Oont had no guns, so he and Mary split her stash. She took the rifle, he the pistol. She also had a shotgun, an old single-shot small-gauge of no particular value.

Loi also was planning an attempt to escape. But it would be carefully designed, not thrown together slapdash like this. She wished them the best, but she was filled with foreboding.

Concerned that she keep up her strength, she ate her egg. "Brian," she said as she returned to the living room, "I want you to eat." She handed him another egg, and he cracked it against the arm of a chair. Bits of shell went everywhere.

Mary put on her canvas hat and Oont buttoned his hunter's vest. Together they looked about as defenseless as two human beings could be. Oont was a pallid man, small, with the eyes of a big puppy and a disposition to match. Mary had her little bit of bluff, but she wasn't going to scare a half-blind housefly for long.

"I want you to think again," Loi said. "We're best off staying together."

"So come!" Mary's voice had a high, edgy note to it.

At that moment they heard a sort of subtle, fluttering sound—more a feeling, really—from under the house. "That's what we had," Jenny Huygens whispered harshly. "That precise noise." She looked at the silent, frightened faces around her. "It's down there right now. Under us."

There was a hurried conference in the Rysdale family. Willie was even more vehement about putting up a fight. His mother's face became the color of old wax. Then Jim stepped forward. "We'll go with you, Mary." Annie Junior buried her face in her mother's dress.

"Thank you, Dad," Willie said. He slapped his weapon. "I wanta get my licks in!"

The fluttering came again, this time strong enough to shake bric-a-brac on the shelf above the TV and rattle the dishes on the table. "There ain't a lot of time, folks," Mary said.

Along with Mary and the Reverend went the Rysdales, a total of six people. "I don't want to be here when it breaks through," Annie explained. "I've been through it, and once is enough."

Loi went to Brian, put her hand in his. Ellen had stuck a big kitchen knife in her belt. She stood before a shelf, examining a portable shortwave radio, blinking the tears out of her eyes. "This work, Bob?"

"I can pick up China with that Sony. But remember we had trouble with my portable."

"You couldn't transmit. But this is a receiver." She turned on the radio, began twisting the dial.

The Yates group went out onto the porch. Loi drew open the curtains in front of the picture window. She saw them get into Reverend Oont's 4×4 and the Rysdales' pickup.

As they were leaving, the earth stirred again. Nancy's bric-a-brac trembled, the ceramic elves shook, the imitation Dresden figurines danced.

"If there's a tunnel getting dug under the house," Bob said, "maybe we all ought to go."

"No! We stay." Loi backed away from the window. One of the figurines fell with a crash from its shelf to the top of the TV. Its head popped off and rolled to the floor.

Outside, the two vehicles were moving out into the road.

From the basement came a soft grinding sound. "I think we're making a mistake," Bob said.

"Why don't you join them, then?" Loi's voice was sharp. Brian was worried about her and Bob. The more this became like war, he thought, the more the buried animosities of these two rival soldiers were apt to surface. They needed work to do, something to focus their energy. Brian searched his thoughts, trying to find a sensible way of fighting back. "We need to locate the facility," he said at last. "That's the key."

Bob nodded, but said nothing.

"You have a way of doing this?" Loi asked.

Ellen came over to them. "It could be anywhere."

"It's here. Everything is happening here. The way I visualize it, they've linked up with some parallel universe, working from my equations and using some incredible hybrid of my equipment."

"Could you also have done this?" Loi asked.

"I was working with the scientific equivalent of a black-and-white photo. Whoever has control of my facility has evolved my equipment all the way to the era of three-dimensional TV."

The group was beginning to move out onto the porch to watch the caravan leave. Brian and Loi followed them.

The air was warm and laced with the fragrance of Nancy's roses. Birds sang, a butterfly fluttered across the lawn. The near view could not have been more normal. But there was also a long loop of ordinary telephone cable lying in the street, and a power line sparking intermittently at the intersection. Reverend Oont's Jeep rolled slowly forward, followed by the Rysdales' pickup. Willie stood in the back balancing against the cab, his Remington in his arms.

Father Palmer began to pray, "Our Father who art in heaven . . ." A ragged chorus picked up the prayer. Brian joined, wishing more than believing.

The two cars rounded the corner. As they disappeared, their engine noise was absorbed by a stand of fir.

Even so, nobody went inside. Far from it, they kept praying.

Not twenty seconds had passed before they heard the unmistakable crack of a rifle. The prayer gained intensity. Veins rose on necks, hands clasped hands, eyes closed. There were three more cracks, then a fusillade. The prayer died, the little group closed in on itself.

Mary's old shotgun boomed once, its echoes slapping off against the hills.

Into the breathless silence that followed, there came a single scream. It was deep and awful, a man's cry. Linda Kelly sobbed. Nancy said, "Kids, get back in the house." As she went in, she herded them ahead of her.

More screams followed, as high and lost as the voice of the wind on a wild winter night.

"God help them," Father Palmer cried.

Crackling sounds erupted, the angry rasp of electricity. Despite the sunlight, purple flashes were visible above the tree line. The screams went on and on, and Brian realized that he was screaming, too, everybody was, everybody except Loi and Bob, who walked side by side down the driveway. They had armed themselves with shotguns.

Brian forced himself to follow. He passed Father Palmer, who was now on his knees, his fists closed and raised in supplication or anger.

With a dull thud a blossom of flame rose into the sky beyond the trees. A single tire, smoking, came rolling down the slight incline and back into Queen's Road. It stopped, fell, and lay in a haze of rubber-stinking smoke.

Dr. Gidumal held his hands to his temples, his eyes wide, his teeth clenched.

As the screaming died, Brian was astonished to hear music. For a moment he was confused, then he realized that it was WRON, the Voice of the Adirondacks out of Glens Falls. They were playing an oldie, Nat King Cole's "Mona Lisa." Only seventy miles away, and they had no idea what was happening here.

Then he saw a long, thin coil rising out of the smoke, rising high above the line of pines that blocked the view of Main. "Jesus Christ, look!" It waved in the air like a vine, and at the end it held something.

Loi and Bob raised their guns, calmly aimed and fired. The vine reared like a snake and a black dot came arcing across the sky, falling right toward them.

Bob fired again and the object was deflected, spinning wildly. It fell into the street twenty feet away.

Then there was silence. The cable or snake disappeared.

"Bring a blanket," Loi called. "Cover it."

Brian saw that it was a head. He recognized Willie Rysdale's young face, frozen in a drum-tight grin. "I'll get one," he shouted.

"Brian," Nancy shrieked as he came through the front door, "Brian, something's *down there!*" She was staring at the entrance to the basement, her eyes wide.

"Get out of here."

"Oh, God, Brian, where will we go now?"

"Hurry up," Loi called. Her voice was as high as a girl's. Brian grabbed the tablecloth and started for the door.

As he returned to the porch, he saw that the head was still somehow alive, the face working.

Loi and Bob both fired at once, fired again and again. The boy's head danced in the street, split as buckshot slammed it.

Brian reached their side, waving the tablecloth. "Loi, be careful. That gun's got a lot of kick."

"I can fire a shotgun, Brian." She pointed with her chin. "Don't let them see. Cover it."

The head was still alive, its left eye blinking spasmodically, the tongue flapping in the mouth with a sound like a moth fluttering against a screen. One blast had gouged the left temple, the other torn off the forehead, exposing an interior complex with thick green folds where the gray brain ought to be.

Brian saw then that the shattered eye was looking at him.

He sensed that this was no longer the face of Willie Rysdale. It was *him* from the other side, a self-portrait.

The eye blinked fast, then the muscle around it tightened. As Brian moved, the eye followed him.

He thought it looked hungry.

Loi fired. Brian threw the cloth at the head rather than covering it. He didn't want to go any closer to it.

More shots followed, and Brian realized that Loi and Bob were not firing at the head, but rather at something farther down the street.

A thick coil had slid across the intersection. It shone in the sun, dripping as if just washed or just born. As the echo of the shots retreated into the woods, he heard a bizarre mix of sounds, the lazy ratcheting of summer bugs, the strains of "Memories Are Made of This" from the radio, and the fan-quick fluttering of Willie's tongue.

Nancy and her boys rushed out of the house. "It's on the stairs," Joey shrieked.

"There's something coming from under the basement door," Nancy wailed, falling into her husband's arms.

"Get a grip," Loi cried. "What's there?"

"Threads," Nancy said, "long black threads."

"They're sticky," Chris added. "Really sticky."

"They're getting thicker," Joey said, "like earthworms get if you touch 'em."

"Bob," Loi asked, "have you got any gas in your garage?"

"Well, yeah, for my lawn mower."

"We have to burn the house."

Nancy's mouth dropped open. "The hell you're

gonna burn my house, you damn *gook!*" She planted herself before the door, her legs spread.

From inside came an ominous sputtering.

"Burn it now," Loi shouted. "Do it, Bob!"

Bob hurried into the garage, came out with a five-gallon tin of gas.

"You are not gonna do this, Bobby West." His wife took the can from him. "Not you." She put it down.

"Get it, Brian. Pour it in the basement window. But you be careful. If anything down there starts toward you, run!"

Brian felt the gas sloshing in the can, looked into Nancy's raging eyes, at their diamond-hard anger, their wet, glistening fear. She spat. Nancy West, a woman he had known since they were babies, spat right in his face. He felt it against his cheek, trickling slowly down. With his free hand he wiped it away, advancing toward the basement window.

"Cover him," Loi told Bob. Then she smashed in the window with the barrel of her shotgun. Methodically, she put it to her shoulder, braced and fired two shells into the basement in quick succession. The response was a dense splash, as if a huge bladder full of oatmeal had burst.

"Dick, Linda, let's go in and get the weapons," Bob said. "But don't take any chances."

The three of them ran into the house, returning moments later with rifles and pistols. "Those things—they're all over inside," Linda said, "oozing along like slugs."

"One of them touched me," Dick said as he distributed the guns.

Brian stepped forward and started pouring in the gas. He could see coils undulating, thick and wet. A segment of heavy black flesh passed the window, and he saw goose bumps form on the skin where the gas splashed against it.

Then the can was empty. Brian looked to Loi. "How do we—"

Before he could protest she squatted, producing a book of paper matches. As she lit one and tossed it into the basement, he jumped back.

A blast of fire roared out of the window and Loi was rolling away, struggling to protect her belly from the violence of the motion.

He grabbed her, brought her to him, pulled her away from the fire-choked window. "I could've done that!"

"This is no time for discussion. We have to act."

A great surging movement began in the basement, in the fire.

"We've got to go to another house." With that Loi got a rifle and crossed the street to the Gilbert Swanson place. Gil and Erica were just gone, like most of the rest of Oscola.

Ellen, who had taken the shotgun Loi had been carrying, now blew the lock off the front door. They entered the house.

Nancy hesitated, looking sorrowfully back at the flames roaring out of her basement windows.

"You would have been caught," Loi said, attempting to console her.

At that moment a gigantic object rose past the smoking living room windows, burning with deep red flames, yellow smoke pouring off its black flesh. It came slopping up out of the basement amid clouds of smoke and steaming, pearl-gray masses of what appeared to be boiling mucus. The house around it disintegrated into kindling, couches and beds and books and appliances tumbling down its sides like foam on a wave. For a moment the humping thing had a roof.

The refrigerator, still festooned with messages and Chris's prized drawings, smashed down into the yard five feet in front of the West family. When it hit it flew open and covered them in frozen steaks and Healthy Choice dinners, vegetables and cans of Coke, leftover green beans and low-fat desserts. "I got a ice cream sandwich," Joey yelled.

Nancy staggered back, soaked in milk and orange juice, and went stiffly in the front door of the Swanson place without so much as a glance at Loi and Ellen.

"Now it knows we'll fight," Loi said. "It knows."

"He knows, Loi. I was with a person. Somebody."

"Very well, Bob. *He* knows."

Brian realized that his wife had just saved them all. She'd fought, just as she said she would, and Bob had fought beside her. He hoped their alliance would last.

This house was not as full as the last one had been. Seventeen people had dwindled to thirteen. Loi inventoried the little cadre. There were Wests, with Nancy in tears and her boys clinging to her. Then Sanghvi and Maya Gidumal, gentle souls, incapable even of firing a pistol. Brian's cousins, the Huygenses, who would probably fight like dogs if called upon. Then there was the priest. She tried to visualize Father Palmer in battle. Forget it.

Her question was, would these people respond to her as a leader? They needed her, she saw that. Unless she gave orders, nothing happened. Not even Bob could assume the role of the officer.

Very well, she would try. "We will wait until sunset, then get out on all-terrain vehicles. We know that things are OK in Glens Falls, from the radio. If we move fast, maybe we can use the cover of dark to make a run for it." Her idea was a good one, she felt, if it could be carried out. "We need to find some ATVs."

"I think we ought to be as quiet as we can, too," Brian added.

"Why?" Father Palmer asked.

"Something operating from underground probably uses sound to find things on the surface. The quieter we are, the better."

"We could create a diversion," Ellen suggested. "Go across the street, turn on the radio in that other house."

"The Cobb place?"

Loi joined in. "After we've found the ATVs, we go upstairs, stay absolutely silent until dark. Then we move."

Would it work? Brian had no idea. But he did know one thing: by their calm courage Loi and Bob had pulled the whole group together. They were no longer a helpless rabble of scared civilians, they were an organized band.

"The hard part's gonna be getting the ATVs," Dick said. "If none of the houses around here have them."

Loi addressed Ellen. "You go turn their radio on. Turn two radios on. And the TV, and the dryer. Leave it on its longest cycle."

"The dryer?"

"Put a shoe in it. We want voices and thumping. Like we're all in there."

Ellen met Loi's fiery eyes, and did not even consider refusing.

"Now," Loi said, "please, at once."

Ellen went into the yard, watching the raging destruction that was still unfolding across the street. The Wests' house was unrecognizable, an exploded belly choked with burning worms. The air was thick with oily smoke that stank like fish that has dropped down into the coals at a cookout. She turned away, her throat closing, and coughed—gagged, really—into her hand.

"Hurry up," came a sharp voice from behind her.

"Right, Loi." As Ellen hurried toward the Cobb house, others fanned out through the neighborhood searching for ATVs.

Only when she had reached her destination did Ellen think of something that even Loi had missed. It was stupid and obvious, too. They couldn't turn on radios and appliances because there was no electricity. They'd been listening to a battery-powered Sony at the Wests'.

There had to be an alternative. What would make noise in a house with no power? Turn on the water? Not in Oscola—each house had its own well, and the pumps were electric.

Fortunately they hadn't locked up, so it was no problem to open the front door and enter the world of these strangers. She had only the faintest memory of them. The wife was chunky, he was tall and had heavy glasses. Children? Yes, there was a toy truck lying on the floor near the television set. On the coffee table was an ashtray full of cigarette butts and a copy of yesterday's *Post-Star*, the Glens Falls paper. No *Gazette*, of course.

She went into the kitchen and tried the water, which ran weakly as the holding tank drained.

What to do?

The recent use of lawn-mower gas gave her an idea. She went into the garage, and found exactly what she needed.

She tugged their power lawn mower into the kitchen, leaning it on its side to fit it through the door. Then she pushed it into the middle of the family room. The mower had a dead-man's bar, which she fastened down with a tieback from one of the living room curtains.

It was a pretty room, if your taste ran to big floral prints and tufted recliner chairs. A game of Scotland Yard lay open on a card table. Beside it were some glasses of Coke, flat and warm. They'd been playing a family game when they'd gotten right up and just gone.

She pulled the lawn mower's starter cord. It was stiff and didn't give easily. On the first stroke, the engine rattled. Again she pulled it. There was a smell of gas now—which reminded her to look in the tank. Nearly empty.

She wondered how much longer she would live, and tasted bitter acid in her throat. "I've never even had a damn baby," she thought, and pulled the cord with a fury. The mower buzzed—and shot off into the couch. Tufts flew as the blade sucked up the ruffle and started eating a cushion. She grabbed the machine and yanked it back, eventually managing to disengage the gears.

Tamed at last, it sat there clattering and vibrating

and belching fumes. She went back to the garage, got a gallon tin of gasoline she found against the far wall, took it into the house and filled the mower's tank until it was brimming.

She went out onto the porch, trotted down the steps and into the street. She was appalled to see that poor Willie Rysdale's head was out from under the cloth. Worse, it had transformed, becoming a mass of black cords with hooks on their tips. When she drew close the cords all stiffened toward her, straining the wicked hooks in her direction.

The intact eye glared at her.

A shot rang out and the thing bounced off up the street in a spray of blood. Loi had been covering her from the porch. Another shot slapped into it and flung it farther. Lying across the end of the street Ellen saw two gigantic black objects like huge, supple tree trunks lying side by side. They emerged from the forest on one side of the intersection and disappeared into it on the other. They must have had a diameter of twenty feet or more. How long they might be she couldn't even guess.

At last the head was lifeless, a limp tangle of cords and vicious hooks. Another look up the street revealed two more of the huge, slick pipe-like objects sliding into place.

People were returning to the Swanson house. Pat Huygens was riding a very new-looking Suzuki Quadrunner. The others had cans of gas, Father Palmer had some bottled water, Dick and Linda Kelly had bread and cereal and other supplies.

To Loi it was a disaster. A single ATV was no help. "Now we go upstairs and wait," she said. "Nobody walks around, nobody talks." She looked at Joey and Chris. "This means you."

"Yes, ma'am," Chris said.

The group climbed the stairs and spread out in the large master bedroom. The boys sat on the bed munching Count Choculas from a box they'd found in the kitchen. After a time Father Palmer moved quietly toward the door. "Come back, Father," Loi said.

"Loi, I—"

"He wants to pee," Ellen said. "Right, Father?"

The priest nodded.

Loi doubted that the old man could be quiet enough using the toilet. "Get a bucket, put a towel in the bottom and do it there. No bucket, then either hold it in or use a corner of another room. You don't want to splash in a toilet or risk a flush."

He crept off.

Loi addressed their situation. "We have the problem of only one vehicle."

"There's a Jeep in the garage," Jenny Huygens said.

"We cannot use a Jeep. Our chance lies in going through the deep forest. No Jeep can do it."

"Then we have to go into town," Dick said. "Henry Fisk's a Suzuki dealer, he's got a bunch of Quaddies."

Father Palmer returned.

Bob spoke. "I look at it this way. The longer we hang on here, the more likely we are to see rescue."

Loi gave him such an appraising look that Brian worried that there might be friction brewing between the two of them after all.

"It's dangerous to wait," she said. As this terrible

day went on, she was becoming more and more uncertain of him. He'd been with the demons, deep in their tunnels and caves. They were invincible, incredibly cruel. So why had he been allowed to leave? Had he been possessed? Was he a spy, or an unfaithful adviser?

Perhaps. But when the two of them fought side by side, it was good.

She returned to her post at the window. The sun was down in the sky, the shadows had grown long. From the Cobb place there came a satisfying grumble of sound. She could feel her friends behind her, sense their desire to live.

This desire was universal, but life belonged only to the lucky and the strong.

Her baby moved within her. She was tired and hungry, and the stretched skin below her belly button ached. When she walked, she could feel the motion of the water in her womb.

Her baby . . . she laid her hands lightly on both sides of her stomach, closed her eyes and imagined that she could hear him dreaming dreams that would one day be woven into the future of the world.

If it had a future.

FOURTEEN

As people must have hidden at the back of caves when the world was still wild, the straggling, miserable band of survivors huddled together in the Swansons' master bedroom.

Loi considered them, Brian's cousin Dick and his wife, Linda, Bob and Nancy West and their boys, Father Palmer, Ellen, Pat and Jenny Huygens. The Gidumals, she noticed, had quietly gone. As long as Dr. Gidumal had been here, she'd felt a little less uneasy about her pregnancy. "Where are Sanghvi and Maya?" she asked in a whisper.

Nobody answered.

Loi had more to say. She spoke as softly as she could and still get some authority into her voice. "Since we didn't find enough ATVs here, we've got to walk into town to get what we need. We must live like fighters. We must give all to the fight."

"I don't think we need VC propaganda to pump us up," Bob said mildly. " 'We must give all to the fight.' That was one of your slogans, I remember it well."

"Then perhaps you'd like to go out and ask the demons to dance."

Bob's face flushed with anger, but he spoke softly.

"I think we can hold out right here if we stay organized and don't get crazy."

"Whisper," Loi said. She was beginning to feel as if she was fighting them for their own lives. "When something comes up through the floor and every other house is gone, then what?"

"That's not necessarily going to happen."

Loi had had enough of his reluctance. "You were with them for hours. What did they do to make you a coward?"

For a moment he looked ready to strike her. Ellen broke in, supporting Loi. "If she's right, what happens? What's your alternative?"

"We're organized. We shoot, and not at random."

Ellen's support helped Loi stand up to Bob, which was not easy for her to do. "When do you imagine that this rescue will take place? Ten minutes from now? An hour?" She tried to use her most reasonable tone of voice, but inside she was ready to scream.

"I don't know when. But inevitably."

This faith in rescue was typically American, and she was afraid that she would be unable to prevail against it. "If we were going to get saved, it already would have happened."

"I don't want to hear that," Father Palmer responded. "I think we should pray and hope."

Pat Huygens went to the window, looked out. "Niagara-Mohawk ought to know that there's a problem here, but where are they? And what about NYNEX? Where are the telephone trucks? We've been cut off. That's the reality of it."

"The demon will *not* let us get away. For whatever

reason, it wants everybody, not just the evil. If we remain passive we have no chance."

Bob regarded her. "I thought passivity was part of your makeup."

Loi would not call Bob a racist, because that would be unfair. But his innocent prejudices could make him seem cruel. She gave him a careful smile. "I left my passivity in the Chu Chi tunnels, Bob."

"We could consider this move," Brian said. "It's better than just sitting."

"Not for me," Dick said. "I agree with Robert here." Linda went close to her husband. "But we oughta do one thing. We oughta write 'help' on some sheets and put them out on the roof."

"I think that's a great idea." Nancy was cradling her younger son in her lap. Without medication, the older boy's burns had begun to hurt, and he was cuddled in the crook of her arm, his eyes closed.

They began to gather sheets and the heaviest tape they could find, to make their sign. There were questions about the number of sheets to use, the size of the letters, on and on. It became a project, a substitute for the real work of escape. They worked with quiet intensity, their silence punctuated from time to time by Jenny's coughs.

Loi waited helplessly as the day wore on. She let them carry out their project without argument. Maybe by dark they would realize that it was hopeless. She prayed that they would be given the time.

At three the Wests and the Dick Kellys and Pat Huygens went to the attic and squeezed through a dormer window onto the roof. They put up their sign, and also added the Swansons' American flag, which they stretched between stacks of books. The sheets were tacked down with roofing nails, but you didn't put holes in a flag. Dick wasn't sure you laid a flag on a roof—too much like putting it on the ground.

Loi borrowed cigarettes from Ellen, smoking and remembering her life before. Even the Blue Moon Bar was preferable to this, even the damnable tunnels. This was worse than that dripping, deadly prison, or the awful numbness of soul she had felt in Bangkok.

She spent time on the bed, sitting beside Brian. From time to time she kissed him. She was beginning to feel close to him again, and she could see that he was glad.

He laid his hand on their little Brian, and she enjoyed that very much. "Do you feel him move?"

"Yeah."

Silently, Ellen came down beside them, sitting with her legs tucked under her.

Loi thought she could work on the two of them. She took them into the hallway, spoke softly. "We must go alone. They will all be caught."

"I hate to leave them," Brian said.

"She's right, Brian," Ellen said. "We've got to move as soon as it gets dark."

Bob soon appeared in the doorway. "What's the big conference about?" he asked.

"Yeah," Pat Huygens agreed, appearing behind him. "No secret conferences."

Loi drew Brian and Ellen away from them. "I think Bob is dangerous."

"That's a hard thing to say."

"Brian, you don't escape from hell. He was sent."

"Loi, that isn't—"

"Hold on, Brian. She makes a good point. He couldn't have gotten away from them. So maybe she's right."

Instead of lowering her eyes as she would customarily have done, Loi gave her husband a hard, challenging stare. "The advice he gives could be from them."

Roughly, self-consciously, Brian hugged her. "I wondered about that myself, at first. But he seems so loyal and so much himself. It's hard to believe now."

"We should go as soon as the sun sets."

"Yes, maybe . . . but won't it be more dangerous at night?"

"Better concealment."

"Let's hope."

As the hours dragged toward evening Loi got more and more nervous. Ellen was completely on her side, at least, but Brian still wavered. The others gave every indication of planning to remain here overnight. Loi did not think for a moment that they would be left alone.

For the sake of her baby, she would leave here on her own. It would hurt, though, more than anything else she had ever done in her life.

Moving carefully to avoid making any telltale thumps, she took Ellen downstairs. She was looking for something—anything—that might be useful. They found an Adirondack atlas and took it back up with them, and spent their time sitting on the bed memorizing the trails that led south out of the Three Counties.

"Why do that?" Brian asked. "I know all the trails. We all do."

"I don't."

He gazed at her. "You have me."

Another hour passed, and Loi became aware of small sounds coming from outside. She thought she knew what they were. But she did not acknowledge them, not just yet. Nobody else noticed, and it was best that way.

Most of them were eating again. Her journey downstairs had encouraged the others to explore also. They'd found a big bag of Fritos in the pantry, and three cans of ranch-style beans.

Loi waited, poring over her map with Ellen.

Soon enough, there came a huge cracking noise. People looked at one another.

"Move quietly to windows if you want to see."

The Cobb place, where Ellen had left the running lawn mower, was heaving and twisting with a sound like continuous thunder.

Dust came up in clouds that were turned a delicate shade of gold by the setting sun.

"My God," Brian whispered.

"And yet you stay here."

Around the house the ground itself was blurring, beginning to melt, to run like a liquid. The rubble shuddered and shook, and started sinking. From its tangled center came a continuous flashing of purple light, so intense that Loi could feel a faint stirring within herself, even from this distance. Chris West pressed his face against the window. Jenny Huygens ran her fingertips along the screen.

"If we left, we'd go south," Brian said.

"Yes. Keep away from Towayda." Loi got the atlas and turned to the Cuyamora County map, pointed to Queen's Road. "We can cross the street and go up the ridge toward Lost Pond, then down to the center of town through Yelling Gorge. We'll come out right on Main, and we'll only cross two roads in the process."

Bob looked at the map. "Those things are out in the woods. They own the woods."

"They're here, too," Loi said. "Obviously."

"What about our sign on the roof?"

"Screw the sign, Bob!"

"Come on, Miss Maas! All I'm saying is we ought to leave a few people behind."

That would be foolish. Loi knew it. She chose her words carefully. "Then we would have to return for them. That would be dangerous."

"Going in those woods is dangerous!"

"If we stay here, we die."

"The Michaelsons tried the woods. I rest my case."

Loi became vehement. "We have to go right away. When they realize we weren't in that house, they're going to try this one." She took Brian's hand. "I have to protect our baby. Please come with me, Brian." She got to her feet, still holding on to him.

"Look, Loi—"

"Be quiet, Bob!" She glared at him. If she'd had a knife, she might have put it in his heart.

They all fell silent, all for the same reason. As the noises of destruction were dying away another sound was rising, the steady mutter of an engine. Everybody in the room had seen the Viper at one time or another, cruising the back roads or racing down the Northway. Those who'd had threatening encounters with it shrank from the windows. The others began to move closer, to try to see.

The car sat in the middle of the street, gleaming and unlikely in this neighborhood of small houses. "What's it got to do with this?" Bob asked. "I just can't understand why they would want a beautiful piece of machinery like that."

Loi saw the meaning: red was the Western color of blood and violence, the lines of the car were mean and lethal and incredibly beautiful all at once, and its speed was dominating. "Power and death," she said. "That is what it means."

Ellen nodded. "The messenger is the message. The car is a tool of communication—a warning, a threat."

"Where's the driver?" Bob asked in a choked, shaking voice. He had gone to the far side of the room.

Brian followed him. "Hey, buddy."

"Where's the damn *driver,* the one I saw when I thought I was going crazy?"

Loi whispered as softly as she could, barely moving her mouth, breathing the words. "Please be still. There is somebody downstairs."

It wasn't footsteps or breathing that betrayed the presence, but rather the creak of boards as a heavy form moved about the house. Loi listened, but the beating of her own heart grew so loud that it interfered.

"It's not . . . walking," Father Palmer murmured.

Loi put her finger against his lips.

The sound dragged slowly along the floor of the living room beneath them. Then they heard the scrape of moving furniture, the stealthy creak of a door.

Young Joey came closer to Loi. Tears were running

down his face. When she wiped his eyes, he smiled weakly at her, and she hoped that her own son would have such courage.

Her thoughts turned to escape routes out of the house. There was only the one stairway down. They might have to jump out a window. But there would be injuries . . . she herself would certainly be hurt.

She had waited too long.

Now they heard a sound at the foot of the stairs, as if bubbles were bursting in thick soup, or something sticky was slowly opening.

Father Palmer's lips began moving in a steady rhythm. What was prayer worth in a world that could produce horrors like this? Where was his God now?

There came a single loud flop, as if a fat beef liver had been dropped onto a butcher's board.

Jenny coughed a little.

"Be quiet," Loi breathed.

Again Jenny coughed, then stifled it. Her throat worked and another small sound came out. Mucus dribbled from her nose, tears of pain squeezed out of her eyes. "You must not," Loi whispered.

Jenny nodded vigorously, then convulsed, grabbing a pillow to stifle the sound.

A pair of black claws appeared at the top of the stairs. Jenny made gobbling sounds as she tried frantically to silence her next cough.

They all watched the claws, lying there as if they would never move again, as if they had always been there. They consisted of two thick, black nails crossed at their curved tips. They were perhaps two feet long, as large as the claws of a predatory dinosaur. They were easily sufficient to slice a man in half. If these had ever been human fingernails, they had been horrendously transformed.

Jenny's eyes were pouring tears, mucus was running in a stream from her nose, she was rocking back and forth, her hands jammed into her mouth.

Loi knew what would happen now, what always happened in war: the weak and the unlucky were about to die.

If only they didn't shoot their guns, if only they kept their heads and remained silent, then some of them might survive.

Father Palmer prayed on in a rhythmic whisper. Pat Huygens had his arms around his wife. Nancy and Bob held their children. Jenny watched with slow, wide eyes. Brian came near Loi. He had a pistol in his hand.

By all gods of luck and wisdom, do not let him be a fool.

Jenny's mouth flew open and she jerked away from her husband, shut her eyes, pitched forward and emitted a long, rolling, wet, barking grandmother of a cough. Her face going purple, her arms flailing, she coughed again and again and again.

With the perfect smoothness of a machine, the claws came up and snapped off her head. There was a sticky click, like the opening of a refrigerator door, and her body toppled.

For an instant the only sound in the room was that of blood hissing in a powerful stream from her neck.

Then both boys shrieked. Pat Huygens opened fire, the blasts of his pistol jarring the air in the small room. "Brian, Ellen, come," Loi shouted into the din.

Brian was staring in fascinated horror as more claws swarmed up the stairs, flowing on their long, supple arms with fluid grace.

When Brian didn't react, Ellen marched up and slapped him across the face. He blinked, seemed to reenter life, and followed the two of them along the short hallway and up the stairs into the attic. The dormer window was still open. Ellen pushed ahead and climbed out. Then she turned around and gave Loi the support she needed.

Brian was behind, and then came the Wests. Inside the house terrible screaming started, and purple light began to flash.

"They're all still in there," Brian moaned. "Dickie and Linda are *in there!*" Then Father Palmer's head appeared at the window and Bob and Brian hauled him up. They shut the window, but it could not be locked from outside.

"We've got to get moving," Ellen said.

The street was filled with long black trunks, six or seven of them. They were sweating thick liquid and exuding smaller limbs, each ending in a claw. They passed into every house, and in the windows the smaller trunks could be seen surging and seething about.

Downstairs, the screams became a high babble, a mixture of crazed delight and abject terror. The house shook. They heard a sound like something cooking in hot fat. A smell came, electric-hot and meaty. Purple light flashed out of the windows, and every flash made their skin tickle delightfully.

Father Palmer looked up toward the pearl-blue sky. "Dear Lord, if you exist, you will come to us now."

"Father?"

"He will come on his fiery chariot, Brian! He will either come in glory right this second or it's all a lie! I tell you, this is too terrible, there has never *been* a human soul bad enough to deserve this, not even Torquemada, not even Hitler!"

"Oh, Father," Chris said.

The priest went silent. "I think a cock just crowed," he mumbled.

The screams became more frantic. Loi could picture the people in the purple light, their eyes bulging, their tongues lolling, shrieks pouring from their twisting mouths. It was a slow process, slow and meticulous and, despite the pleasure, obviously agonizing.

She looked at the old priest, now weeping in shame. "Come," she said in the strongest tone of voice she could manage, "we're going to town."

Nancy stared at her. "To *town?* Just like that, bang, we go to town?"

"Not much choice now, Nancy." She took Brian's pistol, which he had thrust into his waistband. "Bob, I want you where I can see you. You will go on point. And take the correct path, or I will shoot you in the back."

Nancy put her hands to her cheeks. Bob smiled a little, shook his head. "I'm not a traitor to your cadre, Loi. This isn't the war."

They made a rope of the sheets that had been used for their rescue sign, tied it to the radiator under the dormer window.

To test it, Bob climbed down first. It held, and the others began to follow him. Nancy came with the two boys, then Ellen. Loi followed, lowering herself carefully into Bob's arms. Then Brian came.

Father Palmer peered over the edge. "I need help," he said. As if in answer a long, gray arm came out the window, extending three half-formed claws. They were cupped around what looked like a purple jewel or glass eye.

Then they all saw the figure behind the arm, a misshapen travesty of Dick Kelly, his lips ripped back, his tongue splayed across huge teeth like yellow, knotted fists, his left eye darting from place to place with a lizard's jerky glance. A net of veins had grown over the teeth. His skin was a gleaming, chitinous mosaic.

"Oh, Jesus!" Brian gasped.

Bob made a small sound in his throat, then suddenly clapped his hands over his face.

The glass object flickered, then glowed brightly. Father Palmer was hit full in the face with the purple light from a distance of an inch. His head shook furiously, as if he'd been slapped almost senseless. But he laughed.

The horrible remains of Dick Kelly grunted, and they could see that he was engaged in a titanic inner struggle. Part of him was trying to turn the light away from the priest. The arm wavered, the claws snapped, the poor, contorted ruin of his face pulsated with effort.

For a moment the thrall of the light was broken, and Father Palmer began coming down the sheets, falling more than climbing.

"Get his legs, Brian!" Ellen could see black, dripping flesh seething past all the windows of the house. As Brian moved forward, sticky threads floated toward him out of the first-floor windows. Each had an anchor-like hook on the end. As they came near him they went rigid.

Loi cried out. "Careful, Brian!"

Now Pat Huygens slid up beside what remained of Dick. He was glowing brightly, his skin shimmering and undulating. Under it could be seen thousands of yellow-gold shapes, running wildly.

"Oh, no," Ellen said, backing away. "No."

Father Palmer slid fast down the rope, dropping with a resounding thud to the ground.

Miraculously, he was able to walk. "I think I'm OK," he said, looking down at himself. "A hell of a jolt!"

But when he lifted his face into the evening light, Nancy threw her head back as if hit, her boys skittered away, even Bob cried out, a sharp yell that was quickly squelched.

The priest raised his hands to his cheeks, his eyes going wide. He felt along the cobbled surface of his left cheek, his fingers flitting from knob to knob, jerking back when they touched the sharp places. "What—what—"

Ellen said, simply, "The light. You were too close."

It had twisted the priest's features. Had it also captured his mind? Loi touched her pistol. "How do you feel, Father?"

"I—I feel fine." Again he touched his face. "Do I—look . . ."

"Awful," Nancy moaned.

"It felt—dear God, it was the most wonderful, wonderful—" He glanced back, saw all the activity behind the windows of the house.

Without another word the old man started running toward the woods. This was a good sign, and Loi was relieved. It might become necessary to shoot one of them, it was entirely possible. But she wasn't made to shoot people, it wasn't her nature and she dreaded it.

They all followed the priest, stopping in the woods just out of sight of the house. Brian and Loi, the Wests, Ellen and the priest—the group had dwindled terribly.

A sound as of somebody stepping on a gigantic tube of toothpaste was followed by angry buzzing. The husk of Pat had split. "Run," Ellen cried. A thousand of the most terrible hornets imaginable roared out, creatures from the age of giants, with red eyes and fiery, burning bodies. Their wings droned low, and the sound contained a moan, and its tone reminded them all of Pat's voice. As they left him, his skin collapsed in on itself.

The group ran for their lives.

The ridge that rose behind the house was cruelly steep, and their climb was slow and difficult. There was no trail and the underbrush was thick, the trees close together. Nobody looked behind, nobody had the strength. Loi maneuvered Bob to the front of the group. "You will be point man."

"Yeah, you're probably good at picking off point men."

"Very good. Go faster!"

"Get off my case!"

"I will never do that, Bob."

He shook his head, kept moving.

"Baby, are you holding up OK?" Brian asked from behind her.

Loi's heart was rocking in her chest, her legs

screaming protest. "I am full of strength," she gasped.

"You can make it," Bob said over his shoulder.

"There's a bug on me," Chris cried.

Bob came racing down from above, Nancy grabbed her child. Loi went to them. "It's just a wasp," she said when Nancy opened her fist and showed her its remains. "But the next one will not be a wasp. We must hurry."

"I'm tired," Joey said. "It's too steep."

Father Palmer was huffing. Thick blood was oozing down his cheek, which now looked like the skin of an alligator. Flies swarmed around him.

Loi put her hand on Bob's shoulder. "Back to point. Let's go."

"All right!"

Again they started. "Nobody stops for anything again," Loi said.

"I'm tired!"

"I am too, Joey. But if you value your life, do not stop."

That silenced even the children.

These people had to be treated harshly. They were strong and healthy, but unused to even the smallest adversity. As a child she'd seen men beaten to superhuman efforts of tunnel-digging or defense. People are capable of far more than they realize, but this is something they must be forced to discover.

Her mind roved ahead, focusing on Fisk's and the ATVs. They'd move by night, move due south toward population centers, and hope that Oscola and Towayda were the only towns affected. Then the area could be nuclear bombed, pulverized until it was nothing but a crater made of melted stone, and the mountains themselves razed.

The door to the inner world would be sealed again, and a woman could raise a family in peace.

Overhead she heard a drone. It was high, above the top of the thick forest. But she knew what it was. The insects were prowling, looking for them. How far from the house could they go?

Her legs felt like stone, the muscles beneath her belly screamed in pain. She smiled. "We are nearly there," she said. "See, it's not so hard!" She forced herself to hold her head up, to go a little faster.

The drone above the trees grew louder, then fell away. Why didn't the damned things come down? Maybe they couldn't. Or something worse was happening, something they couldn't anticipate.

The droning ceased altogether.

She looked up, but could see only leaves dappled by faded sunlight. Where they broke, there were patches of deepest blue. In some of them stars floated free.

From below came the sound of a horn honking. It honked and honked, and she began to want to know what was happening. She couldn't climb, but others might be able to. Ellen was lithe. "Can you go up a tree and tell me what you see?"

Ellen looked up doubtfully. "I never climbed one of those things in my life."

"I can do it," Chris said.

"No!" His mother grabbed him to her. "Ellen, you try."

They hoisted her into the lower limbs of a maple. With surprising speed she climbed hand over hand into the distant top. Her body grew tiny in the vault of the forest, and finally she was so high that she could see beyond the roof of leaves.

A few moments later and she was dropping down with an agility born of great fear. "It's the Gidumals," she said. "They're in their car and those bugs are swarming over it. Millions of them!"

Far, far away there were high screams. Maya and Sanghvi were being absorbed. Loi could hardly bear to imagine that excellent man being transformed. How could his humanity ever be destroyed? He was too good a man to become anything less. What was going on that the demons were taking good people? Where was the justice?

"Let's go," Loi said. Soon they were climbing again and her breath grew hot as it raced in and out. Her lungs were screaming for more air, the baby within her was jumping. "Your womb is like glass . . ."

Sanghvi. What would she do without him?

She went on, the screams of the Gidumals ringing in her ears and her soul.

As they struggled upward the boys sobbed with effort, their parents urging them on. Then Nancy had to pick up Joey. Chris began to drop back.

Bob suddenly stopped. "We've had it!"

The others caught up with him, gathered around.

"This isn't you talking, Bob," Loi said.

"My kids are exhausted."

"They have to keep on."

"You're right," Bob said. "I'm sorry." He took Joey from his mother. "Come on, big guy."

"So we go." Loi waved them on. "Go." She took Chris's hand. "You can make it with me. I have special strength for both of us."

They walked up and up, and she suffered greatly
from her weight. The flat muscles of her underbelly
began to ache, and a sour, dry taste filled her mouth.
Even holding hands with Chris seemed a great effort. "You thirsty, Chris?"

"Yeah."

"Me too."

Very slowly the woods thinned, became brighter.
Then they abruptly gave way.

They broke out onto the top of the ridge, where
there were only pitch pines and scrub, and long,
wind-polished stones.

From here they could see across Oscola toward
the north, and back south toward Ludlum.

Above them larks spun in the slow air, their wings
flashing in the last sun, their voices whistling shrill
excitement. Loi staggered, Brian caught her around
the waist, Bob gently tried to take her gun.

"I'll shoot!"

"All right! Jesus! Brian, all of a sudden she hates
me!"

"I hate what is in you."

"There's nothing except me!"

"Yes, what's in my husband?" Nancy asked. "What
do you hate, Loi?"

Loi spoke as reasonably as she could. "I think you
know very well that the demons are within you, that
they are trying to use you."

He laughed a little, a miserable, unconvincing
sound.

A moment later the whole group was assembled
on the spine of the mountain. It was Father Palmer
who first looked to the north and noticed Towayda.

He fell to his knees, awed and terrified all at once, whimpering.

The whole sky flickered with purple light.

It infected them with a frenetic sort of elation, like some drug. The two boys groaned and danced from foot to foot. Loi sensed movement inside her. "He kicks hard, Brian."

So at last it was finished, hell had come to the surface of the earth. She took a long, studied breath, observed one of the small secret silences that she used to restore her inner self. "Husband, we must not wait here a moment."

"We can't get away from that," Bob said.

"In our army the defeatist was shot."

"Oh, come on! That's the most ridiculous thing she's said yet! Brian, can't you shut her up?"

"Loi—"

"He was the one who said to stay for rescue. But there was no rescue. Now he says it's all hopeless. That is also a lie." She slapped her belly through her sweat-soaked shirt. "I will live!"

Brian embraced her, feeling her strength, drinking in her power.

"We go," she said. "You in front, Bob."

"No, I don't want to be in front anymore."

"Do it." If the demons attacked, let their own puppet be their first victim.

He stared her down, his expression complex with sadness and hurt, and something that could have been hatred, or perhaps an emotion very much more alien than that.

She did not waver.

The little group straggled off into the spreading

dark, making their way down toward their beloved town.

Above them the larks circled, and to the west the sun set in an increasingly angry sky. Northward in the mountains another world was awakening, savage and cruel, struggling in its ugly purple light to be born.

FIFTEEN

1.

The little party from Queen's Road struggled down the mountain and into Oscola's familiar streets.

Chairs and tables from the Mills Cafe were strewn about in the street. Office furniture, paperbacks and bottles from the drugstore, dozens of boxes of disposable diapers, waterguns, baseball caps, lay in piles. The gas station's pumps had been bent on their foundations so that they stood at crazy angles. Handy's was split like a fish, its guts of magazines and cigars and candy spilled out before it. The Rexall sign, circa 1932, was smashed to bits in the gutter. Even the Village Green was ruined, its gazebo flattened to kindling, its huge shagbark hickories ripped asunder by fantastic and malevolent energy, split down their middles, left with their leaves slowly shriveling.

The destruction had been wanton and extremely violent, but also full of awful, cunning care. Chicken parts were rammed into coffeepots from the Mills, cigars jammed down the throats of dead kittens from the Pet Pantry, car seats lying on roofs, the front half of a large dog dangling from the shattered Citgo sign.

Forgetting their danger, the need to hurry, the little group halted on Main Street, staring in disbelief. Nancy West whispered again and again, "No, no, no." Her husband had assumed the stolid pose that he took at accident sites. Chris picked up an Uncle Scrooge comic book from the street, rolled it up, and put it in his hip pocket. Joey said, "Candy, Mommy," as he touched a Milky Way with his toe.

The destruction had been wrought with a tornado's monstrous attentiveness. A crate of hair dryers had been jammed through the wall of the Excelsior Tower, and they jutted out of the brick surface like some mad work of conceptual art. Ellen's papers and files blew about their feet, and she saw the body of her desk smashed into a counter full of black girdles with red accents from the Mode O'Day. The top of the desk lay on the street, its blotter still neatly in place. She walked closer and found a cabinet, its drawers thrown open and filled with something that looked like mucilage and smelled like wet human skin. She reached down, disgusted but wanting to reclaim her possessions.

Loi knocked her hand aside. "Don't touch it! Nobody touch anything! No telling about diseases."

They went up the middle of the street together, Bob and Brian behind Loi, Nancy and Ellen and the kids behind them. Father Palmer struggled along at the rear, his breath whistling through the twisted black stump that his nose had become.

Getting a heavy enough dose of the light, it seemed, started changes that did not stop. His left eye was fiercely veined, filmed over by a dense, milky membrane. The skin of the left side of his face was now made up of even thicker tiles, like a turtle's back, and each was centered by a fat welt.

The priest's breath hissed, his tongue went around and around, patrolling the fissures that were turning his mouth into a hole.

Absent a mirror, he remained innocent of his true condition. Touch told him that something was very wrong, but he couldn't possibly have imagined just how awful it really was. Nobody could have; his disfigurement was so extreme that it was outside human experience.

A naturally cheerful man, he had even regained some of his good spirits. He'd decided that he had to keep up morale, so he sang as he walked, a catchy old Kingston Trio tune from back in the days when he had a guitar and something of a voice. "Back to back, belly to belly, well I don't give a damn 'cause I done that already." Again and again he bleated out the only verse that he remembered.

"For God's sake, stop him singing the Zombie Jamboree," Nancy West muttered as they passed the Citgo.

"Better be quiet, Father," Bob said.

"I'm sorry. I suppose the Kingston Trio's a little behind the times, isn't it?"

Nancy peered up at the flashing sky and the tumbling angry clouds. "I hate you," she shouted. "I hate you!"

"Mommy, Mommy," Joey shrilled.

"How can you be so noisy?" Loi could walk through dry leaves in total silence. These people couldn't be quiet on a flat street, with all their stomping and roaring.

Father Palmer went to Nancy. "The Lord is here,"

he rasped, attempting to whisper. "The Lord is with us and helping us right now."

Nancy turned bitterly away from him, her face reflecting disgust.

Loi worried that his infection might penetrate very deep. Was his soul being transformed along with his body? She watched him as he humped along leaking fluids, and thought he might bear more scrutiny than Bob did.

How quick her mind was to recapture the habits of that time long ago. She would have thought she had forgotten the sense of careful suspicion instilled in her by Wonmin Kyo, the stern, genial shadow who had been the political officer in her cadre. The men had mostly been entirely indifferent to her, hardly even aware of her existence. He had taught her to listen and report back.

Loi kept on walking, observing and assessing. Even as she scanned windows and roof lines, she evaluated the actions of each member of the group, especially those under suspicion.

"We've got to keep moving," she said. "There's no time for crying about this now." She'd seen villages a thousand years old burned to ashes. People made a mistake being upset by ruins. The first thing was to stay alive, then find a place to start over.

Nobody heard her. Nancy was having hysterics because Father Palmer had embraced her, in a misguided effort at comfort. They were preoccupied with trying to calm her down, and to make the old priest understand why he couldn't. His face grinned hideously, and Loi noticed a net of veins growing across his teeth, which now looked yellow and soft, like big pieces of chewing gum. Only shooting it to pieces had killed the living head of the poor Rysdale boy. She wondered when they would have to begin on the priest.

"Listen to me," she said. Nancy was still sobbing, and now Ellen was having trouble, too, crouching before the remains of her office desk, running her hands over it.

Loi raised her pistol and fired into the air.

The report froze them. "All right," she said into the stunned silence. "No need for me to be quiet, you're all so noisy." She tucked the pistol back into her belt. "Now we go."

They followed her up Main, toward the darkened bulk of Fisk's Garage. "Get food," she said as they passed the devastated ruin of the Indian Market grocery. "But be careful. Nothing with any strange substances on it." The glue-like material was everywhere in and around the store, dripping from tumbled counters, off ruined crates of melons, thickest around burst cans.

A slick of melted frozen food covered the floor, making it treacherous to walk without slipping in melted spinach soufflé and breaded veal cutlet dinners. The fresh-vegetable bins had been upended, as if something had looked behind them for people. The meat locker was wide open, its door pushed up through the ceiling into the second floor, where Caroline Chipman had her art gallery. Like the rest of the food, the meat was ripped up and damaged, but not eaten.

Fisk's Garage was devastated. It was getting dark and they had no flashlights, so they had to pick their way carefully among the glass shards and twisted ruins of yard tractors and all-terrain vehicles to get in.

Gas tanks had been pulled off, axles bent, tires torn to bits. The cylinders and spark plugs from engines that had been ripped open littered the floor around the remains of the vehicles.

"Let's look in the back," Loi said in a brisk voice. "Come on, there's no time to lose."

"No!" Bob was in front of her, barring the door.

She took out her pistol. I will do it if I have to, she thought, although it made her sick at heart.

They faced one another. "Loi, I have this very strong feeling that we shouldn't go in there."

"If we don't find transportation, we're going to get caught, Bob."

"There's something in there!"

Chris ran to his father. He looked from Loi's face to the barrel of her gun, holding his dad around the waist. She felt tears come to the corners of her eyes. "Resolution is the soldier's credo," they had taught her.

"You have to let her through," Ellen said.

"We'll all be killed if we open that door." Bob was sweating. In the gloomy half light, Loi could see that his eyes were glassy with fear.

"I am going to step forward and open the door," Loi said.

Bob gathered up his wife and sons.

Loi threw the door open.

Father Palmer cried out, "Glory to God!"

There stood four beautiful Suzuki ATVs in picture-perfect condition, smelling faintly of gas and new paint, gleaming.

For a moment they were brightly illuminated by a

distant flash of lightning, then long thunder rolled back and forth between the mountains.

Behind her she heard sobbing. She turned to see Bob sinking to the floor, his shoulders heaving. He looked up at her. "You oughta shoot me," he said miserably. "My God, I'm possessed."

"From now on, no matter what you think is right, you trust me."

"I'm going to do everything I can to be loyal to all of us. You're my people. But I have these . . . feelings that make me want to do different."

"Never trust yourself. Never!" She sighed. Maybe he would be all right and maybe he wouldn't. She hoped for the best. For the moment, she saw another problem. "Where are the keys to these things?"

"We can hot-wire 'em in a second," Chris announced, marching up to the closest one. In moments he had them running.

"Where did you learn that?" Nancy asked him.

"I forget."

As Ellen tried the seat on one of the vehicles, Brian and Bob raised the door to the street. Although they were designed for only one rider, each must somehow take two.

"Just one damn minute, you people!"

They all turned. Standing in the shadows of the glassed-in office was the figure of Henry Fisk. He strode to the middle of the room. His scruffy jacket and John Deere cap made him look inoffensive, but he was carrying a weapon that Loi recognized instantly: an AK-47. She became very still.

"What do you think you're doing?"

"Hi, Henry," Brian said mildly. "Just lookin' over some of your machines."

"The hell! You're stealin' 'em."

So deep she felt more than heard it, Loi became aware of the sound of an engine coming in from the outside, loud enough to rise above the steady idling of the ATVs. It was heavy equipment. "We have to leave."

"You sure are right about that, China girl." Fisk turned to Brian. "Get your ass out of my sight. And take Shanghai Lil here with you."

"Take it easy, Henry," Bob said. "You calm down or I'll have to put you under arrest."

"You? You escaped from the psycho ward down at Ludlum Community. They're looking for you from here to Buffalo!"

"They might have been. Not anymore. You know what's happening around here, Henry, as well as we do."

"No, that was a dream, that there. I thought it was real, I sure did. But it was a dream. I mean, Allie's lying on the back porch with a bicycle pump sticking out of the side of her head. That's not real, that's a nightmare! And Junie and Charlie, they—they—oh, shit, Brian, tell me it's a damn nightmare!"

"It's real, Henry. Look at the priest."

Fisk glanced at Father Palmer, then lowered his head. Loi knew how a man feels at such a moment of realization. She laid her hand on the butt of her pistol. He might well put down his weapon. Or he might shoot everybody in sight.

Outside, the engine note was now distinct. It was more than one machine, many more. "We can't get away," Fisk moaned. His head remained down, but his assault rifle was still pointing straight at them.

"We must try to, Henry!" He didn't respond. Loi took a step toward him.

"Don't you move, slant-eyes!"

Bob realized that Fisk was capable of killing her without a second thought. She was nothing to him, just a Chink. But not Bob West. Fisk would hesitate to shoot a man he'd known all of his life, a respected member of the community. Bob stepped in front of Loi. "You put that thing down, Henry. And stop calling her names."

"Bob, I'm warning you."

"Give me the gun, Henry."

"Fuck you!"

"Henry—" Bob took another step.

The AK-47 clicked nastily. Bob could see a vein pulsing in Fisk's neck. He was about to shoot. Another second and they were all going to be dead. He spoke quickly. "You remember that yard tractor I bought from you last summer, the Toro? It's running damn good, Henry." He took another step closer.

The building shook a little. Dust filtered down from the ceiling. That meant only one thing: action in the ground underneath. "Henry, we have to hurry!"

"That was nothing! It was *nothing!*"

"Was Allie nothing? Is Father Palmer nothing? It's all real, Henry. Give me the gun."

Fisk hesitated. Bob approached him. "Hand it over, Henry."

Behind them in the dark somebody made a protracted spitting sound. "My teeth," Father Palmer hissed, pronouncing it "teess." He'd tried to chew some beef jerky he'd picked up along the way. His attempts to drag the mess out of his mouth made a noise like a child playing in wet clay. Henry Fisk watched this, appalled. "What happened to him?"

"Got hit up close by that light."

"Purple light? I seen that. Made me feel funny. Made Junie and Charlie . . . made 'em worse than him." The priest let out a slopping noise, snorted. "I'll get you a towel, Father." Putting down the rifle, he went over to a sink the mechanics used, and brought the priest a roll of paper towels.

Bob picked up the weapon. Loi came close to him. She held out her hands.

"I can do this, Loi."

"I want to trust you, but I'm not sure I can."

"Do you know how to use it?"

She shook her head.

"Then you'd better leave it with me. Somebody could get hurt."

"An AK is easy to use." She grasped the weapon.

They both held it. "Loi, I know something's been done to me. But I can control it. We started this thing as a team, you and I. Let it stay that way."

The floor cracked from one end of the room to the other. More dust sifted down. A growing vibration told of movements beneath the earth.

Loi wasted no time. "We go now."

They got on the bikes, and after a short struggle with the seating arrangements, moved off into the dark. Fisk jogged along behind them nattering about his loss.

2.

The street was a gray strip between the shadows of buildings. Loi was sure she'd heard machinery, but it was nowhere in sight. Then her quick eyes detected movement. "There are vehicles out there," she said in a voice just loud enough to be heard over their own engines. They were coming straight up Main from the direction of the Towayda Road. To escape them, it would be necessary to either go back toward Mound and Queen's Road where they'd come from, or ride out into the woods.

At first the others saw nothing. Finally Bob made out the slowly moving shadows. They were so wide and low that he didn't at first understand what they were. But when he saw them clearly, the shape became familiar. "Those are humvees."

They were absolutely dark. Loi watched carefully. "I count six. Everybody be quiet. Get ready to move out fast."

Bob was astonished at her. "But that's the U.S. Army!"

Suddenly Loi was behind him with her hand over his mouth. "So it seems. But we must be careful. Do you agree?" She pressed the flat side of her gun against his back.

Only when Bob nodded was he released.

Ellen was the first to see the lights that had appeared at the other end of the street. "Oh Jesus, here comes a car."

They all looked. "I think that's Judge terBroeck," Brian said. "That's his car." It was coming up from Mound Road. Loi saw that they were now trapped

between the car and the slowly advancing humvees.
Their only escape route was to go through the alley,
across the yards of the houses behind it, and up
onto the ridges.

There was a flicker of purple light from the front
of the lead humvee.

Nancy started to walk out into the street. Loi put
her hand on her shoulder. "Don't be a fool."

"Look, those are humvees, à la the Gulf War. This
is the American Army and we're saved." She looked
to her husband for support.

"Listen to Loi," he said.

"Get back. You do it."

"But those are our people!"

"We cannot know that."

She came back.

"You've never been in a war," Loi said. "We have
no room for mistakes." She paused. "Do you see the
foot soldiers?"

Nancy looked. "No. There aren't any . . . are
there?"

"There are nine soldiers coming down the street
hugging the walls. They're in full chemical protective dress. They're wearing some kind of night vision
equipment on their faces. They are heavily armed."

"I don't even see them!"

"Whisper! Always!"

"Go easy on her, Loi."

"No, Bob, not if she's taking these risks." She
looked out across the dark. "They are in front of the
drugstore now. Walking parallel to the humvees."

"I see them," Nancy muttered.

To Ellen they looked like robots, with huge mechanical eyes and glistening black metal where their

faces ought to be. Something about their movements was wrong. They came slowly along, looking into doors and windows. The humvees moved along ahead of them.

In a matter of minutes, the soldiers were going to be peering down this alley with their light-amplification goggles.

Loi gathered the group around her. She barely breathed her words. "Get on the ATVs. When the humvees are past, we go out quick. We'll have to hope we surprise the soldiers when we pass them. We'll go as far as Mound, then turn south into the woods. Can everybody get his engine started?"

Quickly, Chris taught his father and Brian which wires to touch together. Ellen had no trouble, and Nancy had already seen him do it. Henry Fisk bristled but said nothing.

As they came closer together, the lights of the judge's car illuminated the first of the humvees. It was a dead, dark black, the blackest color Loi had ever seen.

The first humvee passed the alley, then the second.

With a squeal of brakes, the third stopped, neatly blocking the entrance.

They were trapped. They shrank back into the dark between two buildings. There remained for them only a narrow view of Main, illuminated by the lights of the judge's car.

He came into the lights. He was emaciated, far more so than he had been even two days ago. His dark blue double-breasted suit hung on his frame like a slack sail.

Brian recalled the tall figure he'd glimpsed in the

woods, the time he'd been pulled to the judge's
house. There was that same grave stillness, that
same sense of evil dignity.

"Now listen up," the judge shouted into the dark.
"We've got the U.S. Army here to help us out!"

Loi noticed that he wasn't shouting in any particular direction, or using names. They had not yet
been discovered.

That wouldn't last. The oncoming soldiers were
bound to see them.

"It's all over and we've won," the judge continued,
his voice radiating authority. "There's been a tragedy
here. An experiment being conducted by a scientific
institute failed and a door was opened into something that we don't understand. But the military has
things under control and we're safe. You can come
out now. There's even a field dressing station set up
outside town. So come out, come out all of you!"

Loi saw movement in the dark interior of the
drugstore. Two women and three men whom she
didn't know appeared. Then came Sam Young and
his sweetheart, Henrietta Lohse. Others followed,
hidden by the dark.

"Don't any of you move," Loi said to her group.

"That's bull," Fisk said firmly, speaking for the first
time since he'd reached the alley. "Judge terBroeck is
a fine man." He walked past them and joined the
small knot of people now clustering around the
judge.

Ellen saw this as a rapidly deteriorating situation.
"If we stay here, the soldiers are gonna notice us."

"We have to assume that they already have."

Things were changing quickly in the street. The
soldiers had abandoned their building-to-building

search and were hauling an ungainly black device out of the back of the judge's car. It did not have the appearance of a weapon. Like the humvees, it was so black that it was hard to see. Thick, tapering cables jutted up from it at odd angles and drooped down around the sides. It began to clank, then to emit a low humming sound. The soldiers stepped away. Apparently under its own power, the thing began gliding toward the knot of survivors.

Brian thought it was the ugliest object that he had ever seen. It was squat and fat like the body of an old-fashioned furnace. There were bars on its sides, and behind the bars something shiny, like black glass. It had the squat, dense appearance of something designed for work with great heat.

With a hiss like a bus door opening, its cables stiffened. They pointed at the survivors who had accepted the judge's promise and begun to approach. "Hey, Judge," Young began.

"Now just take it easy," the judge said. "Come on ahead." Again Brian felt that august presence.

A leader, a general, a monarch. Concealed in the body of the judge, him.

The tips of the cables adjusted themselves with great finesse, until each one was aimed at a specific individual. Two were not needed and they retracted with the sound of somebody sucking up spaghetti.

One of the women from the drugstore suddenly broke and ran. "Calm down now, Joanie," the judge called in a gentle voice. "This is just high-tech testing equipment, it won't hurt us."

"That's Joanie Dooley," Father Palmer whispered. "She's one of my deaconesses."

"Honestly, Joanie," the judge said, "I thought you had better sense than this."

She was running like hell now, right down the middle of the street.

Suddenly the judge's left arm slid outward, extending from his sleeve as if made of rubber. As it got longer and longer, people screamed, began to cluster together.

It grabbed Joannie Dooley around the neck and dragged her back with such speed that both of her shoes flew off and spun away. He dropped her in a heap at the feet of the weeping townsfolk, and in the next instant the black glass in the machine glowed a roiling, angry purple, and flashes of light spat from the tip of each extended cable into their faces.

"Shoot him," Brian cried.

The head turned, the eyes flashed. He saw them, the soldiers saw them.

Loi hopped on an ATV. "Go, go, go!" To her horror, the Wests went charging for the street, followed by Ellen. They should have turned around and gone out the alley, the fools! She had no choice but to follow. "Go, Brian, stay with them!"

A series of extremely bright purple flashes erupted as the ATVs worked their way around the blocking humvee. Ellen closed her eyes, but still felt a shudder of unwanted delight.

When she opened them again all nine of the people who had gone to the judge were down on their knees gagging, their fingers gripping their throats. Knotted masses of dark mucus were pouring from their mouths and noses.

The purple light flickered continuously now, bathing them in its glow. They were moaning, but it wasn't a sound of pain. Far from it.

The ATVs roared into the street. "You," the judge roared, "you!"

Bob pulled the trigger of the AK-47 and bullets sprayed, sparked off the hood of the lead humvee, exploded against the sputtering machine, sent four of the soldiers flying up against the far sidewalk, apparently killing them.

To get out of town they had to pass not only soldiers and humvees, but also the judge and his machine.

Ellen could see that the victim nearest her was full of moving humps, kicking and flopping his arms and shaking his head with a furious, impossible energy, like a windup toy gone crazy. The intensity of this motion caused him to rotate slowly in the street. She glimpsed his face, but did not recognize it, such was the distortion.

Henry Fisk made noises like a bird caught in a net, squawks punctuated by piping shrieks. His muscles were full of bulges the size of grapefruits, his face was oozing down the bones of his skull. He struggled, he shook, he groaned like a man in the extremity of sexual excitement. Then his head began to go back and forth, faster and faster, until his pop-eyed stare was just a blur, and spittle and raw muscle and gobs of melted skin were spraying like a multicolored fountain. Now his lips sounded like some kind of berserk lawn-mower motor. A long, thin leg or mandible popped out of his mouth, extended upward, and began sailing round and round his head like a lariat.

"We've got to help them," Father Palmer managed

to gabble. Behind Ellen on her ATV, he threw his arms around her, trying to reach the brake.

"No!"

She gunned the motor, but the machine swerved violently. He'd gotten hold of the handlebars.

The sight of their confusion caused two of the cables to exude from the machine and begin swaying toward them. The sizzling grew louder. There was an almost human quality to it, as if a ten-year-old was trying to sound like the biggest, meanest snake he could imagine.

The machine focused on Ellen and Father Palmer. To give it room the soldiers pressed themselves back against the walls. "It's not painful, Ellen," Judge terBroeck said. She saw now that his mouth didn't move when he talked. His face was a mask. Behind the eyes she could see black, gleaming material, rushing and seething.

"Ellen, come on," Loi cried.

Once more the AK-47 chattered. This time the bullets went through the judge, causing him to flounce but not to fall. Again his arm stretched, and suddenly it had the rifle and was hurling it off into the dark. "We have a right to do this!"

"You have no right," Ellen shouted back.

The judge rose to his full height, lifted his arms. They went up and up, far into the sky, and then came snaking down toward Brian and Loi. But Brian hit the gas and their ATV darted ahead. The arms flopped after them, the hands snatching at Loi's back. She clutched Brian and screamed as they ripped at her shirt, trying to reach around and get to her stomach.

Behind the judge the machine continued its busy

cooking of the ones who had been captured. It was not only sizzling but making sighs, metallic shrieks, and a light, continuous thumping like the excited beating of a heart.

Meanwhile, another part of the machine stiffened a cable toward the departing ATVs. Purple light flashed and Loi felt it like angels caressing her neck and head. She did not turn around, resisted the urge to look into it.

Inside her, the baby began kicking and squirming. "Hurry, Brian!"

But Brian slowed down. "Ellen."

"They're after the baby, Brian! I can feel it!"

Just then Ellen screamed, a long, despairing howl. The machine had pointed cables at her and the priest. As they weaved about on their roaring ATV, the cables swayed, trying to aim. Behind them the humvees were deploying in a line abreast to block escape back toward Mound Road. To surround their ATV, soldiers trotted up both sidewalks.

Brian dismounted. He and Loi were trying to shield their eyes from the light the machine was shining at them, but it was very hard.

Just behind Brian and Loi, the Wests also stopped. "I'll cover you," Bob shouted as Brian went past. He didn't have the AK-47 anymore, but Brian could hear his pistol banging steadily away.

Crouching down behind their ATV, Loi noted that Bob really did seem to have overcome the power of the demon. But this was not easy to believe, and she resolved never to let down her guard.

Ellen was down, Ellen was off the ATV. The judge's hands were extending toward her, racing across the ten feet between them.

Where the survivors had been there remained only masses of waving arms all tangled up with clothes and shoes and hair. Faces were visible in the tangle, faces slack with rapture. The cables from the machine had plunged into the mass, and their sensitive tips raced here and there, buzzing angrily as they flooded this or that remaining bit of human flesh with their light.

A complicated stink rose from the mass, of scorched clothing and melted hair, of sweat, of blood and urine, feces and hot meat.

Suddenly Loi realized that the machine had turned its attention away from Ellen and Father Palmer.

One of the free arms was pointing directly at her. The baby was kicking more than he had ever kicked before. She clutched her stomach. "Brian, *get us out of here!*"

He dashed back to their ATV, leaped on.

Ellen watched him go. For the moment she'd stopped trying to escape. Loi's desperate cry had gone through her like a white-hot blade.

3.

Bob's pistol snapped and the judge began to choke, wrapping his long hands around a hole in his throat.

Loi and Brian disappeared into the darkness, their ATV screaming.

The machine turned its attention to Father Palmer. He was still sitting on the ATV when one of the cables jutted right into his face, flooding it with light. His eyes widened, his arms waved, he began rocking back and forth oozing sighs that belonged to night and the bedroom.

Ellen got back on the Suzuki, pushing in front of him, feeling tingles of delight where the light touched her skin, gasping with pleasure when it entered her eyes. She gunned the motor and the vehicle wailed to life, shot ahead. The soldiers, who had just come up, grabbed at them. Then the humvees snarled to life and began weaving around the spitting machine, coming fast.

Ellen didn't like having the old priest behind her with his arms around her waist. Being touched by the poor man was disgusting. She could hear his breath whistling, could feel his fingers kneading the flesh of her sides as he hung on to her.

She followed the ATV in front of her, staying with it when it turned off the road behind the others. Ellen was clumsy with the unfamiliar machine. It was extremely responsive and she had to drop a good distance behind Chris and Nancy to avoid running them down.

Behind her she heard engines. The humvees had come off the road, too. But surely they were much too wide to maneuver in the forest.

Suddenly the Suzuki screamed and slid sideways. Her reflexive hitting of the brakes only made things worse. They skidded between two trees into the thick woods. "Jesus Christ," she muttered. There was nothing out there ahead of her, nothing but darkness.

Her heart practically flew out through her mouth—she was lost in the woods with a half-monster clinging to her back and at least one humvee from hell somewhere behind her.

Father Palmer coughed. "Where are we?" he asked.

"In the woods."

His hands slid up onto her shoulders. "Are we lost?"

"No!"

He clasped his hands together behind her neck. She could feel his hard, knobby cheek pressing against her back. Sharp things protruding from his torso worked through her clothes, pricked her. She leaned as far forward as she could.

Then she saw a wonderful sight, the tiny red dot of a taillight. "There they are!" The ground sloped up so steeply that she was afraid they'd topple over backward. They went through thick, lashing undergrowth. As best she could she kept her head down. At this speed a twig could put an eye out, a branch hurl them both off the vehicle.

The path grew so narrow that trees scraped their legs, but still they climbed, up and up, seeking that flash of red.

Far off up the ridge ahead, she saw bobbing lights. She took out after them, cursing the ATV because it wouldn't go faster. They bounced across boulders and cracks and the great, gnarled roots of pitch pines. She shouted and Father Palmer hissed and made deep, popping noises in his throat.

The lights went out.

She didn't even slow down.

A moment later the nearest ATV appeared in her headlight. Chris was there, waving. She took her hand off the gas and the Suzuki stopped so fast that she was almost thrown across the handlebars.

"Shut it down," the boy whispered, his voice urgent.

"I have no idea how to do that!" She got off, followed by the priest. He clambered down, his breath a busy whistle. She tried not to look at the black, misshapen hulk of his head.

Chris turned off the ATV by pulling a wire.

They were received back into the group, now haphazardly armed with two shotguns, a rifle and three pistols. "I thought I'd never see you guys again," she said.

Silently, Loi touched her on the shoulder. Nancy came up and pressed a small pistol into her hand. "The safety's in the butt," she whispered.

"Why are we stopping?"

"We're shaking the humvees," Brian murmured.

"But—"

"Whisper," Nancy hissed. "You're louder than I was, Ellen."

"They are looking for movement and light," Loi added softly. "Sound."

"Where are we?"

"About a mile and a half south of town, by my reckoning," Bob murmured.

The night wind blew steadily. To the north, the horizon was now bright purple.

Father Palmer, who had moved off into the dark, groaned. Loi came up to Ellen. She whispered low, barely breathing. "What's his condition?"

Ellen shook her head.

Loi went over to him, draped her arm around his shoulder. There was a murmur of conversation. After a moment she jumped back, uttering a small cry. She returned to the group. "He's not good." She was rubbing the back of her hand. "He says he feels the same as always, but he's beginning to hear a voice in his head. He hears a voice shouting instructions at him. It's telling him to keep us here, not to let us move."

"I've started hearing it, too," Bob said.

Turning away to hide the movement, Loi took out her pistol.

"But it doesn't affect me," Bob continued. He knelt and put his arms around his nearest boy. "*This* affects me."

Chris threw his arms around his father's neck.

Loi looked down at him, now with both of his sons beside him. She thrust her pistol back into her belt.

Ellen, who had seen the stealthy movement of the weapon, realized that Loi would have killed Bob if he'd said the wrong thing. She could kill—even up close, even a person she'd known for years. Ellen found herself feeling a little worshipful toward her, and shook it off angrily.

"How about you, Father?" Loi asked softly, going over to the priest. "Can you resist the one who calls to you?"

"It's angels," he said faintly, his own voice barely understandable, "angels singing the glory of heaven." He raised his tortured face, and in the starlight its mosaic surface looked like a dry, cracked riverbed. His eyes were heavily filmed, his mouth full of what looked like wet modeling clay filled with pumping veins. Then he gobbled out some words. "I'm about done. I want to—want to . . ." His voice sank away.

Loi went back to the others. "He's dangerous." Again her pistol was in her hand.

"Oh, no," Nancy said. "He baptized my babies."

"He baptized all of us," Brian added.

"Whisper! Please!"

Ellen stepped up. "He didn't baptize me."

"I'll do it," Loi breathed.

"I can do it. Give me the pistol." Ellen held out her hand. They all saw how it was shaking.

"Jesus Christ, I'll do it," Brian said, snatching the weapon.

"Go in at the base of the skull, buddy. He'll drop like a bag of flour."

"That's professional advice, Bob?"

"Hell yes it is!"

"Here we go again," Joey said, putting his hands over his ears.

"Wait. We must do it silently." Loi gestured toward the night.

There followed another hushed discussion. They could have hit him with a stone while he knelt praying, but nobody would.

He had begun pulling at his face and making small sounds of chagrin.

Brian was gazing out into the night. "The thing is, I remember we used to come up here and look at the lights of Ludlum."

"So?"

He gestured toward the southern horizon.

There were no lights.

Nancy stifled a sob. Welling up from deep inside Loi was a sensation of obliterating sorrow. If there were no lights in Ludlum, maybe there were none in Albany or New York City or anywhere.

They heard a noise, all of them at the same moment: the rumble of an engine.

"It's a humvee," Loi said in a quiet voice. She pointed along the spine of the mountain. "There." She sighed. "We were too noisy."

Three of the shapes came quickly and quietly along. They were not half a mile away, coming down from the north.

"Let's move out," Loi said.

"Which way?"

"South, always. If not Ludlum, then maybe some other place."

"We can't go that way," Brian said, "it's a cliff! I've climbed it, I know what it's like."

Now the grinding of the humvees' gears came clear, and the rising growl of their engines.

Loi got on their Suzuki. "Come on, Brian."

"I'm telling you, it can't be done!"

Loi flared at him. "Then why did you even stop here?"

"How was I to know they'd get around behind us like that? How could they, in those things?"

"So where can we go?" She wasn't whispering now. Her voice was shrill.

"We could go down the way we came," Bob said.

"Back to town?"

"We skirt the town, cross the Cuyamora where it's shallow up near the Pratt place. Then we go south through the fields. We'll sure as hell make better time than we will in these damn mountains."

It sounded to Brian like a reasonable enough plan. The humvees were now only minutes away. They had no time to consider whether or not it was a mistake.

The instant the first Suzuki started, huge lights flooded the whole ridge with beams brighter than the brightest sun. The ungainly vehicles leaped ahead, rumbling down on the little band of survivors like a herd of maddened rhino.

The ATVs bounced off into the dense woods. They had been expertly turned back in the direction they had come.

SIXTEEN

1.

Brian's ATV bounced and lurched, its engine screaming. Every jerk went right through him. He worried that Loi was going to start bleeding again, and they were so helpless now.

To the north and west the sky glowed purple, and he thought of the forbidden zone, the region of no escape. Was it already too late?

He had conceived of an idea, a long chance. If he was right and his facility had been moved to this area, he might be able to get inside and do some sort of damage that would stop this.

Loi pressed her cheek against his back. "We must turn, Brian. Turn north here."

"Toward Towayda? Is that wise?"

"We've got to go where we aren't expected. We can get around town that way, cross Towayda Road, then go out into that apple orchard the other side of Mound."

"That'll take us right into the center of this, Loi!"

"Where we're least expected."

"I've got to stop. The others'll have to agree." He turned in his seat, trying to see them. In the near distance he glimpsed movement. Farther back, the forest was radiant with light from the humvees.

Loi clutched him tightly. "They'll stay with us."

It was her they trusted. He was no leader. "They'll stay with you."

"Yeah, so let's go."

He made the turn, and the purple glow now lit the glimpses of sky ahead of him. The woods grew thicker, and he had to slow down.

"Go, Brian!"

"Jesus Christ, in this morass?"

"Go, break through it! There is no time!"

The ATV slid and protested, the branches and leaves slapped his face, the bumps came again and again. "Loi, stand up in the seat, you can't risk the shock!"

"Just go!"

Suddenly a yard appeared ahead of them. Then they were crossing grass. Brian recognized the Huygenses' place, now dark and silent. So often he'd sat with Pat under these very trees, discussing town affairs deep into the night.

There were the four green Adirondack chairs Pat had built ten years ago.

"Faster, Brian! This is the most dangerous part."

He crossed the patio, tore through the vine-covered wire fence that gave them privacy from the road—and saw a group of people just ahead. He jammed on the brakes and the vehicle slid to a halt.

A flashlight blazed into his eyes. "State police!"

Loi's pistol came out.

Ellen roared up beside them, the dark lump of Father Palmer huddled on the seat behind her. She gunned her engine, stood over the handlebars, ready to try to blast through the crowd.

The Wests stopped a short distance back.

Behind the light Brian could see state police uniforms, and then familiar faces, friends he had known since he was a child. Among the troopers he noticed Nate Harris.

Bob also saw Nate, his oldest friend in the troopers, his mentor. With them, though, were more of the heavily equipped soldiers with the hidden faces.

The street was blocked. "Loi," Brian said, "we've got to deal with this." He took his hand off the gas.

"All right. Dismount, everybody." They complied immediately, moving now with the speed of a well-trained unit.

The group facing them stirred. "State police," the voice squawked again, "come forward with your hands on your heads!"

Father Palmer wheezed, seemed about to keel over.

Ellen went to Loi. "We're losing him."

"Does he seem dangerous?"

"He was quiet. He groaned a little."

Loi surveyed their predicament. The only alternatives open now were to go down into Oscola or double back the way they'd come. But the humvees were back there, somehow negotiating the woods despite their ungainly shape.

If she could leave a rear guard, they might be able to make the run down through Oscola. She crept over to the priest. "Father Palmer, can you keep watch here for us? Do you trust yourself?"

A rumbling groan.

"Do your best. You're what we have."

He hissed, then his voice guttered low. "I love you all," he said. He may have gasped the word "Jesus," uttered a part of a prayer.

"I'll stay," Chris said. He looked toward the

humped shape that had been the old priest. "He ain't gonna make it." Chris carried a 30-30 almost as large as he was.

Loi gave him a fond glance. She remembered so well what it was like to be a child at war. "We need you with us."

"Come forward with your hands up!" Nate Harris called.

"We're on your side," another trooper said.

"Come on, Bob. You'll all be treated well."

Bob took a halting step.

"Tell Mrs. Kelly to put her pistol down on the ground, Lieutenant. And is that an AK-47 tied to your vehicle?"

Bob took another step. "They've got a lot of firepower, Loi." Then, more softly, "I'm playing for time. Get ready to move."

One of the troopers began walking toward them. "I wanta see everybody's hands," he said as he approached.

There was a slapping sound, the clink of metal. "Stop," Chris shouted. He was aiming his rifle directly at the trooper.

The trooper dropped. The others took positions behind cars. There was a general clicking as guns were cocked. "Unless you throw in your weapons by the count of three, we'll take all of you down," Nate shouted. "One . . . two—"

"I'm bringing a gun in," Father Palmer burred. There was a sloshing sound in his throat. "Somebody give me a shotgun."

Nobody moved. They looked to Loi for a decision. "Yes," she said. Nancy handed him one.

He dragged himself into the middle of the road.

Nate spoke. "Put it down now, Father."

Closer Father Palmer went, moving to within range. "I can't hear you."

"Father, don't take another step."

The priest stopped, his breath gurgling and wheezing.

Nate yelled at him. "Put it down!"

Instead Father Palmer raised it to his shoulder and fired a round of twelve-gauge buckshot directly into Nate's body. There was a blast and a dry smack of sound and Nate flew into pieces—which at once began to jerk spasmodically, the hands clutching, the face working. Black liquid sprayed out of the torso and the neck, and dribbled from the severed arms and head.

Bob was astonished to find that he himself had been following Father Palmer, even starting to raise his hands. Now he reared back in horror, the thrall broken.

Father Palmer's gun roared again and more of them fell. As he fired, appendages grew from his torso and wrapped around the barrel of the gun, attempting to wrest it from him. "By the love of my Lord Jesus," the priest bellowed, his voice suddenly clear and hard and strong, "begone!" Again he fired, and again, and the shotgun's roar rocked the night.

Crowds of black serpentine arms unfolded from him, ripping out through his skin, tugging the gun, snaking around his neck. They squeezed. "Lord," he croaked.

Shots were returned, and the stink of cordite filled the air. For Loi and Bob it was an odor from long ago. Her blood began to run high, his eyes to well.

Yet again, the priest's gun thundered and more of

the crowd of false people was rent into pieces. Father Palmer gargled and grunted and struggled against himself, but he kept firing, again and again.

Loi and Brian and Chris fired. Joey hid behind his mother, his little voice cutting the air with its terrified cries.

Quite suddenly there was silence. As the ringing faded, they all heard the same awful noise in the dark. Pieces of soldiers and troopers and townsfolk lay about scuffling and flopping, their motion chaotic. Hands vibrated, legs kicked like landed fish, lips burbled, torsos wheezed and spilled blood.

Father Palmer ceased firing and began to dance a kind of horrible jig, his hands batting at the great coils that now swarmed from his belly.

"Shoot him," Ellen shouted. "Don't leave him like that!" She fired her own gun, but he didn't react. She was no marksman, and the dark only made it worse.

Bob raised his pistol, but it wouldn't be effective in this light against that gyrating hulk, not from a hundred-foot range. He gunned his ATV, went closer, began to take down the AK-47.

"Bobby, come back," Nancy moaned.

"Daddy!" Joey bellowed.

Chris trotted up beside the ATV. "I've got a few rounds left," he said.

They got to within thirty feet of the priest. This close, the man was a struggling, heaving mountain of fleshy complications.

Now Bob fired, and as usual he didn't miss. The priest staggered, lurched, then toppled. His fluid-filled skin creaked, it was so taut. Liquid spurted from around his knees like water from a burst pipe.

Then the head came to muttering life, the eyes opening wide, bulging until they imparted an appearance of extreme surprise.

Chris fired three shots right into the center of the face.

With a series of wet plopping sounds the priest became entirely transformed, his head, his body, changing into a furiously active tangle of worm-like feelers that probed and pulsated, all seeking the same thing: control of the shotgun that lay before him.

Almost without his realizing it, Bob dropped his gun to the ground.

"No, Dad," came Chris's shout. "Pick it up!"

He looked at it, looked at his boy, who calmly fired two more shots into the bubbling, spitting remains of the priest.

"Goodbye, Father," Bob said, and quietly added a prayer for him. He took the AK-47 to his hip and fired again. The priest's chest burst open, his monstrously deformed head lolled.

Chris tugged his shirt. "Let's move, Dad!"

From long range, Loi fired at the remains of the priest three more times, hoping that this would be enough, fearing the worst. Angry, disgusted, she shook away the tears that had started forming in her eyes. She got up behind Brian and they darted through the dismembered, disorganized rabble that was all that remained after Father Palmer's effort.

From behind them there rose a hideous sound, a high-pitched, raging bellow so filled with hate that it made her cling to her husband's back to drown it out.

They went on.

Just as they were about to hop the curb and get back into the woods, the Viper came speeding up from the direction of Oscola. Its lights were off and it was moving at blinding speed, coming straight at them. But Loi was a good shot. She rose behind Brian and fired over his head.

A blue spark flew off the hood of the onrushing car.

She had perhaps three seconds.

Her next shot dissolved the windshield.

The sound of the engine went high, the car swerved.

Another shot missed. "Goddamnit."

Again she fired, this time into the right tire.

The car careened to the right, narrowly missing Bob and Joey West on their ATV, then rolling off into the dark by the side of the road.

A moment later a series of purple flashes exploded up from the ditch where it had crashed. Out of the flickering explosions there raged a mass of flailing, segmented legs, clashing red mandibles, plates of gleaming red chitin.

It hadn't been a vehicle at all, but a—what? A colony of something?

Before anybody could so much as take a breath, crystalline purple eyes had appeared at the ends of the mandibles.

One of them shot forward.

Loi found herself staring straight into its glittering darkness. She saw the mesmerizing image of a beautiful little baby. He was floating, still attached to the umbilical. He kicked, his whole body jerking with the suddenness of a man waking from an unexpected sleep.

Brian grabbed both of her cheeks and turned her face forcibly away.

Then she was back in this world and they were pulling out, tires wailing protest.

Holding on with one hand, she touched her face with the other. "Did it get me?" she bellowed. Her baby kicked. *"Did it get me?"*

"No!"

"Thank God." As they raced off into the night, she had the bloodcurdling realization that the demon was especially interested in her, and she knew why: it wanted her baby.

Ellen was behind them when she saw, coming up from behind the tree line, something entirely new and completely unexpected. A gigantic, tapering mandible, visible in the dark only as a shadow, probed along behind Loi and Brian's speeding ATV. It was as if the most tremendous, the most terrible of all the dragons of myth had risen from the depths.

For a moment it wavered, as if seeking direction. Then it stopped, focused, and went questing after Loi. On its first pass it came so close that she rubbed the back of her head where it had touched.

"Loi," Ellen shouted, "look out! Look out behind you!"

When Loi turned in her seat she saw a grasping, outstretched hand with fingers ten feet long.

She grabbed Brian's waist and hung on for dear life as they chugged toward the sheltering forest. On her cheek she felt a chill cooler than the wind rushing past, felt it slip around her neck, felt the gentlest of tugs, persistent, getting stronger—then broken.

She was free.

But then the serpent arm flashed back into view,

tremendous fingers waving gracefully in her face. She shrieked, threw herself against Brian's back. Her baby leaped within her. She felt a dull, deep pain. "No, please," she whispered. She tried to force the muscles to relax, but they did not relax. Again her baby jumped. There was a dull, familiar pain. "Oh, no. Please no."

The serpent arm rose high over the ATV, curling in a huge arch. Then its end disappeared into the roiling clouds. She could not see where it was anchored to the ground, or the gigantic creation of which it must be a part. It was large enough to slap all four vehicles to oblivion. "Brian, it's going to hit us!"

The tree line was fifty feet away.

She could feel the thing's presence above like the looming cave-in of a tunnel or a fat client at the Blue Moon Bar sinking down on her. Then the ground shook, the ATV's engine wailed, and the whole enormous thing crashed into the road behind them. The hand closed on air.

Instantly the gigantic apparition rose, stretching its serpentine form to the absolute maximum, and this time swinging out to the side. As it shimmered away into the woods seventy- and eighty-foot pines shattered into matchsticks, their trunks riven, the roar of their fall like the voice of a maddened river.

It came back, sailing toward them at full speed, right beside them, then just beside the rear tires, then just missing, the fingers extended.

They were within twenty feet of the woods.

But the road before them erupted in a geyser of dirt, stones and soil and concrete flying upward as something came bursting out of the earth.

Desperately Brian swerved away. Loi, who had been hanging on by one hand, was thrown hard to the side. She fell, her shoulder glancing off the ground. As she felt the shock blast through her, she screamed in pain and terror. Her womb shuddered like jelly, and long, hot knives of pain penetrated deep.

"Loi!"

She grabbed his back, the far edge of the seat, forced herself up. "I'm OK!"

The other ATVs were coming fast, engines bellowing.

Brian gunned his engine, their ATV leaped ahead—and Loi found herself lying in the road flat on her back. Her mind snatched details, the smell of the exhaust, the faint warmth of the pavement, the gnarled shadowy clouds above.

From underground came a booming, pulsating sound. Her skin felt suddenly shivery, tight. She saw Brian still on the ATV, a look of absolute horror on his face. Then she felt the ground churning beneath her body.

She was falling.

She saw Brian disappear, the sky above him disappear, saw it all become a haze, a blur, then saw it folded away into blackness. She was dropping fast, so astonished that she couldn't even cry out.

From far above she heard Brian shouting, heard her name echoing.

Then she hit something thick and warm, sank into it, kept going down and down, felt it hot around her, breathed, choked, tasted a foul taste, went deeper and deeper and deeper.

2.

Brian threw himself to the ground, began clawing at the pavement, which was still loose where Loi had been absorbed. But the stones soon acquired a sort of crazy, spinning weight, rushing out from under his fingers and back into their places.

Inside of twenty seconds there wasn't a trace of the hole that had consumed her. The only sign that it had ever existed was the presence of pale, friable clay, just like the summit of the mound, or the spot out on the Northway where Bob had been taken.

Deeper silence descended. It was broken when frogs out in forest ponds resumed a tentative chorus. Brian crouched beside their ATV, weeping.

He was unaware of the others as they pulled up around him. Realizing that something was terribly wrong, they'd come back.

Bob leaned over him. "Brian?"

"I've lost her!"

His words sickened them all. She had been their strength. Her belief in escape was what had sustained their effort. She was the only reason that any of them were still alive.

Ellen went down to him, put her arm around his sweat-soaked back. "Oh, Jesus," she said.

It felt as if his heart had been ripped out of his chest. The agony was so pure that he didn't cry out, he didn't even weep. He was there, and Loi wasn't.

"We have to keep going," Nancy said from the dark nearby. "We can't stay here. Loi would want it, Brian. She wanted us to survive." Nancy's voice went low, and a great, racking sob escaped.

Nobody moved. They were all together now, all in one place.

"This could be a trap," Chris said. The boy he had been had evaporated like foam, replaced by this tough little survivor.

Brian looked at him. He wanted a son. He wanted another baby to raise. He wanted Loi. "You go," he told them all.

From deep in the ground there came a cry, long and full of mourning.

That ended what little self-control remained. The anguish came pouring out like lava from the depths of his soul and he raised his eyes to the sky and howled. Then he hammered at the ground, finally leaped to his feet, yanked the pistol out of his belt and emptied it into the road, which sent back little puffs of steam where the bullets struck the asphalt.

Then there came up from the center of him such a feeling as he had never known before. He went beyond agony. It felt as if his soul was congealing in psychic fire. But it also brought him a certain peace, the peace of an absolute decision, of total and complete determination.

"I'm going in," he said. "I'm going to go in there somehow, and I am going to find her and get her back."

"Come on, honey," Nancy said to Bob. Her voice was urgent: they could hear the humvees off in the darkness somewhere.

"We gotta go, Brian," Ellen said. She got on her ATV. The others got on theirs, all except Brian. He backed away.

"I can't leave her." He would not tell them this,

but he was hoping that the thing would return and take him as well.

Ellen got off her vehicle. "You go ahead," she said faintly to Bob and his family, hardly believing her own voice.

"Brian," Bob said, "I've gotta keep going. I have my family to think of."

"You go," Ellen said, "it's dangerous here."

"I can't."

She reached out to him, was glad that he let her take his hand. "Brian Kelly, you listen to me! If you stay here, you'll never have the chance to help her."

"A door that's been opened can be closed," Brian said firmly. "If I can get inside, maybe I can do some good."

A great rush of wind went through the trees, bringing with it cold, intimate smells from the deep forest. "I see a light," Joey hissed.

A hard white light was flitting through the woods, and they all knew what it was. It flew slowly along, almost lazily, winking on and off as it passed among the trees.

Ellen had the horrible, secret thought that they might be looking at part of Loi. She went closer to Brian. It was going to be awfully hard to get on that ATV and leave him behind.

The Wests mounted up. "If we can get help," Bob said, "we'll come back for you, buddy. Both of you." He looked at Ellen. "We've gotta move."

"I'll be going out on my own later," Ellen heard herself say. She was amazed at herself. But the truth was that she had become too committed to Brian and Loi to leave them like this. She just couldn't do it.

Brian's hollow eyes bored into her. His face was a sweaty mask. "Ellen, don't be an idiot." There was something very new in his voice: it cut, it was raw, it was white-hot.

"There's another one," Chris said. A second lightning bug darted across the road. Under them, the ground vibrated.

The Wests left, dashing off into the dark.

Brian nodded to Ellen, almost formally welcoming her to the world of his pain. "I thought he would take me, too."

"Who is he?"

Brian shook his head. He looked down. "That's what I need to find out."

3.

Loi was struggling against the thick, mud-like substance. It was getting in her mouth, her eyes. She had to breathe and she couldn't, she was in agony, her whole body being pressed harder and harder, so hard she couldn't stand it. Her womb was getting tighter and tighter, and she was afraid she was going to burst.

Then she was back in the brothel, spreading her legs and counting, one, two, three. No, she was in real, physical filth, drowning in it.

Involuntarily her mouth opened as she gasped for air. She had to breathe, she had to, *had to!* Mud came sliding in.

Then air.

Air, roaring clouds of it: she hacked, spat, spat harder, shook her head, gasped and promptly choked on little stones and soil, shook her entire body. Debris cascaded around her, plopping to a floor that sounded soft and damp.

Total darkness.

She gulped and belched helplessly, as she'd seen prisoners do in terror of impending torture.

She raised her hands to her belly. Trembling, she felt down to her vagina for blood there, brought up her finger and tasted . . . only her own familiar musk.

She got to her feet—and found just overhead a dense, giving thickness centered by a puckered, rubbery area. It was like an opening in the ceiling, closed by ligaments. She pushed her fist into the center of it, and in a moment dirt ran down her arm.

Then it came to horrible life, tightening as if it was filled with muscle. Her hand was forced out. The lips were rigid now, being held taut. She could not push them open again.

This did not feel like a tunnel or a room or a cave. It was so confined, the air was so bad, that she felt as if somebody huge had his arms tightly around her chest. She flailed against the limits of the tiny space, her hands slipping in the substance that coated it.

She hadn't been sucked into a cave at all, she'd been swallowed. As she ran her hand across the soft floor, the slick, sinewy walls, they shuddered and seethed. This was a living thing. She was inside a huge organ.

That broke her. She slapped the giving walls, kicked the floor, which gave and bounced back like a sponge.

Another fear invaded her, and she felt her face

with frantic little detailed gestures, trying to be sure that she had not changed, that she had not become—

No, her skin remained smooth and soft.

Then she heard something new, a hissing, rattling sound. It was coming closer to her. She drew away from it—and found herself pressed up against the other side of the living chamber.

The space was getting smaller, she could feel the far wall touching her, then pressing against her.

A blazing white explosion of terror convulsed her and she wailed, feeling as she did it all the loneliness of the truly lost.

She did not know how long she screamed, but eventually her howls changed to hard, gulping breaths. The air was even more dense now. Breathing didn't work well. She was being smothered.

Then she knew that something was pressing against her belly. Her reflex was instant—she pushed away, pressing herself into the wall behind her. Dense liquid squeezed out behind her back and oozed down her shoulders and breasts.

Hard, rough hands grasped her thighs, scraped slowly along her sides, again coming to her stomach. Inside her, the baby jerked spasmodically.

She could not move any farther away. The hands came up her sides, up her breasts, her shoulders, her neck. She heard a rattling sound not an inch from her face. Reflexively, she tried to shield herself.

Her hands came into contact with thin wrists as hard as steel pipe, cold and covered with hairs like spikes. The hands came to her hands. They also were hard and cold.

When they tried to close on her hands, she reached out, slapping, hitting.

She came into contact with a face. Undoubtedly it was a face: she could feel the shape of it. But the cheeks were hard, the mouth was complex with parts that tickled her palms as they worked. The eyes were dry and protuberant, feeling under her sliding fingers like the surface of a strainer. They reminded her of the eyes of a fly.

Her baby was jumping and jerking, as if he entirely shared his mother's anguish.

Slowly, the face turned, and her fingers slipped away from the eyes. But there were hard, springy hairs all around them and she clutched these and pulled as hard as she could.

A great caw burst out, blasting straight into her face. The hands came up and closed their hard fingers around her wrists and yanked her arms away. She twisted, she spat, she shrieked.

A feeling of incredible malevolence washed over her with the power of a hurricane stinking of profound rot.

She could not see him glaring at her, but she knew that *he* could see.

"Kill us," she said. She was thinking of the hideous changes she had seen in the Michaelsons and the Rysdale boy and poor Father Palmer. This must not happen to her baby!

A new sound came, a sawing wheeze, coarse, loud, as if it was made not with vocal cords but by sticks rattling together. Even so, she recognized this sound: it was laughter, the laughter of triumph.

He had hunted her and captured her and taken her for one reason: the child.

SEVENTEEN

1.

Ellen and Brian had moved off into the woods and were making their way slowly west, paralleling the town. To their right, they could occasionally hear the falls of the Cuyamora River as it came leaping down out of the mountains. To their left behind a screen of thick forest lay Oscola.

Brian was stricken by his loss, but he had tabled drastic action until he knew what had happened to Loi. If she was dead, then he thought he would want to join her. He had to find out. Rather than paralyzing him, it was the nature of this uncertain grief to drive him to greater effort. His mind was now entirely centered on discovering her fate and the fate of their child.

He watched Ellen riding slowly along beside him. Although he felt gratitude for her support, she could not stay.

Ellen also watched him. She did not know how he kept on. Had she suffered a loss like his, her first impulse would be to just shrivel up and die. She could see his pale ghost of a face, his dark mass of curly hair.

His mind analyzed and deduced. There had to be

a way in, and it must be somewhere in this general area.

The highest probability was that the entrance to whatever remained of the facility would be near the judge's place. He had excellent reasons to think this.

First, the judge had been co-opted early, and the initial manifestations had taken place on his mound and in his root cellar. Second, as they drew closer to the estate, Brian was observing more and more changes in the plant life—subtly twisted limbs, leaves reduced to contorted green knobs, or turning into sticky green-black sheets that stank of mold.

It would have made sense for the scientists involved to move the facility to Oscola. It was close to the Ludlum campus, site of the original problem. More importantly, the town was in the middle of a small but geologically unique area.

The veins of iron and basalt that ran beneath it were among the strongest geological formations on earth. The men who were fighting this war would have wanted that strength, in case they had to try another containment effort.

So he knew where he would find the entrance to the new facility, and that was where he was going.

Ellen stayed with him, even after they moved past a clump of pulsating, bloated saplings.

He called to her. As soon as she stopped she slumped over her handlebars. She was almost done in. "Yeah, Brian?"

"It's time for you to follow the Wests."

"I think I can help."

"Ellen, it's not real likely that I'm going to be coming back."

"But there's a chance we could hurt this thing, isn't there? Or even stop it altogether."

He could not lie to her. "There's a chance. Not a good one, though."

What she wanted was to be in a nice cozy bed with a cup of cappuccino and a sweet, loving husband. But that wasn't to be. She could not turn away from this problem, not if there was any chance at all of doing something useful here. "What would we have to do?"

"Get the equipment turned on—assuming that's even possible."

"Turned *on*? You'd think we'd have to turn something off. Bust hell out of it."

"The link's already been made or this wouldn't be happening. Obviously my colleagues were trying to break it."

"What link?"

"I'm not sure. But I know I'm right about the equipment."

"Which is where?"

"You remember that old iron mine?"

"How could I ever forget it?" The wetness the spider-like thing had left on her legs remained a vivid memory.

"If we go down there, we'll find an entrance, almost certainly."

"We have a couple of pistols. We'll need flashlights. A company of marines."

He smiled at her then, a thin smile. "Listen to the frogs."

Their croaking had risen to hysteria.

"And the crickets," Ellen noticed. They were shrilling wildly.

From all around them there came a continuous rustling, creaking sound. "If we're going to go, we'd better do it, Ellen."

She took a deep breath, blew it out. Then she revved her ATV, put it in gear. "Here goes nothing," she muttered under her breath.

They moved off, deep into the forest.

At first the trip was uneventful, as far as Ellen was concerned. She did begin to notice the twisted limbs, the funny leaves. Then she saw a fern that looked like a pile of seaweed. A few minutes later a black, complicated creature flashed past in her headlight. It was too big to be an insect, too full of spindly legs and feelers to be a bat.

She watched for lightning bugs.

With a soft scratching sound something landed briefly on her chest. She glanced down just in time to see what appeared to be a flying scorpion, its wings still whirring.

Before she could even scream, it had sailed off into the dark.

The closer they got to Mound Road, the more things changed. The trunks of trees were grotesquely twisted, and their leaves were withering like small, closed fists. Purple light glimmered beneath the forest floor. Wet brown tendrils sprouted from the moss, twisting and growing, seeking.

Closer, and the fattened tree trunks were sprouting great black sheets of material in place of leaves.

Along with the trees everything was changing, the ferns turning to flopping, rubbery slabs that exuded black ichor, the mushrooms growing to great size, a fog of mold-stinking gas.

A pearl-white millipede at least eight feet long

glided out in front of her. Before she could stop she had driven over it. With a splash the soft body exploded, slopping her feet with liquid that reeked like clabber.

Despite the rough ground, Brian increased speed. Behind him Ellen's vehicle careened along, bouncing into a gully, then bursting back into the thicker woods.

Now the leaves when they touched her clung a little and felt like leather. Purple sparks played in the soil, and the haze was like dust. She coughed, bringing up something like black tapioca.

Brian kept his eyes focused ahead, watching the dark woods whip past. It wouldn't do to hit a tree. Even letting those crawly leaves touch his bare arms made the gorge rise in his throat.

He wanted only to follow Loi's fate. If she was dead, then he would die. If she had been changed, then he would submit.

The thought of her suffering even a little bit made him twist his throttle and go speeding even faster through the woods, forgetful of the less efficient driver struggling to keep up.

Rough limbs dragged at his chest. His stomach felt as if it was boiling.

A glow flickered in the woods ahead, as quickly died.

Ellen also saw the glow, and sensed her will faltering. Then she fixed her attention on the speeding ghost in front of her.

He swerved to avoid a sapling. At the same moment he saw another flicker off among the trees. He grew wary, began to sweep the area ahead with his eyes. Above all, he didn't want to be destroyed on the way in.

They'd used his equipment to open a door into another world and this was what had come out.

Behind him he could hear Ellen's four-wheeler slurrying and slipping, the engine alternately guttering low, then screaming. She wasn't much good with it. Maybe she'd get lucky and the thing would overheat. She'd be out here alone, but at least she'd be alive.

Off to the left he saw a gray strip. For a moment his heart raced. They were closing in on Mound Road.

They broke out onto the grassy shoulder at more or less the same time. The clouds had parted and they could see the Milky Way overarching the heavens. The moon hung low in the west, above it the evening star.

But their light shone down on a forest that was twisting and lurching and changing, limbs sweeping back and forth against the sky, whole trees splitting with explosive reports, contorting into new shapes, growing great, misshapen leaves as black and slick and floppy as sheets of fungus.

The din was horrendous. The crunching and creaking of limbs, the sighing of leaves in extreme agitation, the bellows and shrieks and ululations of the forest creatures, all combined into a single groaning cry.

When they stopped their ATVs this new sound at first confused them. Then Brian understood. He could hardly bear to do it, for he knew what he would see. But he forced himself to look down the road toward the judge's house.

There, in all its contorted glory, stood the border-land of a new world. Huge, bloated barrels topped by fungoid sheets had entirely replaced the trees. Black, twining vines covered with hair so stiff they looked as if they had been shocked attempted to choke the barrels. Here and there dark forms moved slowly along. Cries rose and fell, gawps and croaks echoed. All stood beneath a purple haze. The farther they looked, the thicker the monstrous forest became, the broader and higher the barrels, the wider the black, mucus-dripping sheets that they presented to the sky.

"I think speed's our only hope."

Ellen got on her bike, turned it around and prepared to escape. "What if we meet up with the humvees?"

"Ellen, the only direction I'll go is forward."

"Into *that*? We'll be killed for certain."

"But we might be able to do some damage."

Under the grass and weeds around them, she began to notice purple flashes and sparks. It was coming, moving like a wave out of the dark, changing everything it touched.

From behind them on the road there came a series of wet snarls, loud enough to be heard over the forest's agony. A bend in the road made it impossible to see what was there. Ellen heard Brian take out his pistol, did the same.

An enormous creature on four segmented legs came stalking around the bend. The legs were at least fifteen feet long. Lurching like a sedan chair in their center was a boxy body that had once clearly been a humvee. Beneath it gnarled, troll-like shadows humped along, seeking the protection of the great beast. They bore long, thin arms. The ruins of the uniforms and chemical protective gear of these creatures who had once been ordinary American soldiers hung in tatters from various appendages.

Where the lights of the humvee had been, the head of the creature had compound eyes that glowed with purple fire.

This light struck joy into their hearts. They did not expect it, and they cried out with the pleasure. Brian stomped his feet and yelled. Ellen staggered in circles, wailing, impotently waving her gun.

It was like being burned to death in glory.

But Ellen also felt it as rape, and the single, tiny spark of anger that this produced was enough to cause her to turn away for a moment.

The thrall broke. Beside her Brian was on his back, supported by heels and shoulders, bellowing and thrusting his pelvis at the oncoming monstrosity with the fury of a sex-maddened rodent.

She leaped on him, pressed her face to his and screamed out his name with every ounce of strength in her body.

Then they were rolling—and not a moment too soon, for the huge walker with its phalanx of trolls had positioned themselves not a hundred feet away. As Brian and Ellen scrabbled, stumbled, finally ran deeper into the forbidden zone, the monstrosity poured purple light into the two ATVs, which belched yellow smoke and began to grow legs.

Ellen, who had been terrified beyond words, now reached another place entirely in her heart, the place where men in battle go, that is beyond pain, beyond fear, beyond hope, beyond everything.

She was a body, bone and blood and brain, sweat

and flying hair, racing between bloated monstrosities through foul purple air, behind a man in a tattered T-shirt who was waving a pistol as he ran.

They went toward the judge's vine-encrusted house and beyond it, now running, now climbing through curtains of vine that shuddered when they were touched. When Ellen slowed for a moment, she felt these vines begin slipping stealthily around her legs, felt leaves plastering themselves to her arms, her thighs. Stifling a scream, she snatched them away. More came, and she could feel all the limbs and twigs and leaves bending toward herself and Brian, could see the fat bodies of the trees beginning to pulsate.

But then they reached the area of the root cellar, and suddenly conditions changed again. Here there weren't so many of the monstrous plants. The brush that had choked the cellar's entrance had given way to sheets of the slick fungus. This had the effect of increasing the opening rather than narrowing it.

Brian sat down on the stuff, began inching toward the hole.

"Brian, don't!"

"We've got to go where we're least expected. There's no other way."

She looked back. With the strange grace of a spider, the enormous machine marched after them. The shadows of the trolls were fanning out, cutting off all escape. Two dead black piles of what appeared to be gleaming meat jerked and heaved in the background: the remains of the ATVs were continuing to mutate.

"We need flashlights, Brian."

"Oh, Christ, you're right." He peered across the

seething lawn. "We've gotta try the house." He sounded sick.

Crossing the heaving, tortured earth, they crouched like soldiers under fire. They kept their faces carefully averted from the oncoming juggernaut, but now even the purple flickering in the subsoil had become bright enough to deliver pleasure.

Every time they as much as slowed down for breath, the grass itself came spinning up around their ankles, the blades having taken on the configuration of thousands of busy, tapered worms.

By the time they reached the porch, these creatures had covered their shoes with a substance so slippery that they could hardly keep on their feet. They entered the quiet, inky black kitchen, feeling their way, unsure of anything.

When Brian inhaled, he noticed a strong odor. "What's that smell?"

"Sweat, I think."

"Is it us?"

"I don't know. Maybe."

"Where would an old man keep a flashlight, Ellen?"

"A cabinet, a drawer?"

She heard a scrape, then clinking. Brian had opened a drawer. Flailing ahead, she found the refrigerator, opened a cabinet above it. Her hands swept the shelf. She snatched them back. There was something slick. It felt . . . organic. She listened, but nothing moved. Licking her paper-dry lips, she stuck her hand in again. "Brian, I've found some candles!"

"Matches?"

"No . . . Yes!" She pulled down a familiar box.

"Kitchen matches. Big box!" Holding them, she grabbed the candles. "Four candles."

He came close to her. They fumbled with their booty like excited children opening Christmas presents. Then he struck one of the matches and held it high.

They both screamed at once, shrieked, really. Standing in the doorway was a seven-foot-tall insect with gigantic, glaring eyes. Lying before it on the floor were five supple arms of the type that had destroyed the Dick Kellys and the Huygenses. They emerged from an unseen source in the dining room. With the easy stealth of a cobra, two of them rose from the floor. Both were carrying purple crystalline eyes.

The insect's mouth parts vibrated and it emitted a buzzing caw. They could hear the excitement.

Then the match went out.

Brian fired his pistol into the dark. In the first flash, the thing's eyes glared, filled with malevolence. In the second, it had spread great, sheet-like wings that looked like black, veined plastic.

In the third, it was gone.

"Let's get out of here," Ellen yelled. She was thinking of those arms.

This time they did not stop at the edge of the root cellar: there was no time to stop. The humvees were in the yard; something was crowing angrily from the roof of the house; the arms were snaking out the kitchen window, their surfaces gleaming in the last failing light of the moon.

Ellen landed on Brian, both of them sinking a foot into the spongy, giving surface that had replaced the earthen floor of the root cellar.

Working with furious haste, Brian lit another match. The room was empty, and the entrance to the mine gaped unattended. They lit candles and went in.

Ellen was so scared that her nervous system was beginning to betray her. She could hardly walk, let alone keep the candle lit in the stinking draft that exuded from the tunnel. "Brian."

"I smell them." He sighed. "If only we had flashlights," he muttered. He was cupping his hand around his guttering candle, leaning into the opening.

"I can't go in there!"

"Where else is there?"

For the first time in her life, the idea of suicide crossed her mind. "Why did I come back? Am I crazy?" She sobbed a ragged sob. It made her mad when she cried, and she choked it back.

"Look. I came back because there's no place in the world I'd rather go. And I have a chance of doing something in here. Out there, none."

"What sort of a chance?"

"There's bound to be something we can do."

"Don't make me think there's hope if there isn't any. Because I think I want to blow my own head off before I get made into one of those . . . things. I don't want to miss my opportunity, Brian."

"If somebody opened a door into another universe—a parallel reality—then the door can be closed. My theories suggested this possibility."

"It's science fiction."

"The Many Worlds Interpretation is accepted physics. Parallel universes are real, I'm afraid."

They went down the mine. The walls were iron,

but the floor was mushy. It was like trying to walk on raw dough.

They went down twenty feet, then fifty.

And they encountered an elevator. "Goddamn that Nate Harris. He's a liar!" Beyond the elevator a tunnel went off toward the surface, no doubt to the main entrance to the facility, which would be hidden well back in the woods.

"The project was classified, Ellen. They probably didn't even let him come down this far."

"They? You mean people?"

"Of course. The scientific team that was working on this."

"They oughta be thrown into the deepest dungeon in the world and left to rot."

He thought he might know the fate of two members of that team: one might have died screaming in the mound, another could have been the woman disinterred from her living grave near Towayda.

To one side was a glass-fronted box with an elevator key in it. Brian broke it with the butt of his pistol and they got the shaft open. Down one side there was a row of ladder rungs. The car was nowhere to be seen.

Without a word, Brian started down, his candle dripping wax into the gloom below. Ellen followed him. She'd never much enjoyed heights—bungee jumping was good copy, no more—and she fought to keep her vertigo from making her lose her balance.

Perhaps an impossible task. "Brian?"

"Yeah?"

"How deep is this?"

"Could be hundreds of feet."

They were now lost in the gloom, two people in a

tiny pool of fluttery candlelight, dropping down and down.

"Hold it," Brian said crisply.

She stopped. Her blood was blasting in her ears, her breath snapping.

"Now come ahead. Be careful."

She hit a surface. There were cables going up. "Where are we?"

Brian pulled open a hatch. "We've gotta go through the elevator car." He dropped down inside, making it bounce. "Shit, lost my light!"

Carefully, she put out her candle and thrust it down in her pocket with her other two.

The darkness was now absolute. "Brian?"

"I'm right here. Just drop."

She slid into the hatch, let go. An instant later she hit the rocking floor of the car. She flailed, felt Brian, then grabbed something thick and cool and wet. "Jesus, it's full of that ick!"

"Strike a light!" His voice was high with terror, and that made her fumble.

Her right hand was covered with goop, so she used her left. "I can't find the matches!"

"Jesus, Jesus, I hate this stuff!"

Her hand closed around the box, drew it out of her pocket. Her candles scattered on the floor. "Brian—" She thrust the matches into his hands.

There was a scrape, a spark, then the small sound of dozens of matches hitting the floor. He scrabbled. "It's OK!"

The match lit, revealing his gray, sweat-sheened face, his bulging, glistening eyes. She looked down at the material on her hand. Black gel. As best she could she rubbed it off against the wall.

Filling the back of the car was a thick, black mass of the material she had touched. It looked like a wet, lumpy garbage bag slathered with ooze.

They stared at it for a moment without comprehension.

Then Brian doubled over, retching loudly. In the semi-opaque gel floated parts of a human being. There were eyes suspended in the mass, connected by tangles of nerve endings to a dark, shriveled appendage, the congealing remnant of a brain. A face, stretched to extremes of distortion, the eye-sockets wide, the lips like red rubber bands, the cheeks crazed by horizontal wrinkles.

"Jesus Christ, it's Bill Merriman! He was our security director." He pointed down into the complex mess. "On his belt—that's his pager!"

"Got a page from hell, I guess."

"Poor guy."

They found the hatch in the floor, and pried up the sunken handle with Ellen's pocketknife, a pitiful little thing with two blades and a fingernail file.

They went on, descending another thirty feet before they reached the bottom of the shaft. The floor was littered with gum and candy wrappers and other familiar debris: lost coins, a half-empty pack of cigarettes—things people had dropped on their way in and out of the elevator. There were stacks of cinderblocks, coils of wire.

"This is only half finished, Brian. It's a mess."

"Yeah." His voice was bitter. "They didn't have enough time. Not quite enough."

A moment later they stepped out into a hallway. Ellen held up her candle. "This part's finished."

The hall was short, the ceiling low. Brian looked

around at the blue pipe that lined the walls. "This is all very familiar. It's a waveguide. The visible part of one. The rest is buried."

"What's a waveguide?"

"When you create an extratemporal particle, it flies off through time and space both. It leaves a sort of track in time. This guides it, so you can detect its passage. But somebody with superior understanding could use its track to literally climb through the ages to reach you."

"From the future? These things are from the future?"

Brian shook his head. "If they're not from some sort of alternate reality, then they must be from the past."

"The past? How?"

"I don't know. Except when you consider that the earth existed for billions of years before the first sign of what we define as life appeared, you can see that there's plenty of room for whole worlds to have come and gone and left not even a fossil behind."

Then they saw a figure lying in the farther shadows. As they went toward it, Brian at once hoped and feared that it was Loi.

It was a young man. The uniform told them where the judge's soldiers had come from: they had been facility guards like this one.

Ellen turned to Brian, put her hands on his shoulders. They held one another in silence, two very frightened and lonely people.

From deep within the complex came a rattle, followed by a long sigh. A wind rose from below, this one foul with odors neither of them had ever smelled before, thick, sour odors, complicated by dense sweetness. It stank like old meat, like rotted fruit.

Then the direction of the air flow changed. What came down from above was fresh by comparison. "What gives, Brian?"

"A ventilation system."

"There's no electricity."

"It isn't our design, Ellen. We vent with fans."

The whole place was quietly breathing.

2.

The first contraction confused her. Despite all the years she'd spent on her back, she'd never given birth. At the Blue Moon Bar girls who didn't get aborted got taken down to the banks of the Chao Phraya River, and they didn't come back.

She'd been aborted seven times, and that was the secret reason she was so fragile inside. Only the doctor had known. "Dr. Gidumal," she moaned, staggering along in the blind dark. "Sanghvi . . . Sanghvi Gidumal . . ."

Now she held her belly, encircling it with her arms. Memories came to her aid, gentle and vivid, of the few good times she had known. But even these memories contained betrayal.

When she was eight, her uncle had dressed her in a beautiful white *bao dai* that was scented with flowers, and taken her from the Chu Chi tunnels to Mai Thi Luu Street, with the Saigon Zoo at one end and the Emperor of Jade Pagoda at the other. Behind the pagoda flowering weeds choked the banks of the Thi Nghe channel, and their aroma scented the grounds.

There had been small bells that tinkled peacefully, and incense that filled the air with the scent of old memories, and the gleaming bald heads of boy monks who had watched her with wide, calm eyes.

In that pagoda was a very special and terrible place, the famous Hall of the Ten Hells. All the torments of the damned were portrayed there, the suffering of those so weighted with karma that they had fallen from the wheel of life forever.

Her two years in the tunnels had taught her about maneuvering in wet and dark, and that training was indispensable now.

She'd been touched all over by those terrible rough hands, and they had left something runny on her that had congealed and become sticky. More than bearing her contractions, she thought now about getting this stuff off her skin.

She did not believe in the contractions.

Brian Ky Kelly would not choose such an inauspicious time for his arrival. He was a glory child, intended to come at the very moment of dawn, under the protection of the sun and the morning star.

Her legs seemed to weigh a thousand pounds, she didn't know where she was, where she was going. There were sparks in her eyes but nothing else, no light.

She must have sinned too much with the perverts who visited the Blue Moon Bar. She had done many things repugnant to heaven and nature. But she had a baby! "I am with child," she cried, a shout she had often heard in the smoky dawn, when the American planes had sailed high and the firebombs had fluttered to the ground with the motion of silver leaves.

She heard a woman sobbing, knew it was her, for

there was no other woman here, nobody else so bad she had been sent to the black bottom of the Ten Hells. She knew she would burn soon, she could smell combustion in the air, hear fire rustling in the walls.

Something brushed against her shoulder, then small threads began dragging across her chest. Reflex caused her to jump away, and the threads disappeared.

She continued walking, trying to hurry now, using her tunnel skills. She kept her head low, waving her hands before her.

Demons, demons, demons.

She cast about in her mind for some deliverance, and found herself returning to the Emperor of Jade Pagoda. There also was a painting of the Guardian Spirit of Mother and Child. "I call on you to help us."

Another contraction came, and this time there could be no doubt: she was going to give birth in hell. At the drumming apex of the pain she sobbed and shouted out, "There is a baby here!" She had also heard this in the quivering waters of the rice paddies, when both sides would be firing bright-burning phosphorus bullets into anybody in a sun hat.

She remembered how the peasant villages smelled in the rain, of rich, damp thatch and sweet cookfire smoke.

Once or twice she thought she'd seen sparks ahead, flickering like candles. But they did not reappear, and so she knew that they were only lights from the tunnels of girlhood.

She would not allow the lamentations that wanted

to rise from her to stop her progress. Brian Ky Kelly was coming! She had to find the sun.

Something trembled inside her, a flutter of the inner belly. Then a hot gush of something poured down her legs. She felt fluid sluicing along her thighs, as if the sea had come out of her. "Do not take my baby!" This had been the cry of her people when the guns roared. Bullets are blind, she remembered, and softly cursed heaven for not letting her keep her gun.

She dabbed at her legs, fearing that this new gush was also blood, a fatal hemorrhage. She lifted the fluid to her lips, tasting, praying.

It was the water of birth. "Help me!" Their baby would see the Hall of the Ten Hells, she had brought him here because of the evil of her life. As if he was already a dead man she grieved for him.

She had heard it coming from under flattened thatch and fiercely burning fire, the cry *help me*. Usually the first answer was that of the mocking parrots. Often, theirs was the only one.

Another contraction came, shooting down from the middle of her belly, causing her to arch her back and cry out, shaking her arms and her head. She nearly toppled back, then staggered forward. She had seen peasant women give birth squatting in a corner of a room, their faces without expression. When she squatted the pain was less.

Finally the contraction passed. Unsteadily, she got to her feet. The way the floor of the tunnel trembled made it very hard to walk. It was like trying to march in a hammock. Worse, the whole place was covered with phlegm, lathered in it.

But when she breathed in, she could smell the

dear damp of thatch, the sweetness of a mud floor. She waved her arms about, but felt only the slick, oozing walls. There was no thatch here, no little hut where a baby could be welcomed.

She was going to have him at the wonderful Ludlum Community Hospital! In one of the beautiful white rooms! Attended by nurses! "Don't forget me, everybody! Dr. Gidumal, I am in need! Dr. Gidumal!"

A sound came like a child drawing the bow across the strings of a *bar-woo*, crackling and guttural.

Instantly she swallowed her cries.

The next contraction hurt so much that she fell to her knees. She was gasping, helpless, lost in the pain. But she would not scream, not if sound drew attention.

When at last it had passed she could taste the salt of her own blood. To keep the screams in, she'd gnashed her lips raw.

She did not try to go forward anymore, she was too exhausted.

This strong woman, who had braved practically every obstacle there was to find a husband and bear a child, was finally being broken. Swelling pain engulfed her, starting down in her center, driving her to slump forward like an abandoned ragdoll. She pushed because she had to push, but every cell of her body wanted to protect her baby. As she arched her back, she raised her arms—and suddenly her hands were in contact with something complicated.

It was cold and wet and warty, and it left a stickiness like slobber in her palms. Gagging, she wiped them uselessly against her soaked jeans.

She crawled then, a few feet, a few more. A slashing sound started overhead, as if somebody was opening and closing huge scissors. A shower of drips rained on her naked back.

Something up there was drooling on her.

She knew, suddenly, why they did not attack her, transform her into a demon with the purple light. They were waiting for the baby to be born. They wanted to eat his sweet and tender flesh. They were up there sharpening their claws.

Crawling as best she could, she silently called on the Goddess of Mothers and Children.

Another contraction broke over her with the power of an explosion, setting her inner thighs afire, sending spears of lightning up her back. She felt something tear within her, felt it give, and suddenly there was deep movement. She went forward to her face, kneeling now with her butt high, her shoulders against the floor. Pulling her jeans away, she reached under herself and felt, and there was Brian Ky Kelly's wet head in her hands.

She turned onto her side, her back, took Brian onto her belly, grabbed a corner of her blouse to shield him from what was above. It came closer and closer, until its hard, warty shell pushed against her belly, her breasts, the still, hot body of her baby.

She pulled him out from under it, felt a pain within herself, realized that he was still attached to the umbilical cord. How to unfasten it? Women must do it somehow, poor women without the simplest tools. She reached down and by stretching took it into her mouth. It was slick, salty, tasting faintly of blood.

Before she could bite down there was the whisper of a blade, very close.

The parted umbilical cord fell away.

She was so exhausted that she couldn't raise herself, could hardly hold him against her breasts. He was squirming, his little hands clutching. "Oh, Brian," she said, "oh, Brian."

Suddenly he was taken from her. A cry tore from her throat. She grabbed for his disappearing body, missed, ended up with her hands clutched against her chest. Even though she was drained dry, she still found enough strength to hammer against the knobbly breast of the thing above her. "Give me my baby!"

There was a crack of sound, sharp and quick. Brian went "Oh! oh!" He gasped, wet, rattling. He cried again, breathed, gasped. Silence. Then he mewed like a kitten.

She hammered the hard body, kicked, screamed. Then a new sound, softer, more easy. He was cooing. As gently as a butterfly dropping through the jungle gloom, he was laid back upon her. She clutched him. He was breathing now, short breaths, very quick, and his arms and legs were moving a great deal.

She took her right nipple and moved it against his face. Despite the dark his lips found it right away.

The air was cold and dank, and all they had was her blouse to warm them. "Brian, my husband," she whispered in wonder, "you have a son."

Behind her she noticed a flicker of light. Turning, she felt a deep warmth in her bones. She'd suffered so much and was so tired that the pleasure almost knocked her out.

But she knew this pleasure, she knew that purple light.

Now that they'd made sure the baby was out, they were bringing their cooker.

Clutching her baby to her breast, she began to slog along. The machine came hissing closer, moving easily. As it came she could hear it sizzling and popping.

Soon the purple light began to touch her back. She sighed, fought down the desire to stop and let the sweet relaxing heat wash over her. She must not let them get her baby!

She ran right into a familiar figure: she knew this coarse hair, these thin, steel-hard arms. Frantically, she pushed away, falling to the floor, bouncing in the giving slickness.

Behind her the purple light strobed furiously. Ahead there was a slurping noise. In the purple flashes she saw a wet cable as thick and alive as an animal's long tongue. As it appeared, it made the sound of a boot being drawn from the sucking bottom of a swamp.

Behind it the compound eyes, in their thousand lenses, were flickering, purple images of a filthy woman with a baby.

Then wet cable was pressing directly against Brian's face and flooding it with that terrible light. She snatched him away, but the cable came too, as if the end of it had been somehow glued to his face. The light flickered, the machine crackled and sputtered, a horrible stink of heat filled the air.

Her baby kicked, he waved his arms, he mewed like a kitten in ecstasy.

Loi could not stop the light, could not detach the cable without pulling her baby's head apart. From deep inside her there came something basic and raw and furious, the tidal wave of savage love that links a mother to her child. Instincts that she didn't even know she possessed came bursting to the surface.

She screamed and screamed and screamed. And as she screamed, she slammed a fist into the cable that was linked to her son's head. He was so tiny, so full of innocent magic, nobody had any right to do anything but cherish him.

There was no time, if she didn't break that connection, he was going to be destroyed. She leaned forward and bit the cable, clamping her jaws like two steel blades. The surface of it cracked and something like hot glue oozed into her mouth. It tasted sweet and alive and stank like old vegetation, the wet rot in the depths of a peasant's compost.

There was a flash of fire that made her groan with pleasure, and suddenly the baby was free in her arms. Wasting not a moment she turned and hurried away from the sparking machinery.

He was still warm, was mewing in her arms, and as she scuttled along she ran her hands over him, feeling his little face, his skin, seeking any sign of damage.

There was none. They had not been able to change him. Her mind raced, turning this over and over again. Of course, the baby had no evil in him, he was innocent, he was not accessible to demons.

She had to get him out, and there was a chance now, a little, tiny ridiculous chance.

Behind her there were squishing sounds, then a great, roaring, furious burr of a voice. Was it speaking words? She didn't know, didn't stop to wonder.

She hurried along the giving floor. She was a tunnel rat again, eight years old and very scared, moving with swift efficiency through the dark.

The great, buzzing roar rose again, and she knew that the demon was in motion now, it was coming fast, bearing down on her like the tiger in the night.

EIGHTEEN

1.

Ellen and Brian heard screams. They raised their candles but they could see nothing beyond the immediate jumble of machinery. The screams faded into the sound of dripping water, which was the chief problem in this ruined place. The water ran along cables, down conduits, fell in streams from the low ceiling, splashed, poured, creating a nervous chorus.

They were well below the water table, perhaps sixty feet down. Pumps had once kept the place dry, but no more. The sweating walls were covered with cables and blue conduits. The floor was made of steel mesh, underneath which could be discerned the shapes of several small machines.

"Generators," Brian said. "This is where they got their power." Overhead, bulbs in black steel cages remained unlit. He knelt on one knee, produced a quarter from his pocket and dropped it through the mesh floor. It fell a few feet, ringing against the equipment, then splashing into water.

It was all so small, so confined, so . . . pitiful.

"If nothing's running, Brian, why is this still happening?"

"I know it's hard to understand. Our people cre-

ated the link back in my old lab in Ludlum. This facility is designed to break it. Which is why it has to
be turned on."

He started down the catwalk, reassured by her
clattering footfalls that she was following him.

He hadn't gone twenty feet before the light of his
candle fell on something strange. "Stop."

Ahead was a gray substance hanging in folds like
a curtain. He touched it and found that it was soft,
giving. When he pushed, it tore, the pieces dropping
lightly away. An odor came out, of mold and acid.

"I don't think we should go in there, Brian."

He gazed at her, a curious peace in his eyes. She'd
seen this expression before. Her father had worn it
on his deathbed.

The odor stung their noses and made their eyes
itch. A greasy taste settled into their mouths, as if
their tongues had been painted with a paste made
from vinegar and toadstools.

He stepped through the rip in the curtain, his feet
squishing into the spongy surface beyond. "It's wet.
Gooey."

Nausea stirred in her.

"We'll only have one chance," he said. "If that."

She came up close behind him. "I want some exact information. What are we looking for? What do
we do when we find it?"

"We've got to get to the control room. Start the
thing up."

"What if we can't?"

"Then we can't."

They set out, two miserable people huddled over
faltering candle flames. They had to wade rather
than walk on the mushy floor.

"It's like the interior of a nest."

"It is the interior of a nest. These creatures are modeled on the same paradigm as insects."

Soon they came to a depression that turned into a sort of hole, fleshy and soaking. He reached in, touched the pliant, slick wall. There was a curious sensuality, a feeling of life.

He pressed himself into the opening. "Here goes something."

Ellen watched as he went feet first into the blackness. Instantly he disappeared, leaving only the orifice behind, gray and gleaming in the light of her candle. She could hear him sliding wetly along. "Brian," she said. Her throat was tight, her skin tingling in the fetid, acidic air.

There was no answer.

Sweat began trickling down her face. He was gone. Just like that, he was gone! "Brian!"

She was in here all alone. She couldn't bear this, she had to get out. She had to get out!

No, wait. Don't panic. "Brian, answer me!"

Silence.

He was gone and she was in terrible danger herself. At any moment whatever had gotten him was going to come out of that hole, and—

She backed away. She was getting out of here.

"Ellen."

"Oh my God, Brian! I thought—wait a minute, where are you?"

"Ellen."

She frowned. What was the matter with him? "Brian?"

"I'm over here, Ellen."

"Oh, thank God! I thought I'd lost you."

"I'm fine."

"Well, you're hoarse. You sound like you've swallowed sandpaper."

"Yeah."

She looked in the direction of the voice. It had been coming out of an opening two feet across, lined with thick, tight-stretched lips—a gigantic, hideously distended mouth.

"Jesus, Brian, are you . . . in there?"

Something inside moved. She had the impression of complicated unfoldings, like a wasp shifting about in the chambers of its nest.

At first she did not understand what she was seeing. The creature was so complex, with so many gleaming angles, that it didn't make proper sense.

Then it did,

The thing was grave and full of dignity, and he had something black and lumpy in the long, narrow hands. A greasy cable came squishing out. Then she saw a ruby eye, and before she had so much as a chance to take a breath felt a white-hot explosion of pleasure down in the depths of her gut. Choirs sang, her mind flooded with delicate, pink-purple light as fine as the first blush of morning. She was peering into a perfect spiral blossom.

The spiral began spinning, turning faster and faster, and Ellen followed it down into the dark, secret heart of the flower.

Far away she heard an urgent voice crying out, roaring her name. Far away . . . Brian was far away, not in front of her at all.

She was dancing in the light.

Then Brian was there, Brian had his hands on her shoulders, he was pulling her back.

The purple light flashed, Brian tugged . . . and a soft sound began, like the clash of beetles in the grass, at once intimate and brutal.

"Ellen, Jesus!"

She was being changed and she'd hardly noticed!

Then the light came back, more powerful than before. Brian had his arm around her neck. She could feel him pull until her bones creaked and her muscles screamed. But he could not break the power of the light.

With every molecule of strength she possessed, she tried to get away. They both pulled, groaning with the effort.

A blasting climax caused her whole body to spasm. She spat, she choked, her back arched, delicious tickling cascaded up from her clitoris.

Again, she climaxed. Again. Again. She dragged in air, saw *him* then, felt *him* in her deep. Again, again. In his many-lensed eyes she saw a thousand reflections of her face. Her lips were slack, nostrils pulsating, tears gushing down sinking, withering cheeks. The pleasure went up and down her spine, a hot agonizing wonderful fire racing from vagina to brain and back.

The pulsations got harder, the hardness began to hurt, then quickly to hurt more. She understood why they cried out in agony and pleasure at the same time, and knew that the voice that was doing it now was her voice.

Pop, pop, pop. Pistol being fired.

Her body was full of swift, sickening movement that wrenched like having dozens of tearing muscle cramps all at the same time. The cable spat purple light and she felt busy itching as her skin liquefied, melting before her eyes.

Brian stood stunned, watching the changes, the drooping of her body, the sudden jutting of bones as they twisted and turned beneath her skin.

To her, it felt as if hot needles had penetrated into her marrow.

He came closer now, getting the light deep into her eyes, deep into her, deep, deep, down into her very essence.

There was a rip inside her, a great bubbling up from her bowels and a feeling of tightness in her left arm. She felt it swelling and knew that she looked the way poor Mr. Michaelson had back in the woods, her appendages bloated, her face and body twisting and distending.

Now it wasn't even a little pleasant anymore. Now it hurt more than she'd thought anything could hurt. Hot waves of agony swept up from her depths, grinding, scraping, churning.

She became aware that *he* had won. She had been destroyed forever, had been captured body and soul. She knew it with absolute clarity.

There was about him something so deeply, fundamentally *wrong* that she almost felt she could taste the evil of him.

He'd been covered by the depths of time, crushed and obliterated and extinguished with all his voracious kind. Their memory lived on only in the hungry cruelty and endless variety of the insect world.

She tried to get away from the hatred he was blasting into her, to return to Brian. She turned— but her body didn't work right. Her body—she saw complicated, stick-like legs flailing, felt herself fall to one side.

But she arose, righting herself as if by magic. To her horror, she leaped at Brian. He skittered away but she was faster, in an instant she was on him again.

She didn't want to, but there was nothing she could do, nothing at all. His pistol flashed.

With a long, long arm she swept the weapon out of his hand.

2.

Brian's candle was snuffed by the onslaught of the thing that had been Ellen.

The fear made him struggle like a man in flames, the sorrow felt as if it might drown his heart.

Something came sweeping up his leg. Kicking as hard as he could, he leaped back, found the sphincter they'd come through to get here, began pressing his arms against it, trying to break the grip of the muscle.

Behind him claws began snapping, at first in a confused clatter, then with more control, then with authority.

He could not return the way he had come. But the undulating floor sloped down and away. Feeling ahead, his body coated with slime, his nose and lungs burning from the acid-cut air, he slithered and slipped away as fast as he could. Blundering helplessly, unable to tell where he was, how close she was, he cried out his rage and terror.

There was an answer, echoing from somewhere ahead.

He knew Loi's voice. Also, that it was a cruel hallucination.

He saw light . . . soft, delicate, purple.

A ruby eye was staring at him from a distance of three feet. It began sizzling smartly.

He threw himself down, rolled away, flailing helplessly.

Then he was falling.

An instant later there was an impact. His confusion was such that he took freezing cold to be blazing heat and breathed in enough water to start himself choking. Forcing himself to clamp his jaws shut, he struggled in the water. His lungs began to ache, then to burn, then to scream for air.

A little water came down his throat. He breathed it, coughed. Another breath came in—more water.

Then he coughed, he knew he was going to gasp this time, to gag, and he was going to start drowning.

His chest heaved, his mouth opened—and he sucked in air. Air! He gobbled, retching, gasping, throat distended, mouth gaping.

Splashing, flailing, dragging himself away from the water, he choked and gagged, then forced calm to his striving muscles, fought down the panic. Treading water, he opened his eyes.

Darkness and silence—but no purple light. He tried to find bearings of some sort. There were none. He swam, throwing one arm in front of the other, paddled aimlessly until his shins hit something hard. Then he felt a steel loop and grabbed it. Hauling himself up, he came onto a sort of shore, which consisted of a floor, an ordinary floor. He felt what seemed to be a broken chair, another beside it.

He realized that he lay on the dark shore of a ruined office.

From off in the gloom there came a droning sound. He listened.

There was something in flight, which meant that it could see in the dark. It was coming closer.

His pistol was gone.

He fumbled about, trying to find something to use as a weapon. The metal chairs were twisted but couldn't be broken. He threw open the drawers of a steel desk, feeling frantically through the paper clips and other debris.

All he found was a letter opener, which he hurled to the floor in frustration.

He began to explore, touching along the walls. He felt steel . . . a door, a locker door. He opened it. Empty. Then a file cabinet. This he also opened. The drawer was heavy, it was jammed with papers. There was what felt like a computer screen on the floor, wires everywhere.

Files, computers—dared he hope he'd reached the control point?

He felt around the jumble—and found something that made him stifle a cry of joy. Frantically he felt for a switch—but what kind of a flashlight was this, what were all these little belts?

It came on, the beam dim. It was a headlamp, the kind miners wore, thus the straps. He put it on, looked around, avid to see. The first thing he laid eyes on was a row of lockers. He threw them all open.

In the last was a kevlar safety vest and a hardhat. On its floor was a beeper. Dead, of course. He threw the beeper against a wall.

The drone of wings began again, got louder.

This light was insane, what had he been thinking? He reached up to flip the switch, but then his eyes fell on a thick manila-backed document. He grabbed it, read the title: "Superluminal Violation Repair Program Structures Integrity Handbook." Another rattling buzz, this one closer. He flicked the light out, shrank back toward the cabinets.

He was right, they'd been trying to fix an earlier break! The problem must have occurred at Ludlum, the first break from the other side. They'd covered that over with concrete, but it obviously hadn't worked.

When the buzzing didn't recur, he turned on his light again. He had to find out more. But the document in his hands wasn't going to tell him, it was just a series of construction protocols designed for engineers and inspectors.

He found a file called "Causality Violations: Kelly Report."

The file was empty. Information about exactly how his work had violated the flow of cause and effect would have been priceless to him right now. As it was, he had to keep guessing, hoping he was right.

Brian threw himself on the files, not noticing the thick black feeler that slipped along the floor behind him, moving swiftly and quietly.

Some of the files were filled, others empty, as if somebody had sorted them, presumably removing the secret material as the facility was abandoned.

A second long, thin cord slipped in beside the

first. They curled about, touching furniture with their delicate tips, seeking, searching.

He read file names, "Causality and Extratemporal Physical Emergence," "Ancient Life Forms in Interaction with Extratemporal Absorbers," "Temporal Flags and Kelly Factor Attacks from Extratemporal Entities."

They had been engaged in a desperate secret war down here, trying to throw back demons called forth from the depths of time.

From the signs of violence all around him, it must have been a near thing, maybe a matter of minutes. The things that had come here were forming a beach head of bloated forests and acidic air. Hordes would come to fill those forests, to breathe that air.

Something brushed his ankle. In the intensity of his thought, he hardly noticed.

But out in the dark water beyond the tilted door there was large movement, very quiet.

Swiftly, easily, eight long arms now uncoiled into the small room. They came across the floor. Their claws opened.

Brian read. This was all quite fantastic. They'd broken into time, not space. It wasn't a parallel universe, but an unknown past that they had unleashed.

When they came, the hands came swiftly and quietly. They closed on his arms, his legs. One of the black arms looped itself around his neck, tightened.

From the depths of the chamber there arose a furious droning buzz.

Brian began to be dragged away. Although he struggled hard, he couldn't even begin to resist. It was like being captured by living steel.

His cries ripped the air, but cries can't overcome steel.

In the blackness, something started sizzling and popping, cooking hot and hard.

He'd waited too long, now he was going to end up like Ellen, he was going to endure that horror, live like that—

He shrieked like a child.

3.

Loi heard the cries clearly, the sounds of a man in gravest anguish. Often enough before she'd heard such sounds. Somebody else had been captured, was being changed.

She held her baby close to her, letting him nurse.

He was her strength, because of the astonishing thing that had happened when the attempt had been made to change him.

Because the demon had been frustrated, he now chased her with unbridled fury, terrible buzzing roars that exploded from him every time he failed to catch this desperate but tunnel-wise mother. She was filthy, steeped in the mucus-like substance that seemed to ooze from the walls. But she would not stop, could not, must not.

While mother rat scuttled along baby rat nursed, then slept on her breast. But she could not run forever, because she was so exhausted that her feet felt like stones and Brian like an ingot of lead. Her throat was burning for water and her hungry baby was eating her alive.

There was a purple flicker in the air, like a storm

nearby. The demon was running, the demon was furious, and when it caught her she knew what it would do. It would not try to change her baby again, it would tear him to pieces with those long claws.

Another scream went echoing through the darkness, and she was reminded of the first night on the mound, how lost and forlorn that voice had been. But this was a man's voice, and closer than before, and there was a tone in it that pierced her very heart.

Oh, Brian. Brian, if only it was you.

She had not reconciled herself to the possibility that she would never see him again, couldn't even begin to do that. But these screams might be another trick of the demon, to get her to come closer.

Her heart breaking, she moved along yet another of the organic tunnels. Little Brian went back on her teat, made a small sound of discontent. Her milk was going, she knew it.

As she crossed a down-spiraling opening, she heard another cry. It was much closer, so close that she was certain.

It was Brian, it had to be him!

Her heart lifted—and then a great pain stabbed it. What if he was being melted?

Another scream, and she heard the depths of his anguish, and her heart all but broke in half.

She hesitated, crouching, trying to think what to do. She gritted her teeth, clutching the baby so close that he wriggled uncomfortably. A shaking hand felt downward, seeking the hole from which the screams were issuing. It was narrow, but she knew she could squeeze through.

Could the demon even kill a baby as fresh and

beautiful as this one, still wet with the dew of heaven?

She couldn't risk it. But then her husband wailed and she thought she had never heard such agony. She entered the hole, descending quickly through its twists and curves, her infant cradled between her breasts.

Brian threw himself about in the grip of the claws. They could have cut him to ribbons, but they only held him. He screwed his eyes closed against the purple light.

"Brian!"

Loi's voice—but where? "Loi?"

"I am here," she replied.

Instantly the hands released him, went questing off into the dark. "Look out, Loi!"

He used his sudden freedom to hurl himself with all his strength in the direction of her voice. As he pulled her down he could hear the claws snapping.

To get her away from them, he shoved her hard. Those sinewy arms could stretch, but not instantaneously. They had a few seconds.

"Be careful," she cried.

Then his arms found her, he felt the familiar coarse Asian hair, felt her shoulder, the softness of her body as he folded her in his embrace.

He realized that she was holding something, something soft and wonderful and deliciously warm. "Oh my God."

Wet cables were oozing out of the machine that *he* carried.

The last moment had come. By making the man scream, he had skillfully lured the agile, tricky woman into his hands. He was just about ready.

Brian's fingers raced over the small body. "Oh, Loi!" The baby made a contented sound.

"This is your son," she said.

Brian went beyond fear, beyond everything but the love that defines the human heart. In wonder and gladness he felt the soft, giving curves of the tiny, naked baby.

He took the little creature from her arms. His son wriggled, seeking a teat. Brian buried his face in the flesh of his child, inhaling the wonderfully sweet smell of his skin. "You're OK," he asked her, "both of you?"

Brian and Loi heard a curious vibration, as if a snake of enormous size was quivering its rattle. The sound was thick with menace, very close.

"He is here with us, Brian, the demon."

Protecting his baby in his left arm, Brian reached out to his wife. She pressed against him. "He could not harm the baby," she said. "The light did nothing."

"Nothing?"

"It doesn't hurt the baby. He did it right in his face."

That terrified Brian. He wished to God he could see—just one little glimpse. He remembered Father Palmer—that horrible, cancerous change—the loamy excrudescences, the stench . . .

Again his hands touched his son. The baby's cheeks felt soft, perfect. Brian ran his fingers along the damp tiny lips, his button of a nose. Shaking fingers crossed the vaporous suggestion of hair on the tiny scalp.

Carefully, he gave back the baby, tucked him into Loi's arms.

Out in the dark there was a splash. Then the purple light started. In its flashes he could see Loi moving off with bird-like speed. Claws snapped the air where she had been.

"Come on, Brian!" He followed her crouching form, moving as best he could through the ruined office. "We've gotta find a way out," she said.

"Not yet!"

"Are you crazy?"

"The controls are around here somewhere. I've got to get to the controls!" He was blundering, feeling his way.

Suddenly there was light—ordinary light sparking in his eyes. Loi was twenty feet away. She'd found a headlamp.

Brian rushed to her, threw his arms around her. "Turn it off!"

"They can see in the dark, so light only helps us. There's got to be a way out around here somewhere."

"We have to find the controls."

When Loi cast the light about, Brian caught a glimpse of black water dancing with wavelets, of a misshapen mass of flesh rising out of it—the source of the long arms and the claws. Ellen? He couldn't bear to consider it.

There was something very different perched on its broad armored carapace, something with huge fly's wings and compound eyes.

The head of this creature turned toward them.

The gaze was so terrible that he gasped as if struck a blow.

Then the thing took flight, came buzzing straight across the small room.

Like quicksilver Loi stepped through a door. She'd been standing right beside it, poised, waiting for the thing to commit itself. "Brian, fast!"

He went racing after her. Her light darted about. "There's a desk," she said. "Block the door."

No sooner had he shoved it against the plywood door than it began to leap on its hinges. Her light flashed from wall to wall. "This is a trap, Brian."

He was looking at the equipment. There was a forest of wires and switches. Here and there were piles of gel filled with the blurry remains of body parts.

He swept the tangle of wires with his eyes. This wasn't his area of expertise, but he knew enough about modern switching techniques to understand a fail-safe system. There were three switches, meant to be thrown at exactly the same time. He stretched, strained, but could not touch more than two of them. It was an "agreement" system like the one used in missile control centers. "Loi, help me with this."

He had to get it turned on. But which side of the forbidden zone was this control room on? Would the breaking of the link catapult Brian and his family into that other world, or leave them here? Best not to think about that now.

The door cracked loudly. In a moment it would burst.

"Brian, we've got to find a way out!"

"Loi, it's our only chance. You have to do this!"

"What do I do?"

"That switch—stand there—turn it—"

The door came off its hinges.

She turned the switch, but not at the right moment. "Honey, we have to do all three at the same time."

Two of the arms came into the room, swarming along the ceiling, their claws cocked wide.

"One, two, three—*now!*"

Something started groaning. A generator? Pumps? He said a silent prayer. Clanging followed, from above, from below, and suddenly a crackle of energy, the hum of one generator starting, another harmonizing with it, a third starting.

Light.

He stood before them with all the dignity of a dark god, this tall, segmented presence—

He came toward them, the buzzing roar so loud that he could not hear, could not think. But the baby regarded him with slow eyes, calm and full of peace.

He faltered.

Loi and Brian saw that they were standing before an awesome tragedy, something proud that had fallen lower than any human being had ever fallen.

He had been glory itself, once, when the world was very, very young.

But then he raised his eyes, and in them there was no glimmer of defeat. Rather, he seemed full of . . . laughter.

With a long, crackling sigh of static, the waveguide started.

Then they were moving, they were sweeping through a blur of changes, into the very well of loneliness and Brian knew that the control room had indeed been on the far side of the zone.

They came to rest in a huge square, a place miles on a side. It was paved with gigantic blocks that reminded Brian instantly of the Bimini Roads, thought to be an ancient geologic formation in the Bahamas.

Loi gasped with surprise, the baby coughed on the yellow, clogged air. A hundred yards ahead there stood a ruined building, once massive, but now tumbled down, its exposed chambers jammed with oozing egg sacs. Thick masses of glowing, red-legged insects swarmed across them, tearing into them and wolfing the contents with complicated jaws.

A high gabble of mad language thundered, and Brian saw that the creatures were so desperate for food that they were eating their own young.

Overhead, wings droned as thousands more flew round and round, seeking something, anything.

This was the heart of the matter: this desperate, dying world was trying to escape its extinction. That was what this was all about.

Using their obvious brilliance and their bizarre science, these creatures had made a link with the living earth, and sought now to possess it and so cheat the darkness that had them in its grip.

Then Brian and Loi were seen. Every eye turned at once, every body grew deathly still. Pincers opened, chitin rattled ominously.

Brian grabbed Loi. Then he saw something truly amazing to him, something that he could not even begin to understand, not for all his knowledge of time and its miracles, and of hidden worlds.

Somehow, the baby in her arms was still connected to their own world, indeed had never left it. It was not an obvious thing, but rather something in the shimmer of light about the child's body, and in the quiet wisdom in those eyes.

We are born to our lives in clouds of wisdom so

great that they are an innocence unsurpassed. The wise child knew, if he did not *see* this place, then—for him—it would not become real.

The dead brown sky split down its middle, exposing a darkness spotted with stars and rolling great planets, a vision of such scope and awe that Brian went to his knees. For the face of God is not a simple thing, nor small, nor made in any image that is known.

Swimming there in the good reefs of stars was the familiar blue earth of today.

The whole mass of creatures saw at once what lay in their sky. A great rumble went through them, a shriek, a hiss, then the blasting drone of wings as they rose in a body, attracted as if to dancing fire.

The things buzzed and roared and struggled.

But their future wavered. Seemingly inside Brian's own mind, the waveguide itself groaned, and the link between the worlds began to falter. He understood what was happening, and why it felt as if it was at once inside him and everywhere: the waveguide was allowing the fundamental order of the universe to be restored.

The earth of the future wavered in the sky. A loneliness like the hollowest hour of an autumn night filled him. His soul ached for the earth that was his own. Beside him his wife choked out a sob.

Brian looked down at his baby, innocently nursing at Loi's breast. The child's eyes met his with a frankness so total that it made him start back in amazement. But there was also tremendous compassion, an openness of spirit that made the old father sob aloud.

Then the angelic presence of the baby focused

him, focused Loi, and they saw that they could not be here, they did not belong here, and nothing could keep them here.

Hope filled them like a rich and dizzying oxygen, and they felt the exhilaration of flight, soaring up, high above the great plaza, the tremendous stone city of the past. Brian saw that it swept to the horizons with its huge shadowed structures, the great blocks with their tiny, frowning windows, and the deep, lightless streets.

Evil had filled every soul in this whole vast place, and they were all corrupt, and so the baby rose above them like a bubble rises in a swamp, and his parents rose with him.

Then they were back where they started, in the dripping, tiny room that housed the control point.

Had it all been a hallucination? . . . or a wish—something from his mind?

The thing they both now thought of as the demon was coming forward in joy and pride, his wings whirring, his long arms spread wide, to greet the horde of his kind that he had so confidently expected to appear.

Instead, Loi and Brian and their baby appeared. The growing power of the waveguide had severed the link between the ages, and the baby's innocence had brought the little family home.

The demon shrank back.

Then Brian saw why: the creature had known better than they what would now happen. A disaster began to unfold. Dark, torn objects started dropping out of thin air—steel-spring legs, pieces of wings, heads with mouth parts still ascramble, glowing, pulpy abdominal segments.

First the pieces dropped, one here, one there. Then they fell in greater numbers, and the demon was jostled by them, moved to protect himself with his cable-thin arms. Then they poured out of the air, and he was thrown back, his howl a jet at full throttle, covered by an avalanche of his own ruined kind.

When he recovered himself, he began moving toward Loi.

Brian pushed his way through the slippery mass of body parts. He had to protect her.

"Brian, no!"

"Get ready to run, Loi."

Closer he went. He could see the segments pulsing, opening and closing to expose bright blue oxygenating organs. This was a primitive creature indeed. This body had been molded when arachnids were the highest form of life on earth. But those eyes—they were very, very smart.

Then Loi did the unexpected, jumping farther than Brian would have thought possible. "Come quick, Brian!" She dashed through the door.

Then what? He'd face that later.

As they ran the lights flickered, and he shuddered with dread. The facility was full of water and in poor repair.

This wasn't over, not at all. If the waveguide failed, or if the demon decided to stop chasing them and destroy it, then all their effort would be for nothing.

They ran up a spiral staircase that had been revealed by the light. In moments Brian's breath came short, his chest burned.

Again the generators ground low, again the lights dimmed.

Little Brian was in full cry, his mother trying to comfort him even as she raced upward.

They reached another surface—and found organic material everywhere lying in limp folds, quivering and dissolving before their eyes.

The outpost he had so carefully fashioned for his people was disintegrating and dying. There was a meaty odor of human blood here, and Brian and Loi both knew that the destroyed creatures in this part of the facility had once been their friends, the people of Oscola and Towayda. Ellen's voice echoed in Brian's memory.

"At least they've died," Loi said. She was also breathing hard.

Brian fought for his bearings. He had no idea where to go to find the exit. But there were limits: they had reached a catwalk, and it only went in two directions. Again the lights flickered. Brian listened—and heard behind them the telltale buzz and clatter of the oncoming creature. "I don't know where the hell we are!"

"We try this way," Loi said.

"You're sure?"

"Just come!"

The buzzing was followed by a great, cawing cry, very different from the roars of anger that had come before. There was blood lust in that cry.

They hurried along, Brian keeping his head down to avoid being knocked senseless by a protruding valve or pipe end. In the light he could see that this place was little more than a few hastily dug tunnels.

They entered a slightly larger room. Brian was amazed: incredibly, Loi had taken them to the main entrance, and there was the elevator shaft. "How did you find this?"

"Too many tunnels in my life, Brian."

He started to push the elevator button, to bring the car down for them.

"No, it's too much of a risk. He can get control of the car from down here."

Brian looked up the shaft. "You can't climb all the way with the baby. It's over a hundred feet."

"I'll carry him as long as I can. Then you do it."

They started up. Brian's chest pain, which had diminished, now returned. His arms shook and his muscles were jelly. Sweat poured down his face. His scars tormented him.

They reached the bottom of the elevator cab. A shaft of light shone down from inside. "I'll pull myself up. Then I'll reach down and take the baby and help you." They were fifty feet from the floor of the shaft.

At that moment there boiled up from below a great, pale cloud, glowing purple within. The lights flashed.

Brian clambered frantically into the car, turned to get the baby. She handed him up, then came herself, moving with the supple grace of a cat.

Absolutely without warning an arm reached out of the gel-covered remains of poor Bill Merriman and grabbed the baby.

Loi threw herself into the mess. She tore at the arm, dug into the gel, throwing gluey body parts over her shoulder. Merriman's enormous glasses sailed past, an eyeball sticking to one of the lenses.

Brian pulled at the mess with her, and together they got their baby back.

"Let's go," he said. They scrambled up through the hatch to the top of the elevator. He had the baby.

With a massive clank and a *whang* the lift cables around them went taut. The elevator began to move downward. Light like a purple sun blasted up from around the car, getting brighter as they dropped.

The ladder was whipping past. "Jump on it," Loi cried.

They leaped, grabbing, clutching, their fingers slipping, holding.

With every ounce of energy they possessed, they climbed. The elevator clicked again and began to return.

"Faster, Brian!"

He fought for every rung of the ladder, tortured by the possibility that he would drop the baby, grabbing for rungs with just the fingers of his left hand. His heart chugged, his breath bubbled.

The car clicked as it came, and the clicks got quickly louder.

Harder they climbed, still harder. But it was no good, Brian could see the car not twenty feet below them. "Loi, as it comes past, jump on the roof! But don't let yourself fall through the hatch." He listened. *Click. CLICK.* "Now!"

Another second and he followed her. She groaned as he landed hard on her. A pain shot up through his leg. He clamped his jaw shut. The baby in his arm cried out in surprise.

"Inside, quick!"

They climbed down into the car.

A moment later it jerked to a stop. Now a doorway

was there before them, but this would only last an instant. Now that they were in it, the car would be brought back down. Brian pressed his fingers between the doors.

He tugged as hard as he could. The doors began to open. But then the elevator moved a couple of inches and they stuck. There wasn't a foot of clearance. Behind him Loi made a stifled groaning sound. He turned. The gel was rising like a slow wave up the back wall of the car. In it the remains of Bill Merriman were coming to life again, but this time they were transforming, moving together, the arms growing thin, the skull changing form, huge compound eyes forming—

He was coming, and in doing so revealing yet another strange ability. He was forming another version of himself out of the man's remains.

They had to get through that door and they had to do it fast.

The baby was easy: Loi pushed him through and set him on the floor outside.

Struggling madly, jerking, twisting, flouncing, she forced her way out. Her breasts stretched agonizingly as she dragged them through, and her own howls made Brian scream, too.

Brian could not make it. He pushed, he shoved, but he was trapped. The creature began to touch him. He felt the purple light beginning to flicker against his back.

Loi pulled and he shoved. His head came out between the doors, then his shoulders. He felt her strong fingers grab him, digging into his scars. "Go on without me," he screamed, "I can't make it!"

She tugged first one shoulder and then the other, and he came by inches.

Within the car there arose a great roaring buzz.

Then he realized that he was out. He was out and crawling, his face scraping dirt.

A long, thin arm came out behind him.

Loi had found some tools and smashed the arm with a shovel, and its surface cracked like a beetle's crisp armor.

Brian realized that she must also have pried the doors with the shovel.

Behind them, the elevator hopped and jumped. Purple light flooded it.

The lamps overhead dimmed, died, then returned, glowing low and weak and red. There came a horrible silence, as if the whole world waited. But Loi gave a shout of joy: not far away was the light of a tunnel entrance.

They had reached the surface.

At that moment a great moan rose from below, the voice of evil stripped naked. There was fierce hunger in it, for the dimming of the lights meant that the waveguide was weakening, and he was gaining strength again.

The cry rose and rose, echoing into the depths, filling the air with its coarse, buzzing savagery.

They covered their ears, they screamed to drown it out.

It ended with the suddenness of a passing storm, and then they heard a scuffling as if of rats, and the sighing of movement in the chambers of the old mine.

He was coming. More slowly now, but still coming. The lights stayed dim.

They moved as fast as they could, dragging themselves toward the entrance, too tired to talk. Brian was sick inside, sick with fear. Now that he knew what was trying to get through, the whole thing was even more awful. What a hideous, hideous fate his experiment had offered the world.

Behind them the scuffling movement of the ravaged demon was getting louder. Brian turned, and could see him in the long corridor, a shrunken, struggling shape all twisted and full of angles, coming along the floor with slow, snake-like undulations.

They went out the facility's entrance, which had been skillfully hidden in the woods between the judge's house and the mound.

They entered a ravaged world.

The alien forest of barrel-like trees was now a desert of sunken bladders. Everything was disintegrating and falling away. Here and there great legs were still attached to huge, dissolving bodies. Shells and carapaces lay scattered about among the leaking, shriveling remains of the trees.

But there was a new scent in the air—new and yet familiar. When dawn is sweet, this is its sweetness. The sun was on the point of rising. Behind the black, torn silhouette of the mound, the morning star floated in pale blue air.

They walked a few steps and sat down. Brian's heart was thundering and his breath was much too short. Loi came beside him and put her free arm around him. Their baby was nursing again, completely content.

"We've got to get help," Brian said. "The facility's got to be kept running!" He could not continue. His grief for his little family expanded into grief for all the world.

"Brian?"

"Yes?"

"You hear that?"

He listened. "Oh God, no." It was the unmistakable sound of humvees. They struggled to their feet. "Loi, I can't go on."

"Yes you can! You have to!"

No. This was the end for him. "I'm sorry."

At that moment a caravan of at least ten of the vehicles came lurching into view, crushing the ruins of the forest beneath their wheels.

Loi turned away from them, heading back toward the entrance to the facility. Somehow, Brian staggered after her. "We can hide in the opening a few minutes. Then we'll think of something else."

But the humvees were fast, and they were already stopping, disgorging their soldiers.

Brian realized that the only thing he could still do for his family was to give them a few extra seconds. As Loi moved away, hurrying as best she could, he turned to face the creatures.

Twenty, thirty, forty soldiers came out of the vehicles, their white chemical warfare suits rustling, their protective masks gleaming in the half light.

With a growl of sheer hate, Brian threw himself at them.

They grabbed him, he shut his eyes against the purple light, snatched at the white cloth, ripped at it. When they took his arms, he fought as best he could, finally yanking away the mask of the closest one.

He came face to face with a perfectly ordinary—

and very scared—kid. "Take it easy," the kid shouted. His breath smelled like chewing gum.

"You—"

"Fourth U.S. Army, mister."

The meaning of this voice penetrated. These were human soldiers. People.

"Loi?" But Loi was nowhere to be seen. From the dark entrance to the facility there came a low, ominous buzzing. *He* was there, his shadow clogging the opening. "Loi! Oh God, no!"

She was not in the entrance: she rose from behind a pile of debris nearby. He watched her come warily forward, her baby in her arms. Her blouse hung in shreds, her jeans were ripped. He went to meet her and they embraced silently. One of the soldiers gave them both jackets.

The buzzing came again, rising like the cry of an insect, then fading to a rumble, sinking. The shadow in the entrance was gone. He was fading like a nightmare with the coming day.

"Listen, you've got to get good generators in there! That facility's got to be kept running at all costs. You've got to—"

"Get in the truck, mister. You're gonna be all right."

"No, for God's sake, listen to me! The waveguide, it's got to be kept on or he'll gain strength again, he'll come out!"

"It's not your problem."

"It's my problem and my fault."

"Mister, this thing is too big to be any one person's fault. Mistakes were made all along the line, way I hear it. Now you get in the truck and let us do our job."

Then Brian saw a huge vehicle trundling down Mound Road, and he recognized what it was: a massive portable generating station of the type deployed in battle. They'd had it outside the zone, waiting for their chance.

Tears came rolling down his cheeks. Somebody somewhere had obviously understood that this would be needed. By getting the guide turned on when they did, he and Loi had given the army its crucial window of opportunity.

They were helped into the backseats of one of the vehicles. The men had some sandwiches and a thermos of coffee. Soon they were lurching and bouncing slowly along the pitted roads of Oscola. Helicopters began landing in the judge's yard, troops pouring out.

"Brian, where are Bob and Nancy and the boys?"

"They went out by ATV."

"They made it?"

"I don't know."

More quietly: "What about Ellen?"

Brian shook his head. "She didn't get out."

She asked no further questions. Silently, she watched the destroyed world going past the window. Suddenly she stiffened. "Stop," she said.

"What the hell for, ma'am?" the driver asked.

Then Brian saw the familiar ruins of the old Kelly Farmhouse, with the burned-out shell of the trailer behind it.

"Just do it, please," she said. "This was our home."

They stopped. "Just for a minute, ma'am."

They got out and went closer to the remains of their old life.

She was solemn. "Even the land is destroyed. Worse than Agent Orange."

Gravely, she offered the baby to his father. "Take him for a second." She marched straight into the fragile, creaking wreck of the trailer. Both soldiers clambered after her.

"Careful there, lady," the sergeant said as she entered the gray, twisted ruins. She reached into the ashes and came up with a blackened lump of an object. "My Laughing Buddha," she said. She rubbed away soot to reveal the familiar rotund figure. "He can be fixed, I think."

The sun rose, and the first shaft of light revealed the true hideousness of the misshapen death all around them. The trees that had surrounded their trailer were dissolving into twisted masses of sludge. A brown, bloated sac of flesh with pincers and spindly legs, and the muscular tail of an opossum, moved slowly across the driveway, dropping chunks of itself, clucking and wheezing as it went.

Dying, it sank down on itself.

But not everything had been reached by the transforming light. A busy cockroach scuttled under a rock, and the dawn chorus began—although it consisted only of a single tattered robin.

Coming out of the rubble, Loi took her baby and held him up to the dawn. "See it, Brian, see the sun."

The baby stirred, smacked, turned his head, seeking instead the nipple. She cuddled him back to her breast. "Our son is going to be so strong."

Brian heard her, but his eye had been attracted to movement in the clear predawn sky. Up very high, a golden contrail went south. "Is that a military jet?"

"Nossir. That'll be a flight coming in from Europe. Probably on its way to New York."

Brian and Loi watched the plane, drinking in its promise with their eyes. The baby, who had finally satisfied his hunger, fell asleep on his mother's arm.

Almost a Bravo

Christine Rimmer

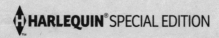

HARLEQUIN® SPECIAL EDITION

Recycling programs
for this product may
not exist in your area.

ISBN-13: 978-1-335-46603-7

Almost a Bravo

Printed in U.S.A.

Christine Rimmer came to her profession the long way around. She tried everything from acting to teaching to telephone sales. Now she's finally found work that suits her perfectly. She insists she never had a problem keeping a job—she was merely gaining "life experience" for her future as a novelist. Christine lives with her family in Oregon. Visit her at christinerimmer.com.

For MSR, always.

Chapter One

When Jaxon Winter entered the waiting room, every nerve in Aislinn Bravo's body snapped to high alert. The housekeeper and the grouchy old foreman from Wild River Ranch followed in his wake. Aislinn hardly noticed them. All she saw was Jax.

He saw her, too. How could he miss her? She was alone in the waiting area and gaping right at him. He gave her that crooked smile, the one she'd never forgotten, the one that tucked a sexy little crease into his left cheek. Too bad there was a crease between his eyebrows, too—a crease that signaled the beginnings of a puzzled frown.

Aislinn shrank in her chair. She not only knew his crooked smile. She knew that almost-frown of his. He didn't remember her. And he had no idea why she was gawking at him.

Stop staring, you idiot!

She tore her gaze free of his and focused hard on a large framed print of the Cape Disappointment lighthouse mounted on the wall opposite her chair. It was one of those mass-produced prints, the solitary lighthouse silhouetted against a wide, gray sky.

The print was dead boring in execution, but Aislinn focused on it anyway to keep herself from sneaking another glance at the tall, broad-shouldered rancher with the thick dark hair.

She heard the brush of footfalls on the carpet as he moved behind her. He spoke quietly to the receptionist. Aislinn stared blindly at that print—until Jax, the ranch foreman and the housekeeper filed into her line of sight and settled into chairs right below the lonely lighthouse.

Now she was staring over their heads, which felt totally awkward all over again. She shifted her gaze once more—downward this time. To her purse, which she grabbed and switched from her left side to her right.

That monumental task accomplished, she crossed her legs and smoothed the skirt of her short-sleeved summer-weight dark blue dress with its cute scattering of tiny white polka dots. The dress had taken her forever to choose. She'd settled on it because the conservative cut and dark color paired with the cheery polka dots said "serious, but with a touch of merriment" to her.

Okay, maybe the merriment part wasn't exactly appropriate in this situation. But a girl had to have a sense of humor, especially at a time like this.

Was her face flaming red? It had better not be.

Stop being weird, she scolded herself. *You're making a big deal out of nothing.*

At least her past obsession with Jaxon Winter was

her secret, one she'd shared only with her closest friend, Keely, who would never betray a trust. Unfortunately, old Martin Durand, Jax's uncle by marriage and also his adoptive father, had known, too.

That unforgettable summer five years ago, Martin Durand had seemed to make it his personal business to keep an eye on her. He used to watch her as if he suspected she might have a criminal past or something. At the time, she'd had no idea that Durand had somehow figured out how she felt about Jaxon.

She'd remained blissfully unaware that the old man knew about her desperate crush until a couple of months ago when Durand had called her out of the blue and announced that Jax's divorce had been final for a year—just in case she hadn't heard.

"He's free now," the old man had said. *"You can go ahead and make your move."*

So bizarre.

At least Martin Durand was never going to say another word about what he knew. According to the letter from his lawyer, he'd died peacefully in his sleep ten days ago. And as for Jaxon, he clearly had no clue that she'd once imagined herself to be hopelessly in love with him.

He doesn't know.

And he would never know.

And it was going to be fine. It was five years ago—yeah, okay. Back then, she'd shamelessly fantasized that he cared, too. But in real life?

Uh-uh. The man had been *married*. He'd been all about keeping his wife happy and he'd hardly known she existed.

As for her, she was so past all that, so over him.

Unwisely, she glanced up—and caught him looking at her with that same perplexed frown he'd worn when he walked in the door. Like she was a puzzle piece and he had no idea where she fit.

This was absurd and she'd had enough of it.

She rose, squared her shoulders and circled the waiting room's central coffee table. Jaxon and the old guy, the foreman—Burt, wasn't it?—got up as she approached. She held out her hand. "Good to see you, Jaxon."

His baffled frown got more so. "I'm sorry," he said in the lovely, low rumble that made her think of tangled sheets and sweaty skin. His eyes were the most beautiful blue swirled with gray, like the sky over the Pacific when the clouds start to gather. He took her hand—just long enough for an utterly unacceptable shiver to slither up her arm. "Do I know you?"

Her smile felt wide enough to crack her face in half. "Of course, you don't remember me. I'm Aislinn Bravo. I worked for you one summer…" She turned to the foreman. "Burt, isn't it?"

The old guy muttered, "Hiya," squeezed her fingers in his rough paw and sat back down.

She aimed a smile at the housekeeper. "Erma, right?"

"Yes," said the housekeeper. "Hello." The older woman reached up and took Aislinn's hand, too, quickly releasing it.

"Wait a minute," said Jax. "I remember now. *Ash*linn, but spelled in that odd way…"

"It's Irish," she replied, just as she had that first day five years ago. "People pronounce it several different ways. But yes, I prefer *Ash*linn."

Jax asked, "Aren't you the one who just disappeared?"

Defensiveness made her draw her shoulders back. She faced him squarely. "I left a note."

"Yes, you did." He looked way too damn pleased with himself that he'd actually recalled some college girl who'd spelled her name oddly and then ran off without giving notice. "It's all coming back to me now. You said in the note that there was a family emergency, that you *had* to go."

"And, um, I did." Not because of any family crisis, though.

"I hope it worked out all right?" he asked, his tone sincere and gentle now. Because he was not only hot and manly, he was also a good person who cared about others.

"Absolutely. Calamity resolved. Nobody died. Everything's fine now."

His frown reappeared. "So you're here to...?"

She really didn't get why she was here. But she shared what she did know. "I got a certified letter from one of the firm's partners, Kip Anders, to attend the reading of Martin Durand's will." Truthfully, that she'd been summoned to the Astoria offices of the old man's lawyer had made no sense at all to her. First off, she hadn't known that he'd died. She felt sorry for that, as she would when anyone died. But why would he put her in his will? He hadn't even liked her—or if he had, he'd had a really strange way of showing it.

She'd considered just blowing the whole thing off, not coming. If Martin Durand had left her something, somebody could mail it to her.

Plus, coming here had meant she was setting herself up for just what was happening now: seeing Jaxon again. It shouldn't be awkward. They'd hardly known each other. Still, she'd had no doubt she would feel uncomfortable. She'd been so right.

And yet she couldn't help but be curious. So here she was.

Burt muttered something under his breath and glared up at her. His unfriendliness didn't surprise her. During those eight weeks she'd worked at Wild River, the foreman had been almost as squinty-eyed and suspicious of her as old Mr. Durand.

"I didn't realize you knew Martin." Jax eyed her warily now.

"I didn't, not really." She felt overwhelmingly defensive, though she had zero reason to be—at least not concerning Martin Durand. "I met him that summer at the ranch, that's all. After I quit, I never saw him again." It was true, but it wasn't what you would call full disclosure. There'd also been that recent unnerving, out-of-nowhere phone call.

"Mr. Winter?" *Saved by the receptionist.* The pretty blonde stood in the arch that led to the inner sanctum. "Everyone." She beamed a professional smile in their general direction. "Mr. Anders is ready for you now. This way, please."

Jaxon gestured Aislinn ahead of him, so she went first. The receptionist led them back to a conference room with a large oval table and a credenza against the wall on which there was a coffee service, including a tray of pastries and doughnuts.

Kip Anders, a slender, balding guy in rimless glasses and a rumpled tan suit, shook Jax's hand and introduced himself to the rest of them. "Please," he said. "Help yourselves to coffee and a bear claw. Get comfortable and we'll get started."

Get comfortable? How long was this going to take? It was a quarter past ten and she'd agreed to help out at her best friend—and now sister-in-law—Keely's art gallery starting at noon. The gallery was about a half hour away from Astoria, on the Oregon coast, in Aislinn's hometown of Valentine Bay. This exercise in awfulness couldn't go more than an hour, could it?

And seriously, why were they even here? Aislinn had worked for a lawyer's office not that long ago. At Deever and Gray they never had will readings. Wills were delivered to the parties concerned. A reading of the will only happened in the movies, because it made for good drama.

Her stomach lurched. Was this about drama, somehow, then?

Oh, God, she really shouldn't have come…

Jax sat at one end of the table. Burt and Erma got coffee and doughnuts and took seats on either side of their boss. Just to have something to do with her hands, Aislinn grabbed a bottle of water. She chose a chair midway down the table. The lawyer took the chair opposite Jax.

"Before you leave," said Anders, tweaking his glasses so they sat more firmly on the bridge of his thin nose, "be sure you each get your copy of the will, which will be waiting for you at the reception desk."

Aislinn almost popped out with, *I think I'll just grab that now and be on my way.*

But she folded her lips between her teeth, set her water on the table and remained in her chair. She was already here and she could spare an hour. Maybe the will contained some complex terms or strange codicils that Kip Anders would need to explain. The lawyer picked up the first paper on the stack in front of him and began to read.

Martin Durand had left bequests of money—ten thousand dollars each—and a series of keepsakes for Burt and Erma. Erma wore a tender look. She seemed sad, but also touched that Durand had thought to leave her something. Who could even guess what that sourpuss Burt might be thinking?

Anders moved on to the next item on the stack. It consisted of several pages paper-clipped together. He removed the clip, set it on the table exactly parallel to the rest of the stack and glanced up to make eye contact— with Jax and then with Aislinn.

"Martin Durand chose to write a letter explaining the main elements of his will," said the lawyer. "His wish was that I read this letter to you, Jaxon, and to you, Aislinn. He also requested that you, Burt, and you, Erma, be present while the letter is read. As you were long-time and faithful employees at Wild River, Martin felt that all four of you should fully understand what he intended and how it should be carried out. The bequests and conditions explained in this letter are also clearly laid out in his formal last will and testament." Anders fell silent for an endless count of five.

Aislinn had the strangest feeling of complete unreality. Her throat felt dry. Sweat bloomed beneath her arms and her pulse raced. She uncapped her water and took a long drink.

Anders asked, "Any questions?"

"Just read," said Jax.

Anders began, "'Dear Jaxon and Aislinn, I never intended for you two to know each other.'"

What?

Aislinn shot a quick glance around the table.

Aside from Anders, serene behind his frameless glasses, they all looked as confused as she felt. How could Durand have *intended* anything when it came to her? He'd never set eyes on her until that summer five years ago.

Anders continued, "'The sad truth, Aislinn, is that I spent the first twenty-one years of your life doing everything in my power never to come anywhere near you. I set myself firmly on pretending that you didn't even exist. And I succeeded for the most part—until five summers ago, when you took the summer job that brought you back to Wild River Ranch.'"

"Back?" Aislinn couldn't keep quiet for one second longer. "But I'd never been to Wild River before that summer, so there is no way that I could have—"

"I know this is bewildering," Anders cut in mildly. "But if you will allow me to read the letter through to its conclusion, most everything will be explained."

Aislinn felt kind of nauseated. She drew in a careful breath through her nose. "Sorry. Go ahead."

With a nod and another quick adjustment of his glasses, Anders went on, "'Such a simple thing you did, Aislinn, to turn my whole life upside down. You took a summer job working at my ranch. And that is how I came face-to-face with the result of the crime I had committed in a split second of opportunity the night of your birth, a crime I've kept hidden for all these years…'"

The night I was born?

She couldn't *not* speak. "I don't get it. Whatever he did, it's got zero to do with me. I was nowhere near Wild River on the night I was born." They were all frowning at her—and okay, yeah. She needed to stop interrupting.

But no. Just *no*.

Durand had it all wrong. Aislinn had been born in Europe, in a tiny principality called Montedoro, where her mother and father and four of her five brothers had traveled when her mom was pregnant with her.

"That right there," she insisted, "what you just read? How could whatever he did involve me? It couldn't. I was born in Montedoro, which is on the Côte d'Azur, in case you didn't know. No way Martin Durand was there when I was born."

Down the table, Burt glared at her. Erma sat silent, her expression unreadable. And Jaxon? He looked like he couldn't wait for this to be through.

Well, neither could she.

And hold on a minute. The letter hadn't actually said that this "crime" of Durand's involved her, had it? So maybe this had nothing to do with her at all. She gulped. "I just don't understand. Why am I here?"

Again, Kip Anders suggested, "If I might just finish...?"

"But it's all *wrong*."

Anders didn't argue, he simply waited.

With a hard sigh, she gave in. "All right. Fine. Finish it, then."

Anders granted her a nod. "Martin Durand writes, 'The morning of the night you were born, Aislinn, George Bravo and his very pregnant wife, Marie, had driven out to Wild River from Valentine Bay to discuss the possibility of their investing in an expansion of our horse breeding and training operation.

"'The investment never happened. But during George and Marie's visit, there was a storm, a bad one. The roads were washed out. Marie went into labor—and so did our then-foreman's wife, Paula Delaney.

"'You see, Aislinn, I had cheated on my wife, Claudia, with Paula. I make no excuse for that. It was wrong. I did it anyway, with the classic result.'"

"What a complete SOB," Aislinn cried. All eyes swung her way. "Sorry. Really." She shot Anders a desperate glance. "And honestly, none of this can be true." They all continued to stare at her. "All right." She waved a hand. "Fine. Just go ahead."

Anders read on, "'When she realized she was pregnant, Paula had come to me. She swore that the baby was mine. She wanted to leave her husband and make a life with me and the child. I wanted none of that. I was happy with Claudia, for the most part. I loved my wife and I liked our life together—and Claudia owned Wild River.

"'Jaxon, you were eight at the time. You'd been with us for four years by then. As I've explained to you many times, in honor of the long line of Winters who had owned and worked Wild River for generations, we had you keep your last name when we formally adopted you. But in all the ways that really count, you were our son. We were a family—you, Claudia and I. I told Paula no. I urged her to forget about me. Use your head, I said, stay with Lloyd where you belong. Paula wouldn't listen. She said she loved me. I was sure there would be trouble, that she would come after me, demand a test that would prove her baby was mine. I would lose everything that mattered to me.

"'I didn't know what to do to get that woman to leave me alone. And then Marie Bravo showed up and went into labor at the same time Paula did. The perfect moment presented itself, both babies in makeshift cribs made of storage boxes, sharing the same room while Claudia, acting as emergency midwife, tended to the new mothers in rooms on either side.'"

Aislinn felt light-headed. Her stomach roiled.

Anders read on, each word painfully slow and clear. "'I entered the babies' room when no one was looking and discovered that the infants were similar in size, both with eyes of that same newborn blue. The hair color was different, one darker, one lighter. But there was so little of it on either tiny head, I dared to hope that no one would notice the difference. I saw my moment and I took it, switching the babies and their blankets, too.'"

Aislinn sat very still, her hands pressed to her churning stomach. She knew if she moved or even dared to breathe, she was going to be sick—just hack up her breakfast, spew it across the unblemished oval of the conference table.

It was all a lie. It had to be. Martin Durand couldn't be her father. Her father was George Bravo, a good man, a loving husband and a doting dad, a man who made each of his sons and daughters feel wanted and secure.

She was a Bravo, born, bred and raised. Her parents had been deeply in love, wonderfully brave and adventurous—and more than a little bit foolish.

They'd had a passion for traveling the world, her mom and dad. They'd lost one son on a trip to Siberia. Finn, eight at the time, had simply vanished—kidnapped for ransom, they all assumed. But the ransom demand never came and Finn had not been seen or heard from again. And then her parents were lost, too, a few years later, on a romantic getaway to Thailand, where they were caught in a tsunami.

Her family had suffered. But they had gotten through

it, together. Her oldest brother, Daniel, eighteen when their parents died, had won custody of all of them. He'd raised them the rest of the way, Aislinn and the six other remaining Bravo siblings. Their road hadn't been smooth or easy, but they'd made it work. Together. And she loved them.

And they were *hers*, damn it. Her people. Not some unknown woman named Paula who'd cheated on her husband. Not crazy, bad-tempered old Martin Durand.

She wanted to scream at them—at Jaxon and Burt, at Erma and the lawyer. She wanted to shout at them, *Stop this! Stop these lies! Stop right now!*

But her voice had deserted her and her throat felt constricted, like brutal hands were squeezing it.

And Kip Anders just kept reading the lying words of Martin Durand.

"'I left those babies, each in the wrong storage-box crib. I ran from that room and I didn't look back—until later, of course, when it was too late, when I realized that if Paula did demand a paternity test, she would find out that not only was the baby not mine, it wasn't hers or Lloyd's, either. She would remember the night of the birth and the other woman's child in the same room with her child. She would figure it out and I would be caught anyway, proved not only a cheater, but also a criminal.

"'As it turned out, though, the crime I'd committed was completely unnecessary. Paula never came after me to take a father's responsibility. Instead, she took my advice and let Lloyd think the child was his. And then a few months later, Lloyd got another job out of state and we hired Burt. I never saw Paula or Lloyd or the child who was really Marie Bravo's daughter again.

"'I told myself there was no harm done. Each woman

had a baby—yes, all right, the *wrong* baby. But they didn't know that, so what did it matter? Everyone was happy. I tried to forget.

"'To Claudia, I was a faithful husband from then on. Twelve years later, when Claudia died, I missed her. I mourned her. She left everything to me with the understanding between us that it would all go to you, Jaxon, at my death. I steered clear of Valentine Bay and any chance I might see you, Aislinn, and know you as mine.

"'But then you showed up at Wild River that summer, looking just like my mother, who had died before I ever set foot in Oregon. At first, I was certain you must somehow have found out who you were to me, that you'd come to make me pay for cheating on Claudia, for switching you with Marie Bravo's child and then just walking away. I watched you, waiting, wondering how you planned to exact your revenge. But all I saw was a girl with my mother's haunting dark eyes, a girl in love with Jaxon.'"

In love with Jaxon...

Aislinn stifled a groan.

Because, dear God in heaven, *why*?

Why that, too?

Martin Durand had no pity at all. He'd died determined to strip her of every last scrap of herself—to steal her identity, take away her family and then go blithely on to out her most shameful secret, that she'd once fallen so hard for a married man, she'd had to run away to keep from throwing herself at him.

Aislinn closed her eyes so she wouldn't have to look at any of them, closed her eyes, braced her elbows on the table and pressed her hands to the crown of her head. Another groan tried to escape her. She swallowed it down.

Anders made a throat-clearing sound.

"Aislinn," Jaxon asked cautiously, "are you all right? Do you need a break?"

She ground her teeth together and refused to open her eyes. "Finish, damn you all. Get it over with."

For a moment, there was silence.

Then at last she heard papers rustling and Anders finally got on with it. "Ahem. Let's see—ah. Here we go. 'And then one day, Aislinn, you simply quit. You vanished without claiming your last paycheck, leaving nothing but a brief note for Jaxon citing some vague emergency. The months went by and I began to accept the truth that you were innocent. You knew nothing. I began to see that I would have to do what I could to make things right.

"'I hired an investigator to find Paula and the missing child who should have been Marie Bravo's daughter. The Delaneys had named the child Madison.'"

At the sound of that name, Aislinn dropped both hands off her head and slapped them, palms flat, onto the table, causing Erma to let out a small squeak of alarm.

Madison Delaney?

No. Uh-uh. Not *the* Madison Delaney. Pure coincidence, it had to be.

Anders went right on. "'My investigator reported that ten years after the Delaney family left Wild River, Lloyd Delaney died. Paula and her daughter then moved to Los Angeles, where Madison pursued a career as an actress— to great success, as it turned out.'"

"This has to be a joke, right?" The question escaped Aislinn without any help from her conscious mind. "This is all a prank. I'm being punked. I'm actually supposed to believe that Martin Durand switched me with the baby who grew up to be *Madison Delaney*? Do you *know* who Madison Delaney is? She's won an Oscar. She's America's darling."

And, dear God, she looks way too much like my sisters.

How had she never noticed that before? Madison Delaney had big blue eyes, like all three of her sisters. And the cutest dimples when she smiled, like both Harper and Hailey. The actress had worn her hair in a variety of colors and styles, but she was naturally blond, wasn't she? Like Aislinn's sisters. And she had a nose that turned up ever so slightly at the tip, just like her youngest sister, Grace.

The others were openly staring at her now.

"What?" she demanded. "Don't you even try to tell me you've never heard of Madison Delaney."

"Of course we've heard of her," said Jax. He spoke gently, as though talking to a crazy person—and maybe she *was* crazy. Maybe she'd completely lost her mind.

Kip Anders made a throat-clearing sound. "May I go on?"

"Please." Aislinn poured on the sarcasm. "Be my guest."

With a dignified nod, Anders continued, "'The sad news, Aislinn, is that Paula Delaney died not long after that summer you worked at Wild River. I'm sorry you will never have an opportunity to get to know the woman who gave you life. I haven't tried to contact Madison Delaney, just as I never told you the truth during my lifetime. I have no idea how everyone will take this news. I'm an old man now. Forgive me, but I can't predict what the fallout from these particular revelations will be. And I don't have the energy to find out. So, I'm leaving all that to you and the Bravo family. The investigator's full report will be available to you immediately.'"

Coward, she thought. He'd left all the tough work for others to do. She wished he hadn't died—so she could kill him herself.

Anders kept reading, "'And as for you specifically, Aislinn, I've had my eye on you since the summer you came to work at Wild River. You haven't married or gotten seriously involved with a man. I wanted to know if you still held out hope that Jaxon might be yours. That's why I called you recently to remind you that Jaxon is free now. I heard the longing in your voice when you demanded that I never try to call you again.'"

It was too much. Of a ridiculousness beyond all insanity. Aislinn straightened and announced, "Come *on*. As if that crazy old man could tell anything from one phone call, a very brief phone call, a phone call that he openly admits ended with me demanding that he leave me alone."

They all just stared at her—as they'd been staring at her almost from the moment Kip Anders began to read Durand's last letter.

Another sound of pure misery escaped her. She ducked her head once more and laced her fingers on top of it. "Sorry. Go on. Just…get it over with, please."

Kip Anders did just that. "'After that phone call, I knew I had to leave you what you want most of all—a chance at a life with my adopted son.'"

"What the hell, Martin?" It was Jax, his voice a rough whisper.

Kip Anders didn't even pause. "'Aislinn, you and Jax are to marry within a week from the date of the reading of this letter. You are then to remain married for at least the next three months. After three months of marriage, you, Aislinn, will receive fifty thousand dollars from my estate. And, Jaxon, you will get the deed to Wild River and all the rest of it, as you should, as I always promised you and Claudia. Once the three months pass, it's up to the two of you whether you choose to stay together or not.

"'You must mutually agree to these terms and carry through with them. Aislinn, if you do not marry Jaxon and live as his wife for three full months, you will get nothing.'"

Nothing. She wanted to throw back her head and laugh.

As if fifty thousand dollars meant squat to her right now.

As if all the money in the world could ever stack up against what Martin Durand had just stolen from her—her pride, her family, her very identity.

Anders droned on, "'Jaxon, if you refuse to marry Aislinn for three months, Wild River Ranch and everything on it will be sold at auction. You will get the proceeds from the sale as well as everything else that belonged to me, minus any other bequests mentioned in my will. Jaxon, you are the son of my heart, and it has been an honor to be a father to you. I want you to have Wild River, but if that doesn't happen, you will at least have plenty of capital with which to start over. I realize that will be little consolation to you, as we both know very well that you love Wild River more than your life. But believe it or not, I am doing this for you—for *both* of you. I think you will make a good match, that you will be good for each other. So I am giving you the opportunity you otherwise never would have had. I wish you both love and happiness and a successful future together. With all my deepest affection and my highest regard, Martin Durand.'"

Dropping her hands from their ludicrous protective position over her head, Aislinn popped up straight in her chair. "That's it? That's *all*?"

Anders blinked behind his glasses. "The, erm, end of the letter, yes. But we have yet to cover several specific conditions and particulars that you'll both need to—"

"Stop." She shoved back the chair and leaped to her feet. "As if I care about your so-called *conditions*. As if I care about that old man's money. As if I care about any of this crap. I am...not that person. Not somebody who was supposed to be named Madison Delaney. I'm Aislinn Bravo. I was born in Montedoro at the villa of Tristan Bouchard, Count of Della Torre. You ask my brothers. They were there, they remember. They..." She lost track of her words as her gaze skittered around the table. They all looked at her as though she'd lost her mind—all of them, Jax most of all.

She could read his thoughts in that look on his face. *She's a nutjob,* his expression said, *and I am so screwed...*

She went ahead and put it right out there, right in his face. "You think I'm crazy."

Jax jerked back. "No. No, I..."

That made her laugh, a bizarre, deranged sort of sound. "Hey, come on. Be honest, Jax. You think I've lost my ever-loving mind. And maybe I have. Because who wouldn't go crazy, after all I've just heard?"

"Aislinn, really, nobody thinks you're—"

"Oh, yes, you do. And to be perfectly honest, you might be right. I've come unhinged. This is all too much and I just can't take any more. I mean, it's simply not possible, that my family isn't my family, that my birth mother and the real Aislinn Bravo moved to Los Angeles, where she became a superstar named Madison Delaney. That all I know to be true about myself and my life is really just a big, fat lie."

The lawyer suggested mildly, "How about if we take a few minutes and—"

"How 'bout if we don't?" Aislinn pinned the lawyer with a hard glare.

It was all so far beyond too much.

Jax tried once more, "Aislinn, if you would just—"

"No." She cut him off cold as she snatched her purse off the chair. "Uh-uh. I need a minute. I need a thousand minutes. I need a lifetime out of this room." She turned for the door.

"Aislinn, wait!" Jax called after her.

She kept walking, not once glancing back, grabbing the door handle, flinging it wide and escaping down the hallway that led to the waiting room.

As she flew by the front desk, the pretty receptionist jumped up. "Ms., er, are you all right?"

"Not really."

"Is there something I can—?"

"Thanks, but no." Aislinn shoved open the entry door and went through it.

Out on the sidewalk under a cool gray sky, she kept walking right into the street. A guy in a red Mustang squealed to a stop just in time to avoid running her down.

"Watch out, you idiot!" he yelled out the window.

She ignored him and kept going until she reached the opposite sidewalk, at which point she suddenly ran out of steam. Halting just past the stop sign, she found herself in front of a three-story building of light-colored brick with a sign that read BPOE on the side.

With no idea where to go next, she ducked into the alcove that sheltered the entry doors. For a moment, she froze and stared at her faint reflection in the glass of the door—a dark-haired woman in a polka-dot dress, someone she hardly recognized.

She shook herself. She couldn't just stand here blocking the entrance.

Wrapping her arms around herself, she slid into the corner on the right side of the door and tried to decide what to do next.

Chapter Two

"Give me a few minutes," Jax said to the others. "I'll talk to her. I'll bring her back."

He went through the door she'd left open and strode down the hallway toward the waiting area.

This was like some nightmare, his worst nightmare. Wild River could be lost to him because Martin had done something really bad way back when—and then decided he needed to make his own brand of twisted amends after his death.

And the woman, Aislinn. She'd seemed completely destroyed by what she'd just learned. It had felt downright evil to sit there at that table, a witness to her suffering, as Anders read that showboat letter of Martin's that said she wasn't who she'd always believed herself to be.

Damn Martin. Damn him to hell and back. Jax had loved the old reprobate, but this was one long, rickety bridge too far.

And then again…

Well, Martin was Martin. He'd always made life interesting. Jax and his Aunt Claudia, both serious, down-to-earth and a little bit shy, had secretly reveled in the excitement Martin brought to their lives. They always tried to hold him back when he got some out-there idea he was itching to pursue. At the same time, they loved it. They were his audience and Martin was the star of their cobbled-together family of three.

If Martin were here now in the flesh, what would he say? Jax knew: *I love you, son. I never wanted to hurt you. But we both know some men need a good kick in the pants to get out there and get what matters most—and who around here needs a good kick?* Martin would grin. *Look in a mirror, Jaxon, my boy.*

Jax felt all turned around. Wild River was in jeopardy. He needed to consider every possibility.

Was the woman really what she seemed? Could this be her doing, somehow?

That bit about being in love with him. What was that, anyway? Had Martin simply lost it in his last days—or had Aislinn Bravo somehow gotten to him? Had she managed, secretly, to cozy up to a lonely old man and whisper in his ear?

But whisper what? *I'm your daughter and you owe me. I'll take Jaxon.*

No. Wrong.

This wasn't the woman's fault. It couldn't be. Even with a possible fifty K in the mix, it didn't quite add up that she was in on this horror show.

No. On the surface at least, this was pure Martin—the drama of it, the insanity and the out-there, over-the-top solution of Jax and Martin's secret daughter getting married and remaining so for three months in order that said secret daughter would get her chance at her heart's desire: Jax himself.

Completely bonkers.

Still, he had to keep his eyes open. That Aislinn Bravo might be the bad guy in this didn't *seem* possible. But as of now, anyway, he couldn't be 100 percent certain of her innocence, either. He barely remembered her from that summer five years ago, and he had no way to be sure who she was deep down, at heart.

And whatever she'd done, whatever her possible part in this lunacy, he needed her on the same page with him now. Unless Anders could come up with some way to break the terms of Martin's crazy-ass last will and testament, Jax was going to need her to be married to him for the next three months.

It was that, or lose Wild River.

And that could never happen. His family had owned Wild River for generations. The ranch was his future and his past. It was everything to him. He would never let it go.

He strode fast across the lobby and pushed through the double doors out onto Exchange Street, glancing left first, then right and seeing no sign of her. Had she vanished around the corner? Disappeared into a Lyft?

But then he looked straight ahead.

And there she was across the street, huddled in the doorway alcove of the Elks building, her arms wrapped around herself, her delicate shoulders hunched. She seemed to be studying the pretty white sandals on her narrow feet.

He waited for a delivery van to go by and then jogged

across the street, slowing his steps when he reached the sidewalk in order not to startle her.

She must have sensed him coming. Her shining chin-length curls bounced as her head came up. He stopped six feet from her, close enough to talk, but not so close he crowded her.

"What do you want?" Her eyes were enormous, dark as black coffee, brimming with hurt and confusion.

If she's acting, she ought to be in movies—just like the other one, Madison Delaney. "Come back inside with me. Hear the rest."

A wild shudder went through her. "Oh, God. There's more?"

"Just the details. You need to hear them. We both do."

"No." She shook her head, setting the curls bouncing again. "No, I don't think I need that. I don't think I *can.*"

A redhead approached pushing a stroller. Her freckle-faced little boy waved at Jax as he rolled by.

Jax stole a step closer to the woman in the alcove. "You don't have to decide anything today."

She scrunched her eyes shut and swiped her inky hair back from her forehead. "I mean it, Jax. I really don't think I can."

"Can, what?"

"Go back in there. I mean, is this really happening? I'm not me. And crazy old Martin Durand is my biological father?"

"I hear you." Another step. She didn't bolt. "It's completely insane."

She pinned him with a shining, furious look. "I hate him. You must hate him about now, too, huh?"

He answered her truthfully. "No. I loved him. I miss him."

She made a tight, angry sound. "You *still* love him? After what you just heard in there?"

"Hey. I didn't say he was an easy man to love. But he made every day an adventure. And he was always good to me in his way."

She scoffed outright. "Oh, please. I saw how he was that summer I worked for you. He let you do all the work while he sat on the front porch in his ratty old bathrobe."

"I like doing the work. And Martin used to work hard, too, back when I was growing up." He watched her closely as he spoke. Did his voice seem to soothe her? Maybe. And at this point, he would try anything to keep her from taking off again. He went on talking. "When I was a boy, we worked together, Martin and me. Aunt Claudia was sick a lot. Martin taught me everything I know about ranching and horses. And then he sent me to college, though I didn't want to go. He said I needed to get out and see what the world had to offer, said I had to be certain that Wild River was my choice, not just the only thing I knew. He also got it right about Judy—my ex-wife?"

She looked at him, wide-eyed. "What about her?"

"Martin said Judy would never be happy at Wild River, no matter that she promised me she would love ranch life. Judy *didn't* love it and she kept after me to move with her to the Bay Area, where her family lived. Eventually, she divorced me and went back to San Francisco."

And whoa. Talk about too much information— bringing up Judy, babbling out private stuff that no one needed to hear. Soothing this woman was one thing, but the verbal diarrhea needed to stop.

Aislinn, still huddled in the corner by the door, was

watching him. And now that he really looked at her, he could see Martin in her—in the soft, full shape of her mouth, the elegant line of her nose.

He held out his hand. "Come back in, won't you?"

She looked at his outstretched fingers, considering. But she didn't take them. "I'm sorry," she said, as he gave up and dropped his arm back to his side. "I can't do it—can't go back in there. Can't do…any of it."

Oh, yeah, she could. She *had* to do it. Impatience coiled like a snake inside him. But he refused to give in to it. Impatience wasn't going to help him get through to her. "What'd I say a minute ago? You don't have to decide right now."

Those doe eyes stayed locked with his. "I'm scaring you. I'm sorry."

"No, you're not scaring me," he lied.

"Yes, I am. And I get it. You'd do anything, even marry a stranger, to keep the ranch you love."

Damn straight, he thought but somehow managed not to blurt out. "Look. It's three months. You live nearby, right?"

"In Valentine Bay."

"A half-hour drive from Wild River. Just think about it. We get married. You live at the ranch, which isn't that far from your job or whatever. Three months. And you're fifty thousand dollars richer."

She looked about to break down in tears. "It's too much. I told you, I can't—"

"Wait." He put up both hands. "You're right. Don't decide now. Just come back inside. That's all I'm asking."

She drew herself up and said stiffly, "There's something I *have* to say to you."

"Go for it."

"No matter what that crazy old fool thought, I am not in love with you."

She wanted him to say he believed her? Not a problem. Whatever she wanted, he would damn well provide it. "I get that. I believe that. You're not in love with me and you never have been."

She frowned, as though judging his answer, turning his words over in her mind, weighing his sincerity. In the end, she nodded. "Good, then. I'm glad we have that cleared up, at least."

A heavily inked couple in matching short-sleeved plaid shirts, bib overalls and Birkenstocks came toward him. He fell back toward the curb a little and nodded as they passed between him and the woman in the doorway.

When he stepped closer to Aislinn again, she was fiddling with the shoulder strap of her purse, all frustrated energy. And then she froze. Her soft mouth trembled. "I'm just having a little trouble processing, you know? I mean, if what that letter said is true, I'm not a Bravo. My sisters and brothers are not actually mine. At this moment, I have to tell you, I don't even know *who* I am. And there's a movie star living in Southern California who doesn't know she's got a whole family of amazing people she's never even met. It's all wrong. It can't be true. I can't even deal."

"You're getting way ahead of yourself."

"You keep saying that."

"Because it's true. Sometimes in life you just need to do the next thing—which, right now, is to go back inside and hear the rest of what Kip has to tell us."

She chewed on her plump lower lip—and the miracle happened. She nodded. "All right. But I'm likely to be late for work, so I need to call in first."

"Do it."

She got out her phone. He turned and went to wait by the stop sign, giving her privacy. A minute or two later, she came up beside him. "Let's go."

Ever the gentleman, Jax opened the door for her. Aislinn went through reluctantly.

The receptionist gave her a too-bright smile as they passed her desk. In the conference room, Burt glared at her and Erma nodded, giving away nothing.

Kip Anders said, "Aislinn. Excellent," as though she'd done something wonderful. "Anyone care for more coffee or whatever?" When no one moved toward the credenza for a refill, he straightened his stack of papers. "All right, then, let's continue."

Aislinn sat down and tried to ignore the frantic racing of her heart. Her hands were shaking. She folded them tightly in her lap to keep them still.

"A few important points." Kip sent them each a cool smile. "As you will see when you go over your copy of the will, Martin instructs that the wedding must take place within a week from today, and that it must also be 'more than in name only.'"

"What does that even mean?" Aislinn asked furiously.

"And how do you enforce it?" asked Jax.

"It is a gray area," Anders replied. "In Oregon, there is no requirement for consummation by sexual relations. That means you will be legally married once you've acquired the marriage license and said your vows before a recognized official—be that a clergy person or a representative of the court. To be married 'in more than name only' in this case will include getting the license, going through with the ceremony and living together at

Wild River for the full three months during which you must remain true to your marriage vows."

I'm not marrying anyone, Aislinn thought with vehemence. But she pressed her lips into a thin line and kept quiet for once. Her embarrassing long-ago crush on Jax aside, she considered him a good man. She *liked* him and she didn't want to mess him over. That ranch meant the world to him. She couldn't quite bring herself to outright refuse to help him keep what he wanted the most. At least not right now, not yet.

She needed to think it over.

And she would. *After* she met with her brothers and they confirmed that this story about Martin Durand being her father had to be a complete fabrication. First and foremost, she needed to reassure herself of the truth from the ones who had been there in Montedoro at Villa Della Torre on the night she was born.

The lawyer said, "To further clarify, after the marriage ceremony, you two must be sexually monogamous for the required three months. You will cohabitate at the ranch house at Wild River. Martin has arranged for someone from Kircher and Anders to drop by randomly in order to confirm that you continue to live together for the entire three-month period required by the will."

"I hate to speak ill of the dead," muttered Aislinn, because she *had* to say something, "but that old man was a terrible, awful, horrible person and I sincerely hope he is rotting in hell."

Burt grumbled something under his breath at that. Erma stared straight ahead. Jax only gave her a sympathetic glance and a one-shouldered shrug, as if to say, *Yeah, I loved him, but I see your point.*

Kip Anders went on to explain that after the wedding,

he would need a copy of the license to prove they had met the requirement of marrying within the week and to begin the countdown to the three-month time limit.

At eleven forty, Kip Anders finally walked them out to the waiting room, where the receptionist gave each of them a blue folder containing copies of Martin's infuriating letter and the will. Tucked in the front pocket of each folder was a contact sheet, which included a secure online address where they could access an electronic copy of everything in the folder.

On the list of contacts was the phone number and address of the Seattle private investigator Martin had hired to find Madison and Paula Delaney.

Aislinn cringed just at the sight of the PI's name. That Martin had hired the man seemed yet another proof that his story might actually be true—though it wasn't.

Absolutely not. So what if Paula and Lloyd Delaney had once worked at Wild River and even had a daughter who grew up to be *the* Madison Delaney?

All that could be true. And Aislinn could still be a Bravo by birth.

Out on the sidewalk again, Jax sent Burt and Erma back to the parking lot to get their vehicle.

Then he turned to Aislinn. "I'm sorry to push you, but we don't have long to get going on this. Can you meet me at the Marriage License Bureau tomorrow to get the license? Just name a time that works for you and I'll be there."

In spite of the panic that kept trying to claw its way along every nerve she possessed, she grinned. "Nice try."

He looked so weary. And worried. "Aislinn—"

"No. Please. I can't agree to anything right this minute."

"When, then?"

"I need a few days, at least."

"We don't *have* a few days."

"I'm sorry, Jax. I know this isn't your fault. But it isn't mine, either, and I need to figure a few things out. I'll talk to you later."

"Aislinn." For the first time since they shook hands in the waiting room, he touched her. His long fingers closed around her arm. "Wait." The feel of his skin on hers made her heart race.

She froze, looked down at where he held her, and then back up at him. "Let go, Jax."

"Sorry." He released her.

"I'll get back to you," she promised because she didn't know what else to say. Whirling on her heel, she headed for her car, walking fast, half expecting him to try again to stop her.

But he didn't come after her. She kept her gaze forward, never once looking back. She knew that if she glanced over her shoulder and saw him standing there, so tall and strong and proud, in good black jeans, town boots and a crisp white shirt, she would give in and agree to do anything he needed her to do.

Keely Ostergard Bravo's gallery, Sand & Sea, two blocks from the beach on Manzanita Avenue in Valentine Bay's historic district, had a profitable afternoon that day.

It was August, after all. The morning fog had cleared, leaving the sky a pure, endless blue. Perfect tourist weather on the Oregon coast.

Aislinn had relieved the manager, Amanda Cruz, who went off to run errands. Aislinn spent the next few hours dealing with a steady stream of customers on her own. That was fine with her. Staying busy kept her mind off the abject awfulness of all she'd learned that morning.

Amanda came back in at four to close up. Aislinn went home to the cottage where she lived with her sisters Hailey and Harper. The two had recently graduated from OU down in Eugene.

The cottage was a family property built in the '40s, a rambling collection of rooms, all on one level, with two baths and four bedrooms. Her ancient great-uncle Percy Valentine had given it to her as a gift for her twenty-fifth birthday with the understanding that she would welcome any siblings who needed a place to stay.

Neither of her sisters' cars were out in front when she got there, which was good. She had this feeling that if they saw her face, they would know something was wrong and they would demand that she tell them everything. She wasn't ready to talk about any of it—not until after she'd met with her brothers, anyway.

Before going inside, she visited Luna and Bunbun, her German angora rabbits. The pair had the run of half of her front porch, which was enclosed, rabbit-proofed and equipped with a roomy hutch they wandered in and out of at will—except on the rare occasions that she needed them caged.

Needing comfort, she got down on the porch floor with them and indulged in a long cuddle session. She buried her face in their enormous clouds of fur, lavished them with rubs and pets, all the while murmuring silly endearments.

Once she'd loved them up thoroughly, she filled their hay racks, refreshed their food and water and cleaned

their litter boxes. And then, leaving them happily nosh-
ing away, she went on into the house.

It was far too quiet inside. All her fury and misery at
what had happened in Astoria that morning came flooding back. She made herself a sandwich, sat at the table
and cried for a while.

She really needed to talk to her best friend. Aislinn
and Keely never kept secrets from each other. If Keely
was here, Aislinn could get it all out, tell her friend everything.

But Keely was off on her honeymoon. Confiding in
her would have to wait.

Glumly chewing her sandwich, Aislinn group-texted
three of her brothers—Matthias, Connor and Liam—all
of whom, so the story went, had been there in Montedoro
when she was born. Daniel had been there, too. But he
was with Keely in Bora Bora and Aislinn wasn't bothering him, either. Daniel and Keely had had more than
enough challenges to face in the past few months. They
deserved their honeymoon in paradise, a beautiful time
for just the two of them, 100 percent free of family drama.

There's something important I really need to talk to
you guys about, she texted her brothers. Beers at Beach
Street Brews? Seven sharp. I'm buying.

Actually, she preferred a little bar called the Sea
Breeze that Keely's mother, Ingrid Ostergard, had
bought, remodeled and reopened just a month ago, on
Independence Day. But Keely's mom would be there.
And Grace, the youngest of the Bravo siblings, probably would, too. Gracie had started working for Ingrid
during the Sea Breeze's remodeling phase.

And the fewer family members around for this particular conversation, the better. Aislinn still hadn't de-

cided how much to tell her brothers. It was all a big mess. *She* was a mess.

A mess who had no idea who she really was.

Her brothers got right back to her. They would all three be there at the brewpub at seven o'clock.

That made her cry again. Who had such great brothers—big, handsome guys who dropped everything to be there if their sister needed them? They were the best. What if it turned out they really weren't even *hers*?

Beach Street Brews was a barnlike place with scuffed wide-plank floors and rows of high-sided wooden booths lining the tin-paneled walls. The acoustics were terrible. On the weekends when they had live music, conversation was impossible.

But early on a Wednesday evening, it wasn't so bad. Matthias had gotten there first. Matt was ex-military. Now he worked as a game warden with the Oregon State Police.

He was out of uniform tonight. When Aislinn slipped into the booth next to him, he poured her a beer from the pitcher he'd already ordered.

"You okay, Ais?" he asked. "You look kinda down."

"Been better," she admitted.

His golden-brown eyebrows drew together in concern, but before he could say anything more, Connor and Liam showed up.

Matt poured them beers and they talked about the warm weather and how Connor was doing over at Valentine Logging. He was running the family company while Daniel was on his honeymoon. Aislinn sipped her beer and watched their dear faces, their gold-kissed eyebrows and tawny hair.

George Bravo had had dark brown hair and blue eyes. Marie was blue-eyed, too, and a natural blonde. All of their children had blue eyes and none of them had hair any darker than medium brown.

Except Aislinn.

Her mom had always claimed that she was special, different. And her dad used to say she took after the Bravo side of the family. He'd had six brothers and a couple of them were dark-eyed with almost-black hair. Her mom used to say she looked French—a little French princess, born in a villa on the Cote d'Azur. Aislinn had loved that, loved being the different one.

Until today.

Matt asked, "So, what's going on with you, Ais?"

"Is everything okay?" asked Liam, burnished eyebrows drawing together.

At home, she'd debated whether or not to tell all and decided she ought to be totally honest, offer full disclosure. But now, sitting in that booth, her gaze bouncing from one well-loved face to another, she just couldn't go there, couldn't tell them outright that she might not be their sister, that she'd taken their real sister's place, while the true Aislinn had gone off to California to become Hollywood royalty.

Later for all that.

"I've been thinking about Mom," she began. "About the story she always told me, that I was born in Montedoro."

"The Montedoro trip." Connor mock-saluted with his glass of beer. "Mom just had to go there, even though she was almost eight months' pregnant with you."

"And, of course," Liam added, "she and Dad took us along—not that I remember a thing about it. I was what, three?"

And Matt had been five, Connor four. Daniel, seven at the time, would probably remember the most of the four of them. Too bad he was off somewhere in paradise with Keely.

Matt volunteered, "I kind of remember the Prince's Palace. Huge and white, up there on that hill overlooking the harbor. And I remember meeting Uncle Evan and his wife, the princess." Their dad's brother, once an actor, had married Montedoro's ruling princess. Matt went on, "But I'm drawing a complete blank on the villa we stayed at—the one where you were born, I mean. Didn't you go to Montedoro to check it out, after college?"

She licked the beer mustache from her upper lip. "I did, yeah, the summer after my senior year. The old count and countess had died. The people living at Villa Della Torre invited me in for coffee and listened politely when I told them that I'd been born in their house. But they had nothing to tell me. They'd never even met the count or the countess. I stayed at the palace during that trip. Uncle Evan and Her Serene Highness were so nice to me. They remembered your visit all those years before, remembered that Mom had been pregnant, but they said that they hadn't realized that Mom had given birth there, in the principality." At the time, Aislinn had been kind of disappointed that they didn't remember—disappointed, but not the least alarmed.

Not like now, when her whole world felt turned upside down, spinning in dizzying circles, way too fast.

She glanced at Connor again. "You sure you don't remember anything?"

He took a gulp of beer. "Mom and Dad were always hauling us along with them to the far corners of the earth. The trips are kind of a blur to me. Sorry, I've got nothing."

Liam said, "Something's off with you…"

"Yeah," Connor agreed. "What's going on?"

Guilt took a good poke at her, for keeping them in the dark. But she just couldn't go there. Not yet. "I was only wondering about how it all happened, you know, on the day I was born?"

Matt tipped his head to the side, studying her. "You've got a problem, haven't you, Ais? And you don't want to tell us what."

She couldn't outright lie to them—but she just wasn't ready to tell what she knew. "It's complicated. I don't want to get into it, not right yet."

"Anything we can do?" asked Liam.

She caught her lower lip between her teeth and shook her head.

Matt put his massive arm around her. "You call. We're there."

She let herself lean into him, as if he could ground her somehow, keep her tethered to dry land so she wouldn't go bobbing wildly off into nowhere, a tiny boat set adrift in a churning, angry sea.

After the disastrous visit to Kircher and Anders, Jax had gone straight back to Wild River and spent several hours in his study finding out everything he could about Aislinn Bravo. She kept public profiles on social media, so he learned a lot there. He also called a few people he knew in Valentine Bay and pumped them for anything they knew about Aislinn and the Bravo family.

The next day, he returned to Kircher and Anders. Kip ushered him back to his corner office and shut the door.

"I've got questions," Jax said, as he settled into a leather guest chair. "Starting with, can the will be broken?"

"I'm sorry, but no. Martin Durand had an absolute right to disburse his worldly goods in any way he chose and his will is legally airtight."

"Wild River belonged to my aunt. She left it to Martin, but it was always supposed to go to me when he died."

Anders adjusted his glasses, braced his elbows on the arms of his swivel chair and steepled his fingers. "There's not a lot of hope in trying to hang a case on that."

"But in his last letter, Martin admitted outright that he and my aunt had an understanding that the ranch should go to me."

"Yes. You could argue that. And the rebuttal would be that he *did* leave you Wild River, just with certain stipulations."

"What about Aislinn Bravo? Is she really his daughter?"

"Jaxon, I have no idea if she is or she isn't. You would need a paternity test to get a definitive answer to that question. And even if such a test proved that she and Martin shared no DNA, the will would most likely stand."

Was Anders hinting at an angle there? "'Most likely'?"

"If you proved she wasn't his daughter, then you could use his last letter as evidence that he included her in his will believing she was his biological child. It's a stretch, but you might challenge the will by arguing that Martin would never have left her anything if he knew she wasn't his."

"That sounds weak."

"Correct. It's weak. And your suit would likely fail. Plus, by the time you obtained DNA samples not only from Aislinn Bravo, but from Martin's remains and then hashed it all out in court, Wild River would already be sold, anyway."

Jax sat back in the guest chair. "You're *my* lawyer now."

Anders granted him a thin smile. "And I'm pleased to help you in any way I can."

"Got any suggestions to get me out of this mess?"

"As your lawyer, I would advise you to marry Aislinn Bravo and remain married to her for the next three months."

"I didn't need a lawyer to figure that out, Kip—and in spite of Martin's claim that the woman was once in love with me, so far she's not jumping at the chance to get my ring on her finger."

"I'm sorry, Jaxon. Truly. But there is no way I can help you with that. Give her a little time."

"Time? There are six days left until we have to be married."

"Look at it this way. If she doesn't agree from the goodness of her heart, maybe she'll think of a use for the money. Not many people would turn down a chance at fifty thousand dollars."

It was just after noon and Aislinn was selling a ceramic sculpture to a regular customer at Sand & Sea when Jaxon called. She had her phone right there on the register counter, set to vibrate. It spun halfway around and lit up with his name, because she'd programmed it into her phone, ready to go as soon as she felt she could deal with him.

"Go ahead," said the customer. "Answer it. I'm in no hurry."

But Aislinn was so far from ready to talk to Jax again. "I'll call him back later." She gave the customer a big smile and let the call go to voice mail.

Later didn't come—not that day, anyway. It was rude of her not to pick up or even listen to the message he'd left, and she was sorry. But she needed more answers before she faced his demands.

When she got off at four, she called Valentine House, where her great-uncle Percy and great-aunt Daffodil lived. They were brother and sister, Percy and Daffy, the last of the Valentines. Neither had ever married and they still lived in the house where they'd grown up.

When Uncle Percy finally answered the phone, she asked him if she could drop by.

"Bring pizza," he instructed. "With the works. Anchovies on the side."

Half an hour later, bearing an extralarge pie with everything on it—except the anchovies, which had their own small separate tub—she mounted the chipped concrete steps leading up to the seven-thousand-square-foot mansion on the edge of Valentine City Park. Aunt Daffy's garden was glorious if a tad overgrown. And to Aislinn, the Italianate Victorian itself looked like something transplanted from the Garden District in New Orleans. Built by Captain Aeschylus Valentine back in 1922, the house boasted a healthy helping of gingerbread trim, an excess of dentil moldings and acres of balconies framed in iron lace. The paint job needed freshening and some of the moldings could use repair, but still.

It was a beautiful old house and it made her smile every time she saw it.

Daffy and Percy greeted her at the door.

"So good to see you, sweetheart." Daffy's thin, dry lips brushed her cheek, light as a cobweb. Aislinn got a whiff of the familiar vanilla and sandalwood scent of the old woman's Arpège perfume. "You're a lifesaver with that pizza. Letha's off today." Letha March cleaned the house and cooked for them. "Let me take that." Daffy whisked the pizza away.

Percy led her into the parlor, where the red carpet had a dizzying pattern of closely woven white lilies overlapping each other. When Aislinn was little, she used to try to count those lilies.

They ate the pizza right there in the front room, paper plates in their laps, clutching paper napkins. Percy talked of the ongoing hunt for her brother Finn, lost in some frozen wilderness on the other side of the world.

He was so sure they would have Finn back home eventually. "We shall never give up the search, never surrender the quest," he declared, like some latter-day Winston Churchill. And then he gave her his sweetest, dottiest smile and asked, "But how are *you* doing, my dear?"

Aunt Daffy, slim and straight even at eighty-plus, her silver hair in soft waves framing her narrow, wrinkled face, piped up with, "Yes. Tell us everything."

Aislinn realized she wanted to—*needed* to—tell someone. Or maybe she was just ready to get it all out. "It has to be only between us, for now, anyway, until I figure out what I'm going to do next, until I'm ready to tell the whole family."

"And so it shall be," declared Daffy, sharing a nod with her brother.

It was so simple after that. She swore them to secrecy and then she told them. Everything. About her summer at Wild River Ranch, her college-girl crush on Jaxon, about Martin Durand, about that letter he'd written claiming to be her father and to have switched her with her mother's real daughter on the day she was born, about the terms of his will—and yes, she had meant to keep all those secrets until after she'd shared everything with Keely. But she really needed answers now.

When she'd told it all, Daffy asked, "Will you marry the man?"

"I don't know."

"Is he a good man?"

"Yes. Yes, I do believe that he is."

"And your feelings for him…?"

"Aunt Daffy, that was years ago."

Daffy peered at her closely. "I think you still like him."

"I do *like* him. And whether I decide to marry him or not in the next week, I'm counting on you two to keep my confidence about all of this."

"We've given you our word," Percy intoned.

Daffy promised, "We will not let you down."

"Thank you. And what I really came here for was to ask you both if you recall how Mom always said I was born in Montedoro?"

Daffy waved a hand. "Ah, our Marie. So full of fun and fantasy."

"But is it true? Was I born at Villa Della Torre?"

Daffy and Percy shook their heads in unison. Daffy

said, "Your mother loved that story. Sometimes I think she even started to believe it."

"Oh, God." Aislinn felt sick to her stomach. "Just tell me the truth, please. I really do have to know."

Daffy patted her shoulder, a touch meant to soothe her. "You were her firstborn daughter, her little princess— and of course you *had* to have been born in a villa over-looking the Mediterranean."

"You're saying she just made it up?" Her heart was a ball of lead in her chest.

"Well, it wasn't only that Marie considered you her little princess, it was that you fell in love with all things royal," Daffy said, as if that explained everything. "You do remember your princess phase?"

"Yeah, I remember." She'd had three princess dresses, in pink, blue and yellow, each with a big tulle skirt and a train. Her mom had made her a princess room, with glittery stars on the ceiling and a bed like a throne. She'd had four tiaras, each more sparkly than the last. And a magic wand, too—because when you're five, the line between princess and fairy is a blurry one.

"You loved the story of your Montedoran birth," Daffy reminded her. "As did your mother. It just seemed harmless and sweet to indulge you both. And, well, the years went by, didn't they? We lost Finn and then your mother and father, and the story simply stuck. Now and then you would mention it, but until now, you've never asked directly if it might actually be true."

And that brought her to the next big question. "So, where *was* I born, then?"

Uncle Percy rose from the circular settee. When he reached her, she stood from her wing chair. He took her hand in his wrinkly one. His faded blue eyes held hers.

"I'm afraid that this Martin Durand fellow had it right about that much, at least."

"Oh, no..." The two words came out as barely more than a whisper.

Percy nodded slowly. "You were born at Wild River Ranch during a punishing storm with catastrophic flash flooding and power lines down across much of the state."

Chapter Three

Before she left Valentine House, Aislinn agreed to contact the PI who'd found Madison and Paula Delaney. She agreed to arrange it so that Percy could get a copy of the final report on the search and ask questions about the case.

Percy, who loved playing detective, promised not to try to get in touch with Madison Delaney until after Daniel and Keely returned from Bora Bora and they could call a family meeting to bring all the Bravos up to speed on the strong possibility that they had a sister they didn't know they'd lost.

Next, Aislinn went to the Bravo family house. The short trip to the house she'd grown up in wasn't really necessary. She believed what Daffy and Percy had told her, that she'd actually been born at Wild River Ranch.

But it had occurred to her that there was one more proof she could easily check.

Gretchen Snow, Keely's aunt and the mother of Daniel's deceased first wife, Lillie, answered the door. The plump, sunny-natured Gretchen was looking after Daniel's twin toddlers, Frannie and Jake, while Daniel and Keely were gone. The twins were already in bed. Gretchen gave Aislinn a hug and then left her alone in the study at the front of the house.

Daniel had a twelve-drawer wooden file cabinet in there that used to belong to George Bravo. In a folder labeled with her name, Aislinn found her childhood immunization record, her original social security card and a few random report cards from middle school and high school. And also, her birth certificate, which listed her place of birth as Astoria, Oregon.

Wild River Ranch had an Astoria address.

It was enough to completely convince her of one thing, anyway. The story of her Montedoran birth was just that: a sweet fairy tale told to her by her mother—or at least, by the woman she'd always believed was her mother.

As she was leaving the Bravo house, she got another call from Jaxon. She ignored it. Instead, she went home, took care of her rabbits and ate some leftovers. After dinner, she went out to the shed she used as a studio.

In the shed, Aislinn made jewelry that she sold online at her Etsy store, via her website, AislinnBravo.com, and at Keely's gallery. She was always promising herself that she would concentrate more on her art. But she tended to get distracted by her various subsistence jobs. She flitted from one job to another, and somehow, her passion for making jewelry always took a back seat to the nine-to-five grind.

Tonight, though, she needed something to get lost in. All her worries faded away as she put her mind and heart into designing a series of lariat necklaces in contrasting materials, each a different length, to be worn as a set. Her sisters came home as she worked. One and then the other, she heard their cars arrive.

At a little past midnight, she returned to the house, passing Hailey's and Harper's cars, parked side by side. The glow of the porch light cut the foggy night, but all the other lights in the house were off.

She spent a little more time with Bunbun and Luna, both of whom were going to need a good clipping soon. When she left the porch, she went to the kitchen, where she brewed herself a restful mug of valerian tea. She was sipping it in the dark when her phone rang again.

Jax.

"All right," she whispered to no one in particular, and took the call. "Hello, Jaxon."

"Aislinn." His voice had a raspy, tired sound. He probably hadn't been sleeping well, with Wild River on the line and the woman he had to marry not answering his calls. "We do have to talk."

"I know."

"Just meet me. Name the place and time." His weary voice did it, somehow. Made her admit to herself that she was going to go through with it, marry a man she hardly knew in order that he wouldn't lose what he loved.

"You know Fisherman's Korner, here in Valentine Bay?" she asked, and then went on without waiting for his answer. "Meet me there at noon tomorrow."

* * *

He was sitting in one of the red pleather booths when she got there. Red plastic cups of ice water, one for each of them, waited on the table in front of him. She pushed in through the glass door and their eyes met. He rose, so stern and handsome in a blue button-down and dark-wash jeans.

She went to him, dropping her purse into the corner of the seat opposite him, then sliding in herself. He didn't sit back down until she was settled. *Always such a gentleman.* The thought almost brought a smile.

The waitress came, took their orders and brought Aislinn an iced tea.

When the waitress left them alone again, Jax folded his big, work-roughened hands on the table and leaned in. His square-jawed face looked drawn. He definitely hadn't been sleeping any better than she had.

She stared into those cloudy-day eyes and decided she might as well cut to the point, put the poor man out of his misery. "All right. I'll do it."

The clouds cleared off in those eyes of his, leaving bright blue fire. He sat back and then forward again. "You mean that?"

She nodded. "Hey. It's fifty thousand, right?" The money wasn't the reason, but no way was she admitting outright that she couldn't bear to see him lose Wild River. It wouldn't sound true anyway.

"Good," he said. "Great. I called the county clerk's office. There's a three-day waiting period after we get the license, but we can fill out a form, pay a fee and get married the same day. So I was thinking Monday. Monday morning. We'll go to the clerk's office, get the license, waive the waiting period and say our vows right then and there."

"Okay."

"We'll need two witnesses. I'll ask Burt and Erma," he said. "Unless you'd rather—"

"Fine. Burt and Erma are fine."

He shifted in the seat, pulling out a folded piece of paper and sliding it across the table to her. "I got this online, a list of everything they'll need to know to provide us with a license."

She smoothed it out and read it, scanning down the list of required information, zeroing right in on the last item on the page.

Applicants' fathers' and mothers' names and places of birth.

She almost threw back her head and laughed out loud. It would have been a thoroughly demented sort of laugh. Because, seriously, at this point, how could she possibly know for sure who her real parents were or where they were born?

He set down his water glass midway through a sip. "Aislinn, what's wrong?"

She drew a slow breath. "I'm fine. No problem, really. I'll bring my driver's license and be ready to fill in all the blanks on the form." She might not know who she was at the moment, but to the rest of the world she was still Aislinn Bravo—and maybe she always would be. It was all too confusing and she refused to think about it now.

The waitress appeared with their food, twin baskets of fish and chips. After pulling the condiment caddy into the center of the table for them, she asked if there was anything else she could get them.

Aislinn shook her head and Jax said, "This is perfect. Thanks."

The waitress moved on. Aislinn sprinkled vinegar onto her fish, same as she did whenever she and Keely met here for lunch. She took a bite. The fish was delicious. Nothing had changed at Fisherman's Korner.

She was the one who had changed. She felt like a fake, an impostor, though to everyone else she was still the same person.

Jax polished off two pieces of fish and wiped his hands on a napkin. "I've been thinking about how to handle this."

What was he talking about? "This?"

"You and me. The marriage." Those gray-blue eyes met hers, so steady and sure. That steadiness of his was one of the many reasons she'd fallen so hard for him during that long-ago summer. He reminded her of Daniel, a little. The kind of guy you could count on to do the right thing, no matter what, the kind of guy you knew would protect his own at any cost. She'd loved the calmness within him. He gave her the feeling that no matter what crisis occurred, he could handle it, could make everything come out all right. "I'm thinking we should keep the fact that the marriage is temporary to ourselves."

"Let everyone think it's for real and forever, you mean?"

"Yeah. Telling people that it's just a business arrangement would mean it's a marriage 'in name only,' right?"

"Right." She took a sip of her iced tea and added with way too much irony, "Can't have that." About then, she remembered the other people who knew the truth. She'd sworn Percy and Daffy to secrecy and they would honor that promise. Kip Anders wasn't going to say anything.

As a lawyer, his job included keeping his clients' business strictly confidential. But Jax's foreman and housekeeper were a whole other story. "What about Burt and Erma?" At his frown, she explained, "Burt and Erma know exactly what's going on."

"They're not going to say anything to anyone."

"And you know this, how?"

"They love Wild River. If it's sold out from under us, they're both out of a job—but I'll talk to them."

"And say?"

"That you and I may have agreed to marry because Martin manipulated us into it, but we both believe in the institution of marriage and we have every intention of making our marriage work." He was still looking at her, his gaze unwavering.

A shiver raced down her spine. "God. The way you say that, *I* almost believe you."

He smiled then, a slow, warm smile. "I've always wanted a wife. You know, a partner in life, kids. The whole thing. Yeah, I blew it with Judy, but you never know. Maybe it *will* work out between you and me."

Where was he going with this? "You're really confusing me."

"I only mean, well, who knows what will happen? Why not approach this unfortunate situation with a positive attitude?"

She understood then. "Right. The easiest way to convince people it's real is to put a little effort into believing it ourselves."

He raised his plastic glass. "To us."

That sounded good. And for the first time since she'd learned more than she'd ever wanted to know about the day she was born, her heart felt lighter. If she had to be married to a virtual stranger until sometime in November, she could do worse than the hunky, kindhearted, level-headed rancher seated across from her, the guy she'd once imagined herself to be wildly in love with.

With a firm nod, she toasted back, "To us—and to three blissful months of happily-ever-after."

"What's up with you?" her sister Harper asked the next morning as Aislinn sat at the kitchen table staring blindly out the window at the tiny sliver of beach and ocean just visible from her chair.

Aislinn blinked, focused on her sister seated across the table and tried to look perky. "What do you mean? Nothing."

Hailey turned from the refrigerator with a carton of eggs. Slim, blonde and blue-eyed, she could have passed for Harper's twin, though in reality Hailey was ten months older. "Don't tell us 'nothing.' There's something going on with you and there has been for three or four days now."

She thought about the wedding on Monday, about sneaking out of the house to marry a man her sisters and brothers knew nothing about. Only Keely knew about the mad crush she'd had on Jaxon Winter five years before. And Keely wouldn't be back in town for another week—days after the damn marriage deadline set out in Martin Durand's horrible, cruel, impossible will.

"Ais-linn," Harper crooned in a musical singsong. "Earth to Ais-linn..."

There was really no way to get out of telling them about the wedding. She might as well face the music now. "I'm getting married on Monday," she said.

The sisters gasped in unison. Hailey almost dropped the eggs.

Aislinn went on, "His name is Jaxon Winter. He owns a horse ranch, Wild River, near the Youngs River. I worked for him five years ago and I've, um, always had a thing for him. We recently got together. He's asked me to marry him and I said yes."

Harper let out a squeal. "Oh. My. God."

"I'm sorry I didn't say anything earlier," Aislinn said, and truly did mean it.

Hailey plunked the eggs on the counter. "Married on Monday? Is that what you just said?"

"Ahem. Yes. I know it's kind of sudden—"

"*Kind* of sudden?" Harper screeched. She jumped from her chair, ran around the table and hauled Aislinn up and into her arms. "Are you crazy?"

Aislinn held her good and tight. "Just possibly, yes."

And then Hailey was there, too, wrapping her arms around both of them. They all hugged it out for a long, lovely string of seconds.

Then her sisters pulled back and started firing questions at her.

"So, you're eloping?" demanded Harper.

"Where to?" asked Hailey.

"Just to the county offices in Astoria. It's going to be really simple. Me and Jax, his housekeeper and the ranch foreman—and you guys, too, if you think you might be able to make it."

"Are you kidding?" Harper took her by the shoulders and gave her a little shake. "Of course we're going to be there. And Matt and Connor and Liam, too. And Gracie. We have to include her."

"They'll probably have to work."

Harper made a sort of snorting-bull sound. "What is *wrong* with you? Screw work. Of course they'll come."

Hailey was nodding. "You can't just leave them out." And then she gasped. "Wait a minute. What about Daniel? He'll be so disappointed. And Keely! Ais, Keely's just plain going to kill you if you go off and get married while she's on her honeymoon."

Glumly, she confessed, "I've been trying not to think about Keely."

"Well, you'd better think of Keely," lectured Harper. "She'll be back a week from Monday. Can't you just wait until—"

"No. No, I can't."

"Why not?" Hailey asked.

Aislinn had never hated Martin Durand as much as she did at that moment. "Long story, but, um, it has to be Monday. It *will* be Monday."

"That makes no sense," declared Harper.

Hailey said, "You need to at least *call* Keely, tell her what's happening, give her the choice of—"

"No. Uh-uh. She's on her *honeymoon*. A couple of weeks alone, just her and Daniel. They never get time alone, and you know it." They had Daniel's twin toddlers to raise and Keely was four months pregnant. They deserved this romantic escape. "I'm not breaking in on that. And I'm counting on you to tell anyone else in the family who gets the bright idea to call them that they'd better not pick up that phone. When Keely gets back, I'll explain everything." She *would* explain everything, to Keely and Keely alone. And when she did, she fervently hoped her friend would understand—and then, once Keely had forgiven her, they would plan the family meeting where everyone would find out they had a sister in Hollywood.

Harper let go of Aislinn's shoulders to plunk her fists on her own hips. "This is just insane."

"Yeah, you already mentioned that."

"Aw, Ais…" Harper grabbed her in another hug and Hailey joined in.

When they let her go that time, Hailey asked, "His name is Jaxon Winter, you said? Will you be moving to his ranch with him?"

"I will, yeah. On Monday, after the wedding."

"Whoa." Hailey widened her eyes. "I mean, of course you're going to go live with him, but, Ais, it's a lot to take in."

Harper burst out with, "The dress! You have the dress, right?" When Aislinn took too long to reply, she answered for her. "Okay, then. We'll need to get the dress."

"And flowers!" chirped Hailey. "You need a nice little wedding bouquet. And what about a wedding band for Jaxon?"

"I don't actually know his size—and come on, can we not make too huge of a deal out of this?"

Hailey scolded, "Getting married *is* a huge deal—but fine. You can get his ring at a later point, maybe shop for one together, the two of you. That'd be sweet."

Harper shook a finger at her. "And right now, you need to call Matt and Liam and Connor and Gracie, too. Real calls. No texting. You need to tell them you're getting married and what time they need to be there."

The calls to her brothers went about as she'd expected. They all said they would be there. But they were also bewildered at her sudden decision to marry some guy they hadn't even known she was seeing.

She just stuck with the story. Yeah, she admitted, it *was* kind of sudden. But it was real love. Jaxon felt the same. They wanted to be married, but without all the hassle and planning of a big wedding.

As the lies fell from her lips, she knew she would have a whole lot of explaining to do eventually.

But all that was for later, for the family meeting after Daniel and Keely returned.

Matt was the most direct about his concerns. "It's a weird thing to ask, I know, but does this have anything to do with the other night, with how none of us could remember your being born in Montedoro?"

She should have just said no, but somehow, when he asked her that particular question, she couldn't make herself spit out the lie. "I can't get into it now, Matt. You need to give me time, okay?"

There was dead air from his end for several long seconds. She pulled the phone away from her ear to see if he'd hung up. But he was still there. At last, he asked solemnly, "Ais, what's going on?"

"I will explain, I promise. I just can't do it now."

"Are you in some kind of trouble?"

Only in her heart, in her sense of herself. Because who was she, really? "I'm not in trouble. I promise you."

Matt gave it up. "All right. I'm here. Whatever you need."

"I love you, Matt."

"Love you, too. See you Monday."

She called her youngest sister, Grace, next. That went a little easier than with Matt. Aislinn trotted out the same lies she'd told the others. Grace got excited. "I'm so happy for you, Ais! I'll be there. Can't wait."

Once she'd invited all of them, Aislinn called Jax to let him know the guest list was going to be a little longer than they'd planned. He didn't pick up.

But an hour later, as she was getting in a little time in her studio before heading to Sand & Sea to relieve Amanda, her phone lit up with his name.

"Aislinn." He sounded worried. Strange how she could tell that just by the way he said her name. "Sorry. One of the fillies sliced up her right flank somehow— and then jumped the fence and took off. We had to track her down and get her stitched up. I left my phone in the house."

"No problem."

He asked bleakly, "Is something wrong?"

She hurried to reassure him. "No, nothing. Honestly."

"We're still set for Monday, then?"

"Yes, we are—and I just thought you should know that three of my brothers and my three sisters are coming, too."

"That's nice," he said.

She'd been so busy dodging their questions, she hadn't stopped to appreciate how they'd all stepped right up to support her on her "special" day. "Yeah. It is nice, isn't it?"

"So that's six, then—plus the two of us. Eight. They allow six at a wedding in the clerk's office, six *including* the bride and groom."

"Well, there will be more than six. And what about Erma and Burt? I mean, I know they've both lived at the ranch forever. Will they be disappointed not to be included?" She felt silly as soon as she asked the question. What did Erma and Burt care about attending a hasty wedding for a marriage between strangers with a three-month expiration date? "Or maybe not?"

"They'll be fine." Something in his voice said they wouldn't be happy about being disinvited, that they might even want to come.

If they did want to be there, she was not going to be the reason they couldn't. "Just bring them."

"That will make ten total. It's not going to fly."

"Bring them. We'll work it out somehow." Right then, she remembered Percy and Daffy. "Er, and Jaxon...?"

"I'm not sure I like the way you said that."

"Well, I just thought of my great-aunt and great-uncle. They would be so hurt if I didn't ask them to be there, too."

"Your great-aunt and great-uncle," he repeated, sounding like maybe he was getting a headache.

She decided they should think positive. "You know what? Don't worry. It's a wedding, after all. I've got a feeling the county clerk won't mind bending the rules a little."

"Last I checked, twelve is twice as many as six."

"Don't be sarcastic."

"Aislinn, I don't think they'll go for twelve."

For a woman unsure of her identity, she did have a lot of close relatives. And now *she* was getting a headache. "I'm going to have to think this over and get back to you."

"You're upset."

"No, really. I just need a little time to work it out."

"Wait. You know what? Don't worry."

"But—"

"I mean it. Bring your brothers and sisters *and* your

great-uncle and -aunt to the Marriage License Bureau just as we planned. I'll take it from there."

They said goodbye and she called Valentine House next. Daffy answered.

When Aislinn invited them to the wedding, her great-aunt said that of course she and Percy would be there. Then she asked, "Are you sure?"

"I am, Aunt Daffy." In spite of her thousand and one doubts about this decision, it came out sounding down-right confident.

On Monday when they all met at the county offices, Aislinn learned that Jaxon had made other arrangements for the ceremony.

They got the license from the clerk, and they had the waiting period waived. And then they all trooped to-gether on foot to a church two blocks away—even Percy and Daffy toddled along with zero complaint, smiling and chatting. They were both in great shape for being well into their eighties.

The church secretary greeted them at the door of the rectory and led them to a small chapel.

It was so pretty, that chapel, with a stained-glass win-dow above the altar and simply fashioned mahogany pews. Aislinn loved it—though she felt just a smidge guilty for the circumstances. God probably wouldn't approve.

Then again, it was a *real* marriage even if it did have a termination date. And she was entering the union with the best of intentions: to help a good man keep the land that he loved.

On second thought, she decided, God would under-stand.

Percy gave her away. The church secretary played the wedding march on an old upright piano as Aislinn walked down the aisle in the white street-length dress Harper had helped her choose the day before. It was sleeveless, the dress, with a layered, high-low A-line skirt. She'd paired it with nude heels and a smart little birdcage veil and she carried a bouquet of white dahlias, calla lilies and roses.

Her groom wore a charcoal-gray three-piece suit with a snowy-white shirt. Just looking at him made her heart beat faster than it should. The way he gazed at her as she came toward him holding Great-Uncle Percy's arm, well, if she wasn't careful she might almost start believing dangerous things.

The short ceremony went by in a hazy kind of glow, like some sweet, old-fashioned dream she was having, where she and Jaxon held hands and promised a forever that wasn't really going to happen. He'd even brought rings for her, an engagement ring in white gold with channel-set diamonds flanking a beautiful round center stone, and a wedding band to match.

Just like a dream, it all flew by so fast.

All of a sudden, the minister said, "You may kiss your bride."

Jaxon folded back her little veil and framed her face between his wonderful, rough hands. Tipping her chin up, he kissed her slowly, gently. She sighed against his parted lips, mindful of her forbidden fantasies five years ago, when she had secretly dreamed of a moment just like this.

She could almost wish…

No.

She wished nothing.

It was what it was and she was happy just for this. A pretty little ceremony, her family—that probably wasn't her family at all—around her. A good man for her groom.

A few gorgeous moments where all the lies seemed true.

Jaxon took everyone to lunch at a great place right on the Columbia River. They had champagne and her family offered toasts to happiness and love and forever. She could have sworn that once or twice even Burt cracked a smile.

Afterward, they all walked out together to their cars in the parking area on the landward side of the restaurant. She hugged them all—her brothers and sisters, Percy and Daffy. They wished her happiness and congratulated Jaxon on being such a lucky man.

They were so dear, really, all of them. She almost hated to see them get in their cars and pickups and drive away. Burt and Erma left, too, but Percy and Daffy lingered.

Daffy began chatting with Jaxon, about the weather, about the history of the four-mile Astoria-Megler Bridge that soared out over the Columbia, visible from there in the parking lot, connecting the Oregon and Washington sides of the river. Percy pulled Aislinn aside to remind her to call the detective agency in Seattle. She promised she would take care of that right away.

After more hugs and well-wishes, Percy and Daffy climbed in the giant Lincoln Town Car they'd owned since the beginning of time and headed for home, leaving Aislinn and Jax standing alone in the nearly empty parking lot under an overcast sky.

"It went well," he said, his gaze holding hers, causing a hopelessly romantic buoyant sort of feeling in the center of her body.

Get a grip, girl. "Yes, it did. Thank you, Jax. For the church, for the beautiful lunch." *For that perfect wedding kiss.* "For all of it."

He gave a careful kind of nod. "I like your family."

"Yeah, they're great. The best…" She didn't know what to say next. Awkwardness had suddenly descended. Their little wedding fantasy was over.

Hello, reality. How have you been?

He asked, "Do you need anything from your place?"

"I have a bag packed for tonight, thanks." She shot a thumb over her shoulder in the general direction of her red CR-V. "And my car's loaded down with a bunch of other stuff I'll need while I'm living at Wild River—I mean, why waste a trip, right?"

He pushed back the sides of his jacket and stuck his fists in his pockets. "I forgot to ask. Do you have to work today?"

"Not until Wednesday." Amanda had disapproved of her getting married when Keely couldn't be there. But in the end, she'd wished Aislinn love and happiness and assured her that Sand & Sea could do without her for two days. "I thought I would take tomorrow to try to move everything else I'll need while I'm living at the ranch."

"Whatever you want to bring, we have plenty of room."

"You sure? I have two German angora rabbits—we are talking *large*. And furry. And I make jewelry, so I'm hoping there'll be somewhere I can set up my jeweler's bench and equipment."

An actual dimple tucked itself into his left cheek. "You have rabbits?"

"I do, yes. Harper and Hailey will take care of them until tomorrow. But where I go, Luna and Bunbun go, too. And they are porch rabbits, meaning that at my house, they live on my enclosed front porch. They're going to need a little room to roam—but on a clean surface, and with a barrier against predators. They can't wander around on the lawn or anything. Their fur traps debris."

The dimple in his cheek got deeper, but he had sense enough not to laugh or otherwise mock her babies. And really, he was being great about this, raising no objections to making space for her workshop and her special-needs pets. "We'll work it out," he said.

They ran out of words then and ended up standing there in the parking lot, just looking at each other as the Riverfront Trolley clattered by on the tracks not twenty feet away.

Funny how easy it had all been, to play the role of newlyweds in love for the family. He'd put his arm across her chair in the restaurant, leaning close to her more than once to whisper in her ear: *"More champagne?"* and *"Pass the water carafe,"* and once even to pay her a lovely compliment. *"Aislinn Winter, you do make a beautiful bride."*

It struck her then, as she stood there with him in the parking lot, struck her like a blinding light shone straight in her eyes. "We are actually, legally married."

He chuckled, a dark and delicious sound. It made her feel like that college girl again, yearning for a certain good and beautiful man who would never be hers. "Yes, we are."

"Legally married, and we hardly know each other."

Hands still in his pockets, he shrugged. "We've got three months together. I'm guessing by the end of that time, we'll know each other just fine."

Three months. During which her possible bio-dad had somehow expected them to discover love and forever— or maybe not. Really, they had no way of knowing what that crazy old man might have been thinking.

And now he was gone. She would never have a chance to ask him.

Jaxon was watching her. He pulled his hands from his pockets. "So, how about we stop by Kircher and Anders to hand over that temporary marriage certificate the minister gave us?"

"All right."

"And after that, we'll go home."

Chapter Four

Wild River Ranch was as green and inviting as Aislinn remembered.

When her car emerged from the cover of the trees that lined the twisting highway, the grassy, rolling land stretched away on all sides with the stable, barns, paddocks and training pens in the heart of it. The Youngs River had cut a twisting path through the low places. All around rose stands of fir and spruce and pine, making a dark green blanket that climbed the nearby hills.

Aislinn followed Jax's enormous gray Chevy Silverado crew cab up the winding dirt driveway to the main house. White, with black trim, the two-story house had a wraparound porch.

The row of three garage doors was around on the far side. Jax led the way there and she pulled up beside him in the wide driveway.

As two of the doors trundled up, Jax signaled her to take the empty space in the middle. They drove in and parked.

He got out and strode around the front of his pickup to meet her as she emerged from behind the wheel. "Let's just bring your suitcase in for now. Leave the rest. We'll deal with it later." He followed her around to the hatch in back. "I'll take it." He grabbed the handle of her bag before she could reach for it.

She followed him through a door to a covered breezeway that led into the house. In the laundry room, he paused long enough to pull open a cabinet and take out two keys, a business-size card and a garage door opener.

He handed them over. "The door opener works for the space where you just parked your car. The big key opens the dead bolts on the front and back doors. The other is the main house key. That's the Wi-Fi password on the card."

She took them with a murmured "Thank you" and dropped them into her shoulder bag.

They moved on, into a large, white kitchen with granite counters and good-quality appliances. He glanced back at her. "Hungry? Want something to drink?" When she shook her head no, he turned and led the way into a big, comfortable-looking family room and from there into a study at the front of the house.

"Come on in." He ushered her in first. There was a seating area across from the desk. He shut the door, set down her suitcase and gestured toward the camel-colored leather sofa. "Have a seat."

Not sure what, exactly, they were going to do in his study, she went where he indicated and took one end of the sofa. He claimed the leather armchair directly across from her.

"I always wondered what the house looked like from inside," she said. That summer she'd worked for him, she'd gone home to Valentine Bay every night. The ranch office where she would pick up her paychecks was in a big trailer near the stables. There'd never been a reason for her to enter the main house. "I like it—or what I've seen of it so far, anyway. It's roomy and simple. Nice and open."

"Judy redid it. It needed a little TLC. And the job kept her happy for a while."

She remembered what he'd told her last Monday, when she'd run from the lawyer's office, that his ex-wife had not been a big fan of life in the country—and a neutral response seemed the best way to go. "Judy had good taste."

"Yeah," he agreed, his cool expression and vague tone letting her know that he didn't plan to dwell on the subject of his ex-wife. "I want to talk a little about what Martin intended for this marriage of ours. The will says we have to live together in this house and not sleep with other people. It doesn't say we actually have to share a bedroom or have sex with each other."

"So, um, you brought me in here to talk about our sleeping arrangements?"

"I did, yeah."

Really? What was there to talk about? "I don't see that it's a problem. Even if whoever Kircher and Anders sends over to check on us notices we have separate rooms, so what? Martin never specified we had to share a bed. A lot of married people don't sleep in the same bed."

"True." He shifted in the chair, bringing up one hard-muscled leg and hooking his ankle across his knee. His jacket had fallen open to reveal his buttoned-up vest over a hard, flat stomach and a broad chest. Though she knew she shouldn't, she let her gaze wander downward to the heavy bulge beneath his fly. He went on, "But we still haven't talked about which bedroom you *want* to sleep in." His voice, in the silent room, was suddenly like raw honey poured out slowly.

Stifling a silly gasp, she jerked her gaze up from his fly. His fine eyes were waiting. He was hiding a smile, damn him. A flush tried to spread upward over her cheeks. She sat straighter and refused to blush or glance away. "What's to talk about? We hardly know each other."

He had those steady eyes on her, pinning her. "We're married." He didn't add, *You had a big crush on me once*, but to her it seemed the words were there, in the way he looked at her, in that smile he wasn't quite letting her see. "We're married," he said again, as though she hadn't heard him perfectly well the first time. And then he added, "And I would very much like to share a bed with you."

Her mouth almost dropped wide open. She really hadn't imagined he would suggest a sexual relationship between them—at least not so soon. He'd always seemed like someone who would want to get to know a woman before jumping into bed with her.

Or was that just her college-girl fantasy of him? Had she made up her ideal man and put Jaxon Winter's face on him?

"Jax." She said it way too sternly.

"Aislinn." He echoed her tone, teasing her.

She sat a little straighter. "We're married, but not *married*. And you're…" She had no idea how to go on.

Sprawled like a lazy cat in that chair, his foot still hooked across his knee, displaying that manly bulge she was not going to look at again, he waited her out.

Until she went ahead and said what she'd been thinking a minute before. "I'm a little surprised. I mean, you just never seemed like the type of guy who falls into bed with a near-stranger."

"You're right. I don't have sex with strangers."

"So then why are you—"

"But you're not a stranger."

She scoffed, "Close enough."

"Uh-uh. You're my wife. And I'm finding I like you, Aislinn. I like you a lot."

"It's all that simple to you?"

"That's right. I'm a simple kind of guy."

Was she tempted to give him a yes? Most definitely. Maybe she'd gotten past imagining herself in love with him. But he still rang all her bells in a very big way.

However, it just didn't feel right to jump into bed with him on her first night in his house—even if he had taken her to a preacher and put a pretty ring on her finger.

"I like you, too," she said. "But the fact remains that five days ago, I hadn't set eyes on you in five years and you couldn't quite remember who I was."

There was a deep stillness in him, as though he were listening very closely, picking up cues most would never catch. Finally, he sat forward and braced his forearms on spread knees. "You're mad at me about that."

"I didn't say I was mad."

"I'm not talking about what you *said*. You *were* angry that I didn't remember you at first."

Was she? "It hurt my pride, okay? But I'm over it."

He actually chuckled, a wry sound, and sat back in the chair again. "Aislinn, I'm a man. Men are stupid and blind sometimes." He held her gaze. "And you have to understand. I was married to someone else five years ago. The only one I was looking at then was my wife."

"I get that. I do. I respect that." It was dangerous, how *much* she liked him. How much she appreciated that he'd come right out and said he wanted her in his bed, that he'd let her know in words where she stood with him, at least about that. "But, Jax…"

"I'm listening."

"I'm still not sleeping with you."

For that, she got a regal nod of his handsome head. "Fair enough." He rose from the chair in a single, fluid movement. "Let me show you your room."

When they left the study, they found Erma in the kitchen rubbing garlic and herbs on a standing rib roast. She gave them each a nod and continued with her work. A real chatterbox, that Erma.

Jax gave Aislinn a quick tour of the rest of the lower floor, then led her into the foyer and up the wide staircase to her bedroom, which had a large window looking out on the front yard, and plenty of closet space.

"You can use the big bathroom at the end of the hall. It was Martin's along with the corner bedroom next to it." He hefted her suitcase onto the bed.

"Martin let you have the master suite?"

"We traded when I married Judy and never traded back. He said he liked the other room better."

"What about Burt and Erma? Where do they sleep?"

"Burt has the foreman's cottage across the yard. Erma has an apartment over the garages."

"It's just you and me living in the house, then?"

He watched her as she checked out the room. "That's right. Just us."

She turned the knob of the door beside the closet. "Where does this go?"

"To my room," he replied as she pulled the door open on a sitting area, with a bedroom beyond. "In case you change your mind."

Laughing, she shut the door. "At least it has a privacy lock." She turned it.

He put his hand to his chest. "You're killin' me here."

She had a powerful urge to go to him right then, to cradle his face between her palms and kiss that tempting mouth of his. She let the urge pass—and found herself thinking that she must have been born in one of the upstairs rooms. "How many bedrooms up here?"

"Six. Mine, yours, Martin's—and three smaller rooms in a row along the hall. When the house was built, there were a lot of Winters living at Wild River. My great-grandfather had six children."

"Is it all right if I see those three smaller rooms?"

"Aislinn. You live here now. The house is yours. Explore all the closets, have a long look in every room."

"Now?"

"Anytime you want."

She went out the door and along the hall, pausing to look into each of the three rooms. They were dim rooms, each with only one small window on the outside wall. She returned to the middle one after she'd had a quick glance at all three. The room had a single bed, a rag rug and a dresser topped with a '50s-era lamp.

Jax had followed her. He stood at her shoulder as she lingered in the open doorway.

She turned to him. "Do you remember anything about the day I was born?"

His brow crinkled and he shook his head. "We used to have a lot of visitors."

"You would have been eight, right? There was a big storm. Two women had *babies* right here in this house. And you don't recall any of it?"

"Sorry, no. I remember my childhood after I came to Wild River as a series of hazy, happy events. Learning to ride and care for the horses, hiking with Martin and Aunt Claudia on one of her good days. In the years before I came here I'd developed a habit of blocking out anything that scared me in any way. I'm guessing a big storm and two women in labor would have had me grabbing my blankie and running for my favorite closet, the one under the stairs."

"Oh, Jax. You still had a blankie at eight?"

"That's right." He faked a tough look. "Wanna make something of it?"

"No, of course not." She did, however, have about a hundred questions concerning his early childhood.

But before she could ask any of them, he said, "Don't feel bad for me. By ten or so, I didn't need that blankie anymore—and I'll bring the rest of your stuff up. You can change, get settled in." He was gone before she could decide which question to ask first.

Half an hour later, he'd brought everything up from her car and gone out to his horses. She put her pretty bouquet of white flowers in a vase Erma found for her and set it on the dresser in the room that would be hers for the next three months.

Unless she joined Jaxon in the master suite.

Her cheeks heated at the thought, and she felt truly silly. Okay, okay. Jax had said straight out that he wanted her. Good to know.

And now, moving on…

Once she'd put her clothes away and changed into jeans and a T-shirt, she sat on the bed and wondered if this was all some kind of weird dream she'd fallen into. She had too many questions that needed answering: Who was she really? She almost didn't feel like the same Aislinn anymore. How would she explain to her best friend that she'd gotten married without even telling her? And the family…

How would she break the news to them that they apparently had a sister they'd never even met?

The blue folder that contained Martin's will, his outrageous last letter and the list of contact numbers sat waiting on the dresser where she'd dropped it when she unpacked her suitcase.

She got up, got the contact list and took out her phone to call the private investigator Martin had hired to track down Madison Delaney.

Jax found Burt in the tack room.

"Rabbits?" groused Burt when Jax had finished explaining what he wanted him to do. "This is a horse ranch. We don't keep rabbits."

Jax had learned from years of experience that the best way to deal with Burt's bellyaching was to ignore it. "There are two of them. They're large rabbits, according to Aislinn. They need a safe, enclosed space to wander around in."

Burt plunked his ass down on a chest full of saddle

blankets. Ace, his border collie, sidled up and eased between his legs. Burt gave the dog a good scratch around the ruff, behind the ears and down his back. "She's gotta have cages for them, right? Rabbits live in cages."

"These particular rabbits need room to roam. I'm thinking we clean out the big shed in the backyard." The shed, which had been Martin's workshop way back when, was well insulated and wired for electricity, with windows and a woodstove. "We can put a fan in there on hot days, and a window-box air conditioner. If she's afraid to keep the stove going with the rabbits loose, we can just use a space heater to keep it warm in winter."

"Winter? She'll be gone by mid-November. And we got stuff in that shed."

"Which is why we'll need to clear it out. Today, Burt. She's bringing the rabbits tomorrow."

Burt muttered something unrecognizable under his breath. Jax knew the man well enough not to ask what he'd just said.

Instead, he moved on to the next point. "She also needs a workshop for her jewelry-making. I'll find out what kind of equipment she's bringing. Maybe we'd be wiser to put the rabbits on the enclosed side porch and use the shed for her workshop."

"The porch is for sitting."

Jax reminded himself that Burt was a good man, a hard worker and amazing with the horses. So he had big issues with the female half of the human race. All men had flaws. "Let me make this clear," he said flatly. "Whatever Aislinn wants Aislinn is getting. We're not losing Wild River because she gets pissed off and leaves before the three months are up."

"Kissing her ass, are you?"

And whatever else she wants kissed. "Be nice, Burt."

Burt grunted. "She's not going anywhere. She wants her fifty grand. And according to that letter of Martin's, she's got a real soft spot for you."

"We don't know what she wants, not really." He still couldn't be sure she hadn't gotten to Martin somehow, gotten to him and convinced him to make those bizarre changes to his will. From what Jax had been able to piece together about her, she went from job to job. As of now, she worked as a clerk at an art gallery and made jewelry. She couldn't be bringing in a whole lot. Maybe the fifty K payoff was huge for her.

Then again, from what he'd learned about the Valentines and the Bravos, they had plenty and they took care of their own. They loved Aislinn. He'd seen that clearly this morning, when they'd all shown up on zero notice to be there for her wedding. That wasn't going to change no matter whose blood ran through her veins. The Bravos would rally around her—whether she needed moral support or help paying the bills. Money didn't seem to be a big issue for her.

Nothing really added up, not to a clear sense of her motivations, anyway. And bottom line, he tended to think she was as blindsided by their situation as he was.

Still, he had to watch himself around her. Already, he liked her far too much. She seemed honest. Sincere. And smart and way too damn good-looking for his peace of mind, with those huge eyes and all that thick black hair in a pretty tangle around that delicate face. And the scent of her...

Sweet and tart and spicy, all at once.

He wasn't quite sure what had gotten into him earlier, to offer a sexual relationship outright. A more experienced man would've had sense enough to be smooth about it, to make a decent move on her, with kisses and slow caresses, letting nature take its course.

Next time he had a chance to coax her into bed, he would do better.

Because there *would* be a next time. Maybe he'd been oblivious to her five years ago. Not anymore. Whatever she might or might not be up to in the grand scheme of things, she'd married him. He wanted her and he was pretty damn sure she wanted him back. Why shouldn't they both get a little pleasure out of this mess Martin had put them in?

Burt was watching him. "You should see your face. She's getting to you. But you don't trust her any more than I do."

"You're wrong. I think she's a good person and all this is as much of a surprise to her as it is to us."

"Sure, you do."

"I want you to get along with her, Burt."

Burt sat there and fumed for a good thirty seconds. Then he pushed to his feet. "Women are nothin' but a nuisance, and that is a proven fact."

"Clean out the shed."

Shaking his head and grumbling in protest, Burt headed for the door.

By the time Aislinn said goodbye to the PI Martin had hired, he'd already emailed her the report on Paula and Madison. She'd instructed the man to email Percy the file as well and to accept Percy's phone calls and answer any questions he might have. After she hung up, she called Percy to let him know that the report was waiting in his inbox for him.

That evening, Erma served the rib roast in the formal dining room. It was the four of them—Aislinn, Jax, Erma and Burt—all of them in jeans and casual shirts. Nothing fancy, except the meal, which was delicious, with fingerling potatoes, a wonderful pear and walnut salad and oven-browned brussels sprouts. Erma might not be a sparkling conversationalist, but she really could cook.

After dinner, Jax and Burt went back out to the stables.

Aislinn helped Erma clean up after the meal, though Erma protested that she always did the work herself.

"Oh, really," said the housekeeper in a breathy little voice. "That's not necessary. I'll take care of it."

Three whole sentences. Erma was growing downright talkative. "I insist." Aislinn used her firmest tone. "Please don't argue."

With a tiny sigh, Erma allowed her to help.

As they cleared the table and loaded the dishwasher, Aislinn tried to get the older woman talking and was marginally successful. Erma revealed that she'd lived and worked at Wild River for fifteen years, since her husband, a salmon fisherman, had died. She had no children. This summer, there were three grooms and a stable hand working at Wild River, all four of whom went home after work.

The minute they had the dishwasher going and the kitchen and dining room back in order, Erma said goodnight and headed for her rooms above the garage.

It was barely seven thirty. Aislinn wanted to jump in her car and drive home to Valentine Bay. She could cuddle with Bunbun and Luna, maybe get in a few hours in her workshop. But there was no going home right now. Her sisters would be all over her, wondering what was wrong.

After all, it was her wedding night. They would demand to know what had gone wrong.

She was just about to go on upstairs and stream a movie on her laptop, when she heard the front door open.

A moment later, Jax appeared from the central hall in his stocking feet. He must have left his boots at the door. For a moment, they both stood there, just staring at each other.

Dear Lord, he got her hormones cooking. The way those jeans hugged his narrow hips, the way he filled out his fly. And those shoulders, so broad and deep, the kind a woman could really hold on to. He wore an old Henley, the sleeves pushed to his elbows. The tendons in his forearms were perfection. She might take up sculpture, make a statue of him, just to try to capture the level of carefully controlled hotness he had going on.

Finally, he asked, "You, uh, holding up all right?"

"All good." It was so weird and awkward—her body humming with his nearness, her words stilted, wooden. Really, what had she gotten herself into here? "I was just going to go on upstairs."

"If you need anything—"

"Nothing. Truly."

Tendons and muscles flexing, manly poetry in motion, he folded his arms over his chest and leaned in the archway. "Tomorrow, I thought we'd have an early breakfast, then we could all head for your place in Valentine Bay around eight."

"All?"

"You, me and Burt. We'll have two pickups, both with

horse trailers if you think you'll need them, and your Honda. Maybe we can make it in one trip."

"Sounds good, thanks."

They did the mutual staring thing again. Her heart had found a faster rhythm, and a strange little shiver raised the fine hairs at the back of her neck. She could just picture herself sauntering over to him, taking his hand, leading him upstairs into her room—but only long enough to pull him through the door that led to his.

And then he peeled his tall frame away from the doorway and came toward her, silent on those stocking feet. He stopped so close that if he took one step closer, her breasts would brush the front of his shirt.

He lifted a hand as if to touch her, and then let it drop. Ruefully, he muttered, "Tell me I don't smell of horse."

"You don't." She stared up at him, transfixed by the blue fire in his eyes. "Not that I would care. I like horses."

"I kind of figured you must, or I wouldn't have hired you back in the day."

She had to press her lips together to keep a goofy giggle from escaping. "It's so flattering, how well you remember the eight weeks I worked for you." His beautiful mouth twitched, but he didn't smile. He lifted that hand again. She smelled soap then—he'd washed up before he came inside.

Catching a curl of her hair, he rubbed it between his fingers. She let him. He held her gaze as he did it, and she almost felt as though he touched her skin. "Silky," he said, his voice gruffer than before. "I love how thick your hair is."

"I had a horse of my own once," she said, her body

aroused by his very nearness, her voice sounding dreamy and soft to her own ears.

He wrapped the curl of hair around his finger. "You want to talk about horses, huh?"

"Why not? You don't?"

"I do. Go on—you had a horse once, you said…"

"Right. He was a sweet dappled gelding named Charlie Boy. My brother Daniel bought him for me, for my twelfth birthday. It was the year after our parents died. I'd been begging for a horse since I was eight. We boarded Charlie Boy at a local stable. Daniel got me riding lessons. I rode every chance I got."

He touched the side of her throat, a slow stroke that stirred every hungry nerve in her body. "You still have that horse? Bring him to Wild River."

She shook her head. "I sold him to a school friend of Gracie's before I left for college in Portland. I was sad to part with him, but I knew I wouldn't be around enough to spend much time with him."

Jaxon's finger trailed upward again. He traced the curve of her jaw. "We'll go riding, you and me. Later this week."

"I would like that. I…" She, what?

She had no idea. Words had deserted her. There were better things to think about.

Like the warm, surprising softness of his lips as he bent his head and kissed her.

"Aislinn." He whispered her name, his breath warm against her mouth.

She made a low, throaty sound, accepting him, welcoming him. His hand curved around to cradle her nape and he pulled her closer, right up against him, her breasts pressing into the hard wall of muscle that was his chest.

Lower down, she could feel him growing bigger, unfurling against her belly.

It felt good. All of it—his mouth on hers, his fingers at her nape, his broad, strong body pressing all along the front of her. He smelled of soap and leather, hay and dust. He tasted salty and clean.

This. Exactly. This was what she had burned for five years ago and finally run away from. A yearning so strong she'd known it was dangerous.

And that was back then, when he'd paid no attention to her beyond the occasional vague, friendly smile.

Too soon, he lifted his head. She gazed up at him, longing surging, a high tide within her, every molecule in her body eager to kiss him some more. He watched her, waiting. His eyes said it all.

The next move was hers. He wouldn't push her.

And she wanted…everything. All of it. His touch and his kisses, his body above hers, filling her, holding her.

A real marriage from this night forward.

Except that it wasn't. And she ought to have sense enough to remember that.

"Good night, Jaxon," she said and turned for the stairs.

Chapter Five

With Jax and Burt's help, Aislinn got all of her stuff moved the next day.

Burt was a jerk to her. He worked hard, though, helping her move and then giving her and Jax a hand to set up her workshop, grumbling under his breath the whole time.

By Wednesday when she left for Sand & Sea, she had her studio ready to go in a large backyard shed—a much nicer one than the shed she used at her cottage. As for Luna and Bunbun, the rabbits were nice and comfy in their new home on the side porch.

They had buyers joining them for dinner at the ranch that night, a couple who ran cattle in the Wallowa Valley and their two little girls. Jax had sold them a pretty pair of fillies and a gorgeous black gelding. Erma out-did herself with the meal and Jax brought out some really nice Oregon wine.

Jax mentioned Aislinn's rabbits and Burt, being Burt, grumbled something under his breath. Nobody asked him what he'd said. Apparently, the buyers were totally on to him and his grouchy ways.

The little girls, who were six and eight, begged to pay the bunnies a visit. Aislinn took them out to the side porch. It was sweet to watch the two of them giggling and cooing over her babies. Luna and Bunbun, always ready for a little attention, loved every minute of that.

The buyers and their children left around eight to spend the night in Astoria. They would return in the morning, load up their new horses and head home to eastern Oregon. Aislinn and Jax saw them off and then ended up sitting out on the front porch together under a cloudy sky watching the night come on.

"Dinner was terrific," she said. "That Erma. Can't get two words out of her. But man, can she cook."

"Buyers love it—dinner at the ranch house, I mean." He stared out at the sky. It was starting to rain, the air heavy with ozone, fat drops plopping on the steps, shining on the leaves of Erma's purple hydrangeas that bloomed along the front of the porch. "After driving a good bargain, they enjoy a great meal and some nice wine."

"Well, you definitely deliver."

He turned to look at her. "The kids loved your rabbits." He gave her a slow smile that sent happy little shivers skating down her spine.

"Everybody loves my rabbits—well, except Burt."

His straight eyebrows bunched together. "He makes you crazy, you let me know."

"I can handle him," she said, and they left it at that.

* * *

But dealing with Burt was a definite challenge. When Jax wasn't near, he sometimes called her Judy, which angered her a lot more than she should have allowed it to.

The first time he did it, she corrected him. But after that, she let it be. Why give him the satisfaction of knowing he was getting to her?

As for Bunbun and Luna, he despised them. She knew that because he seemed to take evil pleasure in saying so under his breath. "Damn, idiot rabbits. All fur, no brains. What's the point, I ask you?"

His dog, Ace, seemed kind of freaked out by them.

Friday morning, when Aislinn was on the side porch changing their feed and water and giving them a little love, Ace barked at them through the screen and then ran in circles on the lawn.

Burt thought that was funny. She heard a cackling laugh and looked up to see him out there with the dog on the grass. He came closer and spoke through the screen. "You know what he sees when he looks at those furbags? Lunch, that's what."

Aislinn couldn't let that stand. "You'd better keep that dog away from them, Burt. Or you'll be answering to me."

He gave her his best crotchety Clint Eastwood scowl. "Think you're pretty scary, don't you now, Judy?"

She decided it was time to make a stand, which was a little discouraging, given that she was only four days into her three-month marriage. "I think we both know the situation here. You're a loyal, longtime employee. I'm the wife Jax has to keep for three months or lose the ranch. If it comes right down to you or me, who do you think will be hitting the road?"

"Got it all figured out, eh, Judy?"

"As a matter of fact, yes. I do." She gritted her teeth and tried for a friendlier tone. "And Ace seems like a nice dog."

"He's a *great* dog."

"Terrific. Keep him away from my rabbits and we'll all get along fine."

Burt put two fingers between his lips and let out an earsplitting whistle. Ace bounded over, stopped dead and sat at his feet. "C'mon, boy," he muttered. "We ain't wanted around here." And off Burt went, grousing about "fool women" under his breath, Ace trotting behind him, feathery tail wagging happily.

As for Erma, she continued to speak only when spoken to. It was like pulling teeth to try to get the woman to carry on a casual conversation. Already, Aislinn had pretty much given up hope that the two of them might somehow become BFFs.

Jax was a sweetheart, though. Whatever she asked for, he made it happen. Wednesday, he'd put a window air conditioner in the shed to keep it cool and hung warehouse-style pendant lights from the ceiling so she could see to work at night. He'd pitched right in to help her bunny-proof the side porch.

He hadn't tried to kiss her again after that first night, though. She couldn't help wishing he would, though she knew it was wiser that he didn't. The chemistry felt achingly right, but sex with her hot temporary husband would only make everything exponentially more complicated.

Friday evening when Aislinn returned from the gallery, she spotted a strange car in front of the house. She put her CR-V in the garage and entered through the breezeway to find Erma at the stove. The housekeeper shot her a strange look over her shoulder.

"Whose Lexus is that in the driveway?" Aislinn asked.

"That lawyer's."

"Kip Anders?"

Erma nodded and Aislinn's heart tripped into high gear, as though she'd done something wrong.

Well, she hadn't. She was living here with Jax just as Martin had demanded and it was a marriage "in more than name only," whatever the heck that meant.

So what if they weren't sleeping together? Nowhere in Martin's preposterous will had it said that she and Jax were required to have sex—and why was she even getting all worked up about this?

Because the whole thing was infuriating, that's why. A visit from Martin's lawyer only served to remind her of the thousand and one ways the dead man had screwed with her life.

"Is Jax back from the stables yet?"

Erma nodded.

"Where are they?"

"Family room," said the housekeeper, never one to utter a whole sentence when two words would do.

Aislinn detoured into the powder room off the kitchen to wash her hands and comb her hair and give herself a little pep talk in the mirror.

"It's going to be fine, no problems, all good," she said to her worried-looking reflection, adding a muttered, "Rot in hell, Martin," as she turned for the door.

In the family room, Kip Anders set down the drink

Jax had poured for him and rose to take Aislinn's hand. "How are you settling in?" he asked.

She played her part, giving Kip her warmest smile. "It's going beautifully. Jax has made sure I have everything I could possibly need for a successful and mutually profitable three-month marriage."

Anders laughed at that. "It is an unusual situation, I'll give you that."

The lawyer stayed for dinner. He praised Erma's pork roast and talked horses with Jax and Burt. After dessert and coffee, he left.

Aislinn and Jax walked him out.

As he drove away, Aislinn couldn't resist asking, "Did he ask to see where we sleep?"

He shook his head. "I took him out to your studio and then to the side porch, where I introduced him to your rabbits. Then I offered him a drink and he accepted. You came home about ten minutes later."

"So we're off the hook on the whole question of sex, then?"

"I'm pretty sure we always were." He was smirking. "But feel free to have sex with me anyway, whenever the mood strikes."

She stifled a snort of laughter and fake-punched him in the arm.

Saturday afternoon when she returned from four hours at Sand & Sea, he met her in the driveway, looking all rugged and yummy in old jeans, a black T-shirt, lace-up work boots and a cowboy hat.

She rolled her window down.

He leaned in. "How about we tack up a couple of horses and go for that ride I promised you?"

"Best offer I've had all day. Give me twenty minutes. I'll meet you at the stables."

He had the horses all ready to go when she got there, two bays—a gelding named Saint John for her and a handsome mare, Lady Jane, for him.

They rode out across the green rolling ranch land and up into the low hills to the east, coming out on a tree-less promontory that looked down over the valley. Dismounting, they hobbled the horses and sat side by side on a big, flat-topped boulder.

"It's beautiful," she said. And it was, kind of misty in the low spots where the river gleamed, everything in varying shades of green—mossy to bright to almost-black. He didn't say anything. She turned to find him watching her. "What?"

He took off his hat, tapped it on his thigh and put it back on. "How're you doing, really?"

"All right. My rabbits are happy on their new porch and my studio is amazing. Thank you."

"Things with Burt?"

She narrowed her eyes at him. "Has he been complaining about me?"

"Only under his breath."

She nudged him with her elbow. "Don't grin when you say that. I might be tempted to get annoyed at *you*."

His expression grew serious. "He's getting on your nerves, then?"

"Burt and I could come to blows, but so far we've kept violence at a minimum."

"Do you want me to—"

"Stop. I'm exaggerating. I'll work it out with him, one way or another." She'd intended to leave it at that, but maybe a little information would help her to understand the crabby cowboy better. "What's his story, anyway? I swear, he hates all women, except maybe Erma. But then, even a hard-core misogynist couldn't hate Erma. She's a great cook, she keeps the house neat as a pin and she never makes a peep unless you ask her a direct question—and even then, she's just as likely to try to answer with a headshake or a nod."

"Erma's shy."

"You don't say."

"As for Burt, he's been married three times. His first wife cleaned out their bank account and ran off with his cousin."

"Ouch."

"His second wife embezzled from the construction company she was working for—and tried to convince the authorities that Burt made her do it."

"Omigod."

"His third wife had a temper problem. She died in prison."

"She hurt someone?"

"Yeah. Burt. She shot him three times. It's a miracle he survived."

"You're kidding about this, right? It's not really true."

But Jax wasn't laughing. "God's truth. Burt has no right to blame *all* women because his three marriages ended in disaster."

"But he does."

"Pretty much. He also didn't get along with Judy."

She couldn't keep herself from asking "Why?"

"Judy complained a lot—about how bored she was and how there was no one interesting to talk to, about how lonely she felt. Horses scared her and she didn't like dogs. She ordered Burt to keep Ace away from the house. They had other points of contention. Lots of them. Burt talked back to her and one night at dinner, right there in front of him, she turned to me and said she wanted him fired."

Aislinn made a mental note not to threaten Burt with losing his job again. "That's awful."

"Yeah. And as you can see, nobody fired Burt, which made Judy unhappier than ever. As for Burt, well, Judy was just one more proof that he's right about women."

"I'll try to be patient with him."

Jax touched her hand. It seemed the most natural thing to weave her fingers with his. His palm was warm and broad. It felt good, sitting here beside him, the sun on her back, the horses chuffing softly as they cropped the short grass behind them. "Don't be too patient," he advised after a moment. "Burt can get a horse to do anything. But when it comes to other people, he really is a pain in the ass."

"I'll manage, don't worry."

"As for Judy, well, I know I'm making it sound like she was the bad guy. She wasn't. Looking back, I can see that we were both talking and no one was listening. She said she loved me and she'd always had a fantasy of living on a ranch—all the while telling me how she missed her family and the city was her home. She never lied about what she really wanted. I heard what I wanted to hear, that's all. And when it came down to it, she wanted to go home and I refused to go with her."

"Because you were already home."

"Yeah. Yeah, I was." He turned her hand over so her engagement ring caught the sunlight and sparkled. "I hope you like your rings."

"I do. Thank you." They were sweet and traditional,

nothing like the bold, unusual pieces she created in her studio. She loved them because he'd given them to her— even if in three months, she would probably be giving them back.

He said, "They were Aunt Claudia's, these rings."

Had they been Judy's rings, too? She pulled her hand free of his, wincing at the thought.

"Hey." He frowned at her in that attentive, focused way he had—until he got what was going on with her. "Hold on. Don't even think it. Judy chose her own rings. She picked them out, told me her ring size and sent me to the jeweler to buy them." He leaned her way enough to bump his arm against hers. "I'm a little thickheaded sometimes, but I like to think I'm not an idiot."

She felt the sweetest little zing in the vicinity of her heart—that he paid attention. That he always seemed to know when something wasn't right with her. The man had clearly learned a lot from what had gone wrong in his first marriage. "You are not in any way an idiot. And I'm sorry to have doubted your good judgment on the subject of repurposing wedding rings."

"You are forgiven." He held her gaze and they shared one of those moments, a moment brimming with prom- ise somehow, a moment where anything seemed pos- sible.

She prompted, "So tell me more about your aunt and Martin."

He leaned back on his hands. "Martin started out on the ranch as a stable hand. He scrimped and saved to buy those rings."

"He really did love your aunt, then, like he said in his letter?" That made her feel hopeful, somehow. Even if he had betrayed Claudia with the foreman's wife—who was probably her real mother.

Seriously, could it get any more twisted?

"He did love Aunt Claudia, yeah," Jax said. "He'd come from back east, with nothing in his pockets. Like me, he never knew his father. His mom was a torch singer, Colette Durand. She played piano and performed in clubs and restaurants to make ends meet. He told me once that she was some kind of grifter, too, always working a con on the men who fell for her. Martin had that in him, too. He had a showman's heart and a tendency to work the angles to get things his way. He was a charmer."

She thought of that grumpy old man during the summer five years ago, sitting on the front porch in his bathrobe, watching her with hard suspicion in his eyes. "A charmer? Please."

"Yeah, he got kind of grouchy when he got old. But while I was growing up, he worked hard. He taught me everything he knew and treated me like I was the greatest thing going."

It eased her bitterness with Martin at least a little, that he'd been good to Jaxon. It was something to focus on when she found herself wishing that he was still alive so she could call him bad names right to his face and maybe strangle him for good measure.

Jax stared out over the land below, his expression far away. "I don't specifically remember what it was like before my mom died. Martin told me later that she'd been disinherited by my grandparents for dropping out of school and hanging with the wrong crowd. I remember she had boyfriends and most of them scared me. I don't think she had a clue of how to take care of a kid. And then she got shot in a convenience store robbery."

"Oh, no. She robbed a store?"

He let out a humorless laugh. "No. It was just a freak thing, she was a customer who got hit by a ricocheted bullet."

"I probably shouldn't ask, but were you there?"

"Uh-uh. It was the middle of the night. She'd left me at the motel across the street, sound asleep."

Aislinn scooted closer to him and rested her head on his shoulder then. She just couldn't stop herself.

He said, "The hotel maid found me the next morning. Child services came to get me. They contacted Aunt Claudia, and she and Martin brought me to Wild River. Here, with them, I had a real life, you know? I got counseling and people I trusted took care of me. I was safe. I knew I'd come home."

Aislinn felt that ache at the back of her throat and behind her eyes—for him, for a little boy who'd lost his mom, but found a home.

In all likelihood, they had that in common, didn't they? Jax had lost his real mother and she'd been taken from hers. He'd found a true home with Martin and Claudia. She'd gotten lucky with Marie and George Bravo, with every one of her Bravo siblings. She sent a little prayer to heaven that Madison Delaney, America's darling, felt the same way about how things had turned out for her.

And thinking of Madison had her wondering about Paula, whom she was slowly coming to accept as her biological mother. According to Martin's last letter and the PI's report, Paula Delaney had died not long after that summer Aislinn had worked here at Wild River.

She would never get a chance to know her birth mother. Loss hollowed her out at the thought.

"Look at me," he said gently and tipped up her chin. "You're a softhearted woman, Aislinn Winter."

She sniffed to keep the pointless tears from getting the best of her. "I'm feeling a little sentimental, yeah, partly just thinking that I'm never going to meet Paula Delaney. And also because I'm glad you felt loved and safe with Martin and your aunt."

He took her hand again and rubbed the back of it with his thumb, an idle, somehow possessive caress that she liked way too much. "Life just seemed full of possibilities with Martin around."

Okay. That was too much. She couldn't let him get carried away saying good things about the man who'd switched two newborn babies, stealing them from their rightful parents, and then simply walked away from his crime, never confessing what he'd done until he was beyond the reach of any retribution. "Come on, now. The guy messed with everyone's lives. And he cheated on your aunt."

"She was always sick."

"That's no excuse, Jax. You know what the vows say, *In sickness and in health.*"

He lifted her hand and pressed his lips to it. She made absolutely no effort to keep that from happening—on the contrary, she melted a little at the touch of his mouth, the warmth of his breath on her skin, the slight scratch of his beard scruff that made her want to feel that soft mouth and that rough beard up close.

"Mostly, Aunt Claudia was devoted to Martin," he said. "But sometimes she would turn on him, treat him like the hired help. I know that doesn't make any of the wrong things he did right. But she hurt him, that's all I'm saying."

"Still. There's no excuse for cheating."

"You're right." And with that, he let it go. For several long, lovely minutes, they just sat there in the late-afternoon sun, holding hands and gazing down at the green, rolling country below.

Sunday, Aislinn clipped Luna and Bunbun—their thick coats and their toenails, too.

She wore an apron to keep the wool from getting all over her and she did the job with the rabbits in her lap, careful not to yank or pull. German angoras had loose skin and pulling at it caused them pain. She bagged the wool for an artist friend who made gorgeous angora hats and gloves and strange, soft tapestries, too. As she was finishing up, with Bunbun on his back while she clipped his belly, she caught movement in the corner of her eye.

Burt. He was standing on the grass a few feet from the porch screen. Really, he was like a bad little boy. Always popping up out of nowhere to torment her and her pets.

"Why'd you cut all the hair off 'em?"

It was a civil question for once and she gave him a real answer. "They're bred for wool production. They need clipping every ninety days or they get matted and when they try to clean themselves, they get wool block."

"Constipated, you mean?"

"That's right. Wool block can kill them."

He was staring at Luna as she nibbled hay. "They look downright pitiful like that." He almost sounded as though he cared.

She set Bunbun on the porch floor. He did look shrunken and scrawny without his enormous cloud of fur. His long, tufted ears suddenly seemed absurdly oversize. But Bunbun wasn't bothered. He hopped away to join Luna, perfectly content.

"Their wool is hot," she explained. "In the summer especially, they love a good clipping."

"What do you do with the fur?"

"I sell it to a friend who spins the wool into yarn."

He frowned through the screen at her and she waited for the insult she knew was coming.

But for once, he surprised her, clicking his tongue for Ace, and heading off toward the stables without another word. Could this be the beginning of a truce with the crabby ranch foreman?

She decided not to hold her breath on that.

Monday, she woke up feeling edgy. Daniel and Keely were due home that afternoon.

Aislinn wasn't on the schedule at Sand & Sea that day. She spent the morning in her workshop making wax jewelry molds. An idea for a whole series of pieces had come to her and she felt energized about her work lately, almost driven.

Maybe it was the ranch. Beautiful. Quiet. A good place for her to concentrate on her work.

Or maybe it was the hit her heart had taken, to learn she wasn't exactly who she'd always thought she was. It seemed to have focused her somehow. Life didn't last forever and at some point a woman had to stop wandering through the days, trying this job and that one, like changing outfits in a dressing room. Eventually, a woman needed to get in there and make her dreams happen.

Her phone rang at a little after three in the afternoon.

She set down the wax ring mold she was smoothing with sandpaper and answered. "Welcome home."

Keely didn't waste words. "We got back a couple of hours ago. Gracie's been acting oddly." The youngest Bravo sister still lived in the Bravo house with Daniel, Keely and the twins. "She just left for the Sea Breeze." Grace worked behind the bar there most nights. "Before she left, she said I should call *you* and ask what's going on."

Aislinn teared up out of nowhere. She blinked to clear the moisture away. "I'm so glad you're home. We need to talk. Alone."

They settled on lunch the next day at Fisherman's Korner.

Aislinn got there first and ordered them the usual. When Keely walked in, looking gorgeous and tanned, her reddish-brown hair loose on her shoulders, her green eyes shining, Aislinn jumped from the booth and ran to her.

"Was it fabulous?" she whispered, as they blocked the entrance with a reunion hug.

"More than fabulous. I love him so much, Ais."

Aislinn squeezed her tighter. "You and Daniel. Completely in love. I get all teary-eyed over it." She pulled back and patted Keely's barely rounded tummy. "How's the baby?"

"No complaints. I'm feeling good and it'll be a while until I'm big as a boat." Keely grabbed her hand. "Come on. Let's clear the doorway."

They took their usual seats in the red pleather booth, leaning close to each other across the Formica table as Keely gave a quick recap of her honeymoon in paradise.

The waitress came with their fish and chips and then left them alone.

"All right," Keely said. "What's happening? Tell me everything."

Aislinn swore Keely to secrecy and told the whole story—from the series of incredible revelations at the reading of Martin's will through her finding out that what Martin had claimed was most likely true, to how she'd married Jax a week ago Monday and was living at the ranch with him for the next three months.

When she finally fell silent, Keely faked a glare. "You should have called me."

"Well, I didn't. And if I had it to do over, I still wouldn't bother you."

"You are *never* a bother."

"Keel. You and Daniel *needed* that trip. And if I'd called, I know you would have come right home for me."

"Of course I would have. Daniel would, too."

"So then. I did the right thing."

"No, you did not."

"Stop. Enough. It's done. Can we please move on?"

Keely faked a glare just to drive home her point. And then she gave that up and widened her eyes. "*The* Madison Delaney is family? Seriously?"

"It certainly looks that way. Percy's going to figure out the best way to reach out to her. We'll see how that goes."

"And you *married* Jaxon Winter."

"Well, I couldn't let him lose the ranch. He loves that place."

Keely bit the corner of her lip. Aislinn knew that look. Her best friend was barely containing a giant, knowing grin.

Aislinn shook a finger at her. "Don't you even think it. It's not like that."

"Why not? You're married and all I have to do is look in those big, brown eyes of yours to see that you've still got a thing for him."

"Right on the first point. As to the second, don't. Just don't."

"Honey." Keely wiped the grease off her fingers and wiggled them at her. "Gimme. Come on." They held hands across the table. "Whatever happens, however it goes, if you feel it for him, make the best of the time you have together. Don't waste a minute. I mean, how long's it been since you were even with someone?"

"Too long." Three years ago, she'd met a talented chain saw artist at the Valentine Bay Sunday Market. They'd become lovers for a little while. But she'd broken it off. He was a great guy. Just not the *right* great guy.

"Think about it, about going for it with Jaxon."

"I will," she promised. Sometimes it seemed it was *all* she thought about. And they needed to move on to the main point. "So, this is the deal..."

Keely ate a french fry. "Tell me."

"Aside from Percy and Daffy, you're the only one I've told that there's a Bravo sister out there who's got a family she doesn't even know about. I was waiting for you and Daniel to come home before telling everyone else."

Keely caught on then. "We need a family meeting."

"Yes, we do."

"Next weekend," Keely said. "Sunday dinner. I'll bully every one of them until they all agree to come."

"Perfect."

Keely frowned. "You look worried all of a sudden. What's wrong?"

"It's just, Martin's will had this stipulation that Jax and I have to be married 'in more than name only.' You, Percy and Daffy are the only ones I've told the whole truth. They all came to the wedding—Percy, Daffy, Matt, Connor, Liam. Hailey and Harper and Gracie. Except for Daffy and Percy, they all believe it's a real marriage, the kind that's supposed to last a lifetime, even if it did happen out of the blue. Jax and I agreed not to make it public knowledge that we only got married so that he can keep Wild River. You can't tell anybody about the three-month deadline."

Keely sat back in the booth, her expression suddenly grave. "What about Daniel?"

Aislinn winced. "Oh, Keel. I'm sorry. Daniel most of all. He thinks he's my dad—he really *is* my dad in a lot of ways. He's a second dad to all of us. He's going to be unhappy enough that I got married without a word to him."

"He's my *husband*, Ais. I can't keep big secrets from him."

Aislinn knew it was wrong to have asked her to. "I never should have told you about the three-month thing..."

"Of course you should tell me," Keely cried. "You have to be able to tell me everything. We've always had that, you and me."

"Not always. You suspected you were pregnant and you didn't tell me."

Keely looked crushed. "That hurt you?"

"Of course not. When you did tell me about the baby, I totally got why you hadn't confided in me earlier. Daniel's my brother—maybe not by blood, as it turns out, but you know what I mean."

"Wait a minute. He *is* your brother. He always will be. Nothing can change that."

"You think?" Aislinn asked in a small voice.

"I *know.*"

Aislinn felt weepy again, and that annoyed her no end. She needed to stop getting all emo about everything. "You're right—and where were we?"

"Ais—"

"No. Really. Let me make my point. When you thought you might be pregnant, you didn't feel it would be right to tell me before telling Daniel. I'm his sister and you didn't want to put that on me. You considered all the sides of the issue and you kept that secret to yourself. You didn't want to put me on the spot in any way. Today, I was just so grateful to finally have you to talk to, I didn't think." Keely's shoulders had slumped. They stared at each other across the table. Aislinn drew a slow, steadying breath. "Okay. I can't do this to you. I get that you have to tell him."

But Keely shook her head. "How 'bout this? I'll keep it to myself for as long as I can. But it's like he's got radar for when I'm not telling him something. If he asks me right out what's going on—"

"I understand. You can't lie to him."

"I don't *want* to lie to him. I *won't* lie to him."

"Agreed."

But Keely wasn't finished. "And you're going to have to at least tell him about the wedding right away. Think about it. Everybody else knows. Are you actually imagining you can keep him in the dark about your marriage until Sunday?"

"Of course not. I will. I'll tell him today."

"And just consider telling him all of it."

"Oh, I don't know, Keely."

"It will make such a difference to him. You know how he is. He still thinks he's everyone's dad. He has to know all the important stuff so he can do everything in his power to protect everyone."

"Yes. All right. I'll consider it." Her mind was doing the hamster-in-a-wheel thing. How to tell her big brother about the wedding *and* about the movie star who happened to be his long-lost sister without him wondering why Aislinn had suddenly decided to marry Martin Durand's adopted son. Aislinn groaned. "This is all getting so convoluted."

"And that is not your fault. It's a convoluted situation that crazy old Martin Durand put you in." Keely reached across the table and squeezed her shoulder in solidarity. "Just take it one step at a time. Come to the house at five thirty. Daniel should be home from the docks by then." Daniel ran Valentine Logging. The family company had its offices at the Warrenton docks. "Grace will be gone, on her way to work. I'll keep the twins entertained and you and Daniel can talk in his study."

Aislinn and Keely both went to Sand & Sea after lunch. Aislinn relieved Amanda. As the owner, Keely had work to catch up on. She disappeared into the office in back for a couple of hours and left at three.

At four thirty, Amanda returned, leaving Aislinn an hour before she had to be at the Bravo house. There was no point in driving out to Wild River, just to turn around and come back. She wandered Valentine Bay's downtown historic district, feeling droopy and forlorn, window-shopping and trying to decide how much to tell Daniel.

Finally, it was time to get it over with.

When she got to the house, Daniel answered the door. He pulled her into a hug and she let herself lean on him just for a minute.

"It's so good to have you home," she said.

He held her away from him to look in her eyes. "Keely says you need to talk to me. Come on in the study." He ushered her in there and over to the grouping of a love seat and two club chairs across from his desk. She took the love seat and he settled into a chair.

She gazed across the low table between them. He was tan and relaxed-looking, his blond hair bleached even lighter by the tropical sun. A trip to paradise with Keely had been good for him.

And she had no idea where to even start. "How much did Keely tell you?"

"Just that you needed to talk to me."

"Well, okay. I'll start at the beginning, then. Right after you and Keely left for Bora Bora, I got a certified letter from Kircher and Anders, Attorneys at Law…" And from there, everything just came pouring out. All of it. She even told him about the three-month deadline.

Somehow, now that she was here, sitting across from the brother who'd raised her, she didn't know how *not* to tell him. Her sisters—Grace especially—had had conflicts with Daniel. They resisted his need to take care of them, to keep them safe. Not Aislinn. She appreciated all he'd done for their family, getting custody of all of them, helping them make it to adulthood after their parents were killed. She trusted his judgment, had often sought out his advice.

When she finished telling all of it, he said, "You like

this guy you married." It wasn't a question. "You think he's a good guy."

"I do, yes. And he *is* good, Daniel."

"I believe you."

"I couldn't let him lose his ranch. That ranch is everything to him."

"I get that."

"And hey." She tried for lightness. "There's a fifty K payoff for me when it's over."

He grunted. "I know you better than that. You wouldn't marry anyone for a payoff."

She swallowed around the sudden lump in her throat. "I love you, Daniel."

"I love *you*—and with Keely's help, I've been making a real effort lately not to butt in, trying to let you and our brothers and sisters run your own lives, make your own choices."

"Shut the front door." She couldn't help grinning. "You, staying out of our business. That's a lot to ask."

"Tell me about it."

"Another thing, Daniel. I, um, agreed with Jaxon that we wouldn't tell anyone the specific terms of the will. Martin put this phrase in there that the marriage had to be 'more than in name only.' It just seemed wiser not to go around telling people we have an arrangement so that Jax can keep Wild River. I've let everyone else think it's a marriage like most marriages. For love and forever."

"But I can discuss it with Keely?"

"Of course. She knows everything, too."

"It's your choice how you want to handle that. I won't tell anyone—and you said Percy's already looking into contacting Madison Delaney…" He shook his head. "I can't believe it. We have a sister we've never even met."

"Yeah. It's a lot to deal with, huh?"

He said nothing for a moment, but his sea-blue eyes were watching her. "You are still my sister," he said quietly. "That will never change."

Her vision blurred and her throat clutched. "Oh, Daniel…"

"Come on, now." He rose, came around the table and pulled her up to wrap her in his arms. She held on tight until he took her shoulders and pulled back. "It's not only blood that makes us a family," he said. "It's all the years, together—every loss, every triumph, every trial we came through, stronger than ever. You are a Bravo. You always will be." He put on his sternest look, the one he used to wear when she'd done something she shouldn't have. "You'd better remember that."

"I will." She pushed the words out around the big lump in her throat.

"Don't make it necessary for me to override Keely's wise advice and go full-out substitute dad on your ass."

That brought a pained chuckle. "Can't have that."

He squeezed her shoulders and then released her. "I'm going to call Percy, get him to bring me up to speed on what's happening with Madison Delaney."

"That'll work." She told him about the family meeting Keely was setting up and realized she felt better, now that he knew what was going on. Keely had been right. She'd needed to tell him.

"Stay for dinner?" he asked.

She thought of Jax. He was probably wondering where she'd run off to. In the eight days they'd been married, she'd always returned to the ranch by five or so. "Not tonight, thanks. I need to get back."

* * *

She'd left her phone in the car. When she slid in behind the wheel, she saw that the little blue light was blinking with a text from Jax. Everything okay? Are you coming home for dinner?

Home. Already Wild River kind of did feel like home.

Did she need to watch herself, to make more of an effort not to get too attached?

Her phone rang in her hand. *Jax.* She couldn't help smiling just at the sight of his name. She put the phone to her ear. "Sorry. I'm still in Valentine Bay. I had some stuff to deal with, but I'm on my way now. I'll be there in half an hour or so."

"We'll wait dinner for you, then."

"No. Really. It isn't necessary."

"We'll wait," he said again, that low, almost-gruff voice of his reaching right through the phone to her, sending warmth curling down inside her, making her belly feel all fluttery.

Sheesh. *Keep your pants on, girl.* "All right. See you soon."

At Wild River, the house smelled of savory roast chicken and fresh-baked bread. She washed her hands and joined Jax, Erma and Burt at the table.

Burt just had to make a snide remark. "So great you finally joined us, Princess."

Jax said, "Burt," in a warning tone and Aislinn had to hide a smile. Princess, she decided, was a definite improvement over calling her Judy.

Burt mumbled something else. Aislinn couldn't make out the words—not that she cared what the old sourpuss said. She sent the foreman a dazzling smile and asked Erma to pass the chicken.

After dinner, she helped to clean up after the meal. Burt disappeared, but Jax pitched in, too. With all three of them working, the job took no time at all.

The minute they were done, Erma headed for her rooms, leaving Aislinn and Jax alone in the kitchen. It seemed as good a time as any to confess to him that two more people knew the particulars of Martin Durand's will.

"Got a minute?" she asked.

He reached for her hand, his fingers closing around hers. His touch felt too good, too exactly right. Like her hand had been waiting all her life for him to be the one holding it.

Oh, she was a complete fool for this man. No doubt about it.

Out on the back porch, the sun was still up but hovering close to the western horizon, the sky splashed with layers of purple and orange. They sat on the steps leading down to the unfenced backyard, which consisted of a wide, grassy area rimmed in box elders, maples and alder trees.

He still had her hand in his and he didn't let go. Instead, he pulled her closer and rested their joined hands on his hard thigh.

He leaned in and his lips brushed her cheek. She felt his breath across her skin and wished that this moment might never end. Really, she needed to watch herself or she would tumble into love with him all over again.

"Stuff?" he whispered in her ear.

"Hmm?"

"On the phone, you said you had 'stuff' to deal with in Valentine Bay."

It was as good a lead-in as any, she supposed. "I had lunch with my best friend, Keely, who recently married my oldest brother, Daniel. I told her everything, about Martin switching me with Madison Delaney on the day we were born, about you and the three months we have to be married so that you can keep Wild River and I can get a fifty-thousand-dollar payoff, about all of it. And then I was late for dinner because I went to see Daniel and told him everything, too."

For a long chain of uncomfortable seconds, Jax didn't reply. He did keep holding her hand, though. Was that a good sign?

Finally, he said exactly what she'd been expecting he would. "I thought we'd agreed to leave the terms of Martin's will out of it, to tell people we got married for real and forever." His voice was too careful.

And she suddenly felt contrary. "Well, at least the for-real part is true. We are really married."

"Not the point. And you know it."

He was right. Damn it. "I'm sorry. Truly. But I needed to tell Keely. And she convinced me that I should tell Daniel." She looked at him and waited for him to finally meet her eyes. "And now that I've broken our first agreement, I'm not expecting you to believe me, but that's it, Keely and Daniel. That's all. I won't tell anyone else and neither will they." And then she thought of Percy and Daffy. She'd told them, too.

He read her so easily. "Who else?"

She scrunched her eyes shut and let out a moan. "I have such a big mouth."

"Who?"

"My great-aunt and -uncle. I told them, too."

Did he sigh? She couldn't tell for sure, with her eyes shut. But it seemed that maybe he had.

He let go of her hand.

"Oh, Jax." She made herself look at him. "I really am sorry."

And something wonderful happened. His cool expression warmed. He put his arm around her and pulled her in nice and close against his side. His lips touched her hair. "You know, maybe we're making too much of this."

"Too much?" She leaned into him. He was so strong and solid and it felt so good, just to be there on the porch with him as the sun set, her head on his shoulder, his cheek against her hair. "You think so?"

"Yeah. We have a real, legal marriage, however long it's going to last. Nobody's defrauding anybody. We live together and we support each other."

"We *like* each other," she added, because that mattered. Yeah, okay, marriage was supposed to be all about the love. But two people needed to like and respect each other, too.

He put a finger under her chin and she looked in his eyes again. "Tell whoever you need to tell."

She let out a huff of a laugh. "Well, I already pretty much have."

"It is what it is," he said. "And we don't have to lie about it."

"Good. Because I don't *want* to lie about it."

"Aislinn." He said her name so tenderly. And he touched her hair, a lingering stroke of his big hand. That slow, sweet caress wrecked her in the most wonderful way.

They were married. Truly married.

Maybe it wasn't forever. But when you got right down to it, what was?

She wanted him, all of him. So very much. "Jax, I…"

"Yeah?"

She tipped her head back and they shared a long glance. Heat ricocheted through her. She whispered his name again as she lifted her mouth so their lips could meet.

Chapter Six

Jax took his time with that kiss.

He loved the taste of her mouth, the feel of her body in his arms, the way he could look in her eyes and sense if something was bothering her. He'd never had a clue what Judy might be thinking.

But Aislinn...

Aislinn tried to be careful, to be logical, to puzzle things through, to guard her tender heart.

But her nature was to be open. Willing. Already, after being married to her for a week and a day, he was just next door to certain that Martin had been right. She would make an ideal wife for him.

She seemed to like living at Wild River. There were no sulky looks, no hints that she found ranch life empty and boring. She had her workshop and her enormous, good-natured rabbits, her large family not that far away.

She kept busy. She knew how to handle herself on a horse, and she even managed to treat Burt with tolerance and a smile.

Jax pulled her closer. He nipped at her lower lip. She made the sweetest little moaning sound. He could eat her right up.

Yeah. He might as well admit it to himself. When their three months were over, he was going to want to make it forever.

Was he too easy, too eager to start seeing her as a companion for life?

Burt would say, *Hell yes!* But Burt had zero confidence in the trustworthiness of any woman.

Jax didn't believe that she'd manipulated Martin. But even if she had, well, so what? Martin had owed her a lot more than the fifty thousand she would get when the terms of his ridiculous will had been satisfied.

Her mouth gave beneath his, those plump lips parting. He slipped his tongue in and tasted her sweetness more deeply.

She sighed and snuggled closer. He turned her, lifting her, until she was sitting across his lap, her soft arms around his neck. He groaned at the feel of her round bottom, brushing him, making him harder, hotter, as their kiss went on and on.

He hadn't known that a kiss could be like this, slow and sweet and hot and—*more*. Painful, too, but in a good way, the best way. He was thirty-four years old and he'd been with three women before her: his ex-wife, his high school sweetheart and the girl he'd dated in college. When it came to sex, he'd thoroughly enjoyed all three.

But this, with her, felt different somehow. Hotter. Better. More intense—and there was that word again: *more*.

She broke the kiss to settle back into the cradle of his arm. Her sooty eyelashes fluttered open and she regarded him through those black eyes she'd gotten from the father who'd denied her from birth. "I want to be with you, Jaxon. *Really* with you. It's probably foolish and definitely too soon. But I don't care. I want you to take me upstairs to my room. I want to open that door to *your* room…"

He bent close again, captured her lower lip between his teeth and bit down gently, loving the soft fullness of her flesh there, swiping his tongue over it. A tiny groan escaped her. He drank in that hungry sound before he let go. "And then what?" he asked, because he needed to hear her say it out loud.

She didn't disappoint him. "I want to go through that door with you, to your room. To your bed. I want tonight with you."

"I want that, too. I want all the nights."

A husky little whisper of a laugh escaped her. "Let's start with this one. See how it goes. See if we still feel the same way in the morning."

"I already know how I'll feel in the morning."

Those dark eyes gleamed. "Oh, yeah? How's that?"

"Satisfied. And ready for more."

She laughed. And then she wriggled free of his hold and stood. "Let's go inside." She held down her hand.

Jax took it.

He followed her willingly in the back door, across the kitchen, down the central hall to the stairs and up them. She pulled him into her room and through the inner door to his.

As she led him across his sitting area, he stopped and pulled her against his body, her back to his front. "I can't take it." He whispered into her hair. "I need to have my hands all over you."

"Yes," she replied in a tender little whisper.

He buried his face in the curve of her neck and she leaned back against him with a sigh. Pushing the wide neck of her shirt out of the way, he scattered a string of kisses along the satin flesh leading out to her shoulder. At the same time, he brought his open hands up over the cage of her ribs until he could cup her breasts in either palm.

They were round and firm. Just the feel of them sent a fresh surge of blood to his groin. He plucked at her nipples through her clothes. She wriggled against him, murmuring his name, "Jaxon," pleadingly, like she wanted everything from him.

Well, everything was exactly what he wanted to give her.

He was starving. He really was. Starving for her, for her kind ways and her beautiful skin, for the things a woman has that a man needs—heart and tenderness, the promise of understanding, so that life could be more than work and a decent bank balance.

More.

Yeah. It really was the perfect word for what she offered. *More.*

"Say it again," he instructed. "Aislinn, say my name."

"Jaxon." It came out just right, all breathless and wanting.

"Again."

"Jaxon. Jaxon. Jaxon…"

"Woman, what you do to me…" He brought his hands up to her shoulders and turned her to face him, so he could have her mouth again, so he could taste the hot sweetness beyond her parted lips.

She twined her arms around his neck and pressed her body close to him. He felt caught by her, captured. A willing victim, the enthusiastic engineer of his own total defeat.

He clasped her waist and lifted her. She knew what he wanted and wrapped those fine legs around him. Her low-heeled sandals clattered to the floor as she hooked her ankles together at the small of his back.

Kissing her, drawing her tongue into his mouth so he could taste her even more fully, he carried her to the bed. When he tried to set her down, she leaned backward, pulling him with her.

They went to the bed together, both of them laughing through the unbroken kiss.

She caught his head between her slim hands. "Condoms." Her face, flushed and so serious, enchanted him. *Enchanted?* It was one of those words he never used. Not even in his mind.

Until tonight.

He was a goner. No doubt about it now. He gave a nod, repeated, "Condoms."

"I don't have any, Jax. Do you?"

He did. He'd bought them three days ago, the last time he went into town. Because when a man wants a woman, he needs to be ready if the moment comes when she wants him, too. He shifted off her enough to switch on the bedside lamp, slide open the nightstand drawer and pull out a chain of them. "Will these do?"

Her smile bloomed wide. "Yippee."

He dropped them on the nightstand and turned back to her. "Now. Where were we…?"

"Right here." She lifted her mouth to him. He took it for another one of those long, delicious kisses.

But he still had his boots on. The boots had to go.

With definite reluctance, he sat up. "Don't move."

"Yes, sir."

"I really like the way you say that."

She tugged on his shirt. "Get back here."

"I'm working on it." He whipped off one boot and then the other and tossed them away, his socks, too. Then he turned to her, grabbed her shoulders and pulled her up to a sitting position. She blinked at him, kind of stunned, as he pulled her silky shirt out of her jeans. And then she caught on. She lifted her arms for him. He took the shirt up and away.

Her bra was white lace, with a little satin bow between the swells of her pretty breasts. He could not resist. He bent close and opened his mouth over her left nipple, sucking right through the lace, drawing her in.

"Jaxon..." She cradled his head. "Keep doing that. Never stop..."

"Too many damn clothes." He sucked her other nipple as he reached behind her and undid the clasp. A moment later, he was tossing the bra over his head. "Everything else," he commanded. "Off."

She got right to it, those dusky-tipped breasts bouncing as she wiggled out of her jeans and took her panties down with them. When she had them off, she kicked them over the side of the bed. "You, too." She leaned his way and poked his chest with her finger. "Stop fooling around."

He could take an order. Especially one that meant he'd end up naked with her, skin to skin. He stripped fast.

And then he reached for her.

She came to him, so willing, wrapping her soft, slim body around him, pulling him down to the mattress with a happy little moan. They rolled together, kissing, hands roaming everywhere. He buried his face in the dark, silky cloud of her hair, caught her earlobe between his teeth and worried it as she pulled him closer and let out a hungry, throaty sound.

There weren't enough kisses to do her justice. But he tried anyway—starting with her breasts, and not only the nipples. He kissed every inch of them: the soft upper slopes, the tender sides, the round curves beneath. He kissed them and he took them in his hands, pressed them together, kissed them some more. When she giggled and rolled over to her stomach, that didn't even give him pause.

He kissed the points of her shoulder blades, the sweet trail of bumps all down her spine. He dipped his tongue into each of those twin dimples where her backbone met her hips.

She let out soft, sweet little mewling sounds as he kissed the perfect swells of her bottom, right side first. On the left, he kept going, moving on down to the tender crease where her thigh began and lower. He lingered at the back of her knee, licking and nipping the taut, pale skin there.

About then, she grew impatient and rolled to her back again. If she hadn't been so quick about it, he would have grabbed her and held her in place to continue downward—to her calves, her ankles, the vulnerable soles of her feet, each and every pretty toe.

But she gave him a direct order. "Come up here. Kiss me."

"Yes, ma'am." He moved up her body and fused his

mouth with hers. Her kiss lit him up like a five-alarm fire. It was deep and so right.

As she kissed him, she reached down between them to wrap her fingers around his aching erection. He was the one moaning then, the one begging her name as she stroked him, her grip nice and tight, each pull just right—firm. A little bit rough.

Too soon, he had to catch her wrist and stop her or he would have finished without her.

For their first time, that wouldn't do.

Pushing her back onto the pillows, he kissed his way down the center of her to the neatly trimmed patch of dark hair at her mound. He pressed his lips to that tender crease where her thigh met her torso. She wriggled and sighed, clutching at his shoulders to pull him back up again.

No. Not yet.

He needed to taste her, there at the musky-sweet center of her. He nipped at her, gently guiding her thighs to part.

And then, at last, he kissed her, opening her with his fingers, delving in with his tongue.

She said his name some more then, so sweetly, pleading with him. "Jaxon. Oh, yes. Jax. Oh, please…"

He played her, using his fingers and his eager tongue. She reached down and clutched his head as he worked her. And she whispered husky, hungry encouragements, her hips rocking into him as he coaxed her higher.

And then, with the sweetest cry of triumph and abandon, she came. He drank her up, so wet and musky, tasting just right on his tongue.

And then she was clutching him again, pulling him

up, urging him to cover her. "Jax. Come here. I need…"
The words became a moan.

He couldn't wait to give her just what she needed—
and his eagerness almost got the best of him. He surged
up over her.

And pulled back with a groan in the precise second
before he buried himself in her welcoming heat.

"What?" She looked up at him, stricken.

"Condom." He growled the word.

Those big black eyes widened farther as she gasped.
"I forgot, too—oh, hurry, please! I can't wait…"

He'd never agreed with anyone more. He lifted away
enough to tear a condom off the strip, get it out of the
pouch and rolled down over himself.

"Jax." She reached for him, flattening her hands on
his chest, sliding them down to brush the base of his
erection. "You're so big, so beautiful…"

He was gone over her, done for. So much so that he
didn't even bother to tease her that a man should not be
called beautiful. Instead, he concentrated on the moment, which was just about as perfect as a moment could
get. He settled between her open thighs and she lifted
her hips, reached with her arms, tried to wrap herself
all around him.

He braced up on his elbows to get a little control,
hissing a breath through gritted teeth at the incompara-
ble feel of her. She was tight. It must have been a while
for her, too.

Tight, but so warm and wet. He took it slow, though
he almost had a heart attack holding himself back.

Her soft hands were all over him, stroking his shoulders, digging into his sides, grabbing his butt and hold-

ing on like she couldn't get enough of him, like she would never let go.

She whispered, "Yes," and, "Like that," and, "Oh! Oh, my!" the words punctuated by sharp gasps of pleasure along with little moans of discomfort as her body slowly opened for him.

Finally, he was all the way in, surrounded by her. She yanked him down, close and hard. He groaned when she did that. He didn't want to crush her, but she was insistent. In the end, he gave in and buried his head against her throat.

"Jax." Her breath across his cheek, her soft lips against his ear. "Oh, yes, Jax…"

That did it. Something broke loose in him. He couldn't wait anymore. He had to move.

He slid out to the tip and back in again. She gave him a soft, eager "Yes!" so he did it a second time.

And then she was moving, too, matching her rhythm to his. Everything got gloriously fuzzy, perfect and hot, frantic and so fine. She was on top and then they were on their sides, facing each other, moving more slowly, together, just right. Her eyes were all pupil, so dark and wide, miles deep.

He felt her rising to her peak. Somehow, he held off, managed not to lose it until she went over, clutching him so tightly, with a tender, wordless cry.

That did it for him. The end came searing along his backbone and the pulsing began. He wrapped his arms around her and let the pleasure take him down.

It was dark in the bedroom when Aislinn opened her eyes. The clock on the nightstand gave off a soft glow.

2:22 in the morning. The lamp had been on earlier. Jax must have switched it off.

Jax...

He was all wrapped around her, his warm breath stirring her hair, his big arm resting in the curve of her waist, his hard, hairy thigh caught between her smooth ones. She could close her eyes and stay here forever, satisfied and protected in the shelter of his embrace.

But all at once, out of nowhere, her heart was racing, knocking against her rib cage, urging her to go. Her mouth tasted of copper, sharp and all wrong.

They shouldn't have done this.

Yes, it had been glorious. But she wasn't ready for this.

She hardly even knew who she was anymore. She couldn't just fall into some hopeless love affair with Jax, no matter how great a guy he was. They were here because the father who had turned his back on her and changed the course of her life on the day of her birth had forced them into it. She needed to remember that.

What had she been thinking last night? This wasn't real. She had no idea what *was* real. Not anymore.

And she needed out of this bed. Now.

Panic clutched at her, urging her to hurry, get up, get out of here.

But she didn't want to wake him, so she tried her best to take it slow, easing out from under the weight of his arm, scooting an inch away at a time, toward the edge of the bed.

She slipped over the side, rolling out from under the blankets and down to the rug. And then she darted around in the dark snatching up her clothes, managing to find her jeans, panties, shirt and one sandal, but not the other one, or her bra.

Too bad. She could get them in the morning.

She tiptoed to the door that led to her room and reached for the door handle.

"Aislinn?" She heard the covers rustling. Jax switched on the lamp.

She whirled to face him, her clothes clutched against her nakedness, feeling utterly foolish, blinking against the sudden brightness.

"Aislinn." He sat up, the covers falling away to reveal his broad chest, heavy with hard muscle, a gorgeous trail of hair across his pecs, and leading down...

She gulped. "I'm just going to my own bed, that's all. Go back to sleep."

"Stay here. Don't go." He raked a hand through his sleep-scrambled hair. "I want you here." He looked at her so tenderly, like he couldn't stand it if she left.

Oh, God. He really seemed to mean it—and she wanted to stay.

But she couldn't. She simply couldn't. "I just need to, um, go, okay?"

He pushed the covers down and swung his feet to the floor. "Wait."

"I...can't, I..."

But then he was coming for her, completely naked, all man, so beautiful, so right, so...everything.

She stared with her mouth open like some kind of hypnotized fool.

When he reached her, he put his big, warm hands on her shoulders. She almost melted in a puddle of pure longing when he did that. Because oh, she did want him, to love him, to hold him and have him hold her. But she had to remember that this just...wasn't real.

"What is it?" His eyes searched her face. "What's happened?"

She didn't know how to explain herself. "I just... It's all too much, okay? Too fast. Tonight, I went overboard. And now I really need to go."

But he didn't release her. "You're shaking."

And she was. She was quivering all over. "Please, Jax..."

That did it, somehow. His hands fell away from her. She whirled for the door again.

"One thing," he said, still right there behind her, where she could feel him, the size and heat of him, at her back.

She froze. "What? Say it." *Make it fast.* "Go ahead."

"I'm here. If you need me." His hand came over her shoulder and pressed flat against the door. "I'll be right here on the other side of this door."

"Um." She clutched her wad of clothing and swallowed convulsively. At least the shaking seemed to have subsided. "Thank you. I, well, it was perfect, tonight. You and me. I loved every minute of it. But I have this little problem."

"What problem?"

"See, um, I don't really even know who I am anymore."

"Because of what Martin did? Is that it?"

"Yeah. I guess so, essentially—but, Jax. I just can't."

"Can't?"

"I can't talk about it now."

"You're still the same person you always were—a person I am finding I want to know better."

His quietly spoken words helped. But not enough. "I

like you, too. I do. But I'm kind of confused now and I really have to go."

He was silent behind her. And then his powerful arm vanished back over her shoulder. "Good night, Aislinn." He stepped away. She felt the loss of him, a coolness at her back.

She grabbed the knob and turned it. The door swung open. She stepped through, closing it behind her.

And engaging the lock.

Chapter Seven

By the time daylight came, Aislinn was nowhere near ready to deal with Jax again.

Her heart felt scraped raw. Last night had been everything she'd ever dreamed it might be, if he could be hers.

So how had it happened that the very rightness of it felt all wrong now, like some twisted, ugly joke? Her forbidden college-girl fantasy crush had come true. He wanted to be with her. He'd said it right out loud. He wanted them to go forward, together, as a couple.

She wanted that, too. So very much.

But right now, she couldn't do it. She longed for him, but she couldn't reach out for him. Not when she felt like an impostor in her own skin.

Her solution to all this confusion: hide.

Yes, hiding was childish and accomplished exactly nothing.

She hid anyway, remaining in her room until she knew that he and Burt would have finished breakfast and left for the stables. Creeping downstairs on tiptoe, she found the house empty. Out the side window, she spotted Erma at work in her vegetable garden.

Aislinn ate a bowl of cereal, spent some time with her rabbits and then wandered out to her workshop, where she attached colored glass beads and silver charms to silver filigree bookmarks for a standing order from Valentine Bay Books. It was mindless work, really. Perfect for a day like today when her concentration was pretty much shot. At eleven, when she ran back to the house to change for work at Sand & Sea, Erma was still in the garden.

Upstairs, Aislinn found her white lace bra on the bed and her missing sandal at the foot of it.

Jax had left a folded note beside the bra: *Figured you might want these back.*

For the first time since she woke in a panic the night before, she almost smiled. She was acting like a crazy person and he was being so sweet and patient.

That evening, at dinner, she shifted her glance away every time he tried to catch her eye.

Really, she was starting to piss herself off. She needed to talk to him, to apologize for freaking out on him. Whatever did or didn't happen next with them, she owed him some kind of explanation for running out on him last night.

Unfortunately, she didn't understand her own behavior, so her actions were going to be pretty difficult to explain.

After dinner, the men went back out to bring in some colts they'd left to graze in a far pasture. She helped

Erma clean up after the meal and then spent an hour with Luna and Bunbun.

When she left the side porch, she felt restless and edgy. She returned to her studio until after midnight, losing herself in working out certain design issues in the new series of pieces she'd been planning.

The house was quiet when she went inside. Upstairs, she showered and got ready for bed. When she turned off the light, she saw the glow beneath the interior door.

He was awake.

And she needed to make her apology. *Now*—if he even wanted to hear it. She considered changing into something other than her Snoopy Snooze-Time sleep shirt and cropped sweats, but that would only be an excuse to stall.

Before she could lose her nerve, she turned the light back on and marched to the inner door. Her heart sounded like a wrecking ball to her ears, but she wasn't about to chicken out now. She knocked.

"It's open," came his deep, wonderful voice from the other room.

She twisted the lock and pulled the door wide to find him propped up on a pile of pillows wearing a T-shirt, track pants and black-rimmed glasses, reading a paperback.

He tossed the book aside and took off the glasses. "Hey."

She gave a ridiculous little cough because her throat had locked up tight. "Hey."

"Come in." He swung his legs over the side of the bed and sat up.

She padded on over there and sat down beside him.

There was empty air. Several endless seconds of it.

Finally, he asked, "So how're you doing?"

Drawing a bare foot up and tucking it in against her other thigh, she turned to him. "I swear I'm not usually a nutjob after sex."

One side of his mouth twitched, an almost-smile. "You weren't."

"Uh, yeah. I was. And I'm sorry. Did I tell you it wasn't your fault? If I didn't, well, it wasn't. What happened with us in this bed was amazing and I loved it."

He did smile then. "It was so good, you couldn't get away from me fast enough?"

"No. Honestly. It wasn't the fabulous sex that freaked me out. I think I've just been through one too many changes lately, that's all."

Very slowly, giving her every chance in the world to duck away, he lifted his hand and guided a stray curl of her hair behind her ear. "I want to grab you and take off that Snoopy shirt, you know that? And those sweats and whatever else you've got on underneath there."

Little, happy shivers chased themselves along her arms, down the backs of her knees. "That sounds so good…"

He must have heard her hesitation in her voice. "But?"

"Well, it's like this. I'm me, but I'm not me. I live here, but only for three months. You're my husband, but we married for other reasons than love—oh, and in twelve weeks or so, we can get divorced and I get fifty thousand dollars. I wasn't really born in the villa of a Montedoran count on the Riviera as my mother always told me. Instead, I was switched at birth with America's darling. My mom wasn't really my mom and my real mom is dead now. I'll never get to meet her." She waited for him to say something. Anything. When he just looked at her with panty-melting tenderness in his eyes, she demanded, "You hear what I'm saying? The craziness is extensive, you gotta admit. And last night…" Her throat clutched. Again.

He gave her ten seconds before prompting, "Last night, what?"

She sucked in a big breath to relax her voice box and made herself go on. "You still don't know, do you, how much I wanted you five years ago? How bad I had it for you. You just don't get it."

"Aislinn, I—"

She put up a hand. "Wait. Let me finish, okay?"

"All right."

"I was so gone on you, Jax. I made up a whole life with you, one where you left your wife and ran off with me. A lovers' getaway to the Riviera where you were thoroughly impressed by my princely relatives was definitely involved."

He started to reach for her again, but he stopped himself and said quietly, "Aislinn, nothing happened five years ago. You did nothing wrong."

"Oh, but I *wanted* to do wrong with you. I was on fire to make a serious move on you. Remember that time in the stables, when I *accidentally* stumbled and landed in your arms?"

He opened his mouth, and then shut it without saying a word.

"Omigod. You're actually drawing a blank on that, aren't you?" Shaking her head, she buried her face in her hands. "You don't even remember how I threw myself at you." With a slow, deep breath, she straightened her spine and made herself face him again. "The good news is, that kind of did it for me—that you caught me and steadied me and asked politely if I was all right. Even in my love-addled condition, I knew you didn't have a clue how I felt. I knew you weren't the least interested in me or my not-so-secret passions. I realized that if you *had* known what was going through my mind, you wouldn't have been able to run away from me fast enough."

"But I didn't know. And it doesn't matter now."

"Not to you, maybe."

He suggested, "You could just...let it go."

"I'm trying. I am. But I was so ashamed. You have no idea. So I wrote you that note about a family emergency and I left that afternoon and never came back—not until my supposed biological father decided to play matchmaker from the grave."

There was another extended silence. Finally, he asked, "Is that all of it?"

A snort-laugh escaped her. "Don't you think that's enough?"

"It *is* a lot," he finally admitted. "But if you're beating yourself up for being attracted to a married man, stop. You were young and nothing happened. And as for all the rest of it, none of that is your fault."

She wrapped her arms around herself and stared down at her bare toes. "I'm still not sure who the heck I am." She slanted him a glance. "I know I keep saying that, but it really is bothering me. And I just think it's a bad idea for you and me to fall into bed together again."

Something changed in his face. A darkening. A shutting-down. She wanted to cry out at the loss of him—a loss she had just asked him for.

"*I* didn't fall," he said kind of stiffly. "For me, what happened in this bed last night was a choice."

She couldn't backpedal fast enough. "I'm not saying I didn't *want* it to happen. I did. Very much. And you're right, last night was a choice for me, too. Just kind of a hasty one."

"Now I'm a *bad* choice." His voice was flat.

She could not read him at that moment. "I didn't say *bad*. I said *hasty*."

"And I would call that a distinction without a difference."

"But there *is* a difference. And, Jax, are you teasing me? Or pissed off? I can't tell."

He took time to give her question some thought. Eventually, he shrugged. "Maybe both."

She'd definitely overstayed her welcome. "Well, I…"

"Good night, Aislinn." He got up and went to stare out the window that overlooked the moonlit yard, those fine, wide shoulders set against her.

Yep. No doubt about it. Time to go. "Good night."

She made it all the way to the open door between their rooms before he spoke again. "Did you ever consider that you can't just let yourself go for it with me because then Martin would be right?"

She turned to find him watching her. "You're wrong."

His eyes held hers. In spite of her determination not to end up in his bed again tonight, longing burned and twisted down inside her.

When he spoke, his voice was low and lazy. "Your face is flushed and your mouth is trembling. Come on over here. I want to remind you of why you should be spending every night in my bed." His eyes promised everything—another glorious night. A whole, thrilling, satisfying string of nights. Even across the room from him, she could feel his heat. She ached to run to him.

But she held her ground.

More denials would not prove her right. Still, she

couldn't stop herself from offering them. "It has nothing to do with Martin. I didn't even *know* the guy."

"It has everything to do with Martin. You're so mad at him and, yeah, you have a right to be. But you could look at it another way. He put us in this situation because he was trying to give you what he thought you wanted."

She outright scoffed at that. "Meaning you."

"Meaning you and me together, which he believed would turn out great for me, too. I can't speak for you, but for me, Martin's matchmaking is right on the money."

She knew that whatever she said next would not be helpful.

Apparently, he knew it, too. "Go on." He gestured at the open door behind her. "Go. When you change your mind, it's really simple. My side of that door will be open."

Alone in her room with the door shut and locked between them, she fumed.

When she changed her mind?

Jax had an arrogant side. She'd never noticed that about him before. Not when she was twenty-one and following him around like he was Justin Timberlake and she was a love-struck thirteen-year-old drooling over the hottest guy in her favorite boy band. Not in the past couple of weeks when she'd married and moved in with him.

Above all, then and now, she'd always considered him a really nice guy.

Tonight, she'd learned differently.

He wasn't above a little in-your-face jerkishness. Hitting her with all that stuff about how Martin was only trying to give her what she wanted. Calling the two of them having sex together really *simple.*

It wasn't simple. There was so much to consider. Who knew how it would all work out? The man had broken her heart once while simultaneously hardly knowing she existed.

This time, if she let him, it could be exponentially worse.

When, he'd said. *When you change your mind,* like it was inevitable that she'd be walking through that door.

Uh-uh. No way. She was going to sleep in her own damn room for the required three months, help him out so that he wouldn't lose the ranch he loved above anything or anyone. And make herself fifty thousand dollars in the process.

Win/win. End of story.

Distance.

As the week crawled by, they had distance, she and Jax. They spoke to each other politely, but only when they had to, avoiding direct eye contact whenever possible.

She scrupulously resisted the urge to try the door between their rooms at night just to see if his side really was open. If she tried the door, who knew what might happen next?

She wanted to find out.

But uh-uh. For once in her life she was taking the cautious path. So far, caution didn't have a lot to recommend it. Caution made her droopy and sad.

Too bad. She was sticking in there, staying away from him, even though he'd offered to show her why she ought to be in his bed and all her lady parts had pined for an immediate demonstration.

Forget that. *Caution* was her catchword.

Because he'd said *when* instead of *if*. Because he'd dared to suggest that Martin Durand had turned their lives upside down for *her* sake. Because he'd shown her his jerkish side and now she knew for sure he wasn't perfect.

Friday was payday at Sand & Sea.

Keely called Aislinn into the office to give her the check and to talk about the future. "So, what do you think? I would love to keep you on the schedule."

"How about this? Hire someone and I'll stay to help until the new clerk is up to speed. And any time you need me to fill in, I'm here."

"Got something on a salmon troller?" Keely teased. It was an old joke between them. Whenever Aislinn got a yen to change jobs, she would threaten to try joining a fishing crew, which paid pretty well but included long hours, grueling work and a fair amount of physical danger.

Aislinn answered Keely's joking question honestly. "I want to concentrate on making jewelry."

"Can't argue with that." Keely was always encouraging her to spend more time in her studio.

"Something's changed in me. I don't get so easily distracted, you know? I can sit at the bench for hours now. I've designed some pretty, affordable pieces for my Etsy store and they're selling like crazy. And I'm working on some higher-end stuff, a whole collection, if you can believe it."

"*I can* believe it. I can't keep your pieces in the store—and okay, you're fired."

"Perfect. Thank you."

"In a couple of months, we need to discuss a show for you here at Sand & Sea."

"A show of my own?" Aislinn's current state of droopy sadness lifted a little. Her work had been included in a few group shows at the gallery, but her own show would be a big step, and she wanted that.

Keely was nodding. "We'll make plans for it when you're ready. Just let me know."

Before Aislinn left, they discussed the upcoming family meeting.

Keely said, "Neither Matt nor Liam can make it to dinner this Sunday. So I set it up for next Sunday. Dinner at four and the meeting after. Everyone can come for that, including Percy and Daffy. Does that work for you?"

"It's fine."

Keely peered at her searchingly across the desk. "You okay? You seem kind of down."

Aislinn sagged back in the guest chair and blew out her cheeks with a sigh. "Everything in my life feels up in the air, you know? At the same time, I realize it's always been that way. I used to like it, being open to adventure and the next, new job. Never letting myself get tied down to a paycheck or a relationship. But lately..." The sentence died unfinished. She tried again. "Suddenly, I want something to hold on to, you know?"

Keely rested her arms on the desktop and leaned closer. "It's natural for you to want consistency right now, I think."

"Well, it just feels depressing."

"You've had a big shock, found out everything isn't what you'd always believed it to be. It's huge. It would hit anyone hard."

"And then I went and had sex with Jax." She hadn't realized she'd said it out loud until she saw the look on her best friend's face. "Oops."

Keely maintained a serious expression. "Was it good?"

"Oh, yeah. But the next night I told him we couldn't do it again. I don't think he believed me."

"*Have* you done it again?"

Not yet. "No."

"But you want to. A lot."

"You know me too well, Keel. You always did."

"And you don't have to mistrust your own heart just because your life got turned upside down. You've always said that Jaxon's a good man."

"But jerkish. Sometimes he *can* be jerkish."

"Often?"

"Well, no. Once, though."

Keely looked at her patiently. "I get that you hate the position Martin Durand put you in, but that doesn't mean you can't make the best of it."

"Jax said something similar. I got mad at him when he said it. But when *you* say it, it kind of makes sense."

"Ais, you wanted that man so bad once. It's obvious you want him now. He's your *husband.* Frankly, I think you need to get out of your own way."

"Okay, now I'm starting to get a little mad at *you.*" She actively pouted.

Keely shrugged. "It's all right. I can take it. Just consider what I've said."

"I will," she promised. *Maybe.*

Or maybe not...

Jax had decided his best move was no move. He was actively keeping out of Aislinn's way, letting her come to him.

By Friday night, he'd begun to see the flaw in his plan. She kept her distance and he kept his. At this rate, their three months could speed on by without the two of them sharing more than the most basic kinds of conversation. He would never get his arms around her again.

His plan wasn't working. He needed to change his approach—or rather, he needed *an* approach. Because staying away from her only made it easier for her to avoid admitting how good they were together.

Saturday at lunchtime, Aislinn's sisters drove up. The three pretty blondes in jeans, T-shirts and sturdy boots got out of the car as Aislinn came running down the steps to greet them.

Jax, Burt and Ace, on their way in from the stables to grab some food, halted halfway across the yard to watch as the women fluttered around, hugging each other, emitting happy, birdlike cries of glee. Watching them, a man would think they hadn't seen each other in years.

Burt, as usual, muttered bad things about them to no one in particular. Ace gave an eager whine. Unlike Burt, Ace loved women. To him, the female of the species usually meant kind words, lots of strokes and pats and just possibly a treat or two.

As for Jax, he was hiding a grin. If he played it right, the three blondes could present a great opportunity to remind Aislinn of what a thoughtful guy he was, a guy she needed to stay married to indefinitely, a guy she wanted to sleep with—tonight.

And every night to come.

Inside, Erma had lunch ready. The men washed up and they all sat down to eat. The sisters chattered away about their jobs and the summer weather. Aislinn promised them a quick tour of her new studio and a stop on the side porch to visit the rabbits.

Jax seized his moment. "Aislinn, why don't you bring your sisters out to the stables for a tour? You can go riding—I mean, if you all have the time."

Burt sat there glaring, no doubt at the prospect of a bunch of talkative women invading his domain. But at least he kept his mouth shut.

Not that Jax even cared about Burt's predictably crappy attitude. Aislinn had turned that gorgeous smile on him. "Thanks, Jax."

Now, this was more like it. He asked the sisters, "Are you experienced riders?"

Grace said, "I've ridden a few times."

"I've ridden, but not often," said Harper.

"Me, too," Hailey volunteered. "But not in the past couple of years."

As soon as he and Burt got back to the stables, Jax chose three older, steadier horses and had one of the hands tack them up, along with Saint John, the gelding he already thought of as Aislinn's, and the mare, Lady Jane, for him.

When the women appeared, he handed each a complimentary Wild River Ranch cap and showed them around, after which he had two of the grooms bring out four of the five saddled horses, leaving Lady Jane out of sight.

Grace, the youngest, spoke right up. "Jaxon, aren't you coming with us?"

He modestly suggested that maybe the four of them would prefer to have the time on their own. "Aislinn's an experienced rider, so you should be fine."

The blondes protested. They wanted him to come, too. Aislinn was watching him, a small almost-smile on her face.

He was beginning to worry she wouldn't speak up. But then she said, "Jaxon. Please. Join us?"

He called for Lady Jane and the groom brought her right out. Aislinn didn't roll her eyes—but close. "That was quick."

He was definitely busted, and he didn't even care.

The ride went well, he thought. Aislinn's sisters were pretty green. They were damn cute, though, three blondes and a hot brunette, their shining hair poking out from under their Wild River caps. It seemed to him they all enjoyed themselves. Things got iffy only once when Harper let her mare have her head and nearly ended up on the ground.

But the mare was a sweet-natured old gal. She knew she was losing her rider and slowed up. With a "Whoopsie!" Harper dragged herself up into the saddle again and everything worked out fine.

Back at the stables, the girls volunteered to unsaddle their mounts. He'd planned to let the grooms take over, but the sisters seemed sincere in their desire to do the job. And it was good for any horsewoman to put in the time to take care of an animal she'd ridden.

He and Aislinn led them through the process of which

strap to uncinch in what order. Once they had the sad-
dles off, they gave the animals a nice brushing and he
even showed them how to check their coats for sores,
bumps and dry spots and how to pick any bits of rock
and debris from their feet.

Finally, it was all done. The grooms took the horses
away. The sisters thanked him for playing hooky from
his workday to take them horseback riding.

Aislinn brushed his arm. "This was great, Jax." Those
big coffee-brown eyes gleamed up at him and he had to
actively restrain himself from hauling her up close and
slamming his mouth down on hers.

"Thanks for inviting me along," he teased.

She gave a little giggle, like they had a secret joke,
the two of them. Best of all, she lifted up and brushed
a kiss across his lips. He felt about ten feet tall and he
couldn't wait for the evening, when he would pull out
all the stops to get her to maybe sit out on the porch and
watch the sunset with him—and yeah, he kind of hoped
for a little hot, sweaty, amazing sex later, but he wouldn't
push her. There was time to convince her that she needed
to spend the rest of her life at his side.

When he got back to the house at a little before six,
the car Aislinn's sisters had arrived in was gone. He went
on inside and found Erma at the stove. She said dinner
would be ready in half an hour and added, "Aislinn said
to check your cell phone."

"She's not here?"

Erma shook her head. "She left with her sisters."

Disappointment made his steps heavy and tightened
the muscles at the back of his neck. Saturday night and
she'd gone off without him.

Not that he had any real claim on her Saturdays. She

had a right to time with her family and he needed not to start acting like a jealous fool.

"Where'd she go?" He tried to sound casual about it, like it didn't matter all that much to him where his wife had run off to.

But it did matter. He wanted Aislinn and he'd gotten his hopes up and now those hopes had soured.

Soured hopes brought Judy to mind. They'd always been out of sync with each other, him and Judy. He'd been such an idiot, just accepting her word for it when she'd said she had a yearning to live in the country, paying no attention to the other signals she was giving off.

After the divorce, he'd told Martin that he didn't understand women and marriage wasn't for him.

Martin had laughed. *You've got "born to be married" written all over you, son. You just need to hook up with the right woman and you'll be fine.*

In her wispy little voice Erma said, "Valentine Bay."

"What?"

"Aislinn went to Valentine Bay. Check your cell phone."

"Uh. Yeah. Cell phone. Got it."

He went upstairs to look for the damn thing and found it on his dresser, deader than a hammer. It still wouldn't work when he plugged it in. So he left it to charge a little and jumped in the shower.

Five minutes later, dripping wet with a towel hooked around his hips, he padded back to the bedroom. The phone was working by then.

Aislinn had sent him a text. He instantly felt better about everything, that she'd thought of him, thought to touch base with him when she was going out.

Having dinner with Harper and Hailey at the beach cottage. Afterward, we're going to the Sea Breeze. Did I tell you Keely's mom bought it and fixed it up?

She had. And he knew the Sea Breeze. The bar was a Valentine Bay landmark.

The good part came next.

We should be there around eight. Come meet us. I'll buy you a drink.

Chapter Eight

At the Sea Breeze, the small parking lot was full, the place all lit up. Rock music blared from inside.

Jax had to drive a couple of blocks up Ocean Road and take a side street to find a parking place. When he got back to the bar, the parking lot was still packed and the music was still loud.

Inside, there were potted palms and café tables. One of those roll-up doors spanned the wall facing the ocean. The door was open. More tables and chairs, all of them taken, filled a patio under the cloudy, darkening sky. There was a lull in the music. For a second or two, he thought he could hear the waves lapping the beach out there beyond the reach of the lights.

"Jaxon!" It was Grace. She stood behind the long bar topped in a mosaic of sea-colored glass tiles. He elbowed his way over there. "You made it." Aislinn's sister beamed at him. "She's over there, in the corner."

He turned and looked where Grace pointed. Aislinn had already spotted him. She waved, a big smile on her beautiful face, like she was really glad to see him. He'd never been all that hot to get out and party on a Saturday night. But right at that moment, with his eyes locked on Aislinn's across the room, he was ready for some fun.

He turned back to Grace and shouted to be heard over the band playing '80s hard rock. "A beer for me, whatever's on tap." He glanced over his shoulder. Aislinn was still grinning at him. With her sat Hailey, Harper, their brother Matt and some other guy Jax had never seen before. Jax added to his order. "And a round for the table, whatever they're drinking."

Grace started setting up the drinks. "Go on, have a seat. I'll get Ginny to bring the drinks over."

He worked his way through the sea of tables. Aislinn stood when he got close and held out her hand. He took it and she pulled him around behind her sisters and into the chair next to hers.

"You came!" She looked so pleased that he had.

He saw his chance and he seized it, putting his arm across her shoulders, drawing her close, brushing a kiss across those perfect lips and breathing in the sweet and spicy scent of her skin.

She didn't pull away. In fact, she smiled so soft and sweet against his mouth.

"Love." The guy across the table next to Matt gave a loud groan. "Freedom's better."

Love. It sounded pretty damn good to Jax. And Aislinn hadn't stopped smiling. Maybe love sounded good to her, too.

Not that he was pushing it with her. Uh-uh. He was taking it slow and easy. One step at a time.

Hailey laughed and shook her head. "Ignore Jerry. He thinks he's a player."

"Yes, I am." Jerry pounded the table once to emphasize his point, causing their drinks to jump. "And proud of it. I like to keep my options open—and wouldn't you know? There are a lot of fine ladies out there who like to keep their options open, too."

Matt introduced them. "Jaxon, this is Jerry. He's been my friend since first grade."

Jerry, a bearded ginger, with freckles across his nose and all over his muscular arms, offered Jax a hand across the table. "He means there's no getting rid of me. And he is *right*."

"Good to meet you, Jerry." They shook.

A cocktail waitress brought their drinks and the band started another song, this one a ballad. A slim, older woman with purple-streaked hair strummed a guitar and sang about love in a small town.

Aislinn leaned close. "That's Keely's mom, Ingrid. She wrote that song."

"And she owns this bar and she's also a rock star, right? With Pomegranate Dream?"

"Wow. Impressive—but the band's a thing of the past. Ingrid's back in town to stay."

Her soft cheek was so close. He dropped a kiss there and she let him. It all felt like a dream. The best kind of dream, the kind that happens to be real.

The band finished that set, took a break and then started playing again. Jax nursed his beer and let himself enjoy the evening, with Aislinn at his side, the place packed with people having a good time.

Jerry seemed to know everyone—especially all the women. They came by the table, one by one and in groups of two, to flirt with Jerry and to try to get Matt's attention. Aislinn's brother showed little interest in any of the pretty women angling to catch his eye. He was friendly enough, but there was something in his eyes that said *taken*.

Outside on the patio, people pushed the chairs and tables to the side and made a dance floor under the sky.

Jax was a lousy dancer. He'd never had much practice. Still, tonight, with Aislinn beside him, he got the appeal. A slow one would make a good excuse to hold her in his arms.

"Dance?" he asked.

"Yes." She flashed a smile that made his stomach flip.

And then they were up and moving. They wove their way through the crowded tables out to the open space. The night air was damp and cool, smelling of salt and sea. The overcast sky hid the stars, but the moon appeared now and then, showing its ghostly silver face and then vanishing again behind the clouds.

He took her in his arms. She fit like she was born to be held by him and he wished they could just dance on and on forever, with the music soft and slow, the sound of the waves rolling in out there on the beach and the moon playing peekaboo in the cloudy sky.

They stayed until a little after midnight.

Aislinn had left her car at the cottage. Jax tried to talk her into riding home with him.

"I'll drive you in tomorrow and you can get the car," he said as he opened the passenger door of his truck for her.

She got that look, the one that said she'd made up her mind and no man was changing it. "That's an extra half hour each way in the car, sixty minutes of our lives we'll never get back." She hopped up to the seat and he pushed the door shut. When he got in on the driver's side, she said, "Take me to the cottage. I'll get my CR-V and follow you home."

Forty minutes later, they pulled into their side-by-side spaces in the garage at Wild River. She got out before he could run over there and open her door for her.

But when they converged onto the breezeway, she stopped and turned to him. And then she put her hand on his chest, right over his suddenly racing heart. "I had a good time tonight—a wonderful time."

"Me, too." He clasped the smooth curves of her waist in either hand.

And she swayed in close, sliding both hands up to hook around his neck. "I've missed you the past few days, Jaxon. Missed you a lot. Even with us living in the same house."

He tipped up her chin and kissed her. She tasted so good, like everything he wanted, everything he'd once given up hope of ever finding, ever having. When he lifted his head, he said, "Come back to me." She simply gazed up at him, eyes so dark and deep. He tried a smile. "Wait. Was that a yes?"

It worked. She laughed. And then she grew serious again. "I do want to be with you tonight."

His heart did a little jig inside his chest. "Will you think I'm easy if I just keep saying yes?" When she only gazed up at him, eyes wide, mouth silent, he prompted, "Go ahead. I *am* listening."

She chewed the corner of her lip, hesitating. But she

finally came out with it. "If I need to get up and go back to my own room, I need to know you'll be okay with that."

He wouldn't, not really. But whatever she needed, he intended to deliver. "All right. When you want to go, I won't try to talk you out of it."

She frowned. "If. I said *if.*"

He fell back a step. "Why do I get the feeling we're about to have an argument?"

Now her sweet mouth was trembling. "You probably shouldn't put up with me. I'm an emotional disaster lately."

He moved in close to her again. How could he not? She drew him to her without even trying. He traced the shape of her ear and smoothed her hair back with a stroke of his palm. He loved her hair, loved the warmth and the thickness of it, the way it curled around his fingers, dark as midnight in his hands. "I just want you, Aislinn. What you said before is true. It *is* simple for me. I keep trying to remember that it's not so simple for you."

She turned her mouth into his hand, her eyes drifting shut. He felt those soft lips and the warm touch of her breath against his skin. Every nerve in his body heated. Burned.

When she looked up at him at last, she said, "Let's go upstairs."

They went in through her room again, so that she could unlock the inner door and leave it wide open.

For her future escape, he thought with equal parts desire and exasperation.

He hung back, watching as she crossed the sitting area to the bed. She kicked off her pretty high-heeled sandals and folded back the covers the way any wife might do. When she turned to him again, she held out her hand.

He couldn't get to her fast enough.

They shared a long kiss. And then, simply and quickly, they undressed.

Naked and so beautiful, she reached up her arms to him. He gathered her close and took her down to the sheets.

The other night had been perfect.

But tonight felt even better.

Simpler. Truer.

He touched her and she lifted herself toward his hand. She was slick and ready, opening like a flower in the sun.

He took his sweet time with her, dipping two fingers in, and then three. She came apart so sweetly, rising, shattering, rising again.

When she reached for him, he knew he wouldn't last long. And when she took him in her mouth, he was absolutely certain it was all over.

But somehow, he held out, held on, as the need to go over sang in his blood. He muttered dark promises of what he would do to her, burying his hands in her hair, holding out until he couldn't hold back any longer.

She drank him down, every drop.

They collapsed against the pillows. He pulled up the sheet to cover them and wrapped his arms good and tight around her.

They whispered together.

She said Keely had fired her at her own request. "I want to focus on my work in the studio. Lately, I have a lot of ideas and I'm going to explore every single one."

He said he had buyers coming next week. "They'll be here Tuesday."

"And stay for dinner after?"

"Yeah. They have a five-year-old son."

"I'll introduce him to Bunbun and Luna—oh, and next Sunday, I have to go to Daniel and Keely's for dinner, with a family meeting afterward. I'm nervous about it. I don't know how it will go."

"You're telling them about Madison Delaney?"

"Yeah." She faked a bright tone. "'Guess what, everyone! You have a sister you've never met!' Ugh. My great-uncle Percy will be there. I'll probably just let him do the talking. He's the one who's reaching out to Madison Delaney, letting her know she has a family in Valentine Bay."

Jax smoothed her hair and pressed his lips to her forehead. "I'm going with you."

"What?" She pushed against his chest. The mutinous curve of her mouth said it all.

He tried again. "Please, Aislinn. Take me with you."

Her expression softened, but not completely. "It's going to be weird and awkward. You don't need to be there."

"I *want* to be there."

She flopped back against the pillows and glared at the ceiling. "I'm so on edge over this. I don't even know what to say to them. And I feel that I already should have told them. I mean, I spent all day with my sisters today and I didn't say a word. They'll probably be furious at me for keeping it from them."

"They love you. They're not going to be mad at you."

"You don't know. You can't be sure how they'll take it."

"All the more reason I need to be there."

She turned her head and looked at him then. "No. It's a bad idea." Her mouth was set, determined.

But he refused to give up. "It's a family dinner, right?"

"Didn't I just say that?"

"I'm your husband. Doesn't that make me one of the family? And this is an important meeting. What are they all going to think of me if I don't show up to support you for this?"

She narrowed her eyes at him and he knew that he had her. She could refuse him if he was going for her sake. But she didn't want her family thinking less of him. "Okay, fine," she grumbled. "You might possibly have a point there."

He pushed his advantage. "I'm going. Accept it."

She rolled to her side and cuddled close to him again. "I surrender—about this, anyway."

Something in her voice alerted him that there was more she wanted to say. "What else?"

She tipped her head back and scrunched up her face at him. "You're not going to like it."

"I'll decide about that. Tell me."

"Well, as soon as the rest of them know about Martin and the switch, they're going to start wondering about the way we suddenly got married when I'd never even mentioned you before."

"They don't know that you worked for me once?"

"Even if they remember my eight-week summer job five years ago, Keely's the only one I ever told about my thoroughly inappropriate crush on you. They're not going to make any connection between then and now. But they *are* going to suspect that there must be a correlation between our out-of-the-blue marriage and what Martin did—and hey." She laid her hand against his cheek, pressing enough to make him meet her eyes. "This is not your happy face you're wearing."

He tried really hard not to scowl. "You're right. I don't like where this is going. Everybody in the world doesn't have to know the whole truth about everything. Sometimes it's just not their business."

"But I *love* them. And I trust them. And it will hurt them to wonder, to know there's stuff I'm keeping from them about something that's really important to all of us. Jax, they have a sister they've never even met. They're going to want to know the whole story behind that. And we've both agreed already that our marriage is real, even with an expiration date. No, I don't want to run up and down the streets of Valentine Bay telling everybody I meet about what Martin did. But my family isn't 'everybody.' My family needs to know."

"No, they don't."

"Yes. They do. They need to know, and when we tell them, they're going to understand. It's not our fault that Martin Durand decided to manipulate us from the grave. This ranch is everything to you, and you'll do what you have to do to save it. I'm willing to help you. And I'll make some money in the process. It's an honest transaction. And hey, it turns out we like each other—in bed and out—so it could be a lot worse."

"You were planning to tell them all along," he accused.

"Not always. But in the last few days I *have* been thinking that honesty is the best policy when it comes to this—for them, I mean, for my family."

"I don't like it."

"I don't blame you. This situation is seriously twisted. But at least we're doing the best we can with it."

"I was hoping to get along with your brothers. So much for that."

She did a little double take. "What are you talking about?"

Even deeply annoyed with her, he couldn't help thinking how beautiful she was, those black eyes gleaming, her hair the color of a raven's wing, wild now, tangled around her face. He skated the back of his index finger down the creamy skin of her arm. "I never had a sister, but if I did, I'd beat the holy crap out of any man who put her in a situation like this."

"Oh, Jax." She actually chuckled. As if there was anything the least bit funny about it. "You didn't put me here. I'm a volunteer."

"I was kind of looking forward to being your hero next Sunday, supporting you with your family. Now I'm just the douche basket who took advantage of your tender heart."

"You are not a douche basket."

"Yeah. I kind of am."

"Uh-uh. You're a hero." She tucked her head under his chin, nuzzled his throat. "My hero."

He grunted. "Calling me a hero doesn't make it so. And you're not giving me a choice, are you? We're owning this mess Martin put us in."

She dropped a string of kisses down over his Adam's apple, ending with a flick of her tongue in the hollow at the base of his throat. "That's right—and, Jaxon?"

"Yeah?"

She nipped a kiss on his chin. "I wouldn't want to be in this mess with anyone else but you."

"Watch out. I'll hold you to that indefinitely—like say, for the rest of our lives."

For a moment, her face went so soft and open. But

then she put on a flirty look and teased, "Hmm. I don't know. It's a little soon for any big commitments."

Was it? Didn't feel that way to him. "We're already married. That's a pretty big commitment."

"You know what I mean."

"Come here." He drew her closer, kissed her temple and the space between her eyebrows, one cheek and then the other, after which he claimed her softly parted lips.

The magic began again.

They took their time, with long, wet kisses and slow, arousing caresses.

When he pulled open the bedside drawer for a condom, she whispered urgently, "Jax. Hurry. Please..."

He couldn't suit up fast enough.

She reached for him again, opening to him. He buried himself in her tight, wet heat. She was the best thing that had ever happened to him.

And one way or another, he would make her see that he could be the same for her.

Later, he pulled her in close and they dropped off to sleep. That night, at least, he was certain she would stay with him.

But at a little after four in the morning, he woke suddenly to find she was gone.

To Aislinn, the next week sped by. She went to see Percy and Daffy and they agreed that, come Sunday, they would share the whole story with her brothers and sisters.

Other than the visit to Valentine House, she stayed on the ranch, spending long hours every day in her studio working on her new collection and keeping on top of a lovely avalanche of orders from online sales.

Her nights belonged to Jaxon—up to a point. At bedtime, they went upstairs together. In his room, they made beautiful love, and afterward, she fell asleep in his arms.

The peace never lasted, though. She always woke before dawn, frantic and panicky, her eyes popping open, her heart pounding in her ears—and she just couldn't be there. She had to get out.

More than one of those nights, she sensed by his breathing that Jax was awake. But he kept to their agreement. He never tried to stop her as she tiptoed from the room.

Saturday came and with it, a rising anxiety. Sunday was too close. She would have to face the family, tell them everything she knew. It wasn't her fault, that they'd lost a sister, that she'd taken their real sister's place.

It wasn't her fault.

So why did she feel so lost and guilty and alone?

She probably needed some serious counseling. But she really wasn't ready to face therapy, either.

After Sunday, once everyone in the family knew what she knew, she would feel better. The undeserved guilt and the uncalled-for tension would fade.

David Hanes, the buyer from Tuesday night, returned to Wild River on Saturday afternoon. David's wife and their little boy remained at home on their farm in northeastern Washington.

The Hanes family had decided to go for it and buy that other gray filly they liked so much. Erma put dinner on early and David joined them. He spoke of his farm and proudly announced that he and his wife, Louella, were expecting a second child.

They all raised a toast to Louella and the coming baby. Aislinn liked David. She was glad for him and his family—and for the distraction of company for dinner. For a little while, she almost forgot all her apprehensions about tomorrow.

By seven, David had the filly loaded up in the horse trailer and all the paperwork in order, and was on his way home to Holly Tree Farm.

Jax came in smiling. It was turning out to be a profitable summer for Wild River.

"Movie?" he asked her. "Your pick."

"Sure."

He ran upstairs for a quick shower and she wandered into the family room, turned on the big screen and started scrolling the Netflix options, thinking about tomorrow, her stomach kind of knotting up.

"Aislinn?"

She blinked up at Jax, who was freshly showered, his wet hair slicked back, and realized she'd just been sitting there, staring at the menu on the screen. "Sorry…"

He took the remote from her and turned off the TV, then sat down beside her. "Not really in a movie mood, huh?"

She leaned his way and he wrapped an arm around her so she could rest her head on his shoulder. "I've been sitting here thinking how I really don't know for sure that Martin is my biological father. I was considering asking Daniel to do a sibling DNA test with me, just to prove we're not brother and sister, after all—but really, with all the information I have, I'm reasonably certain that Martin and Paula were my real parents and Madison Delaney is the biological child of George and Marie Bravo."

His lips brushed her hair. "Freaking out about the family meeting, are you?"

"Smart-ass." She gave him a sharp elbow to the ribs, which didn't seem to bother him in the least. "There actually is one other possibility. Lloyd Delaney could be my father. Think about it. How could Paula have passed Madison off as Lloyd's if she hadn't been sleeping with him at the same time as she was having an affair with Martin? And excuse me, but ew. It's just wrong that I should have to even think about people who might have been my parents having sex."

His arm rested on her shoulder and he was wrapping a curl of her hair around his index finger. "There is a resemblance between you and Martin—your eyes, a little around the mouth. Your coloring, too. And sometimes, the way you tip your head just so, when you're listening? I see Martin in you then."

"Proves exactly nothing."

"Maybe not conclusive proof, but a clue and a convincing one."

"Yeah, maybe."

"No. Definitely."

"Still, I'm never going to know for sure—unless I try to have Martin exhumed for a DNA test." She dropped her head back against the cushions and glared at the ceiling. "Exhuming Martin. Now, there's a cheerful thought."

"You really are freaked out about tomorrow." He bent his elbow, wrapping his arm around her neck and pulling her closer. Pressing his wonderful lips to her cheek, he whispered, "It's going to be okay. I promise you."

"Thank you for being so patient with me. But there is no way that you can know for sure how it's going to go tomorrow."

He nuzzled her ear. "You're serious about wanting some kind of proof that Martin was really your father?"

"Of course I'm serious. Everyone wants to know who their father was."

"Yeah. Well, everyone *doesn't* know. Some of us will never know."

She let out a moan. "Oh, God." And then she turned, caught his beard-scruffy face between her hands and kissed his mouth. Hard. "I'm sorry. I didn't think. I'm a selfish pig." She went all the way with that, adding, "Oink, oink."

He gave her a hint of a smile. "It's okay. *I'm* okay. It was hard when I was a kid. I really did want to know my dad, at least to know who he was. But my mother didn't put his name on the birth certificate. And by the time I was old enough to insist on answers to my questions, she was dead."

"And so you think of Martin as your dad."

"Yes, I do." He said it strongly. Proudly.

Her eyes burned. She blinked the moisture away. "I guess that's something. He couldn't have been all bad. I mean, *you* loved him."

He caught her hand, wove their fingers together, brought her knuckles to his lips and kissed them one by one. "Stay here. I'll be right back." Rising, he went to the low cabinet against the sidewall and returned with one of those old-timey picture albums. "Here." He opened the album on the coffee table in front of them and dropped back down to the cushions beside her.

There were four faded photos on the first page, all of a woman who was probably in her twenties. The woman was dressed in high style—for the end of the 1950s or maybe the early '60s. She had thick black hair and big dark eyes and a sort of sultry movie-star vibe, posing with a sexy smirk over her shoulder in one shot, a hand braced on her hip in another.

"Martin's mother, the torch singer?" she asked.

Jaxon nodded. "Colette Durand, your grandmother. Don't tell me you don't see it. She looks just like you." He turned the page and she saw more shots of Colette, two with a baby in her arms.

Aislinn took over, turning the pages herself: Martin as a toddler, at around five and maybe seven. There were more pictures of his mother. In some, Colette was all dressed up in glittery, clingy evening gowns, her hair up-swept, wearing dangly rhinestone earrings. There were more shots of Martin, too, as he grew into a teenager in shiny, pointy-toed black leather shoes and tight jeans with way too much product in his inky hair.

By the last page, Colette was in her forties, possibly fifty, lying in a hospital bed, frail and way too thin, her black hair gone gray. Martin was a young adult, a hand-some guy in a New-York-Mafia-wannabe sort of way.

She flipped the album closed. "Okay. You're right. I look like both of them. I guess Martin can stay buried."

"Hey." He reached for her. She went to him will-ingly, curving her body into his steady strength. "Feel any better?"

"Strangely, yes. A little."

"Marie and George Bravo are still your parents, too, in all the ways that really count. I know you lost them too soon, but you loved them. They loved you. You had a good childhood."

She nodded against his broad chest, grateful for his strong arms around her, for the comforting beat of his heart beneath her ear. "Madison had a great childhood, too. All the tabloids say so."

"You've been researching her online?"

"Guilty. She gave a long interview to *Vanity Fair* about growing up on ranches all over the Northwest, about how her dad was her hero and after he died in a fall from a horse, Madison begged her mom to take her to Hollywood so that she could be in movies. And Paula did it, moved the two of them to LA and took a bunch of low-paying jobs to support them until Madison got her first big break on *Memorial Hospital*. Maybe it's all crap. But I believed it while I was reading it."

Jax stroked her hair and curled a lock of it around his finger the way he loved to do. "Were there pictures of Paula?"

"A few. One really sticks with me. It showed Paula and Lloyd and Madison together. Madison was maybe five years old, looking like Harper and Hailey with a little touch of Grace, in pigtails on a palomino, Paula on one side and Lloyd on the other, both of them beaming up at her like she was the most perfect child ever born. Paula was slender, with dark hair. Lloyd was a big, blond guy. I could see how he never would have questioned that Madison was his." She tipped her head back to meet Jax's eyes. "Let's skip the movie and go upstairs. I need a distraction from obsessing about tomorrow."

"What kind of distraction?" As if he didn't know.

"I want you to do that thing you do."

"Which thing?"

"All the things."

He gave her the slow smile she'd grown to love way too much. "There *are* a lot of them, now that I think about it." He eased his arms from around her and rose. "Come on. We'd better get started."

Upstairs, for a glorious couple of hours, Aislinn's dread at facing tomorrow faded away.

But when she woke in Jax's arms at two thirty in the morning, it all came rushing back. She returned to her room and spent the remaining hours of darkness staring at the bedside clock, willing herself into a sleep that never came.

Chapter Nine

For Sunday dinner at the Bravo house on Rhinehart Hill, there were twelve of them: Aislinn, her seven Bravo siblings, plus Percy, Daffy, Keely and Jax. Keely had dropped off the twins, Jake and Frannie, at their grandmother's house for the night.

They ate at the long dining room table. There was laughter and easy chatter. Aislinn sat with Jax on her left and Matt on her right and thought how much she loved them all—and she fervently wished to be anywhere but here.

After the meal, everyone pitched in to clear the table. Keely served coffee in the family room with its high coffered ceiling, gorgeous glass-fronted bookcases and the giant fireplace where they all gathered on Christmas mornings to open their presents.

Today, they made themselves comfortable on the

leather couches and chairs in front of the bow window that looked out on the front porch. Aislinn ended up on one of the couches between Jax and Liam.

Percy asked her, "Would you like to say something first?"

She gulped and shook her head, grabbing for Jax. He took her hand and gave it a reassuring squeeze. Beloved faces looked at her in confusion and concern. Somehow, she found her voice. "Thanks, Uncle Percy. But I would rather if you would just go ahead."

"All right, then." Percy picked up the sheaf of folders he'd set on a side table and handed them out. Aislinn let go of Jax's hand to open hers. Martin's last letter was inside. Percy went straight to the point. "It seems you all have another sister." He let them have a moment for that to sink in before continuing, "In your folders is a copy of a letter that accompanied the will of one Martin Durand." He quickly went on to explain the rest of it, everything that Martin had laid out in the letter, after which he shared all of the reasons that Durand's claims were most likely true.

He saved the name of the missing sister for last. "Your missing sister, as it turns out, is a famous celebrity, Madison Delaney."

Grace let out a cry. "Madison Delaney, the *actress*?"

"Yes."

Before Percy could get out another word, Harper turned to Hailey, "What'd I always tell you?"

Wide-eyed, Hailey nodded. "That we could have been sisters…"

Connor said, "Wait a minute. I thought Ais was born in Montedoro. This makes no damn sense at all."

Liam brushed Aislinn's arm. When she looked at him,

he said, "That night at Beach Street Brews—that's why you asked us if we remembered the day you were born?"

"Yeah." She glanced from Liam to Connor and then to Matthias. "I'm sorry. I didn't want to believe Martin's story. But Uncle Percy and Aunt Daffy set me straight."

Daffy said, "You all knew your mother. She loved to make things exciting and fun. She made up that story to please Aislinn when Aislinn was little. There never seemed to be any pressing reason to set the record straight."

"Until now," Aislinn finished for her.

"Ais?" Matt was watching her, worry etching new lines in his face. "Are you okay?"

Aislinn made herself nod. "Fine. Yes. Really."

Nobody believed her. "Oh, Ais!" cried Grace and jumped from her chair.

A moment later, Jax had moved out of the way to make room for Aislinn's sisters and Keely and Daffy.

They surrounded her, pulling her up from the couch to hug her and say how much they loved her.

She opened her mouth to tell them how much she loved *them*, but what came out was, "I feel so awful. I'm such a fraud."

"No way," announced Gracie.

"Not a chance," Hailey declared.

Drama queen, much? She certainly felt like one, stealing the spotlight this way. Still, all the love and attention did soothe her battered heart.

"You should have told us sooner," Harper scolded.

"Yeah," agreed Hailey. "We're really annoyed with you about that."

"I'm sorry. I just couldn't figure out where to start—and I'm okay, I truly am." They looked at her as though they didn't quite believe her. Not surprising. She didn't quite believe herself. But her ongoing identity angst wasn't the reason they were here. "There's more to tell you. We need to let Percy finish."

Reluctantly, her sisters returned to their seats.

Aislinn looked around for Jax. He stood several feet away. Both Connor and Liam eyed him with suspicion.

"Leave Jax alone," she warned her brothers. "He's been a hero through this, taking care of me, making sure I love living at Wild River with him. We really are married, however bizarrely it all came about." She made herself add a big dose of the L-word to settle her brothers down completely. "I love him and he loves me."

That seemed to quell Liam and Connor. They did that nodding thing men do to each other, dipping their heads at Jax like they'd come to some big agreement, all without actually saying a word. Jax nodded back.

Aislinn held out her hand to him and he came and sat with her again.

Harper fired a volley of questions at Uncle Percy. "So, have you talked to her, to Madison? Does she know about us? When can we meet her?"

"Slow down," cautioned Daniel. "Let Percy talk."

"It's all right," said Percy. "I'm sure everyone has a thousand questions. Unfortunately, the answers I have are unsatisfying."

"What do you mean?" Hailey cried.

"You haven't talked to her?" demanded Harper.

"Settle down, you two." Daniel sounded like the father he'd essentially been to all of them. "Think about it. Big celebrities have layers of intermediaries you have to get through to even get a message to them."

Harper and Hailey both drooped in their chairs.

Grace said, "But you tried, right?"

"I have, yes," said Percy. "And I've also engaged the private investigator Martin Durand first hired to find your missing sister. We've both left messages that have not been returned."

Grace spoke up. "I think I read in *People*—or maybe it was *In Touch*—that she's on location in Madagascar."

"That's right." Hailey was nodding. "And did you hear? She and Bolt Marcovik are going to be making another movie together. Before she left for Madagascar, they did an interview, Madison and Bolt, about how she'd signed on for the new project with him. Most of the interview was the two of them denying rumors they're a thing."

"They're not a thing, my ass," Harper scoffed. "'We're just good friends,' they always say. Right. As if anyone believes that."

Percy gave a little cough. "Ahem. If I might continue…"

Harper winced. "Oops. Sorry."

Grace urged, "Yes. Please, Uncle Percy, tell us the rest."

"All right, then," said Percy. "The investigator has spoken to someone at Madison's agent's office and to her manager's receptionist. I got through to her housekeeper and to her personal assistant. I had asked the PI to proceed with caution, and he did. He told both the agent's office and the manager's receptionist that he needed to speak with Madison on a personal matter."

Harper snorted. "Well, I know that got him exactly nowhere."

"You're right. They gave him the runaround. He'll keep trying, though, until he gets through to the higher-ups."

"What about the housekeeper and personal assistant?" asked Grace.

"The housekeeper took my number and hasn't called back. The personal assistant asked me for more information. I said that we had credible evidence that Madison Delaney's biological parents were George and Marie Bravo of Valentine Bay, Oregon. The assistant gave me an address and said to mail the proof to her and she would get back to me. I mailed a copy of the letter you have in your folders along with a note explaining how I know that Marie Bravo gave birth to a baby girl on the same night that Madison was born, and at the exact same location. I also sent links to your Instagram accounts."

"Whose?" demanded Grace.

"Yours and Harper's and Hailey's, in the hopes that pictures showing the obvious physical resemblance between you three girls and Madison might help her to see the truth. And I offered to set up a series of sibling DNA tests. I'm assuming that none of you would object."

"Bring it," said Liam, and the rest of them nodded agreement.

"That was two weeks ago." Percy's white eyebrows drew together in a frown. "I called again last week and couldn't reach Madison's PA. Instead, I got another woman who said that Madison was on location in Madagascar and would I like to leave a message."

"So you gave up?" demanded Harper.

"Of course not. I left another message."

"And?" asked Grace.

"Nothing as of now. We have more avenues we can try, and we will. But you're all going to have to be a little bit patient."

"Patient?" Hailey slapped her hands to the sides of her head and opened her mouth in a silent scream.

"What if she's already received your messages?" asked Harper forlornly. "What if she's *telling* her people to blow us off?"

Both Grace and Hailey cried, "No!" And Grace added, "Why would she do that?"

"Any number of reasons," replied Percy patiently.

Connor said, "Think. She probably gets a lot of cranks claiming to be her long-lost best friend or relative or whatever."

Aislinn shifted on the couch cushions. She wasn't surprised in the least that Madison hadn't gotten right back to them.

Jax leaned close and whispered, "Tell them. Help them understand."

"Understand what?" Hailey looked so disappointed.

Aislinn gave a weary shrug. "It's not necessarily easy to find out that the people who loved you and raised you aren't your blood parents. It can be disorienting. It can call into question everything you are and all you know about yourself. I loved Mom and Dad. I hated finding out that strangers could be my birth parents. From what I've read about Madison Delaney, she loved her parents, too. So, it's not only that she has so many layers of protection from anyone trying to contact her. It's very possible that she'll resist the news—at first, anyway."

"At first?" Harper echoed.

"Denial," Aislinn said.

Percy nodded. "It's the classic initial response to learning a truth we'd rather not face."

Aislinn continued, "But I'm guessing from my own experience that Madison won't be able to quit thinking about what she's learned. The Delaneys probably told her she was born in Oregon at Wild River Ranch. She'll begin to wonder if maybe her parents never gave her the whole story. And I would bet that eventually she's going to want to know the truth, however painful it might be for her. And when that happens—"

"We'll be right here," said Grace. "Ready to welcome her to the family with open arms."

Percy leveled his gaze on Aislinn. "We can do the tests for you anytime you're ready. Sibling DNA is very reliable. It could prove that your brothers and sisters are a biological match with you, that Martin Durand was either lying or delusional, that the switch never even took place."

Aislinn considered Percy's offer and shrank from it, even though the night before she'd been talking about exhuming Martin's remains to find out the truth. Most likely, testing would provide the final proof that she wasn't a Bravo, after all.

Was she really ready to find that out for certain?

Not yet.

"I'll wait," Aislinn said. "When Madison Delaney finally gets in touch, we'll all test then. Together."

"It wasn't so bad, was it?" Jax asked that night. They were out on the side porch. "Your family still loves you and your brothers didn't kill me. Things could be a whole hell of a lot worse."

She sat on the floor with Bunbun, petting him, rubbing his head and stroking his coat, which was already filling in two weeks after clipping. "I'm just glad it's over. They all know everything we know. I don't like to keep secrets and now I don't have to."

Luna lifted up to rest her front paws on Jax's leg. He picked her up and she settled right down on his lap. As a rule, Luna hated sitting in laps. But apparently Jax was some sort of rabbit whisperer. "You said you love me." A half smile tugged at one side of that sinfully sexy mouth of his.

No way was she going there. "I had to do it, for your safety. You saw the looks Liam and Connor were giving you."

He rubbed Luna's ears. Luna had never liked anyone fooling with her ears—but she sure didn't seem to mind it if Jax was doing it. Jax could do whatever he wanted to her, apparently. "And here I thought you really meant it."

She gave him a long, steady look. "I like you a lot. Okay?"

"You were in love with me once. Who's to say lightning doesn't strike twice?"

"That wasn't love. That was a bat-crap crazy, obsessive crush. Believe me, neither of us wants me feeling like *that* again."

"I don't know. I might be ready for the crazy in you now."

"Why are we talking about this?"

"Because it's fun." In his lap, Luna wiggled contentedly, making soft, happy sounds as he continued to fool with her ears. "Your face is flushed. I love when that happens."

"Jax. What's the matter with you? You're downright lighthearted. Like the hero in one of those '40s movies where people dance in the rain."

Did he look hurt? Maybe a little. "You like me better when I'm grim and serious?"

She could not tell that lie. "No—well, I do like you when you're serious. I like you however you are."

He was smiling again. "Now you're talking."

"And it's great to see you this way, too."

"If I'm lighthearted, it's all because of you." He held her gaze. It was a lovely moment. She didn't want it to end.

But then again, it seemed a little unsafe, somehow, to get too carried away with talk of love. Tomorrow marked their three-week wedding anniversary. They had a long way to go until the three-month deadline. And they were already having amazing sex together. Wasn't that enough intimacy for now?

Some part of this strange relationship they'd been forced into ought to be done slowly, with care.

Like talking about love.

She changed the subject. "You know, I think somebody cleaned out the cages in here and refilled the hay racks while we were in Valentine Bay."

"This upsets you for some reason?"

"No. It's just, well, we know it wasn't Burt. I'll talk to Erma tomorrow, tell her she doesn't have to deal with the rabbits. She's already got way more than enough to do."

"I like your rabbits. Maybe Erma does, too."

"That doesn't mean she has to take care of them."

He lifted Luna and gently set her down. She hopped toward the cages and started munching pellets. "Nobody asked her to do it, so unless there's some other reason you don't want her helping out with them, why not just thank her and leave it at that?" He got up, brushed rabbit wool off his jeans and held down his hand to her. "Ready to go in?"

She let him help her to her feet and stepped in close.

"Thank you." She fiddled with his shirt collar, feeling wifely and affectionate and grateful—and a number of other more dangerous emotions. "It really helped that you were there with me for the meeting today."

"I wanted to be there." He dipped his head and captured her mouth.

She gave it up willingly, sinking into his kiss, sliding her hands up over his chest to wrap around his neck.

A few minutes later, he led her upstairs.

The next morning, after breakfast, when it was just Aislinn and Erma in the house, Aislinn thanked the housekeeper for tending to her rabbits.

"But really, Erma," she added. "It's not necessary. You've got way more than enough to do already. I'll take care of them."

Erma put the last plate in the dishwasher and pushed it closed. "Wasn't me," she said in her tiny voice.

Aislinn didn't get it. "Jax was with me, so it couldn't have been him." A shocking thought occurred to her. "Not Burt…"

Erma shrugged and shook her head. "Not me," she said again, and turned and disappeared into the laundry room.

Aislinn stared after her. *It has to be Burt.*

Come to think of it, Burt hadn't called her Judy for a couple of weeks. They'd reached a kind of détente in the little war he'd started in those first days after she married Jax. Now he called her Princess. Somehow, she didn't mind that at all.

She went out to the side porch and sat with the rabbits for a while. They seemed fine, jumping around, nibbling hay, doing all the things healthy rabbits do. As far as she could tell, Burt hadn't done anything but freshen their food and water.

And come on. Burt had a bad attitude toward women—and rabbits, too, at least at first—but he'd never struck her as the kind of man to harm an innocent animal.

She decided to let it go. If the crabby foreman wanted to be friends with Luna and Bunbun, more power to him. She went on out to her studio and got to work.

That following Thursday, Kip Anders showed up again. Aislinn greeted him with a warm smile. For all she cared, the lawyer could head straight up the stairs and check the bedrooms. Her marriage to Jax was the real thing now in every way.

Well, except for the time limit. That was still in effect. And she'd yet to spend a whole night in his bed.

And there was also that vague feeling she had, that none of this was real. Because *she* wasn't real.

Not anymore.

But they were good together, she and Jax. She cared for him, she really did. And she loved spending her nights in his bed, even if she couldn't quite make herself stay with him till dawn.

Anders never asked to go upstairs. He had a drink, joined them for dinner and left before eight.

"Pretty clear he's just going through the motions," said Jax as they watched the lawyer drive away.

The weeks kind of flew by. Uncle Percy called a family meeting the last Sunday in September. The news was disappointing. Madison had remained unavailable. All attempts to reach out to her were met with polite promises that Madison would be in touch "soon."

Grace, Harper and Hailey instantly started brainstorming ways to make Madison return Percy's calls. Percy and Aislinn talked them down off that particular ledge, reminding them that the next move was in Madison's hands. They had to respect their lost sister's wishes.

Grace cried, "But if we could only *talk* to her."

Harper said, "We have to find a way to get through to her, to meet with her," as Hailey nodded in complete agreement.

Percy tried again. "If she doesn't want to see you, forcing a meet would be wrong."

Grace let out an outraged cry. "But she needs to—"

"Stalking," said Matt. "That's what we'll be doing if we push this too far."

"Stalking's a little harsh," grumbled Harper.

Keely was sitting on the couch with her. "Patience." She wrapped an arm around Harper for a quick side-hug. "She'll reach out eventually."

There was more grumbling, but the sisters finally gave it up and promised to let Madison Delaney decide when and if to get in touch.

Monday, Kip Anders stopped by the ranch again. He came in the early afternoon, not long after lunch. Jax and Burt had already gone back out to work with the horses and Aislinn had volunteered to clean up after the meal so that Erma could get going on her afternoon chores.

The doorbell rang and Aislinn called out to Erma upstairs, "I've got it!" She opened the door and there was the lawyer. "Come on in." She stepped aside and ushered him into the foyer. "Have you eaten?"

Anders gave her his odd little smile, lips pursing, the corners curving up. "Just coffee would be great."

She led him through to the kitchen, offered a seat at

the breakfast nook table and brewed him a cup. "Jax is out with the horses. Half the time he forgets to take his cell with him, but I'll try giving him a call."

Anders waved a hand as she set the cup in front of him. "Don't bother him." She got the cream from the fridge and he poured some in his cup. "I'll just drink my coffee and be on my way. Join me?"

Suddenly wary for no real reason, she chirped out a bright "Sure," grabbed the half-finished iced tea she'd poured herself at lunch and took the chair across from him.

"So how's it going?" he asked.

Resentment. That was what she felt. To be put on the spot like this just so that Jax could keep the land that was rightfully his anyway. "It's going beautifully, thank you."

Anders didn't miss the fury beneath her aggressively cheerful words. "You're angry," he said kind of wearily as he brought his cup to his lips. He took a sip. Swallowed. Set the cup back down. "I can't say that I blame you. I honestly tried to talk Martin out of the terms you are living with. But he was determined. He said that you and Jaxon were made for each other and he couldn't see how you would ever get together. So he was going to set things up to *make* it happen between you."

"How generous of him—love and happiness by force."

Anders sipped more coffee. "I'm just his attorney. It's my job to do what my client wants—within the confines of the law, of course."

"Of course." Now she felt deflated. Because really, none of this was Kip Anders's fault. "And I'm sorry to be hostile. I'm not what you would call at peace with Martin's memory, if you know what I mean."

"I completely understand."

No, you don't. Nobody does.

Except maybe Madison Delaney, possibly. If the actress had even received the information Percy had been trying so hard to share with her.

"But it's obvious that you do love Jaxon," said the lawyer. "And he loves you. At least Martin was right about that."

What could she say? She did have her part to play. "Yes, exactly. Love. There's that."

Anders said goodbye a few minutes later. Aislinn put his coffee cup and her tea glass in the dishwasher, wiped off the table and counters and then returned to her studio.

When she sat down at her bench, a long breath escaped her. She rolled her shoulders. The tension of dealing with Anders, of living with all the ways Martin Durand had screwed with her life—it all just drained away as she returned to the project at hand.

Most of the time she felt as insubstantial as the morning fog that crept up from the beach in Valentine Bay and then faded to nothing with the light of the sun.

There were only two places she felt almost real—at work in her studio.

And in bed with Jax.

The next day, Tuesday, Keely came out to Wild River for lunch. Aislinn gave her a tour of her workshop and showed off her big project, a whole line—everything from rings to bracelets, pins, necklaces and a range of pieces designed to be worn in piercings. She'd used heart-shaped motifs throughout, in the ceramic elements, in the metalwork, even in the way she mounted semi-precious stones. She was calling the collection Patterns of the Heart.

Keely declared them all "gorgeous, original and so romantic."

They agreed on a solo show of the collection at the gallery.

"We'll open your show the last Friday of January and carry it through the month of February," declared Keely. "It's perfect. Patterns of the Heart for Valentine's Day." Aislinn said how thrilled she was, but Keely wasn't buying. "Something's wrong. What?"

Aislinn reassured her friend that she was fine, there was nothing wrong. She could see in Keely's eyes that her friend didn't really believe her, but Keely didn't push.

"What's going on with you?" Jax asked that night after dinner, when it was just the two of them alone in the family room. He grabbed the remote and turned off the thriller they'd been watching. "You're staring at the screen, but you're not watching the movie."

She blinked and looked directly at him. "I think it's Burt who's been feeding my rabbits."

"And what? You want me to tell him to stop that?"

"No."

He dropped the remote. It clattered as it hit the coffee table.

"You'll break that one of these days," she warned.

"Forget the remote. What's eating at you?"

"All of it." She leaned back against the couch cushions and stared straight ahead.

"Could you maybe be a *little* more specific?"

She rolled her head his way and met his eyes. Such beautiful eyes. He really was a terrific man.

And she needed to get honest with him—as well as with herself.

With a slow, deep breath, she sat up straight again. Jax looked bewildered. "All of what?"

"I've been thinking lately that the only time I feel real is when you're with me, touching me, kissing me..."

His eyes changed. They went liquid and lazy. "You've got no idea how happy you make me. Come here." He reached for her.

"Wait." She put her hand on his chest to stop him, to keep him from wrapping those muscular arms around her, soothing her anger and growing discontent, making her feel real—for a while, anyway. His heart beat, strong and steady and a little faster than usual, against her palm. *Patterns of the Heart.* "And my work," she added. "When you're making love to me and when I'm working. Those are the times I feel real."

He put his hand over her hand and curled his hot, rough fingers around it. "So then, how 'bout I get busy making you feel real?"

With a low groan of frustration, she yanked free of his grip. "Please don't make light of this. It's not a light thing."

His face fell. He was trying so hard and she should be more appreciative of him. "But what is it, exactly? Tell me what's wrong."

"I am. It's what I just said. When I'm not working or touching you, I feel like there's been a zombie apocalypse."

"Whoa. You're saying that you're afraid, somehow?"

"No. I don't have to be afraid because I'm already one of the walking dead."

His eyes burned into hers. "A feeling of numbness, you mean?"

"Yeah."

"Because of the whole mess with Martin?"

"Pretty much. The good thing is that learning I'm not who I thought I was has shocked me into finding a real focus in my work. And I'm glad for that. It was time I found that. I can trust in that. But you and me…"

She had to give him credit. He waited for her to finish. But after several seconds dragged by without another word from her, he grew impatient. "Just say it. You and me, what?"

"I'm in love with you, Jaxon."

His whole face lit up. "You are?"

"Oh, Jax. Don't you get it? It's all wrong, you and me."

"No, it's not. Aislinn, I love you, too."

She scooted away from him. "I knew you would say that."

"Because it's true, damn it."

"Jax, I can't…trust you. I *don't* trust you."

She had never seen him look so shocked. "Why the hell not?" he demanded in a near-whisper.

"You know why."

"No. I don't."

"Because when you're loving me, it's all real and immediate and beautiful and true. But then, I wake up in the middle of the night, and I have to get away, run back to my room, lock the door between us. Because I love you, and to you I'm just a placeholder. I'm not anyone all that special to you."

"That's not true."

"It is. You didn't even remember who I was that first day at Kircher and Anders."

"We've been through that already. You said you understood. Why are you dragging it all up all over again?"

"Because I need to be realistic. I need to remember that I'm only a good fit for you, a convenient wife for the life that you love. I'm the wife who knows horses and likes living in the country. I could be any reasonably attractive woman as long as I checked all the boxes."

He shot to his feet and towered over her, scowling. "You're really pissing me off about now. You know that, right?"

"I know I'm telling the truth. You getting mad at me for being honest isn't going to make what I said any less true."

"Aislinn!" he practically shouted. With what appeared to be considerable effort, he moderated his tone. "I just said I love you and you told me I don't. You said that you're nothing more than a placeholder to me. Of course I'm angry. I love you and I kind of want to pick up that damn remote you're so worried I'm going to break. I want to pick it up and throw it at the far wall."

"Please don't."

He continued to glower down at her. She glowered right back. The stare-down went on for what seemed like a year and a half. Finally, he said, so quietly and evenly, "I've had enough of this for tonight. I'm going upstairs."

She answered in kind. Quietly. Without inflection. "All right, then. Good night."

Chapter Ten

"What's going on between you and the princess?" Burt was brushing down the filly he'd just been putting through her paces.

Jax picked a burr out of his mount's hoof. "No idea what you're talkin' about."

The filly had attitude. She snorted and nipped at Burt. Just with her lips, but still. Burt gave her a light whack on the rump. "Behave yourself, Aphrodite." The filly gave another snort. "Okay, then, get on with you." He slapped her rump again and she took off through the open gate.

Jax sent his mount after her and then closed the gate. "I should get in some work with Popcorn in the round pen."

"The yearling can wait." Burt hooked his thumbs in his belt loops and glared from under the shadow of his ancient straw hat. "Let's get a water." They kept bottled water in a cooler in the tack room.

"I don't want to talk about it, Burt."

"Did I ask you what you wanted?"

Times like now, Jax felt like a green boy again. And an angry one at that. "Aislinn and I are having issues, is all. It'll be fine." It had been six days since they both said *I love you*, after which she'd informed him that he *didn't* love *her*. Like he didn't know his own damn heart—or worse, like he was some lying dog, the kind who would tell a woman he loved her just to keep her in line, the kind who wanted a woman because she was *convenient*.

Six days of mutual avoidance, of speaking to each other only when absolutely necessary, and even then taking care to use as few words as possible.

He missed her and it hurt like hell. Missed her in his bed, yeah. But in all the other ways, too. Her soft body pressing against him as they watched a movie in the great room. The two of them on the side porch entertaining the rabbits and talking about anything that came to mind. The sound of her laughter filling all the empty spaces, lighting up the darkest places...

Crap. Was that a rhyme he just made?

A man knew he was in trouble when he started making bad rhymes about his woman.

"Get in here," ordered Burt, striding through the open doors into the stable, Ace at his heels.

Jax was just miserable enough to follow the old horse wrangler back into the tack room. He took a water from the cooler and hitched a leg up on an empty saddle stand.

Burt grabbed a water, too, and sat backward on an old straight chair. "Okay, what's going on?"

"I do not believe I'm talking to you about this."

"Well, you are. Talk."

"Fine. She thinks I'm just with her because she's convenient."

Burt gave a snort of laughter. "And you tried to explain that you're with her 'cause you have to be or lose Wild River? Bet that went over big."

"Burt. Your rotten attitude is not helping. Yeah, at first it was all because of Martin's will. But even with that, I always liked her—and she knew exactly what the deal was. Now, though, it's more. So much more. She's everything to me now. But she didn't believe me when I told her so."

Burt was silent. He sipped his water and petted his dog. Jax got to thinking the old troublemaker would keep his mouth shut. And really, that didn't seem like such a bad idea.

But then Burt spoke. "Don't you tell her I said so. I got my reputation as a horse's ass to uphold. But over the last couple of months I've been forced to face the hard fact that I have judged her wrongly. She's a good woman, a keeper. She's got heart, she's smart and she pitches in. I can see why you don't want to lose her. This thing with Martin, though, I think it's messed with her mind."

"I think you're right about that."

"You gotta tread that fine line between being there for her and giving her the room she needs to find her feet again after Martin knocked the stuffing out of her."

"How do I do that?"

Burt snorted. "That's the billion-dollar question, all right. It's also way above my pay grade, son."

That night, Jax helped clear the table. It didn't take long. Erma left for her rooms.

Before Aislinn could run off, he stepped close to her at the sink and said, "Please. I want to talk to you."

She flipped on the faucet and rinsed the sponge she'd been using to wipe down the counters. "I have to take care of Bunbun and Luna."

He was ready for that one. "Let Burt do it." She turned off the water and wrung out the sponge—but not before slanting him a skeptical glance. He shrugged. "Burt has come to the logical conclusion that you're a good woman. You've got heart, you're smart and you pitch in. His words."

She turned toward him, but avoided his eyes. "Wow. I never saw that coming."

"Well, don't tell him I told you. He doesn't want you to get the idea that he's a good guy or anything."

"Okay, now. That sounds more like him."

"He likes you *and* your rabbits. And you were right. He's the one who's been keeping an eye on them."

"Burt likes my rabbits. Amazing."

He wanted to slide an arm around her, pull her close, tip up her chin and take her mouth. But he knew it wasn't kisses she needed right now. He said, "I asked him specifically to check their feed and water, to freshen their hay and spend some time with them tonight so I could talk to you. He's out on the side porch right now."

She still held the sponge. Turning back toward the sink, she flipped open the little door above the lower cabinet and slipped the sponge into the holder there. She shut the door with a snap.

He gently clasped her arm. "Aislinn." She still wouldn't look at him as he guided her around to face him again. "I'm sorry. I know none of this is easy for you, that what Martin did was really bad and completely wrong on so many levels. He committed an unforgivable crime on the day you were born. Then he compounded his wrong against you by putting you on the spot in his will. I had years with him, good years. I loved him and was grateful to him for becoming a father to me. All you know of him are the bad things. He's messed with your life and left you to try to make sense of it, to pick up the pieces and put it all back together again."

She still wouldn't look at him.

He stared down at her bent head, sure he was getting nowhere with all this talking. Actions counted more than words. But sometimes, a man did need to put a little effort into explaining himself. "Yes, you're right in what you said about the way we fit together. I see the way we fit as a *good* thing, though. I love that you know horses, that life here on Wild River suits you same as it suits me. For me, that you can live here and be happy here in no way makes you a placeholder. You are not replaceable. You are all the things Burt says you are and more. You are brave and strong and good and kind. And so damn beautiful. You are everything to me." A small, tight sound escaped her. He waited, for her to look up at him, for what she might say.

When she remained silent, her dark head tipped down, he didn't know what else to do but keep talking, keep trying to get through to her. "What you said, about not being certain of what's real anymore. I can see that, how you might feel that. But I do love you. I'm *in* love with you. It's real. And it's deep. It hurt me when you belittled what's in my heart for you. I acted like a jerk—and I'll say it again. I am truly sorry and I hope that you—"

"Jax." Her head came up at last. The shattered look on her face and the gleaming tear tracks on her cheeks hollowed him out like a punch to the gut.

"Aislinn. Please." He dared to lift a hand, to cradle her beautiful face, to rub at the wetness with his thumb, willing it gone. "Don't cry. I know I'm making a hash of this and I—"

"Jax," she whispered his name again. "You're not making a hash of anything."

"But I—"

"No." She pressed two soft fingers to his lips. "What you said was perfect. Don't you dare take a single word back."

That left him speechless.

Which worked out fine because she threw her arms around his neck and lifted her mouth to him. "Kiss me."

At last. It felt like a lifetime since he'd held her in his arms.

He claimed her lips. She tasted so good, of the salt from her tears and such sweetness, too, as she opened for him, letting him in. Her scent of spice and honey swam around him.

His confidence soared. They would make it, he felt sure of it. When the three months were up, she would still be his.

He nipped at her lip, trailing a hungry line of biting kisses down over her jaw and along the side of her neck. She shoved her fingers up into his hair, moaning as she arched high against him.

"Upstairs." He nuzzled the collar of her shirt aside and kissed the smooth slope of her shoulder.

"I love you, Jax. I do."

"And I love you. And now that's settled—"

She laughed and took his hand. "Upstairs. Yes. Great idea."

Right then, in that moment at least, Aislinn felt that all was right with the world. She loved Jax and she believed at last that he really did love her.

They pulled off their clothes as they raced up the stairs to his room, dropping them to the floor as soon as they cleared the threshold.

She let out a squeal of surprised delight as he grabbed her up, slung her over his shoulder and carried her to the bed. Tossing her onto the mattress, he followed her down.

Swiftly, they tore off the few items of clothing they still wore.

And then he was kissing her and she was holding him and every last doubt and fear, every worry, every hurt—it all spun away into nothing.

There was only the two of them, Aislinn and Jax, together the way they were meant to be. And when he settled against her, when he moved inside her, she knew that she'd found all she'd ever wanted in his strong arms. She was sure they would make it, together, that everything would work out right.

Hours later, she woke with Jax wrapped around her.

The panic didn't come. She lay there in the darkness listening to his even breathing, grateful for his warmth, for the possessive way he held her even in sleep. He made her feel that she was his in the truest way. She wanted to stay.

But her mind grew uneasy.

Carefully, she slipped out from under the shelter of his arm, hardly stirring the covers, making no sound as she ducked over the edge of the mattress and slid to the floor. On swift, silent feet, she crossed the shadowed room and went through the open door, shutting and locking it between them as she'd done every night she'd spent with him.

Her empty bed was waiting. With a sigh of regret for running away again, she eased under the covers and closed her eyes.

Sleep was coming for her, settling over her.

But she woke at the sound of a muffled tap on the door—not the one she'd just come through. The one to the hall. "Aislinn?"

It was Jax. Out in the hall.

She sat up and turned on the bedside light. Holding the covers to her breasts, she called, "It's open."

The door swung wide. He stood in the hallway, naked. The light from her lamp revealed him, tall and broad, with that thick chest tapering down to narrow hips and heavily muscled thighs dusted with dark, wiry hair.

It touched a warm chord in her, to see him standing there, to know he'd chosen the outside door instead of the inner one between their rooms. That choice seemed to say he wasn't assuming anything.

"Can I come in?"

"Um. Sure."

He came toward her, his eyes shadowed and sleepy, his hair sticking out every which way. The most beautiful man. Her love. He stopped at her bedside. "Are you all right?"

"I...couldn't stay."

"But you're all right?"

"Yeah. I'm okay."

He studied her face, seeking answers she didn't have. "Good enough, then." He turned to go.

And she simply could not bear that. "Jax. Wait." He stopped and looked back at her.

She lifted the covers, inviting him in. He arched an eyebrow. *Are you sure?*

At her nod, he came back to her. She raised the covers higher. He joined her in her bed.

"The lamp," she said.

He switched it off and stretched out on his side facing her. She turned her back to him, scooting up close. Reaching back to take his hand, she positioned his arm into the dip of her waist. He pulled her in a little closer and settled his body around hers.

"You just tell me," he whispered, "if you want me to go."

"Stay," she said, and closed her eyes.

When she opened them again, morning light peeked around the edges of the window blinds and Jax was still there with her, warm and solid.

And real.

The next night was the same.

They made love in his bed. And ended up in hers.

It went on like that for a week and a half. And then came the night she went to sleep in his bed—and didn't wake up until time for breakfast the next day.

After that, it might go either way. They would sleep in his room through the night—or move to hers.

On a Tuesday night toward the end of October, after they'd moved to her room, Aislinn started to snuggle close to him spoon-fashion, her favorite position for sleep.

But she had something she really needed to say, so she turned on her other side and faced him. "I've been wanting to tell you…"

"What?" He reached out and idly smoothed the wild tangle of her hair.

"That summer I worked for you?"

"Yeah?"

"I used to wish with all my heart and soul that your marriage to Judy would fail."

"You mentioned that before." He eased his warm fingers around to cradle her nape, pulling her close enough to kiss the tip of her nose. "And wishing never makes it so."

"When Martin called me and told me you were divorced and had been divorced for over a year—I just felt like such a terrible person. Wishing for the destruction of a marriage. That's low."

"My marriage to Judy died because of Judy and me. We own that. Whatever you might have wished had nothing to do with it."

"Yeah. Well, then we can talk about what I *did*— which was to try to put a move on you."

"And then you realized how wrong that was and removed yourself from the situation. Sometimes people want what they can't have. Wanting isn't a sin. It's cheating and stealing to get what isn't yours, that's where the evil is."

She met his eyes through the shadows. "I never felt so guilty in my life as that day at Kircher and Anders. I felt like Martin had reached into the darkest corner of my soul and brought my most shameful secret out into broad daylight for everyone to see."

He combed her hair back from her temple with his fingers, a gentle, rhythmic sort of touch. "You think maybe that's a guilt you can learn to let go of?"

"I'm working on it."

Leaning in again, he brushed her lips with his. "What else?"

She smiled against his mouth, that he had read her so well—and then she gave a nervous sigh. "Two weeks from tomorrow, the terms of Martin's will are satisfied."

He pulled away. "Something in your voice tells me I'm not going to like what you say next."

She needed just to say it outright, like ripping off a bandage. No sense in dragging it out. "Once we're all settled up with Kircher and Anders, I want to move back to Valentine Bay."

His eyes remained locked with hers through the gloom. "Why?"

"I need to."

"Because?"

"I need…a separation between this, you and me, living out the terms of Martin's will. And you and me as just us, doing what *we* want to do, building the life we choose, together."

"Are you going to divorce me?"

"Never. I fully intend to come back and live here with you. I just need some time. I need coming here to be *my* choice."

He was quiet, his eyes reproaching her. The silence stretched out.

Finally, he asked, "When will you come back to me?"

"I'm sorry. I don't have the answer to that question yet."

There was another silence. A long one. "I'm not happy about this," he said at last.

"I didn't think you would be."

He pushed back the covers and got up. "I'm going to sleep in my room."

"All right," she said. "Just remember I love you. And it will all work out."

Jax tried to stay angry at her. He lasted through the next day.

But then he realized that he'd just wasted a whole day he could have had with her. If she did leave, she would be going way too soon.

Fourteen days remained to him. He'd been an idiot to waste a single one of them. Refusing to speak to her wasn't going to help him convince her to stay.

He went out with Burt after dinner in the pouring rain to check on a sick mare. The mare seemed better. But they found a fence down. A couple of fillies and a gelding had gotten out. He and Burt herded them back where they belonged and fixed the broken fence.

It was past nine and still raining when he got back to the house. He could hear the TV going in the family room, which meant Aislinn hadn't gone up to her room and closed the door—yet.

He left his boots by the back door, washed up quick in the downstairs half bath and dried off his shirt and jeans with the hand towel as best he could. Then he went to find her and make amends.

She turned off the TV when he entered the great room. "Wet enough for you?"

He went and stood by the sofa where she sat. "I still don't like it."

"Yeah." Biting the corner of her lip, she looked at him through those big eyes he saw in his dreams. "I got that loud and clear. But I need to do it."

"Do I get to be with you while you're living in that beach house in Valentine Bay?"

"Yes, please."

"What? Like for dates?"

"Well, yes. I was hoping we would go out. I don't know. Take walks. I'll cook you dinner. Sometimes maybe I'll come here. You know, like couples do."

"And we'll still be married?"

"Yes, we will."

"Just separated."

She licked her finger and hissed through her teeth as she made an imaginary mark in the air. "Good one."

He looked down at his thick socks. "I'm being a jerk again, huh?"

"Yeah, pretty much."

He held out his hand. "Will you come up to bed with a jerk like me?"

She got up and put her hand in his. It was all the permission he needed to pull her in tight and kiss her hard and deep.

They went up the stairs with their arms wrapped around each other.

The next fourteen days were gone in an instant.

All of a sudden, it was the first Tuesday in November and Jax and Aislinn were leaving the offices of Kircher and Anders. Fifty thousand dollars had just been direct-deposited into her checking account. And Jax was now the sole owner of Wild River Ranch and everything on it, along with a number of stocks and investments and the key to Martin's safe-deposit box at a nearby bank.

She offered to go to the bank with him if he wanted to check out the safe-deposit box.

"I pretty much know what's in it," he said.

"So then that's a no?"

He looked at her bleakly. "I could not care less about the damn safe-deposit box right now," he grumbled. "When are you leaving?"

"I thought I'd get started moving my stuff today."

He eyed her mournfully—with maybe a teaspoon of bitterness. "Where will you stay tonight?"

Was she tempted to steal one more night in his bed? Undeniably. But she did mean to do this and she needed not to wimp out. "I'll be at my cottage, Jax."

His big shoulders slumped. "Fine. Let's get moving."

At the ranch, he and Burt and Erma all pitched in to help her load her things into her Honda and the two pickups with horse trailers. They packed up and loaded the studio, the rabbits and all the rabbit gear, along with Aislinn's personal belongings from upstairs.

At five, after a shy goodbye hug from Erma, Aislinn climbed in her CR-V and they caravanned to Valentine Bay.

Harper and Hailey were waiting at the cottage with takeout for everyone. They ate quickly and got to work. By nine, with everybody pitching in, they had it all unloaded and the rabbits set up in their old home on the enclosed front porch.

Burt was eager to go.

Aislinn offered him her hand. "Thank you, Burt."

Scowling, he took her fingers and gave them a quick

shake. "This is a dumb-ass idea, Princess," he griped. "Say the word and we'll load everything right back up again and take you home where you belong."

She almost threw her arms around him and burst into tears.

But he must have sensed her intention. His eyes widened in alarm. He spun on his heel and headed for his truck, muttering loud enough that she didn't miss a word, "Women. Even the good ones are crazy half the damn time."

Harper and Hailey said goodbye to Jax and went inside.

That left her standing outside between the cottage and her work shed with her unhappy husband. It was starting to rain.

She pulled up the hood on her canvas jacket and took a key from her pocket. Catching his hand, she laid the key in his palm and folded his fingers over it. "Anytime you want to visit, come on in."

"Your sisters okay with that?"

"Of course. You're my guy."

The grim lines of his face eased a little. "Great. I think I'll stay over." She didn't miss the light of challenge in his eyes.

He was expecting her to send him away.

Not a chance. "What about your horses?"

"I'll get up good and early. Burt won't even know I was gone."

She slid her arms around his waist and tipped her head back. "All right, then." Raindrops—big, cold ones—splattered her cheeks and forehead. "Stay the night. I would like that a lot."

"Aislinn." He growled her name as he claimed her

lips, his tongue spearing in to invade her mouth in the most delicious way.

When he lifted his head, she took his arm and led him inside.

It was still raining when she woke at dawn the next morning. And Jax was gone. She missed him already.

In the kitchen, her sisters gave her funny looks.

Harper poured her some coffee and handed it over. "What's going on, really?"

"Yeah," Hailey chimed in from her seat at the table, where she was shoveling in her usual Honey Bunches of Oats. "You're married. You love the guy. It's obvious he loves you. But still, you're back here."

"And he stayed the night, didn't he?" Harper sounded bewildered.

Hailey paused with a mound of milky cereal dripping from her spoon. "Makes no sense." She stuck the spoon in her mouth and chewed, frowning. "Are you separated?"

"No way. I love him."

"But you're here and he's there."

"I know. But it's not a separation so much as a little pause."

"Ais," said Harper. "You are making no sense at all."

Aislinn leaned back against the counter and looked into her coffee as though an answer to everything might be lurking in there. "I don't really know why I'm doing this. I just have to do it."

Harper moved in close. Aislinn appreciated the comforting touch as her sister hooked an arm around her waist. "Is this about your getting switched?"

She let herself lean on Harper a little. "Yeah. It's

about taking back my life, you know? Starting over with Jax, doing it in a way that works for me."

Hailey crunched more oats. "You mean you and Jaxon are going to be dating?"

"Essentially."

"Wow," said Harper. "Dating your own husband…"

"It's all backward, I realize that. Too bad. I just need to do it."

"Maybe a little therapy wouldn't hurt," Hailey suggested gingerly.

Aislinn shrugged. "Maybe. We'll see how it goes."

"I try not to say bad stuff about dead people." Hailey picked up the orange juice by her bowl and drank it, plunking the empty glass sharply down. "But sometimes I hate that old man, Martin. What he did was unforgivable."

"But think." Harper's arm around Aislinn tightened a little. "If he hadn't done it, Ais wouldn't be our sister."

"Fine." Hailey let out a hard sigh. "Some really good stuff happened because of what he did. But only because God or fate was willing to help out a little. As for Martin Durand, though? I'm not giving him credit for squat."

Aislinn spent most of that rainy day setting up her studio.

When she finally got down to work, she felt cramped in the small shed and kept having to stop and search for her tools. She missed the bigger, more comfortable space at Wild River—oh, who was she kidding?

She missed Wild River, period.

She missed Jax, too, though she'd spent last night in his arms. She missed Erma's steady, comfortable presence. She even missed Burt, which was something she would once have sworn could never happen.

She texted Jax twice. At around ten in the morning: Did you get home okay?

And later, in the afternoon: Just so you know, I love you.

He didn't answer either text. She hadn't really expected him to. His phone was probably sitting on the dresser in his bedroom, in need of a charge.

When she took a break to scare up some dinner, the house was empty. She kept her phone on the table to the left of her plate, just in case Jax might get in touch.

Nothing.

She took care of Luna and Bunbun, worked until ten and then went to bed, waking from a fitful sleep when the mattress shifted. Cold air made her shiver as the covers were lifted.

"Jax?"

"You were expecting someone else?" He was gloriously naked. And his skin was cool.

"Brr." She cuddled in close to help warm him up—and because where else would she ever want to be? "What time is it?"

He stroked her shoulder, pressed his lips into her hair. "Late."

"You have to leave early?"

"In about three hours."

"You'll be exhausted." She sighed and pressed a kiss to the center of his chest.

"I wasn't going to come," he said in a gruff whisper, his lips close to her ear. "I held out until after midnight. But I couldn't last."

"I'm glad. It's selfish of me, but I am."

He made a low, grumbling sound. "I love you."

"I love you, too. I texted you my love."

"And to ask me if I got home okay—which I did. I got both texts when I charged my phone after dinner."

"But you didn't answer."

"I'm here," he said, as if that explained everything—and really, it kind of did. His big arms gathered her even closer. "Go to sleep."

She felt a little stab of guilt, to be putting them both through this absurdity, with her wanting to be back at Wild River with him and his driving to get to her in the middle of the night because he couldn't stay away.

It was all completely unnecessary. She wanted to be home—and yes, somehow in the three months she'd been living out the terms of Martin's will, Wild River had become her home.

What was she waiting for?

She had no idea.

She only knew that in a few days something would click within her and she would be ready to pack up her stuff all over again and go back where she belonged.

Chapter Eleven

The click she was waiting for?

Never happened.

Not that week or the next.

She worked long hours in her studio, not stopping until Jax arrived, which he did nearly every night, only to leave before dawn the next morning.

He was doing all he could to make this thing she just had to do easier on her. He even took her out—to dinner one Saturday night, to a show the next.

In bed on the following Tuesday night, a week and two days before Thanksgiving, she asked him if he would go with her to Daniel and Keely's for the holiday dinner. He said he would and she suggested, "Bring Burt and Erma, too."

"Erma always goes to her sister's in Tacoma when there's a holiday. But I'll invite Burt."

"Perfect."

He was silent. Too silent. Finally, he asked, "Are you ever coming home, Aislinn?"

"Of course, yes."

He reached over, turned on the lamp and sat up. As she blinked against the sudden brightness, he said, "Got any idea yet when that's going to happen?"

"Soon, I'm sure."

He glowered down at her. "I would do anything for you. But I'm not understanding why this is necessary. You think you're getting even with Martin somehow?"

"No. Of course not."

"Good. Because there's really no getting even with a dead man, in case you didn't know."

"I do know. Yes." Her voice sounded doubtful to her own ears.

"You want me to sell Wild River and move in here with you?"

Had she heard right? He would never sell what he loved most of all. And she didn't want him to. "Of course not."

"For you, I would do that. What we have—or what we will have as soon as you work through what's eating at you—it's everything to me. *You're* what matters most to me now."

"But what about Erma and Burt? They're family. What about them if you sell the ranch?"

"I would create jobs for them, ask them to come along, work with me, whatever I ended up deciding to do. If I sold Wild River, there would be plenty of money for me to find something else. My degree's in veterinary medicine. I could do something with that. Anything's possible. Whatever you need to move forward, you're on. You just say the word."

Tears flooded her eyes that he would offer such a thing, that he would sell his home for her sake. She sniffed and swiped the tears away. "Don't be crazy. You love Wild River. And so do I."

"You sure?"

"About Wild River being home? Beyond a doubt."

"Then what are we doing spending our nights here?"

"I just…" She scrunched her eyes shut, *willed* the answer to come. But there was nothing. "I just don't know."

"It's been two weeks. When *will* you know? Can you give me a hint? Can you say, 'New Year's Day' or 'Two and a half more weeks'?"

When she still had no reply for him, he threw back the covers and reached for his clothes.

"Jax. Come on. It's almost midnight. Where are you going?"

"Home." He yanked up his boxer briefs, grabbed his jeans and shoved his feet in them. "I'm going home and I'm going to try my damnedest to stay there. I want to be a good husband, a man who supports his wife. I want to be with *you*, no matter how hard you make that. But I'm starting to feel like one those enablers, like I'm just making it easy for you to mess up the good thing we have together. Because, Aislinn, we are *married*. We can't go back and pretend to start over. We are where we are and I *like* what we made, together, out of what Martin dumped on us. I'm not ashamed of it. I'm not resentful of it. What we are together makes me proud. I love what we have and I love you." He pulled on his second boot, grabbed his jacket off the bedside chair and started for the door.

"Jax, wait…"

He stopped and turned. "I'm listening."

"I love you, too," she cried. "I love you so much."

"Then work it out. And when you do, please come home to me."

Jax didn't come back. Or call. Or text.

Not later that night, not on Wednesday or Thursday.

She moved through those days in a weird gray haze. Thinking of the things he had said before he left, seeing the truth in them, loving him with her whole heart. And doing nothing to fix what she'd broken.

By late Thursday afternoon, she knew she had to do something—call a friend. Get a therapist. It did warm her heart a little to think of how many people she could reach out to who would be at her side in an instant. Harper and Hailey were right there if she needed them. She could call Keely or Daniel. Or Matt, Connor, Liam or Grace.

Instead, at six that evening, she went to Valentine House carrying a large supreme pizza, anchovies on the side, in her hands.

Daffy answered the door. "Aislinn!" she exclaimed with real delight. "And with pizza, too."

"Come in, come in!" said Percy, right behind her.

Daffy kissed her cheek and took the pizza. Percy enfolded her in a hug.

They ate the pizza in the living room the way they always did. She felt nervous to say what she came to say and resorted to counting the lilies in the carpet.

But then Percy said, "Come now. Whatever it is, it can't be that bad."

And just like that the floodgates opened. She started

talking and didn't stop until she'd told them how she loved her husband but couldn't seem to go home to him, how she was stuck in the beach cottage, longing for the life that could be hers with Jax at Wild River, the life she somehow kept throwing away.

When she was finished, she cried on Daffy's shoulder. They sat together, she and Daffy, on the ancient green velvet circular settee.

Percy paced the lily-strewn carpet, his hands clasped behind his back. "So then," he said in his most thoughtful analytic style. "You are finding yourself unable to accept the life you've come to love. *Why?* we must ask ourselves. What stands in your way?"

"It's Martin," she sniffled.

"Ah, yes. Martin."

"He messed with my life. He claims to be my father and yet he denied me. Well, okay. I didn't need a dad like him, anyway. But he couldn't just leave it at that. He had to switch me at birth with another innocent child. And then he had to come after me from the grave, too."

Percy stopped, turned and raised an eyebrow at her. "You consider him an evil man."

"Yes!" she replied with enthusiasm.

"And yet, as it turned out, at least some of his manipulations have worked quite well for you."

She remembered what Hailey had said the morning after she returned to the cottage. "That was God or fate helping things along, that's all."

"Yes, well. Who can say what higher power had a hand in all that's happened? Is it fair, though, to say that Martin Durand, your biological father, chose to take a series of actions that have had a powerful and continuing effect on your life?"

"Yes. And I hate him for it."

"Because your life is a disaster."

"Wait." Aislinn lifted her head from Daffy's shoulder and glared at her great-uncle. "No. I didn't say that."

"Of course you didn't. How could you? You've taken what Durand perpetrated upon you and made it work in some rather excellent ways, haven't you? That is, until this little downward spiral you've been indulging in recently."

"Indulging? Uncle Percy, that's not fair."

"Sweetheart," said Aunt Daffy. "We love you very much, which is why, when you come to us, we do our level best to give you what you're looking for."

"And this evening," said Percy, "you came to us so that we could tell you the simple truth. And the truth is, your husband has it right. I hate to sound like a Disney song. But you need to let all that go. That's the job of the living, to let the dead go. We have to learn to be grateful for what we've been given and forgive the wrongs that can never really be made right."

"Forgive," she whispered. Daffy handed her a tissue and she blew her nose. "I have to forgive Martin?"

"Are you ever going to have a chance to confront him?"

"Not in this life."

"Exactly. Leave him to heaven, Aislinn. Let the dead go and live your life. Let yourself be happy with the man that you love."

When Aislinn left Valentine House, she almost took the turnoff to Wild River. She could send Harper and Hailey a text so they wouldn't worry.

But she had Bunbun and Luna to consider. She needed

to give them fresh food and water to last them till to-morrow and maybe grab a toothbrush and a change of clothes.

When she reached the cottage, neither of her sisters' cars were there. But a heart-stoppingly familiar Silverado crew cab was parked near the front steps.

It was dark by then, but the porch light and the light in the rabbit's enclosure were both on. She could see Jax through the storm windows, sitting there with Luna in his lap.

Aislinn looked at her hands clutching the wheel. Her knuckles were white.

What if he was fed up with her? What if he'd come to tell her he'd had enough and he was filing for divorce?

"Breathe, damn it," she muttered to herself.

She took a couple of slow, deep breaths and made herself let go of the steering wheel. Jax loved her. He really did. A man who didn't love her would never have put up with her crap the past few weeks. He might be totally put out with her, but the love was still there.

It had to be.

Up on the porch, Jax lowered Luna to the floor, brushed off his jeans and stood. He was looking right at her, though he couldn't see her, out here in the dark. But he would have heard her drive up, would have seen her headlights. He knew someone was there.

She got out of the car. One foot in front of the other, she marched up the steps and opened the door to the rabbits' enclosure.

"Aislinn," he said. "Here you are." For an endless moment, they just stared at each other. His eyebrows drew together and he asked so tenderly, "Have you been crying?"

"A little. Oh, Jax." Arms outstretched, she threw herself at him.

He caught her, grabbed her close and buried his face against her neck. "What's made you cry?" He lifted his head so he could look in her eyes.

"I'm just so glad you're here."

"Aislinn." He said her name with yearning. With hope and with tenderness. And then he was kissing her and she was kissing him back.

They needed those kisses. So many kisses, all the kisses they hadn't shared since he'd left her two endless nights before.

When the storm of kissing finally passed, he said, "I couldn't stay away. However long this takes, I still need to see you, to hold you, to be with you."

"You're a brave man, Jaxon Winter—and I was just going to feed the rabbits, grab my toothbrush and come home."

He went still. His eyes shone down at her. "Home? You're coming home to Wild River?"

"Yes. Tonight. To *you*."

"What happened? What changed?"

"Everything. Nothing."

He gave her a crooked smile. "Well, that about covers it."

She laughed. "I went to talk to Uncle Percy and Aunt Daffy. They set me straight. I've been spinning in circles, so angry at Martin. They told me what you told me. That I need to move on. I guess I've finally heard it enough that it actually got through to me—plus, I do love you. And I want everything for you. I haven't been a good wife to you the last few weeks. I've been making both of us suffer for a dead man's sins."

"I was too hard on you."

"No. You were amazing. When you put up with me. And when you drew the line."

He touched the side of her face. "I have something for you." He took an envelope from his back pocket and handed it to her. "I finally checked Martin's safe-deposit box."

She stared down at the envelope. *Aislinn*, it said in a bold, back-slanted scrawl. Her hands were shaking all of a sudden, but somehow she managed to peel open the flap. Inside was one sheet of paper, a small silk jewelry pouch—and a cashier's check made out to Aislinn Bravo. She looked up at Jax in disbelief. "A hundred thousand dollars?"

Jax shrugged. "Martin had a lot of investments. He was good with money." And then he grinned. "You look so shocked."

"Well, duh." She stuck the envelope and the check in the front pocket of her jeans. "You're not?"

"Not in the least. Martin would have wanted you to have something no matter what, but he wouldn't have wasted the leverage of making you believe you *had* to marry me or get nothing. He was ruthless. And he was wrong in so many ways, but he wasn't heartless, Aislinn. I think he really believed that you and I should be together. I think making that happen was his idea of making things right."

She opened the folded sheet of paper.

Aislinn,
I have not in any way been the father I should have been to you. I have failed you and I have cheated you of your rightful place in the world, of your

very identity. But in the past few years, since an accident of fate brought you again to Wild River, I have made it my business to learn all I can of you. What I discovered is that providence has treated you much better than I did. You love the family you found and they love you, unconditionally. You are kind to others and generous in spirit. I also believe that you still long for a chance with my adopted son, Jaxon.

So yes. I have given you that chance. And whatever has happened as a result, I wish you love and happiness, always.

And I do realize that you will want to know beyond a shadow of a doubt what I have known since I first set eyes on you. So I have had my DNA collected and profiled at a reputable lab for comparison with yours. Contact the lab with the information below. They will arrange to collect a sample from you and get back to you with results within a week.

The locket was my mother's. When she died, she instructed me to give it to her first granddaughter.

Live well, Aislinn. Make better choices than I did.

With all the love I never gave you,
Martin Durand

Below his signature were instructions for contacting a lab in Portland.

And she was still shaking. The paper crackled in her hands. She passed it to Jax.

He scanned the lines. "Martin," he said ruefully when

he glanced up at her again. "Just when you want to punch him in the face, he does something right."

She opened the pouch and turned it over. The heart-shaped silver filigree locket on a delicate silver chain dropped into her palm. Inside were two pictures—of a young Colette Durand with her hair pinned up and a sexy smirk on her full lips. And of Martin in his wannabe-Mafia-man phase, glaring at the camera with a scowl on his face.

Patterns of the Heart...

"Oh, Martin..." She blinked the tears away, closed the locket and handed it to Jax. "Put it on for me?" She turned and lifted her hair out of the way.

He hooked the clasp for her and then guided her back around to face him. "It looks beautiful."

She pressed her hand over it. "It feels right."

He kissed her, quick and sweet. "I love you, Aislinn Winter."

She beamed up at him. "I love *you*, Jaxon Winter. Forever and always—now, just let me freshen the rabbits' feed and water. Then I'll grab a few things and we can go to Wild River."

"We'll go in the morning," he said.

"You sure you don't want to go home?"

"Home is where you are," he whispered and lowered his beautiful mouth to hers once again.

First thing the next morning, Aislinn contacted the Portland lab. Jax drove her down there that day so they could swab her cheek. They warned her that she might not have her results until the Monday after Thanksgiving.

But she got lucky. The following Wednesday morning, her results were posted at a secure online location.

They proved what she'd already come to believe: that Martin Durand was her biological father.

When Jax came in from the stables for lunch, she shared the news.

He pulled her close. "You're okay with this, then?"

She beamed up at him. "I feel good. Peaceful. I mean, I already knew in my heart, I really did. But it's nice to have proof."

He kissed her then, slow and sweet and deep.

She whispered, "I love you."

He replied, "And I love you. So much. More than I know how to say…"

The next day, Jax went with her for Thanksgiving at Daniel and Keely's house.

Burt came, too. As it turned out, the crabby horse trainer had a soft spot for kids. He got down on the kitchen floor with the two-year-old twins, Frannie and Jake. Jake offered his ratty stuffed rabbit to kiss. Burt didn't hesitate. He laid a big smacker on the stuffed toy. Frannie handed him her giant toy cell phone and he pretended to make a call.

All the Bravos were there, and Uncle Percy and Aunt Daffy, too. So was Gretchen Snow, Keely's aunt and the mother of Daniel's deceased first wife, Lillie. And Keely's mom, Ingrid, who had changed her hair to a blue-green so vivid it almost looked radioactive.

There was barely room for everyone at the table.

But they all fit, somehow.

Gretchen said grace, after which Ingrid raised a toast to life, love, happiness and rock and roll. "And babies," she added, grinning at Keely, who was in her third trimester.

Keely patted the big mound of her stomach and smiled down the table at Daniel, who had never looked happier.

Jax took Aislinn's hand. She leaned in close to him and they shared a quick kiss. Thankfulness filled her.

Life had thrown her a curve or two. But she'd worked her way through all the confusion and doubt to find what mattered most. She wore her grandmother's locket, she had her family around her and the man she loved sat close at her side.

* * * * *

Watch for Matt Bravo's story,
Same Time, Next Christmas,
coming in December 2018,
only from Harlequin Special Edition.

Madison Delaney's story
will be available in May 2019.

And for more great Bravo stories,
check out the beginning of
The Bravos of Justice Creek miniseries:

Not Quite Married
The Good Girl's Second Chance
Carter Bravo's Christmas Bride

Available now wherever Harlequin books
and ebooks are sold!

CHAPTER ONE

"THIS IS TOTALLY LAME. Why do we have to stay here and wait for you? We can walk home in, like, ten minutes."

Daniela Capelli drew in a deep breath and prayed for patience, something she seemed to be doing with increasing frequency these days when it came to her thirteen-year-old daughter. "It's starting to snow and already almost dark."

Silver rolled her eyes, something *she* did with increasing frequency these days. "So what? A little snow won't kill us. I would hardly even call that snow. We had way bigger storms than this back in Boston. Remember that big blizzard a few years ago, when school was closed for, like, a week?"

"I remember," her younger daughter, Mia, said, looking up from her coloring book at Dani's desk at the Haven Point Veterinary Clinic. "I stayed home from preschool and I watched Anna and Elsa a thousand times, until you said your eardrums would explode if I played it one more time."

Dani could hear a bark from the front office that likely signaled the arrival of her next client and knew she didn't have time to stand here arguing with an obstinate teenager.

"Mia can't walk as fast as you can. You'll end up frustrated with her and you'll both be freezing before you make it home," she pointed out.

"So she can stay here and wait for you while I walk home. I just told Chelsea we could FaceTime about the new dress she bought and she can only do it for another hour before her dad comes to pick her up for his visitation."

"Why can't you FaceTime here? I only have two more patients to see. I'll be done in less than an hour, then we can all go home together. You can hang out in the waiting room with Mia, where the Wi-Fi signal is better."

Silver gave a huge put-upon sigh but picked up her backpack and stalked out of Dani's office toward the waiting room.

"Can I turn on the TV out there?" Mia asked as she gathered her papers and crayons. "I like the dog shows."

The veterinary clinic showed calming clips of animals on a big flat-screen TV set low to the ground for their clientele.

"After Silver's done with her phone call, okay?"

"She'll take *forever*," Mia predicted with a gloomy look. "She always does when she's talking to Chelsea."

Dani fought to hide a smile. "Thanks for your patience, sweetie, with her and with me. Finish your math worksheet while you're here, then when we get home, you can watch what you want."

Both the Haven Point elementary and middle schools were within walking distance of the clinic and it had become a habit for Silver to walk to the elementary school and then walk with Mia to the clinic to spend a few hours until they could all go home together.

Of late, Silver had started to complain that she didn't want to pick her sister up at the elementary school every day, that she would rather they both just took their respective school buses home, where Silver could watch her sister without having to hang out at the boring veterinary clinic.

This working professional/single mother gig was *hard*, she thought as she ushered Mia to the waiting room. Then again, in most ways it was much easier than the veterinary student/single mother gig had been.

When they entered the comfortable waiting room—with its bright colors, pet-friendly benches and big fish tank—Mia faltered for a moment, then sidestepped behind Dani's back.

She saw instantly what had caused her daughter's nervous reaction. Funny. Dani felt the same way. She wanted to hide behind somebody, too.

The receptionist had given her the files with the dogs' names that were coming in for a checkup but hadn't mentioned their human was Ruben Morales. Her gorgeous next-door neighbor.

Dani's palms instantly itched and her stomach felt as if she'd accidentally swallowed a flock of butterflies.

"Deputy Morales," she said, then paused, hating the slightly breathless note in her voice.

What *was* it about the man that always made her so freaking nervous?

He was big, yes, at least six feet tall, with wide shoulders, tough muscles and a firm, don't-mess-with-me jawline.

It wasn't just that. Even without his uniform, the man exuded authority and power, which instantly raised her hackles and left her uneasy, something she found both frustrating and annoying about herself.

No matter how far she had come, how hard she had worked to make a life for her and her girls, she still sometimes felt like the troublesome foster kid from Queens.

She had done her best to avoid him in the months they had been in Haven Point, but that was next to impossible when they lived so close to each other—and when she was the intern in his father's veterinary practice.

"Hey, Doc," he said, flashing her an easy smile she didn't trust for a moment. It never quite reached his dark, long-lashed eyes, at least where she was concerned.

While she might be uncomfortable around Ruben Morales, his dogs were another story.

He held the leashes of both of them, a big, muscular Belgian shepherd and an incongruously paired little Chi-poo, and she reached down to pet both of them. They sniffed her and wagged happily, the big dog's tail nearly knocking over his small friend.

That was the thing she loved most about dogs. They were uncomplicated and generous with their affection, for the most part. They never looked at people with that subtle hint of suspicion, as if trying to uncover all their secrets.

"I wasn't expecting you," she admitted.

"Oh? I made an appointment. The boys both need checkups. Yukon needs his regular hip and eye check and Ollie is due for his shots."

She gave the dogs one more pat before she straightened and faced him, hoping his sharp cop eyes couldn't notice evidence of her accelerated pulse.

"Your father is still here every Monday and Friday afternoons. Maybe you should reschedule with him," she suggested. It was a faint hope, but a girl had to try.

"Why would I do that?"

"Maybe because he's your father and knows your dogs?"

"Dad is an excellent veterinarian. Agreed. But he's also semiretired and wants to be fully retired this time next year. As long as you plan to stick around in Haven Point, we will have to switch vets and start seeing you eventually. I figured we might as well start now."

He was checking her out. Not *her* her, but her skills as a veterinarian.

The implication was clear. She had been here three months, and it had become obvious during that time in their few interactions that Ruben Morales was extremely protective of his family. He had been polite enough when they had met previously, but always with a certain guardedness, as if he was afraid she planned to take the good name his hardworking father had built up over the years for the Haven Point Veterinary Clinic and drag it through the sludge at the bottom of Lake Haven.

Dani pushed away her instinctive prickly defensiveness, bred out of all those years in foster care when she felt as if she had no one else to count on—compounded by the difficult years after she married Tommy and had Silver, when she *really* had no one else in her corner.

She couldn't afford to offend Ruben. She didn't need his protective wariness to turn into full-on suspicion. With a little digging, Ruben could uncover things about her and her past that would ruin everything for her and her girls here.

She forced a professional smile. "It doesn't matter. Let's go back to a room and take a look at these guys. Girls, I'll be done shortly. Silver, keep an eye on your sister."

Her oldest nodded without looking up from her phone and with an inward sigh, Dani led the way to the largest of the exam rooms.

She stood at the door as he entered the room with the two dogs, then joined him inside and closed it behind her.

The large room seemed to shrink unnaturally and she paused inside for a moment, flustered and wishing she could escape. Dani gave herself a mental shake. She could handle being in the same room with the one man in Haven Point who left her breathless and unsteady.

All she had to do was focus on the reason he was here in the first place. His dogs.

She knelt to their level. "Hey there, guys. Who wants to go first?"

The Malinois wagged his tail again while his smaller counterpoint sniffed around her shoes, probably picking up the scents of all the other dogs she had seen that day.

"Ollie, I guess you're the winner today."

He yipped, his big ears that stuck straight out from his face quivering with excitement.

He was the funniest-looking dog, quirky and unique, with wisps of fur in odd places, spindly legs and a narrow Chihuahua face. She found him unbearably cute.

With that face, she wouldn't ever be able to say no to him if he were hers.

"Can I give him a treat?" She always tried to ask permission first from her clients' humans.

"Only if you want him to be your best friend for life," Ruben said.

Despite her nerves, his deadpan voice sparked a smile, which widened when she gave the little dog one of the treats she always carried in the pocket of her lab coat. He slurped it up in one bite, then sat with a resigned sort of patience during the examination.

She was aware of Ruben watching her as she carefully examined the dog, but Dani did her best not to let his scrutiny fluster her.

She knew what she was doing, she reminded herself. She had worked so hard to be here, sacrificing all her time, energy and resources of the last decade to nothing else but her girls and her studies.

"Everything looks good," she said after checking out the dog and finding nothing unusual. "He seems like a healthy little guy. It says here he's about six or seven. So you haven't had him from birth?"

"No. Only about two years. He was a stray I picked up off the side of the road between here and Shelter Springs when I was on patrol one day. He was in a bad way, half-starved, fur matted. As small as he is, it's a wonder he wasn't picked off by a coyote or even one of the bigger hawks. He just needed a little TLC."

"You couldn't find his owner?"

"We ran ads and Dad checked with all his contacts at shelters and veterinary clinics from here to Boise with no luck. I had been fostering him while we looked, and to be honest, I kind of lost my heart to the little guy, and by then Yukon adored him so we decided to keep him."

She was such a sucker for animal lovers, especially those who rescued the vulnerable and lost ones.

And, no, she didn't need counseling to point out the parallels to her own life.

Regardless, she couldn't let herself be drawn to Ruben and risk doing something foolish. She had too much to lose here in Haven Point.

"What about Yukon here?" She knelt down to examine the bigger dog. In her experience, sometimes bigger dogs didn't like to be lifted and she wasn't sure if the beautiful Malinois fell into that category.

Ruben shrugged as he scooped Ollie onto his lap to keep the little Chi-poo from swooping in and stealing the treat she held out for the bigger dog. "You could say he was a rescue, too."

"Oh?"

"He was a K-9 officer down in Mountain Home. After his handler was killed in the line of duty, I guess he kind of went into a canine version of depression and wouldn't work with anyone else. I know that probably sounds crazy."

She scratched the dog's ears, touched by the bond that could build between handler and dog. "Not at all," she said briskly. "I've seen many dogs go into decline when their owners die. It's not uncommon."

"For a year or so, they tried to match him up with other officers, but things never quite gelled, for one reason or another, then his eyes started going. His previous handler who died was a good buddy of mine from the academy, and I couldn't let him go just anywhere."

"Retired police dogs don't always do well in civilian

life. They can be aggressive with other dogs and sometimes people. Have you had any problems with that?"

"Not with Yukon. He's friendly. Aren't you, buddy?
You're a good boy."

Dani could swear the dog grinned at his owner, his
tongue lolling out.

Yukon was patient while she looked him over, especially as she maintained a steady supply of treats.

When she finished, she gave the dog a pat and stood.
"Can I take a look at Ollie's ears one more time?"

"Sure. Help yourself."

He held the dog out and she reached for Ollie. As she
did, the dog wriggled a little, and Dani's hands ended
up brushing Ruben's chest. She froze at the accidental
contact, a shiver rippling down her spine. She pinned her
reaction on the undeniable fact that it had been entirely
too long since she had touched a man, even accidentally.

She had to cut out this *fascination* or whatever it
was immediately. Clean-cut, muscular cops were *not*
her type, and the sooner she remembered that the better.

She focused on checking the ears of the little dog,
gave him one more scratch and handed him back to
Ruben. "That should do it. A clean bill of health. You
obviously take good care of them."

He patted both dogs with an affectionate smile that
did nothing to ease her nerves.

"My dad taught me well. I spent most of my youth
helping out here at the clinic—cleaning cages, brushing
coats, walking the occasional overnight boarder. Whatever grunt work he needed. He made all of us help."

"I can think of worse ways to earn a dime," she said.
The chance to work with animals would have been

a dream opportunity for her, back when she had few bright spots in her world.

"So can I. I always loved animals."

She had to wonder why he didn't follow in his father's footsteps and become a vet. If he had, she probably wouldn't be here right now, as Frank Morales probably would have handed down his thriving practice to his own progeny.

Not that it was any of her business. Ruben certainly could follow any career path he wanted—as long as that path took him far away from her.

"Give me a moment to grab those medications and I'll be right back."

"No rush."

Out in the hall, she closed the door behind her and drew in a deep breath.

Get a grip, she chided herself. *He's just a hot-looking dude. Heaven knows you've had more than enough experience with those to last a lifetime.*

She went to the well-stocked medication dispensary, found what she needed and returned to the exam room.

Outside the door, she paused for only a moment to gather her composure before pushing it open. "Here are the pills for Ollie's nerves and a refill for Yukon's eyedrops," she said briskly. "Let me know if you have any questions—though if you do, you can certainly ask your father."

"Thanks." As he took them from her, his hands brushed hers again and sent a little spark of awareness shivering through her.

She was probably imagining the way his gaze sharpened, as if he had felt something odd, too.

"I can show you out. We're shorthanded today since

the veterinary tech and the receptionist both needed to leave early."

"No problem. That's what I get for scheduling the last appointment of the day—though, again, I spent most of my youth here. I think we can find our way."

"It's fine. I'll show you out." She stood outside the door while he gathered the dogs' leashes, then led the way toward the front office.

After three months, Ruben still couldn't get a bead on Dr. Daniela Capelli.

His next-door neighbor still seemed a complete enigma to him. By all reports from his father, she was a dedicated, earnest new veterinarian with a knack for solving difficult medical mysteries and a willingness to work hard. She seemed like a warm and loving mother, at least from the few times he had seen her interactions with her two girls, the uniquely named teenager Silver—who had, paradoxically, purple hair—and the sweet-as-Christmas-toffee Mia, who was probably about six.

He also couldn't deny she was beautiful, with slender features, striking green eyes, dark, glossy hair and a dusky skin tone that proclaimed her Italian heritage—as if her name didn't do the trick first.

He actually liked the trace of New York accent that slipped into her speech at times. It fitted her somehow, in a way he couldn't explain. Despite that, he couldn't deny that the few times he had interacted with more than a wave in passing, she was brusque, prickly and sometimes downright distant.

His father adored her and wouldn't listen to a negative thing about her.

You just have to get to know her, Frank had said the

other night. He apparently didn't see how diligently Dani Capelli worked to keep anyone else from doing just that.

She wasn't unfriendly, only distant. She kept herself to herself. Did Dani have any idea how fascinated the people of Haven Point were with these new arrivals in their midst?

Or maybe that was just him.

As he followed her down the hall in her white lab coat, his dogs behaving themselves for once, Ruben told himself to forget about his stupid attraction to her.

When they walked into the clinic waiting room, they found her two girls there. The older one was texting on her phone while her sister did somersaults around the room.

Dani stopped in the doorway and seemed to swallow an exasperated sound. "Mia, honey, you're going to have dog hair all over you."

"I'm a snowball rolling down the hill," the girl said. "Can't you see me getting bigger and bigger and bigger?"

He could tell the moment the little girl spotted him and his dogs coming into the area behind her mother. She went still and then slowly rose to her feet, features shifting from gleeful to nervous.

Why was she so afraid of him?

"You make a very good snowball," he said, pitching his voice low and calm as his father had taught him to do with all skittish creatures. "I haven't seen anybody somersault that well in a long time."

She moved to her mother's side and buried her face in Dani's white coat—though he didn't miss the way she reached down to pet Ollie on her way.

"Hey again, Silver."

He knew the older girl from the middle school, where

he served as the resource officer a few hours a week. He made it a point to learn all the students' names and tried to talk to them individually when he had the chance, in hopes that if they had a problem they would feel comfortable coming to him.

He had the impression that Silver was like her mother in many ways. Reserved, wary, slow to trust. It made him wonder just who had hurt them.

Don't miss Season of Wonder
by RaeAnne Thayne,
available October 2018
wherever HQN books and ebooks are sold!

COMING NEXT MONTH FROM

H HARLEQUIN®

SPECIAL EDITION

Available October 16, 2018

#2653 THE MAVERICK'S CHRISTMAS TO REMEMBER
Montana Mavericks: The Lonelyhearts Ranch • by Christy Jeffries
Wedding planner Caroline Ruth comes to after a fall off a ladder believing she's engaged to Craig Clifton—but they've never met before! The doctors don't want Caroline getting too upset, so Craig goes along with the charade. But what's a cowboy to do when his fake feelings turn real?

#2654 THE MAJORS' HOLIDAY HIDEAWAY
American Heroes • by Caro Carson
Major India Woods thought house-sitting in Texas would be just another globe-trotting adventure—until her friend's neighbor, Major Aidan Nord, shows up. But their hot holiday fling is interrupted by his two little girls, and India thinks she might have just found her most exciting adventure yet!

#2655 A STONECREEK CHRISTMAS REUNION
Maggie & Griffin • by Michelle Major
Griffin Stone is back in town, this time with a little boy in tow! Can Maggie forgive his disappearing act? And will Stonecreek win over a tech CEO to host their new headquarters? Find out in the anticipated third book of the Maggie & Griffin trilogy!

#2656 AN UNEXPECTED CHRISTMAS BABY
The Daycare Chronicles • by Tara Taylor Quinn
Tamara Owens is supposed to be finding whoever has been stealing from her father's company. But when she meets prime suspect Flint Collins—and his new charge, infant Diamond—she can't bear to pull away, despite her tragic past. Will Flint be able to look past her original investigation to make them a family by Christmas?

#2657 WYOMING CHRISTMAS SURPRISE
The Wyoming Multiples • by Melissa Senate
Moments before walking down the aisle again, Allie Stark finds her presumed-dead husband at her door. Little does he know, he became the father of four babies in his absence! Can this reunited couple make their family work the second time around?

#2658 THE SERGEANT'S CHRISTMAS MISSION
The Brands of Montana • by Joanna Sims
Former army sergeant Shane Brand's life has stalled. When his new landlady, the lovely Rebecca Adams, and her two children move in, he finds he's suddenly ready to change. Now it's his new mission to be the man the single mom deserves, in time to give them all a dose of Christmas joy.

YOU CAN FIND MORE INFORMATION ON UPCOMING HARLEQUIN® TITLES, FREE EXCERPTS AND MORE AT WWW.HARLEQUIN.COM.

HSECNM1018

How hadn't he heard her first knock?

And then she saw the carrier on the chair next to him. He'd
been rocking it.

"What on earth are you doing to that baby?" she exclaimed,
nothing in mind but to rescue the child in obvious distress.

"Damned if I know," he said loudly enough to be heard
over the noise. "I fed her, burped her, changed her. I've done
everything they said to do, but she won't stop crying."

Tamara was already unbuckling the strap that held the
crying infant in her seat. She was so tiny! Couldn't have been
more than a few days old. There were no tears on her cheeks.

"There's nothing poking her. I checked," Collins said,
not interfering as she lifted the baby from the seat, careful to
support the little head.

It wasn't until that warm weight settled against her that
Tamara realized what she'd done. She was holding a baby.
Something she couldn't do.

She was going to pay. With a hellacious nightmare at the
very least.

The baby's cries had stopped as soon as Tamara picked her up.

"What did you do?" Collins was there, practically touching her, he was standing so close.

"Nothing. I picked her up."

"There must've been some problem with the seat, after all…" He'd tossed the infant head support on the desk and was removing the washable cover.

"I'm guessing she just wanted to be held," Tamara said. What the hell was she doing?

Tearless crying generally meant anger, not physical distress.

And why did Flint Collins have a baby in his office?

She had to put the child down. But couldn't until he put the seat back together. The newborn's eyes were closed and she hiccuped and then sighed.

Clenching her lips for a second, Tamara looked away. "Babies need to be held almost as much as they need to be fed," she told him while she tried to understand what was going on.

He was checking the foam beneath the seat cover and the straps, too. He was fairly distraught himself.

Not what she would've predicted from a hard-core businessman possibly stealing from her father.

"Who is she?" she asked, figuring it was best to start at the bottom and work her way up to exposing him for the thief he probably was.

He straightened. Stared at the baby in her arms, his brown eyes softening and yet giving away a hint of what looked like fear at the same time. In that second she wished like hell that her father was wrong and Collins wouldn't turn out to be the one who was stealing from Owens Investments.

Don't miss
An Unexpected Christmas Baby *by Tara Taylor Quinn,*
available November 2018 wherever
Harlequin® *Special Edition books and ebooks are sold.*

www.Harlequin.com